New York Times bestselling author
Patrick A. Davis "delivers the goods"
(*Kirkus Reviews*) in these acclaimed novels!

THE SHATTERED BLUE LINE

"More twists and turns than a cattle show. . . .
A gripping military thriller."  McBain

"A chilling murder mystery . . . head-scratching clues,
twists, and dead ends."
—*Publishers Weekly*

"A crafty, detail-rich mystery. . . . Deft characterizations."
—*Booklist*

A SLOW WALK TO HELL

"Davis knows how to tell a terrific story by creating characters that matter."
—thebestreviews.com

"Enthralling. . . . A peek through the usually obscured
doors of political intrigue."
—*Old Book Barn Gazette*

A LONG DAY FOR DYING

"The tension builds with every stone overturned. . . ."
—*Publishers Weekly*

THE COLONEL

"Fans of Nelson DeMille will find this one entirely satisfying."
—*Booklist*

THE GENERAL

"A terse, gung-ho military-thriller. . . . Lots of action."
—*Kirkus Reviews*

ALSO BY PATRICK A. DAVIS

★ ★ ★

The Shattered Blue Line

A Slow Walk to Hell

A Long Day for Dying

The Commander

The Colonel

The Passenger

The General

PATRICK A. DAVIS

DECEPTION PLAN

POCKET BOOKS

New York London Toronto Sydney

This book is a work of fiction. Names, characters, places and incidents are products of the author's imagination or are used fictitiously. Any resemblance to actual events or locales or persons, living or dead, is entirely coincidental.

An *Original* Publication of POCKET BOOKS

POCKET BOOKS, a division of Simon & Schuster, Inc.
1230 Avenue of the Americas, New York, NY 10020

Copyright © 2006 by Patrick A. Davis

ISBN-13: 978-0-7434-9976-7
ISBN-10: 0-7434-9976-X

This Pocket Books paperback edition December 2006

10 9 8 7 6 5 4 3 2

POCKET and colophon are registered trademarks of Simon & Schuster, Inc.

Cover design by Jae Song
Cover photo by Time Life/Getty Images

Manufactured in the United States of America

For information regarding special discounts for bulk purchases, please contact Simon & Schuster Special Sales at 1-800-456-6798 or business@simonandschuster.com

To the memory of my U-2 brethren
who have flown their final high flight:
Rich Schneider, Marty McGreggor,
Randy Roby, Chris Coffland, and Scott Ward.

Acknowledgments

As usual, many people contributed to making this book a reality. First, I'd like to express my deepest appreciation to my muse, Kaitie Sessler, who patiently tolerated my insecurities and tirelessly guided me into crafting something readable. I'd also like to thank her husband Bob, for his advice and encouragement, and my former U-2 colleagues, Nathan Green, Dave Markl, Paul Memrick, and Jeff Gruver, for keeping me straight about aspects of the plane I'd long since forgotten.

Special kudos also go to my brutally honest circle of proofreaders: Ginny Markl, Dr. Carey Page, my nephew Erik Olson, my niece Charlotte Steiner, Colonel Neal Barlow and his wife Diana, Cecil and Barb Fuqua, Kathy and Bob Baker, Becky and Dennis Stefanski, Karen Amyx, and Susan and Mike Farris. In addition, I need to thank Lieutenant Melissa Prince, Korean linguist extraordinaire; Kevin Smith, easily the best editor in New York; and Karen Solem, agent, guru, and friend.

Finally, I'd like to thank my wife Helen, who makes everything in my life possible, and my parents, Betty and Bill Davis, who continue to inspire me.

DECEPTION PLAN

★ Prologue ★

SPRING 1993, EIGHT BRIDGE PARK, OLD CITY,
SHANGHAI, CHINA

She was young, midtwenties, and at five-ten, tall for an Asian. She wore sunglasses, no makeup, and was dressed simply in gray slacks and a bulky coat. It didn't matter. As she stood at the edge of the small pond, people stopped to look. They couldn't help it. She was a striking beauty and possessed a flawless face that belonged on magazine covers, perhaps a model or an actress.

She was neither.

Several brazen young men strolled by, calling out suggestive comments and generating laughter. Oblivious to them, the woman continued to toss bits of bread from a paper sack into the water. Several goldfish broke the surface with a splash, and a feeding frenzy ensued. Throwing out more bread, the woman appeared completely calm. Only someone looking closely could notice the slight tremor in her lower lip.

From behind, she heard a slight cough. Then a demand whispered: *"Oe-di iss-oe-yeo?"* Where is he? He was speaking Korean, not Chinese.

"*Dwi-e o-run-chok-e. Choeng-saek-ot. Bi-man-han-da.*" Back to the right. Blue suit. Fat.

A man sitting on a stone bench behind her turned the page of a newspaper. As he did, his eyes casually flickered to a heavy man standing beside a pagoda-shaped fountain. The woman's ever-present shadow.

Shielding his face with the paper, the man on the bench said, "*Hoe-ham-i wi-heom-hangeoshi-da.*" This meeting is dangerous.

"*Gwan-shim-i eop-seo-jeot-da. Sae-ro-un Roe-sha yeo-ja e-ge gwan-shim-i eop-seo-jyeot-da.*" The Dear Leader is losing interest. The Russian girl is his new favorite.

"*Seong-gyo?*" The sex?

"*I-ju ha-na man.*" Only once this week.

The man swore softly. The Dear Leader was Kim Jong Il, the North Korean dictator. A sexual deviant who watched porn constantly, Kim usually had sex with his mistresses several times a day. "*I-nae. A-jik chul-hal-su-eopt-da.*" Patience. We can't pull you out yet.

"*I-il-e Pyong-yang e chul-bal hae-yo.*" You must. We leave for Pyongyang in two days. Her voice desperate.

"*Hal-su eopt-da.*" Impossible.

"*A-ni-ya—*"

"*Nae ga gal-a-ha-gi-jeo-ne mot gan-da.*" I say when you leave.

"You son of a bitch," she blurted out in unaccented English.

Behind the newspaper, the man's face registered surprise.

Neither said anything for a few moments. The woman wanted to spin around, scream to the man that she couldn't do it any longer, couldn't screw that sick pervert again.

Instead, she let out a breath. And calmly fed the fish.

Matching her perfect English, the man said sarcastically, "Does your American father know you fuck for us?"

The woman's face smoothed into a mask. When she spoke, her voice was barely above a whisper, but there was no mistaking the disdain.

"*Ne-il. Ne-il chul-bal hae-yo.*" Tomorrow. I leave tomorrow.

"*Chat-a-nae-get-da. Chul-bal-an-he-yo.*" They'll find you. You'll never get away.

She emptied the bag of bread crumbs into the water, saying softly, "*Ab-eo-ji e-ge jeon-ham-yeon, ab-eo-ji ga ne rul ju-kil-geo-shi-da.*" Then I will get a message to my father. And when he learns you made me a whore for my country, he will kill you.

The man was silent.

"*Ne-il,*" she said again. Tomorrow.

She walked away.

The entire fortieth floor of the Shanghai Intercontinental Hotel was reserved for the North Korean entourage, the halls guarded by a small army of secret police. The rooms for Kim Jong Il's mistresses—four had accompanied him on this trip—were clustered at one end, near a private elevator. Once summoned, the women were immediately whisked to his penthouse. When Kim Jong Il wanted to get his rocks off, he didn't like to be kept waiting.

As was the current pattern, the Russian had been the only one called out to service the dictator. A statuesque blonde with a baby-doll face, she had been a recent purchase from a white slave trader.

The woman from the park had gone to bed around midnight. At a little after 3:00 A.M., she awoke with a start, realizing something was pressing down upon her. At first, she thought she was dreaming . . . a nightmare. Then she felt a wrenching pain. She tried to fight, kick out, but strong arms locked her to the bed. Panic flooded through her. She struggled to scream through a gloved hand gripping her mouth.

The curtains were pulled back and she realized the windows were open, ropes dangling outside. *Ropes? Why would they use—*

And then it hit her, who her assailants had to be.

In the moonlight, she could clearly see the two dark figures hovering over her. Both were short and powerful, dressed completely in black. Neither wore a mask and her eyes widened in sickening recognition. She knew one of them.

Her eyes focused on him pleadingly.

He smiled menacingly.

Her panic turned to terror. She became aware of the smell of alcohol and felt a pinprick on her arm. She struggled violently, but the hands holding her were like vises.

In minutes, her body relaxed and she became light-headed. She blinked, trying to focus. She felt drunk, sick. The hands weren't pressing down on her anymore. The window started moving toward her. She knew she should still be frightened, but she was so tired.

The window stopped moving. Softly, she heard, *"Jal haesseo-yo."*

The woman's head jerked toward the man she'd recognized. He had just told her she'd done well.

With her mouth still covered, her eyes shot him a tacit question. *"U-ae?"* Why?

"Haeng-jin," he mouthed.

Orders.

She never saw or felt either man move. But an instant later, she was startled by the wind whipping past her face. Everything began to spin and she was aware she was falling.

She opened her mouth to scream . . .

★1★

From somewhere above the droning noise, Colonel Ed Coffin became dimly aware someone was calling him. Then he felt a hand shake his shoulder.

"Colonel, sir. Wake up. Sir . . ."

Colonel Coffin's eyes cracked open. He was lying in a darkened metallic tube and an attractive young woman with boyishly cropped red hair and wearing an even more boyish-looking flight suit was peering down upon him with concern.

"Jesus," she said, smiling with relief. "You had us worried. I'm been trying to wake you for the past five minutes, sir."

"Wake me? Give me a second."

His groggy mind slowly processed his surroundings. Open walls filled with wiring, cargo pallets wedged around him, the telltale hum of engines. It clicked; he was the lone passenger on a C-141 military transport, flying from Hickam Air Base, Hawaii, to Korea. Easing upright from the web seats he'd been lying on, he smiled apologetically at the woman. As the plane's loadmaster, she was responsible for the cargo and the care and feeding of passengers.

"I took a sleeping pill, Sergeant," Coffin said. "Guess it worked."

"I'll say, sir. You been out for almost seven hours."

Her eyes lingered on his with more than a passing interest. It was a reaction Colonel Coffin was accustomed to, and not only from women. People were curious about his ethnicity— his mother was Asian, his father white—and the mismatch between his youthful appearance and the eagles on his blue Air Force uniform. With his black hair, spare frame, and boyish good looks, Ed Coffin just didn't look old enough to be a full colonel.

But at forty-three, he was.

"The pills were prescription. Migraines." Rubbing the sleep from his eyes, Coffin glanced out a window. It was a clear night, and peering downward, he was surprised to see they were still at cruise altitude, well out over the water.

"We're not landing?"

"Not for another two hours, Colonel."

"Two hours?" Coffin felt a trace of irritation. "Mind telling me why you woke me?"

But the loadmaster had keyed the mike on her headset. "The colonel's okay, Captain Beale. You want him up front or—"

Motioning Coffin forward, she said, "Go on up to the cockpit, sir. Captain Beale's reinitiating the phone patch now."

"Phone patch?"

"Osan Command Post, sir. They want to talk to you."

She waited expectantly, but instead of rising, Coffin removed a battered Korean-English dictionary from his shirt pocket and began studying it.

The seconds passed. A minute. Coffin kept reading. The loadmaster began a nervous two-step; he pointedly ignored it.

Listening to her headset, she finally said to Coffin, "Sir, Captain Beale has the CP on the line."

"Congratulations," Coffin grunted, without looking up.

Her mouth cycled open and closed. As a sergeant, she certainly couldn't order Coffin forward. "Right," she said into the mike, "I told him, Captain Beale. But the colonel doesn't seem to want to—"

"Correct, Sergeant," Coffin interrupted her. "Tell Captain Beale to relay to the CP that I'm on leave for the next week."

She relayed the message. To Coffin, "Sir, the CP says it's urgent."

"It isn't."

Coffin knew precisely what the problem was; he'd even anticipated this eventuality. A fast burner in the promotion game, Ed Coffin had spent his twenty-year career carefully choosing assignments with the sole purpose of making rank. A master at manipulation and blessed with natural charm, he'd pinned on full colonel years ahead of his peers. Setting his eyes on the next rung of the ladder, Coffin had lobbied to become a four-star general's executive officer—a crucial job because it guaranteed him a powerful sponsor. After a few years of filling squares in various command billets, Coffin finally landed his coveted exec job, working for General Marvin Ford, the four-star in charge of all Pacific Air Forces. For the past fourteen months, Coffin had run the general's life, coordinating everything from appointments and briefings to picking out civilian suits for the general to wear. Hell, Coffin even picked up his laundry and walked the general's dogs.

Demeaning chores for a colonel—not that Coffin minded. To him, all that mattered was ingratiating himself to Ford and ensuring his support.

But nothing is forever and attitudes change.

Recently, Coffin had taken stock of his life and come to

the painful realization that he'd been mistaken all these years. He'd always believed that success, professional success, was a precursor to happiness. But the truth was, he was miserable. He had no life, no purpose outside his work. With few close friends and no serious relationships—he'd only proposed to one woman and she'd turned him down—there was no one with whom to share his success. In past, his parents had been there for him, but they'd died in a car accident, leaving him alone.

And loneliness was a feeling that was all too familiar to Coffin. Until seven, he'd lived in a Korean orphanage and, as a mixed-race kid, he'd been regarded as something of a pariah. Adoption had been his salvation, affording him an opportunity for a far better life. Still, his early childhood branded him, and he never forgot that feeling of loneliness, the acute sense of exclusion. It's what fueled his constant need to prove himself.

But, at what cost?

That was the question Coffin had finally gotten around to asking himself. And he didn't like the answer.

The next step hadn't been easy. It took Coffin a week to summon the courage to tell General Ford that he no longer wanted to be his exec.

"You understand what this means?"

"Yes, sir."

In a year, Coffin would meet his primary board for general, when he had his best chance for a star. Without Ford's signature on his annual evaluation, the odds of making it were slim to none unless a miracle occurred and he was promoted early.

"General, I have my reasons . . ."

"They'd better be good, Ed."

Apparently, they were. Once Coffin explained his rationale, the general didn't try to talk him out of it. He just wished him the best and initiated the transition process. As of next week, Coffin's babysitting assignment would be officially over, his replacement already in place.

And that, of course, was the problem behind the command post request. Coffin's replacement.

Ford's new exec was a cocky guy who'd waltzed in like he was the new sheriff in town and made it clear he had no intention of taking advice. That was fine with Coffin. Instead of wasting time training the guy, Coffin opted to take a week of leave.

But he figured he'd get a panicked call when the new exec realized he wasn't the Shell Answer Man and discovered Ford had a low tolerance for foul-ups. Well, screw him; the guy had his chance.

Smiling grimly, Coffin checked his watch. Almost 1830 hours, Korea time, and he tried to recall when he'd last eaten. Pocketing the dictionary, he rummaged under the seat for his box lunch. The loadmaster began two-stepping again.

"Relax, Sergeant," he said, offering a smile, "odds are it's only a misplaced briefing or itinerary."

Her pretty face went blank.

Coffin sighed, motioned for her headset and mike. "Captain Beale, Colonel Coffin—"

"Yes, sir."

"Tell the CP I'll phone on a land line when we land—"

"Hang on, sir. The CP's calling again. I'll put the HF on intercom so you can hear."

The operative word was hear. Coffin's mike was intercomonly; he couldn't transmit over the plane's radios.

As he waited, he fished out a ham sandwich. Ten hours ago, it had probably been edible. He shrugged; as a bachelor, he'd eaten worse.

Moments later, he heard the telltale hiss of a high frequency radio. Then: "Razor, two-four, Osan CP. Inform Colonel Coffin his leave is canceled and he is ordered to come to the radio."

"You get that, sir?" Beale said to Coffin.

Coffin's mind kicked into gear. One thing was certain; this had nothing to do with the new exec.

"I'm coming up."

Rising, Coffin felt the beginnings of another headache.

Finishing off the sandwich in two large bites, Coffin made his way forward to the cockpit. He knew he looked like hell and was tempted to slip into the lav and clean up. But any additional delay would be pushing it; someone with serious clout was already irritated with him.

Likely candidates? General Ford? Didn't figure. He's the one who approved the leave, insisted Coffin take it. General Gruver, the three-star Seventh Air Force commander in Korea? Possible. But Coffin and Gruver had worked together before and gotten along. Besides, how would Gruver know Coffin was en route to Korea? Another general? Someone from the embassy?

Shaking his head, Coffin gave up and went up the short metal stairs into the cockpit. The two pilots and the flight engineer twisted in their seats, looking at him. The pilots were rail-thin captains who looked about sixteen; the flight engineer, a grizzled master sergeant. The FE handed Colonel Coffin a headset. "It's all set, sir."

Coffin keyed the mike. "Command Post, Colonel Ed Coffin. I understand you have a message . . ."

"Yes, sir," a man said. "Stand by."

Coffin glanced out the windscreen. In the blackness ahead, he could make out the faint lights of the Korean coast.

It was a sight he was familiar with; he'd spent countless hours flying high above it.

Moments later, a voice came on the radio, a woman's voice. The instant she began to speak, the blood drained from Coffin's face.

"Oh, my God . . ."

The words just came out. The cockpit crew stared at him in surprise. Since Coffin hadn't keyed the mike, the woman continued to talk, unaware of his reaction.

Coffin's mouth felt like sand. He stood with his heart pounding. He kept telling himself it couldn't be her, that it had been a long time ago and he must be mistaken.

But that *voice* . . .

He listened. The voice was deep and seductively husky, with a distinctive accent that was more Northeast than New York.

Jesus . . .

The woman cryptically told Coffin an emergency had occurred and that his leave was canceled so he could conduct an investigation. "Lieutenant General Gruver personally assigned you to the case, Colonel," she added. "The matter is confidential and you'll be briefed on the details when you land."

"Nothing else you can tell me now?" Coffin asked, managing to sound calm.

"Not over an unsecured frequency."

"Does General Ford know?"

"Yes."

"And he approved this?" Ford knew the trip to Korea was important to Coffin.

Another pause.

"He didn't, did he?" Coffin said.

"He said it's your choice."

"So I can decline."

"Neither General Gruver nor General Ford believe you will."

Like hell, Coffin thought. In the past, his job had always trumped his personal desires. But not this time.

"I decline," he said.

"You don't know the specifics. When you do—"

Coffin cut her off. "It doesn't matter. Tell General Gruver to find someone else."

For almost a minute, there was no response. The crew continued to fixate on Coffin with something approaching shock. It didn't compute, a colonel bucking a three-star.

Then the woman said, "I just spoke with General Gruver; he said to remind you that your leave is still canceled."

"Now hold on a minute—"

"Command Post out."

Coffin's jaw clenched. But the hissing radio told him she'd terminated the call. No doubt about it, he thought. It was her.

She always had to get in the last word.

Shaking his head, he handed the headset back to the FE.

"Wonder what they want you to investigate, sir?" the sergeant said.

That was only one of two questions that bothered Coffin. The second was why they specifically wanted him. There were thirty thousand American troops stationed in Korea. It wasn't like he was only colonel who could lead an investigation. Unless . . .

Unless it was something only he was qualified to do.

When he heard the FE mention they were being diverted from their intended destination, his hunch became a certainty.

"We're not landing at Osan?" Coffin asked.

"No, sir. The runway is closed. We're going into Kunsan."

Bingo, Coffin thought.

At precisely 2036 hours, the huge transport touched down at Kunsan Air Base, ninety miles south of Seoul. Coffin barely felt the landing; the pilots might be Opie Taylor clones, but they knew what they were doing.

As the plane exited the runway, Coffin rose from the cockpit observer's chair and leaned against the windscreen. A snowstorm had passed through and foot-high snowdrifts were visible on the infield. Turning down a taxiway, the big jet lumbered past seemingly endless rows of F-16 fighters. A major U.S. Air Force installation, Kunsan was second in size only to Osan.

"Welcoming committee, sir," Beale announced, tapping the brakes and cranking the nosewheel steering.

Coffin nodded.

They were turning onto the base operations ramp. A marshaler with glowing wands guided them into parking, an air force staff car and several uniforms visible behind him. Under the bright ramp lights, Coffin scanned the small group. A lieutenant colonel, a captain, and sergeant.

None were female.

The plane lurched to a stop and the engines wound down. Pulling his overcoat off the chair, Coffin threw it on over his uniform jacket. In contrast to his earlier appearance, he now looked every inch the air force poster boy. Even if no one had been expecting him, Ed Coffin would have meticulously groomed himself and donned a fresh shirt. With him, image was everything. It was only recently that he'd learned it wasn't the only thing.

"You going to take the job, sir?" the FE casually asked, as Coffin reached for the stairs.

The young pilots squirmed in their seats, uncomfortable that the FE had dared voice this question. But as a senior NCO, the master sergeant had been around too long to be intimidated by a colonel.

"You really want to know, Sergeant?" Coffin asked him.

"Not particularly, sir." He grinned. "But I got a bet with Captain Beale that says you aren't crazy enough to tell a three-star no."

Coffin had to smile. "Pay up, Captain."

Beale's head bobbed, clearly embarrassed. The FE laughed.

On this point, the generals had been correct. There was no way Coffin would turn down this investigation.

Even if he still wanted to.

The loadmaster met Coffin at the foot of the stairs, breathing hard. "I took your bags outside, sir. This sure isn't Hawaii. Jesus, it's cold."

Coffin smiled his thanks and donned gloves. Worming on his flight cap, he peered through the open passenger door and saw the staff car moving toward the plane, the waiting committee hurrying behind it. As he was about to exit, Coffin suddenly closed his eyes and massaged his forehead.

"You okay, sir?"

"Fine. Never better."

But as he left, he took out several pill bottles from his jacket and hurriedly swallowed pills from each.

"Right," the lieutenant colonel barked into a radio. "The colonel is on the ground. Start your engine and pass CP an ETA to Osan."

Strolling up to Coffin, the light bird saluted, as did his men. He spoke in a rush, saying, "Welcome to Korea, sir. I'm

Lieutenant Colonel Kelly, the base operations commander. Everything's a go." He glanced to an air force blue hangup bag and civilian suitcase sitting on the ground. "Those yours, sir?"

"Yes, but I need to clear customs—"

"You've got a waiver, sir. We need to hustle. Orders straight from General Gruver. He's hot to have you at Osan. Rich. Ben."

As Kelly nudged Coffin toward the staff car, the captain and sergeant grabbed the bags and tossed them in the trunk. Practically shoving Coffin into the backseat, Kelly followed after him. To the driver, he said, "Pad six."

The car made a U-turn and sped across the massive ramp.

"Pad six?" Coffin said.

"Your ride," he said, pointing. "Got in no more than twenty minutes ago. Had to hump it to get it refueled."

Leaning forward, Coffin spied a Blackhawk helicopter less than a hundred yards away. Moments later, the engines whined and the rotor blades started to spin.

"They tell you why they want me in Osan?" Coffin asked.

Kelly did a double-take. "You don't know, Colonel?"

"No."

Kelly shrugged. "Hell, don't look at me, sir. It's way above my pay grade. All I was told was to get you out of Dodge and pronto."

"What about the plane crash?"

Another stare, this one accompanied by a frown.

"Wasn't there a plane crash at Osan?"

"News to me, sir."

"But the runway is closed . . ."

"Repairs."

"I see."

But Coffin didn't see. As a pilot and former flying squadron commander, he knew plane accidents weren't normally regarded as top secret items. While the public might not be immediately told, certainly an in-theater base-ops commander would be kept in the loop.

Arriving at the Blackhawk, Coffin recalled something else that concerned him. It was the woman on the radio. Her presence. Unless she'd changed jobs, she wouldn't normally be involved in an aircraft accident investigation.

He had a bad feeling as he crawled from the car.

It was like walking into a wind tunnel, a loud one.

Ducking low against the Blackhawk's spinning rotors, Coffin waited as Kelly and the driver slung his bags up to the flight engineer crouched in the cargo hold doorway. The FE scurried to stow them, then motioned Coffin up the steps.

Inside, the lighting had been shifted to red for night flying. Web seats ran down either side and Coffin strapped into the one closest to the door. After shutting the cargo door, the FE handed Coffin a headset, shouting into his ear. "Press this button for intercom. Flight should take about twenty minutes, sir." He grinned. "Lieutenant Colonel Hardy sends his regards."

A name from the past. "Is he your detachment commander?"

"Yes, sir. Took over last month."

Coffin nodded, donning the headset. To his left, he could see into the glowing cockpit, the faces of the pilots barely visible.

Up to now, Coffin had assumed he was alone in the back. But as his eyes adjusted to the gloom, he became aware of a figure sitting in the opposite corner. Something thumped hard inside his chest.

Mother.

★2★

Mother was silent, watching him.

Instead of the required air force uniform, she wore a stylish overcoat with a fur collar, a signal she hadn't changed jobs. Even in the dim lighting, he saw she'd aged little. While her blonde hair was shorter perhaps, she still possessed the freshly scrubbed quality of the Minnesota farm girl she'd once been. A small, compact woman with pleasantly rounded features, she'd never be considered a beauty, not that Coffin cared.

All he knew was that he'd loved her . . . once.

Mother's large eyes held him in an unblinking gaze. For a moment, Coffin thought she was trying to unnerve him. But after she made a couple of false starts to speak, he realized she was reacting to the tension between them. It was more than a feeling of awkwardness. Much more.

It was a wall.

Once again her mouth opened. This time over the headset, Coffin heard: "It's been a long time, Colonel."

"Yes, it has."

Another silence; neither knew what to say next. Slowly, as if with great reluctance, Mother shifted forward, sliding into the seat next to him. Coffin thought he detected an air of sadness to her, but that was probably wishful thinking. This woman didn't feel normal emotions, not her. If she did, she couldn't have left without explaining—

Mother abruptly addressed the pilot in command over the intercom. "Captain Gentry, I need the crew to turn off their intercom."

"We'll have to wait until we're airborne, ma'am. For safety."

Mother acquiesced with a nod. Facing Coffin, she said in his ear, "Colonel, this won't be easy on either of us. If we can't work together . . ."

"Colonel? A little formal—"

"Sir, please . . ."

"I don't foresee a problem, Mother."

"What about our . . . issues?"

"Buried in the past."

Mother searched his face. "I wish I could believe that, sir."

"It's the truth. I've moved on." He flashed a disarming smile, to convince her.

She nodded her acceptance. But Coffin could tell she didn't believe him, not that he faulted her. She'd known Coffin as a hard, uncompromising man with more than his share of ego. Guys like him don't forget and they certainly don't forgive.

Was it worth telling her that he wasn't the same man, that he'd changed? Coffin decided against it; she'd never believe that either.

The crew chief glanced back to confirm they were strapped in and jerked a thumb skyward.

"Sir," Mother said to Coffin, "I'll brief you en route."

"Okay, but knock off the sir."

No response. But once again, Coffin thought he detected a sadness.

With a shudder, the Blackhawk rose into the air.

The helicopter leveled off and chattered north. Mother was quiet, looking straight ahead. Coffin sneaked a glance at her left hand. Her gloves didn't appear to show the bulge of a wedding ring. Maybe that's why she did it. Maybe she wasn't the marrying kind and couldn't tell him.

Maybe.

His eyes crawled up, following the lines of a face he knew well. The bridge of her nose, her lips, the slope of her throat—

He felt a sudden excitement. Disgust immediately followed.

How could he feel anything for her? After what she had done to him.

How?

Turning away, he willed his mind back. Forcing himself to remember.

The memories returned in a rush. They'd met five years earlier, at Osan. He was an operations officer for a flying squadron and Mother was a criminal investigator with the Office of Special Investigations, the air force version of the FBI. Their first meeting had been like a scene from *Top Gun*, where they played eye-tag through the smoky haze of the crowded Officers' Club bar.

She'd made the first move, camping down beside him and announcing, "My name is Marva Hubbard, but most people call me Mother; get it? No, I'm not married and don't have kids. Yes, I'll dance, but I'm not a fanatic about it. What I'd really like to do is get to know you, decide if you're worth my time."

Just like that.

Coffin could only grin at her brazenness. "Let me guess. You teach courses in self-esteem and self-confidence."

She snorted. "I *look* like a teacher?"

"You're not wearing a uniform. Usually, the civilian women are DoD teachers—"

She tossed something on the table. Coffin did a double-take. Then realized it fit.

Picking up her OSI credentials, he handed them to her. "Special Agent in Charge Hubbard. Impressive. You're what, a major?" OSI credentials never revealed a rank, the theory being that suspects and witnesses would be less cooperative if they knew they were being grilled by someone they out-ranked.

"Something like that." She watched him for a beat. "That it?"

"Am I supposed to say something else?"

"A polite good-bye is customary." She shrugged, motioning toward the door. "Last guy that found out I'm a special agent ran for the hills."

"Guilty conscience."

"And you're completely innocent," she said dryly.

"Not completely." He smiled.

"You married?"

"No."

"Ever been?"

"You practicing your third degree?"

She ignored him. "Girlfriend?"

"Not lately."

"How lately?"

"A couple years."

She squinted suspiciously. "Two years? You straight?"

Coffin didn't miss a beat. "Like a board."

Her face relaxed into a grin. "Well, hell. You'll do."

That meeting was the beginning of a torrid affair. Coffin never could explain what it was about Mother that attracted him, except that she was like no other woman he'd ever met. Larger than life, she could be loud and crude one moment, sultry and kittenish the next. In bed, she was an animal and made love with a passion he'd never experienced. She also took a perverse pleasure in pushing his buttons, to keep him off balance. It was the most infuriating relationship Coffin had ever been involved in and he told himself to end it.

But he couldn't. Something about her was addicting. An excitement. He couldn't stop seeing her.

After one month, he suspected what the problem was; after the second, he knew.

For the first time in his life, he was in love.

Unlike Coffin, who was permanently stationed at Osan, Mother was on temporary assignment. With her departure imminent, Coffin did something completely out of character. He acted on impulse.

At a downtown jewelry shop, he bought the biggest diamond ring he could afford. He told Mother to meet him that evening at a local restaurant, where he'd reserved a private room and filled it with flowers. Ten minutes before she was to arrive, he went out on the sidewalk to wait.

But she never showed.

An hour passed, then two. After his frantic phone calls went unanswered, Coffin finally accepted that he'd been stood up and went to her BOQ room. No one answered his knock even though he saw movement through her blinds.

The next morning, he learned Mother had left on the first flight to the States. There'd been no message or note. He made attempts to contact her, but she never responded. She completely disappeared from his life.

The base gossip machine went into overdrive, and Coffin had never felt more humiliated. For years afterward, he'd resented and perhaps even hated her. And that's precisely what Coffin was attempting to do now, rekindle a little of the resentment and hate.

Because falling for her again sure as hell wasn't an option.

"Agent Hubbard," Captain Gentry announced. "Interphone is all yours. We need to be back on before landing."

They were perhaps fifteen hundred feet up, skirting a valley of frozen rice paddies. The stable winter air made for a smooth flight. "I'll need fifteen minutes, Captain," Mother said.

"I can give you ten, ma'am."

Before addressing Coffin, Mother watched each crewmember push buttons on the com consoles. A characteristic of a good criminal investigator; never assume anything.

"First things first," she said to Coffin. "You on board for the investigation, sir?"

"The name's Ed, remember? We're not kids, Mother."

"It's better if we keep this professional—"

"Don't flatter yourself."

The words came out harsher than Coffin intended. Mother thrust out her jaw, doing a slow burn. She didn't lose her temper often, but when she did—

"Easy," Coffin said. "I was out of line. Sorry."

She appeared genuinely startled by his remark. Another reaction Coffin understood. Apologizing had never been his strong suit.

He said, "Assuming we're talking about an accident investigation . . ."

"One of your boys went down this morning."

The confirmation he'd been seeking. As a new colonel, Coffin had commanded the First Strategic Reconnaissance Squadron based at Osan. The First flew the high-altitude U-2 spy plane. Another of Coffin's suspicions was verified—the reason for his selection.

The U-2 community was small, with few full colonels in its ranks. Regulations required that a full colonel, preferably one with U-2 experience, head the crash investigation. As far as Coffin knew, he was the only person in the Pacific Theater who fit the bill.

"The pilot survive?"

"For an hour. Died in the hospital without regaining consciousness."

"His name?"

"Major Erik Olson."

Something lurched in the pit of Coffin's stomach. Olson had been his exec and training officer.

"Lost control on a landing. Managed to eject—"

"Start at the beginning, Mother."

"There's no time. It'd be better if you saw the tape. I made you a copy." She dug out a videotape from her purse and passed it over.

Videotaping was a peculiarity U-2s shared with naval carrier aircraft, and for the same reason. Since the U-2 was extremely difficult to land—the plane's long wings generated excessive lift, which caused it to wildly pitch up unless completely stalled from flying speed at touchdown—the squadron videotaped most landings, to provide the pilots feedback on their performance.

"The highlights, then," Coffin said, slipping the tape into his overcoat pocket.

Mother reluctantly complied. Major Olson's flight was scheduled for an 0500 departure that morning, a routine mission to keep tabs on North Korea. Everything went smoothly until takeoff, when Olson began flying erratically. The mobile officer—a backup pilot monitoring the flight—became alarmed enough to order Olson back to the field. When Olson tried, he crashed while attempting to land.

"Crap," Coffin said, when she finished.

Mother blinked.

"Crap. Erik's got over two thousand hours in the jet. He can land the damn thing in his—"

He stopped. She was giving him an odd look, a sort of knowing half smile, and Coffin had an inkling what was behind it. It was time to clear up a third question.

"Your involvement," he said. "You're convinced this is a criminal matter—"

"Yes."

". . . and *not* a case of pilot error causing an accident."

"Relax. I know it wasn't."

"Define 'know.' "

From her purse, she produced an envelope, opened the flap, and removed several papers. Borrowing the FE's penlight, Coffin scanned them. The first three pages were primarily a grid, various values filled in. Off to the side were lists of medical-sounding terms, including the names of familiar drugs.

"It's the lab report on Olson," Mother said.

Standard procedure. Whenever a pilot was involved in an accident, his blood was screened for alcohol and drugs. Going down the entries, Coffin saw nothing but negative marks under the various tests.

Until he got to the third page.

A positive.

Coffin was stunned. Dammit, he knew Olson.

He angrily flipped to the fourth page. A doctor's handwritten summary of the results. Coffin didn't bother to finish the paragraph before thrusting the pages at Mother. "I don't give a damn what the tests show. Someone in the lab screwed up—"

"They didn't."

"Olson *wasn't* a druggie. A little too much booze now and then, sure. But not drugs. C'mon, Mother. Ask yourself what pilot in his right mind takes drugs before a flight—"

He broke off. Once again, Mother had that odd little half smile.

She said, "Olson tested positive for isoflurane."

"So . . ."

"That's why Dr. O'Malley, the flight surgeon, contacted me. Isoflurane is a powerful anesthetic, not a recreational narcotic. It's usually used during surgery to depress cardiovascular and pulmonary function. Dr. O'Malley is convinced Olson didn't take the drug voluntarily and so am I. People don't get high on isoflurane; they pass out."

Her remarks floated toward him, picked up speed, and landed hard.

"My God," he said. "You're actually suggesting—"

"Suggesting, hell. I'm *telling* you Erik Olson was murdered."

Just then they heard a soft click and the voice of Captain Gentry. He sounded almost cheerful.

"Osan's in sight and you're getting curbside service."

★3★

The rice paddies ended and familiar landmarks began scrolling by. The garish red-light district nicknamed "the Ville," the Osan Air Base main gate, and the taxi stand crowded with drunks, the rows of crackerbox BOQ buildings and the sprawling Officers' Club, the darkened rectangle of the K-COIC (the hardened intelligence center) and the black expanse of the golf course.

As Coffin watched out the window, none of what he was seeing registered. All he could think about was Mother's conclusion and its damning inference.

The helicopter gradually descended and the runway lights appeared. A gloved finger slid by Coffin's face, pointing to a cluster of trucks near the approach end. Light stands illuminated a blackened area, strewn with debris.

"The larger stuff is already in a hangar," Mother said.

"So a crash team has been assembled?"

"Essential specialties only. The operation is under a security blackout. Until my investigation is completed, General Gruver doesn't want to risk any leaks."

In an accident investigation, essential specialties were defined as flight operations, maintenance, and medical. Ancillary functions varied depending on the situation, but always included weather and ground control. Since Coffin knew the cause of the crash, this was a constraint he could accept.

The Blackhawk angled from the runway and a brightly lit compound the size of a football field came into view. It was the U-2 squadron and they were heading right for it. A truck was rolling through the gate and Coffin could make out what looked like a chair on the back.

But, of course, it wasn't a chair.

Turning to Mother, he said, "You mentioned Olson ejected . . ."

"Right."

"The U-2 has a zero-zero seat. Even on the ground, he should have been able to eject safely."

"The isoflurane actually killed him. It shut down his vital functions. Nothing the docs could do."

Coffin struggled to make sense of all this. Couldn't. "Isoflurane? How accessible is it?"

She shrugged. "You know the Korean black market."

He did. Anything could be had for the right price. "What about motive? Everyone liked Erik. Enlisted and officers alike. No one would have a reason to want him dead."

"You've been gone for several years—"

"I've made trips back."

"Olson could have enemies you didn't know about."

"He didn't."

"He made at least one."

"Not from the squadron."

"Ah, I see where this is going, Ed. You're still playing commander, trying to protect your former— Something funny?"

He had a slight smile.

She sighed, realizing she'd slipped and called him by name. "Guess old habits are hard to break."

"Apparently."

"Fine, okay. We'll keep it informal." But she was less than thrilled. Mother hated making concessions.

Abruptly, the helicopter broke off its descent and began hovering over the compound. The pilots waved and pointed, as if trying to signal someone. Looking down, Coffin saw the problem. Vehicles and equipment were everywhere.

"Guess the First didn't get the word we were coming in," Mother said, voicing the obvious.

People gazed up, watching them. No one seemed to know what to do. A black officer in a flight suit and a stocky man in a green Battle Dress Utility uniform—the newer version of fatigues—ran from one of the two giant hangars, waving and gesturing. Bodies scurried and vehicles started clearing the landing zone. A flatbed carrying the U-2's shattered tail swerved to miss a forklift, clipped a pickup and sent it careening. The stocky man and the officer stared in disbelief, then took off running.

"Man, what a goat rope," the FE called out, crouching by a window.

An understatement. The drivers involved in the accident jumped from their vehicles and began arguing animatedly. A shoving match ensued and the black officer had to separate the two men.

"Lieutenant Colonel Hardy part of the team, Mother?" Coffin asked, watching with amusement as the irate officer reamed out both men.

"Your deputy. Really wanted the job. Practically begged General Gruver for it. Hope he's got his shit together more than he's showing so far. You know him, huh?"

A reference to the FE's comment when he'd boarded. Coffin hesitated, picking up a note of disapproval. "We're friendly," he said cautiously. "Why?"

"Can't figure him out. Whenever we run into each other,

he won't give me the time of day." She shrugged. "But hey, it can't be anything personal. I barely know the guy. Could be he's a Neanderthal with a thing against women or he just doesn't like cops."

Her eyes bored into Coffin's, anticipating a response.

"Yeah, that's probably it," he heard himself say.

She nodded, accepting his remark. It was a lie.

"Won't be long," the FE said. "Chief's playing traffic cop. What's that in his hand?"

Looking down, Coffin and Mother saw the heavyset man in BDUs standing in the center of the compound, waving what looked like a stick at the vehicles.

"It's his cigar," Coffin said.

The FE grinned; Mother rolled her eyes. Chief Master Sergeant Jim-Bob Sessler was one of those people everyone seemed to know, and for good reason. Married to a Korean, the chief had spent most of his career at Osan, becoming something of an institution.

"The chief's on the team," Mother said. "First guy the general picked."

Another note of disapproval. Only this time, Coffin understood it.

A cigar-chewing good ole boy from Texas, Chief Sessler possessed none of the spit and polish normally associated with a ranking NCO. Opinionated and outspoken, he cared little for military protocol, even less for his appearance, and relished knocking heads with those who disagreed with him. What Sessler did care about was his men and his airplanes, and he regularly busted his ass for both. When Coffin took over the squadron in the late eighties, the maintenance record was abysmal and he took a chance on Sessler, making him the head of the section. When word reached his superiors, they reacted as if Coffin had lost his mind.

"Colonel," a general told Coffin, "that man is a disgrace. He's twenty pounds overweight and exhibits a complete lack of military bearing. His character is also questionable as hell. For chrissakes, he's been investigated by the OSI."

"The Korean police cleared him, sir." Through his wife's family, Sessler owned several businesses downtown and had been accused of offering bribes and kickbacks.

"For a lack of evidence, not because he was innocent. Word I got is he bought off the police."

"Sir, that's only an allegation."

"Colonel, I don't trust him and I want him removed. Is that clear? What's this?"

Coffin handed him a computer printout. "Our launch reliability for the past two months, sir. Not a single U-2 flight was canceled for mechanical problems under Chief Sessler's watch."

"And before that?"

"We've scrapped a flight every ten days, sir."

For the rest of Coffin's tour, the U-2s set a record for reliability and the general never mentioned Sessler again.

"All clear, sir," the FE called out to Captain Gentry. "The chief's waving us down."

"I see him, Sergeant."

As the Blackhawk resumed its descent, Coffin checked his watch. Almost 2200. They'd wasted eight minutes.

"By the way, Ed," Mother said. "He agrees with me."

He frowned at her. "Chief Sessler?"

"Please. General Gruver. He agrees the killer has to be someone from the squadron."

Typical Mother. She was going to keep pressing this point until he agreed. He said flatly, "The general is wrong."

"Come on. There are over a hundred people in the First. How can you possibly know—"

"I know."

"You're convinced it has to be someone else? An outsider."

"Right."

"*Look.*" Mother gestured to the window. "Ask yourself who else could access this compound, avoid the guards, and enter the hangars unobserved—"

"Erik could have been drugged before he showed up."

Mother nodded as if she agreed with Coffin, then flung back, "Not a chance in hell, Ed."

She went on, speaking fast. "Isoflurane is quick-acting, within seconds. We know Olson showed up for the flight feeling fine. We know he passed the preflight physical with flying colors. We know he suited up in the spacesuit and prebreathed oxygen for an hour without incident. We know he was lucid during the time he got into the U-2 and taxied to the runway. We know that he first displayed signs of distress within seconds of takeoff. So much distress that he lost control of the plane. You're the U-2 expert, Ed. You tell me how that happened. How could an outsider sneak in and rig either his spacesuit or the plane to feed Olson enough isoflurane to kill him?"

Coffin passed on a response. She had him and they both knew it.

This was the chilling inference that had worried Coffin. Mother was describing sabotage. Since a U-2 was a classified asset, only those who worked on it had the access and knowledge to pull something like this off.

Someone he'd once commanded was a killer.

★4★

A bump. The Blackhawk settled to the ground.

Removing his headset, Coffin unlatched his belt and started to rise. Mother immediately jerked him back down, saying, "A couple other things we need to get straight—"

"Make it quick." He glanced toward the cockpit, realizing the pilots had shut down the engines.

Noticing his reaction, the FE said, "We're hanging around to pick up a DV, sir. A general."

That explained the curbside service, since full colonels normally weren't considered distinguished visitors.

"Ed," Mother said, keeping her voice low, "this is a criminal *and* a crash investigation. While we'll be working both aspects simultaneously, you have to understand the criminal takes priority."

Translation: She'd ultimately call the shots. "All right."

"Taking orders from me won't be a . . . problem."

"You a full colonel yet?" It was possible. He'd made his promotions in minimum time, pinning on eagles six years early.

"Does it matter?"

Another translation: She wasn't. "Relax, Mother. I don't have a compulsion to be in charge."

She snorted derisively. "Since when?"

"Still pushing buttons, I see."

Her face turned to stone. Miss Sensitive. Coolly, she said, "I'll need to know how the isoflurane was administered. By tonight."

Their eyes locked. She was giving him his first order. Testing him.

"Sure, Mother," he said lightly. "I'll get right on it."

She tried to appear unsurprised . . . and failed.

The rotors stopped and it was quiet. The FE opened the door and they heard voices. As Coffin reached for his bags, the FE said smoothly, "I'll get them, sir."

"Thank you, Sergeant. Here." Returning his penlight, Coffin rose. "Who's the DV?"

"Some Korean general, sir." The FE shrugged.

"General Cho," Captain Gentry called back. "The chairman of the South Korean joint staff. We're flying him to the Blue House—I say something, sir?"

Coffin stood frozen, his mind racing.

The Blue House meant the South Korean president. And General Cho was arguably the country's second most powerful man. It didn't make sense. Someone of Cho's stature would never become personally involved in the crash of an American plane. Certainly, the Korean president wouldn't. But since this was also murder . . .

Shit. *Shit.*

He swung around to Mother accusingly. "You're holding out on me. You knew General Cho was here. You knew of President Rhee's interest."

"Yeah. The ROKs are pressuring us for answers big-time."

"Why?"

"You read the papers. The north supposedly has nukes, remember? Since the U-2 is the only thing that's regularly monitoring those facilities, it's understandable that the ROK government would become concerned whenever—"

He cut her off. "The U-2s will keep flying. Erik Olson's death doesn't change that. Cho has another reason for coming here. What?"

"Suppose you tell me." She managed to sound both sarcastic and amused.

The crew was hanging on their every word, but that wasn't why Coffin didn't reply. Frankly, there was no point. Mother knew damn well why General Cho had flown here and why the Korean president was apparently interested in the crash of a U-2.

The killer could be an outsider, after all.

A swarm of green BDU uniforms converged on the helicopter. Most were enlisted maintenance technicians, with a few contract civilians thrown in. Normally, they would have greeted their former commander with crisp salutes and welcoming smiles. But tonight there were no smiles; they'd lost one of their own.

Emerging from the helo, Coffin heard a shout. In a darkened area by the hangars, dim figures inspected the dented pickup. The silhouette of an arm waved and Coffin waved back.

At the bottom of the ladder, Coffin impulsively extended his hand to Mother. A mistake. Slinging her purse over her shoulder, she coldly ignored him and climbed down on her own. Coffin felt his face get hot, aware that the crowd had caught the snub. Frankly, he couldn't understand what had gotten into Mother; her sudden disdain. She was the one who had left him. Yet, she was acting as if she were the wronged party.

And it was getting to him.

Facing the crowd, Coffin saw a wall of somber faces looking back. A few diverted their eyes, as if embarrassed for him. A demanding, no-nonsense commander, Coffin had sacrificed popularity for respect, not that it mattered now. He was one of them and they were hurting.

"Hell of thing about Major Olson," a sergeant said quietly. "Damn shame."

"I still can't believe it," a civilian added. "We all thought he'd make it."

"I saw the whole thing, sir," someone else said. "He just . . . crashed."

More people spoke up. They needed to talk, let their emotions out. Coffin voiced words of reassurance, tried to be sympathetic. Stepping away, Mother briefly conversed with two of her agents, a dark-haired man and a blonde woman. After pointing out a concrete building to the right of the hangars, the agents left. The FE unloaded Coffin's bags and asked what he should do with them. Before Coffin could reply, he spotted two men hurrying toward their group. It was Lieutenant Colonel Samuel Hardy and Chief Sessler.

They looked angry.

The accident.

Coffin initially assumed Hardy and Sessler were upset about the accident involving the pickup. But as the men approached, he realized he was mistaken.

Their eyes were fixed on Mother. They never left her. Twice Lieutenant Colonel Hardy even shook his head in disgust.

The snub, Coffin realized.

"Outta the way," the chief's gravel voice barked out. "Coming through. Time's a-wastin', people, and you got work to do. Jensen, take the colonel's bags to my truck. Chop,

chop. Christ, what a fucking cockup. Last we heard, you were landing on the pad, Colonel."

"No harm, no foul, Chief."

The crowd quickly disbanded. A mop-topped airman darted forward and snatched the luggage from the FE. The chief and Lieutenant Colonel Hardy stopped before Coffin and Mother. As usual, the chief wore a rumpled uniform, which matched his even more rumpled face. By contrast, Hardy stood lean and long, his form-fitting flight suit immaculate, the toes of his boots gleaming.

Jamming his unlit cigar between his teeth, the chief threw Coffin a sloppy salute while Hardy remained motionless, his chiseled face locked on Mother. A former college tight end, he was giving her the same dead stare that he'd used to unnerve opposing players.

But apparently Mother didn't play football. She snapped, "You got a problem, Colonel?"

Hardy's jaw flexed into ropes. "You're damn right. Where do you get off—"

Coffin immediately cut Hardy off, saying sharply, "Stop, Sam."

Hardy blinked.

"Stop," Coffin repeated. "We all need to work together."

Slowly Hardy's face relaxed. He nodded.

"Not so fast," Mother said to him. "I want to know what the hell your problem is, Colonel. You've got something against me. What?"

Hardy's eyes crawled over to Coffin. "She doesn't know?"

"I never told her."

He snapped Coffin a textbook salute. "Long time no see, roommate."

Mother's mouth fell open.

Hardy laughed and laughed.

*

Mother's response surprised Coffin.

Once she recovered from her shock, she should have been furious, spitting mad. But as Hardy laughed, she just stood there silently, taking it.

Moments later, Coffin noticed something even more astonishing. Mother meekly turned away, looking upset and hurt.

The laughter stopped.

None of the men spoke. They all frowned at her, puzzled by her reaction. That she could be so sensitive. Coffin tentatively reached out. "Mother . . ."

She jerked away.

"Colonel Coffin! Sir!"

From the direction of the squadron operations building, a woman jogged toward them. They recognized her as the admin clerk. "Colonel Coffin," she called out, "the general would like you and Agent Hubbard—"

"Hold it right there, Dee Dee," the chief said. "They'll be with you in a minute."

"Chief, I'm supposed to—"

"*In a minute.*"

The clerk jerked to a stop, her expression confused.

An awkward silence fell upon the group. No one said anything, they just watched Mother. Waiting.

Finally, she faced the three men, her hurt replaced by a cold expression. Sam Hardy began, "Look, I didn't mean—"

"The hell you didn't." She shot Coffin a withering glance. "What'd you tell him, Ed? That I'm a heartless bitch who gets her rocks off leading men on?"

Coffin knew better than to reply.

Mother swung around to the chief. "You know, too, huh? What? The whole damned squadron know what happened? Christ, this is unbelievable."

"I only told Sam," Coffin said.

Mother's gaze was like ice.

"Blame me," the chief said to her. "My family owns the restaurant. I was there the night the colonel was waiting for—"

He gave up; Mother wasn't listening to him. She was shaking her head, saying, "Everyone thinks I'm a bitch. That I left you for no reason. But that wasn't it at all. I'm not like that. I was only trying . . . to hell with it . . . I don't have to explain . . . I don't because . . ."

She trailed off, staring into the dark. Lost in her thoughts.

Watching her, Coffin felt his pulse quicken. All these years, never knowing . . .

He signaled Hardy and the chief with a look; they were already moving away.

"What reason?" Coffin softly asked Mother. "What did I do?"

Silence. She didn't seem to hear him.

"Mother . . ."

A slow blink. When she focused on him, he saw the hurt had returned. "I'm not made of stone. I have feelings . . ."

"Mother, I . . ."

"Jesus, you think it was easy for me. Walking out on you. Well, it wasn't. Despite what you think, I loved you."

Coffin felt a sudden pain in his chest. "Then why? Tell me why."

"I . . . can't."

"I have a right to know. You owe me at least that much."

"You blew it, Ed." She sounded sad. "We had something and you blew it."

She turned away from him, saying nothing more.

A wrenching disappointment. Again.

Backing away from Mother, Coffin desperately searched

the past. But there was nothing there, no reason he could find. Dammit, he hadn't done anything.

A lie? Was she lying to him? Trying to shift the guilt—

"Ed," Hardy said. "You and Mother better get going."

He and the chief were standing by the admin clerk, Dee Dee, who appeared on the verge of panic.

"Go where?" Coffin asked dully.

"A briefing in the conference room, sir," Dee Dee squeaked. "It's already started."

Coffin glanced to Mother. She was moving away, unhooking her portable radio from her belt. He said, "Mother . . ."

"You go, Ed. The general will have questions and I need to check with my office, for updates."

Mother walked until she was out of earshot, confirming to Coffin that she regarded their cooperation as a one-way street.

Shaking his head, Coffin started to leave. But after a half dozen steps he pulled up. Another few minutes wouldn't matter. Besides, this was the kind of meeting you don't interrupt twice.

Seeing Coffin was going to wait, Dee Dee began to squirm. The chief whispered to her and she hurried back toward the squadron.

Hardy and the chief came over to Coffin. "Sir," the chief said, "I'll take care of your bags, get you checked into the Q."

"Thanks, Chief." Coffin appreciated the gesture; the chief rarely displayed this kind of personal attention for an officer.

Coffin's eyes drifted to the leftmost hangar. The massive doors were open and he watched people crawl over a relatively intact U-2 fuselage and a large section of a wing. Smaller remnants of the plane had been placed off to the side. He asked, "How much longer until the recovery is complete?"

"By early morning," Hardy replied. "Cleaning up the fuel slowed us down."

"You get the word Mother thinks Olson was murdered?"

The men nodded grimly. "Some kind of gas," Hardy said.

"She also thinks he was killed by someone in the squadron," the chief added, scowling at Mother. "She's fucking crazy, sir."

"Careful, Chief."

"Well she is, if that's what she thinks," the chief insisted stubbornly. "Hell, everyone in the squadron loved the guy."

Coffin let it go. The chief was only doing his job, defending his troops. "Our first priority is to find how the gas was administered. The obvious way is the oxygen tanks . . ."

"Except," Hardy said, "Major Olson breathed from the tanks for a good twenty minutes before he took off, and I understand the stuff acts fast."

Coffin nodded. This bothered him, too.

"Can't be the tanks, then," the chief concluded. "But I'll have the boys pull them ASAP. We'll know for sure soon. Do me a favor, sir. Talk to Agent Hubbard and get her to back off. Her agents are messing up the entire operation. Every time I look around, they're hauling one a' my troops in for questioning." Chewing on his cigar, he added sourly, "What'd I tell ya? Those assholes are at it again."

They watched the female OSI agent lead two maintenance troops into the concrete building used by PSD. The physiological support division technicians were responsible for maintaining the spacesuits and dressing the pilots for their flights.

"It's bullshit and a waste of time, sir," Sessler said, throwing up his hands. "How am I supposed to get any work done? You tell Agent Hubbard she's pissing in the wind if she thinks it's one of us. I should have my head examined for not retiring." Hitching up his pants, he lumbered toward the hangar.

"He's right," Hardy said dryly, glancing at Mother. "She probably could piss in the wind."

"Knock it off, Sam."

Hardy's head jerked around. "What's *this*? The ice lady shows she has a few feelings and you suddenly change your tune."

"It's more than that."

"Let me guess. She told you she dumped you because she's really into girls, so that makes everything okay. I mean it's not like there was another guy, so your ego—"

"I'm not laughing, Sam."

"That makes two of us. What the hell is your problem anyway?"

"*My* problem?"

"Damn straight. You haven't answered my emails or phone calls for months. On top of that, you didn't let me know you were coming to Osan. Imagine my surprise when I learned my old college buddy—"

"I didn't know you were here."

"You *read* my emails, Ed? I'll bet you don't know I got engaged."

Coffin stared at him.

Hardy looked disgusted. "Christ, you're unbelievable, you know that?"

"Sam, I got a lot going on . . ."

"Yeah, yeah. Too busy bucking for general. Your first-look board met what, last month? When you get that star, it'll be good-bye, Sam. After all, general officers can't mix with the help—"

Hardy's words hit a nerve. "Dammit," Coffin shot back, "that's not true. You know me, Sam. You know I'd never forget—" He broke off; Hardy was grinning.

"You son of a bitch," Coffin said, catching on.

Hardy winked. "Gotcha. You should have seen your face. You thought I was really one pissed off Jose."

Coffin sighed, nodding.

He clapped Coffin on the back. "So we don't stay in touch, so what? We're like family, am I right?"

"You're right."

"You better believe it, kemosabe. Why the hell do you think I volunteered for this dog and pony show? Took some fast talking, I can tell you. General Gruver wasn't crazy about assigning a rotor head to investigate a fixed-wing crash. But I told him we'd worked together before and you needed me to set you straight."

"Thanks, Sam."

They became quiet, looking at each other. Old friends recalling a shared past.

"Hell, I had to do it," Hardy said with feeling. "I owe you, remember?"

"No one's keeping score, Sam."

At the sound of clicking heels, they turned and saw Mother approach, clipping her radio to her belt. Coffin whispered, "Sam . . ."

"I'll be nice."

Moving forward, he flashed Mother a smile. "I'd like to apologize for my big mouth."

"I'll survive, Colonel. I'm a big girl."

"Call me Sam."

"Let's not rush it."

He grinned. "Hell, I deserved that. I'll either be in the hangar or on the runway. Best way to get me is the radio. My call sign is Recovery One."

As he strolled off, Mother watched him thoughtfully. "Did I hear Sam say he owed you?"

"Yes."

She looked at Coffin expectantly. The cop in her curious, wanting to know.

"Any breaks in the case?" he asked.

"No."

Shrugging, he turned on a heel and headed for the operations building. If she wanted to keep secrets, he could also.

★5★

Don't tell anyone. Promise.
I promise, Sam.

Hardy had always believed fate brought Coffin and him together. Why else would two people with nothing in common become friends?

They'd met during their sophomore year at college. Hardy was a larger-than-life football star who was on the verge of flunking out; Coffin, the engineering and ROTC student selected to tutor him. Because of their disparate backgrounds, they spent their initial meetings feeling each other out, but over the months developed a genuine bond.

"Just get me to graduation and you got a car, Ed. Any kind you want."

"Get your millions first and we'll talk."

"You want a Porsche? You'll be the only lieutenant with one. Be like Tom Cruise in *Top Gun*. Girls will be all over you."

"Sure, Sam. A Porsche would be fine. Let's go over those history questions again."

Getting Hardy to study was like pulling teeth. He was so sure he was going to make it to the NFL. In truth, so was Coffin. Hardy had the speed, the size, and the ability. What he didn't have was something even more important—luck.

When a devastating knee injury the following season ended Hardy's pro dreams, the effect on his psyche was profound, and he became depressed to the point of being suicidal. A product of inner city Cleveland, he saw no future and feared returning to the projects.

One night, Coffin received a hysterical call from Hardy's girlfriend. Hardy was drunk and talking crazy and had driven off in his car. At first, Coffin thought she was overreacting. Then she told him what Sam had taken from the house.

After several hours of looking, Coffin was about to give up when he spotted a lone car in the stadium parking lot. It was Hardy's. Walking up to it, Coffin saw Hardy slumped at the wheel and feared the worst.

But Hardy raised his head when Coffin approached.

"Leave me alone, Coffin."

"It's not the end of the world. So what if you can't play football. You can still go to school."

"Shows what the hell you know."

"I never took you for a quitter, Sam."

"Fuck you. I can't handle the academics. You know I can't."

"I'll help you. I'll tutor you."

"Why? What's in it for you? You some kinda Boy Scout looking for a merit badge? Help the poor black kid—"

"Don't do this, Sam. I only want to help."

"By *judging* me. You don't know what it's like to be poor and black. Growing up, I never knew my father and barely knew my mother. I lived with four brothers and sisters in a one-room apartment with no heat. Everyone I grew up with is either dead or in prison or strung out on drugs. You think I'm a quitter. Well screw you, man. I'm no quitter; I'm a *survivor*."

"Join the club," Coffin said softly.

"What's that supposed to mean?"

So Coffin described growing up in the orphanage, how he was treated as an outcast, a *chu-bang ja*, a mixed race nonperson. He told Hardy about being beaten and spat upon and other constant humiliations. He told him about the loneliness of being ostracized and how much it hurt. He told him everything, leaving nothing out.

Afterward, Hardy said nothing. Coffin tried to read him, but couldn't tell if he'd gotten through.

"Look," he asked, "you want my help or not?"

"I got no money. I can't pay you."

"Who's asking you to?"

"Why are you doing this?"

Hardy would sense a lie, so Coffin went with the truth. "I don't know."

Hardy nodded, accepting. He was quiet for a while, staring at the darkened stadium. "I was good, wasn't I?"

"One of the best."

He gave Coffin a little smile. "Don't laugh, but I've been thinking about all the stuff you talked about. How you're going to be a military pilot and all . . ."

"Okay."

"I was wondering . . . you know. If maybe I could do it, too? Become a pilot?"

Again, Coffin went with the truth. "Maybe. If you work hard enough and bring your grades up."

"Hard work is all I know. I told you I'm a survivor."

"Prove it now," Coffin said quietly. He came forward and held out his hand.

Their eyes met. Hardy appeared embarrassed.

"I wasn't going to do it, Ed. I swear to you."

"I believe you."

"Don't tell anyone. Promise."

"I promise, Sam."

Hardy finally passed over the gun.

Since the First Strategic Reconnaissance Squadron only had a complement of three permanently assigned pilots—the commander, operations officer, and assistant ops officer—and four TDY pilots who rotated in on two-month tours from the home base in California, the operations building was the smallest on the compound and easily the most dilapidated. Roughly the size of a double-wide trailer, the structure should have been renovated a decade earlier, but in a fighter-pilot-dominated air force, money for intelligence programs was hard to come by. But at least it was heated and the roof didn't leak . . . much.

The entrance was off to the side, adjacent to a barbecue pit that had seen better days. Angling toward it, Mother and Coffin skirted a dime-sized parking area crowded with official vehicles, including two Ford Mustangs used by the mobile officers—the backup pilots responsible for chasing after and talking down landing U-2s. As they went by a staff car flying a three star flag, they noticed the driver slumped forward, asleep.

Coffin rapped sharply on the window.

The driver jolted upright with a look of panic.

Coffin and Mother headed down the walkway without breaking stride. She said, "You almost gave the kid a heart attack."

"Better than letting General Gruver catch him sleeping. By the way, Chief Sessler would like your people to back off their questioning, at least until the recovery is completed."

"What part of murder investigation doesn't he understand?"

"He has a point. We're only talking a few hours—"

"Inform Chief Sessler he can kiss my ass."

"Any particular style? Full juicy lips or a quick peck—"

"Not funny, Ed."

They came to the ops building door, which had the unit's logo, a black cat, painted on it. As Coffin started to play gentleman and open it for Mother, he hesitated, looking at her.

"It's okay," she said. "I'm sorry about what happened earlier."

"No problem. I enjoy being emasculated in public."

"Listen, I made it clear from the beginning I wanted to keep it strictly professional between us."

"Got it. No touching or displays of courtesy."

"Ed . . ."

"Just want to make sure I understand the rules."

He rudely brushed past her and entered the squadron. Sure, he was being petty, but he didn't give a damn. He was tired of being the nice guy. From behind, he heard her mutter, "Asshole."

They were standing in a dingy paneled hallway lined with photographs of men wearing spacesuits. Former squadron commanders. The pictures were in chronological order, which placed Coffin's the second from the door. "You had more hair then," Mother said.

Ouch.

The hallway made a ninety-degree turn to the left. A door to the right said simply *Ops*. It was the pilots' room and they could hear voices coming out.

"I'm questioning the pilots after the briefing," Mother said.

Coffin had figured as much. "Who was Olson's mobile?"

"A good friend of yours, apparently . . ."

"Oh?"

". . . Major Caralyn Barlow." And she looked at Coffin in a suggestive way.

Coffin sighed, tempted to ignore the inference. But Mother would continue to pester him. He said, "You shouldn't listen to rumors."

"What rumors?" Her face was blank, innocent.

"Caralyn's father ran the ROTC unit at my college. When U-2s were opened to women, he asked if I could her get in. Caralyn and I got to know each other and became friends. That's all there is to it."

"Only friends, huh?" She drew out the remark, making it sound dirty.

"She's *married*, Mother. I don't mess around with married women."

"*Was* married. I understand she got divorced after she joined U-2s."

"Because of the TDYs. U-2 pilots are constantly gone from home. It's tough on any relationship—"

He stopped. Mother's face lit up and he realized she'd only baited him to get a reaction. And this time, she'd finally succeeded in hooking him.

A caustic response was out because that was her goal, to get him to lose his cool. And one thing he'd learned from babysitting a four-star general was how to keep cool.

"You got me. Congratulations." He sounded as if he meant it.

She was taken aback by his response. "Uh, thank you."

"You're welcome."

As they moved down the hallway, Mother continued to toss Coffin puzzled glances and he resisted the urge to smile. She wasn't the only one who could play mind games.

"Thank God, sir," Dee Dee said, appearing from

around the corner ahead. "The general just asked for you again. You can go right in. There are two open seats at the back."

Coffin and Mother made the turn. Dee Dee waited by the closed door of the briefing room, a short, bookish ROK Army lieutenant colonel beside her. He seemed familiar, but Coffin couldn't place him at first.

Then the Korean turned his head, revealing a fleshy nub where his left ear should have been.

Mother caught her breath, but Coffin's expression never changed. Smoothly, he said, "*Dae-ryeong eu ro jin-geup haet-da.*" You've been promoted, Lieutenant Colonel Kwan.

Kwan made a tight formal bow. Bent at the waist, the back straight. "*Cho-eun gi-eok ess-eo-yo.*" Politely complimenting Coffin's memory.

As he reached out to open the door, Mother tensed, staring at his left hand. It was missing the ring and little fingers. Kwan watched her through his black-rimmed glasses, amused by her reaction.

"*Os-se yo,*" he said, ushering them inside.

"*Gam-sa ham-ni-da,*" Coffin replied.

They entered the darkened briefing room. It was thick with smoke and packed with military uniforms, Koreans along the far wall, Americans near the door. Seated at the conference table were a total of eighteen stars, counting both shoulders, and two full colonels. General Cho, the ROK chief of staff, sat slumped in an overstuffed chair, quietly smoking a cigarette. A small man with a worn, haggard face and a stooped laborer's back, he could have passed for a retired farmer instead of a revered military figure. Per military protocol, General Gruver, the burly Seventh Air Force three-star, occupied the seat to Cho's left. The two men were a study in contrasts. With his putting-green scalp and Popeye-the-sailor jawline, Gruver looked like a general straight out of central casting.

"Looks like you've decided to come on board, Colonel Coffin," Gruver said, kicking back in his chair.

"Yes, sir."

"Mother, you bring him up to speed?"

"Yes, sir," she answered.

"Anything turn up on your interviews?"

"Not yet, sir. We're planning on working through the night."

Gruver contemplated Coffin for a beat. "This thing is a bucket of worms. Believe me, if it wasn't, I wouldn't have asked for your help. You're doing me a helluva favor, Colonel."

A curious remark. Since when did an imperial general use the word favor when talking to a subordinate? "Glad to help, sir," Coffin said.

Gruver gave him a look that said "bullshit." Jerking a thumb, he said, "We saved you a couple of seats. General Yee is chief of army intelligence. He's briefing us on their latest information."

"Yes, sir."

A pair of ROK and American one-stars were also at the table, but Gruver was referring to the diminutive two-star standing at the podium. Major General Yee was another face familiar to Coffin. And like the lieutenant colonel outside, he was also someone who'd been promoted.

Yee watched Coffin with a sense of expectation. Waiting for Coffin to acknowledge him. But Coffin had no intention of doing so.

Turning, he started to follow Mother to their seats.

"You're late, Colonel," Yee said suddenly. "It's disruptive

and unprofessional." His English was impeccable, his sarcasm unmistakable.

The nearby American officers seemed puzzled by the remark. Coffin wasn't.

With a sigh, Coffin faced Yee. "My apologies—" He forced out the word. "General."

An arrogant smile. The response Yee had been seeking.

The two open chairs were beside a young Korean lieutenant manning the audiovisual equipment. As Mother and Coffin sat down, two dozen pairs of eyes watched them. But Coffin was only aware of one.

General Yee continued to fixate on him with that arrogant smile.

Mother whispered, "Yee doesn't seem to like you."

"What was your first clue?"

On the wall-mounted screen, a slide with a top secret header showed a high-altitude, overhead shot of a cluster of enormous concrete buildings. The most photographed installation on the Korean Peninsula.

Yongbyon, the North Korean nuclear facility.

"A waste of time," Mother muttered. "There's no connection to the murder. There can't be."

Obviously, the Koreans thought differently.

★6★

As General Yee resumed his briefing, images flashed on the screen at a dizzying rate: various pictures of Yongbyon, photos of long-range Scud missiles, schematics of possible warheads, intelligence summaries of recent North Korean troop movements, and talking points outlining the current North Korean political situation and the harsh realities of the country's economy. The information was comprehensive to the point of being numbing. It was also information Coffin had heard in intelligence briefings before, except for one significant difference.

Everything was presented not as an intelligence estimate, but as a fact. Yee was stating unequivocally that North Korea had not only developed nuclear weapons, but had married warheads to operational missiles.

It was a stunning revelation and should have generated shocked looks and a flurry of questions.

But it didn't.

The Americans sat calmly, showing no reaction. They obviously weren't buying what Yee was selling. Coffin certainly wasn't. Something this big, American intelligence would have passed along months ago. The fact that they hadn't meant this was at best an exaggeration or at worst an outright—

Then Yee mentioned the woman.

"An agent," he said. "A young female KCIA operative. She represented our deepest penetration into the North Korean leadership. Until her infiltration, we could only guess at the North's intentions and capabilities. But now, we *know*." Yee paused for effect, looking right at General Gruver. "She had access to the highest levels of the North Korean government."

Gruver went with it. "How high, General?"

"She was a mistress of Kim Jong Il."

Gruver sat up fast. "Jesus."

"She became a favorite of Kim Jong Il," Yee went on. "She gained his trust and for over a year has provided us with intelligence that has proven consistently reliable. General Gruver, I'm sure you recall the assassination team we apprehended last summer . . ."

Gruver nodded, as did most of the Americans. It had been a big story, picked up by the news services. The North had tried to slip in assassins along the coast, ostensibly to kill President Rhee. They were captured when an alert fisherman spotted them and notified authorities.

"Our agent was the source for that information," Yee said. "Her reliability is unquestioned, which is what makes her latest revelations so troubling. Several months ago, she informed us that Kim Jong Il intended to attack the South. Initially, we discounted her assessment. But she explained that he was acting out of desperation. With his economy in shambles and the growing unrest in his military, he feels he has no other choice if he wants to avoid being overthrown. According to our agent, the attack will come in the early spring, possibly in March—"

Up until now, Gruver had been nodding as he listened. But this was too much.

"Wait a second," he said. "Why in the hell would Kim Jong Il reveal military war plans to a mistress? That's frankly . . . insane."

"Kim Jong Il *is* insane, General," Yee said.

Gruver swung around to Cho, but the ROK four-star ignored him. Puffing away on his cigarette, Cho appeared detached, as if he wasn't following the conversation. But Coffin knew that wasn't the case at all. As the senior Korean officer, Cho was choosing to let Yee run the show, so he could remain in the background, watching and observing until he had a reason to speak up.

Apparently, this wasn't it.

Gruver coughed suggestively. Cho yawned and massaged his eyes.

Taking the hint, Gruver gave up and addressed Yee. He said, "You'll have to do better than that, General. Kim Jong Il would have security people all over the place. If he had a loose mouth, they would know. Take precautions with the women—"

"They did, General."

"Meaning . . ."

"Our agent was terminated." Yee shrugged.

"So you can't produce her. Pretty damned convenient."

Yee's jaw tightened at the insinuation. But the truth was that the ROKs had a history of exaggerating threats posed by the North. In an era of congressional budget cuts, the last thing they wanted was for their U.S. allies to pull out.

A tense moment followed as the two generals played the staring game, neither willing to back down. Yee cracked first, becoming visibly angry.

"General," he said tersely, "may I remind you—"

Cho finally spoke up, and in a dramatic manner. In a

harsh, angry flurry of words directed at Yee, he said, "*Ip eul jo-shi ha-sae-yo.*"

Yee looked to General Cho in surprise.

"*Da-bo saek-i ya.*" The old man emphatically jabbed a bony finger. He appeared completely disgusted.

Yee bowed low. "*Ui-mi ha-ji-ant—*"

"*Mal-han geo-seul meol-ji-ant-da.*"

"*Ne?*" Yee reddened. "*Joe-song ha-shim-ni-da.*"

The conversation continued. Everyone in the room was transfixed. "What's going on?" Mother whispered to Coffin.

"Cho is telling Yee to remember that Gruver is his superior. Yee tried to point out that Gruver questioned his truthfulness; Cho isn't interested."

"*Ji-gum bu-teo,*" Cho said severely. "*Yam-jeon ha-ge-gul-eo-ya dwae.*"

"*Ne, ne.*"

More obsequious bowing from Yee. He looked embarrassed, which was precisely Cho's intention. Humiliation was a preferred way to deal with minor missteps by subordinates. For more egregious acts, superiors administered beatings, often brutally. In a well-publicized incident, a colonel beat a soldier to death for falling asleep on guard duty.

In the ROK Army, discipline was everything.

After a final, effusive bow, Yee barked an order to the lieutenant at the back. The young officer frantically rifled through a box of slides. Around the room, the other Korean officers stared at the floor, not daring to make eye contact with Yee. But Coffin chose the opposite tack and stared right at Yee.

He enjoyed seeing the man sweat.

Addressing Gruver, Yee said sullenly, "I must apologize for my rudeness."

"Accepted."

"General Cho would like me to prove our agent exists. We have . . . photographs."

"Fine."

"Huh?" Mother said. "Why didn't he just show them before?"

Coffin wondered the same thing.

The lieutenant stuffed several slides into a tray, inserted it into the projector. At a nod from Yee, a picture appeared on the screen.

It was taken with a telephoto lens, showing a woman standing at the edge of a pond, in what looked like a public square or park.

Another nod and click. A closer shot of the woman in the park. They saw her face clearly.

Appreciative murmurs from the Americans. It was a visceral reaction. The image had that kind of an effect. "My God," Mother said, "she's beautiful."

"Very," Coffin said.

They now understood why the Korean dictator had told her secrets. Any man might have done the very same thing, to build himself up in her eyes, impress her. She was that beautiful.

Staring at the picture, Coffin couldn't shake the feeling that he'd seen her before. But a face like that men don't forget.

"You said she was terminated?" Gruver asked Yee.

"Yes."

Another slide came up. A body lying on a slab in a morgue. Yee nodded and a close-up appeared, revealing a battered and bloodied face.

"Aw, Christ," Gruver said.

"They threw her out of a hotel window," Yee said. "Fortunately for us, she'd already passed along her information."

Gruver was obviously shaken. As a fighter pilot, he wasn't used to seeing death up close and personal. "We've seen enough."

The image disappeared.

"Does the CIA know about this?" he asked Yee.

"Yes."

"And their reaction?"

A diffident shrug.

"Nothing," Cho said with feeling.

Gruver looked to him in surprise.

"Nothing," Cho repeated in heavily accented English. "America does nothing. America is afraid of China." He shook his head angrily. "*Geom-jaeng'i.*"

The Korean officers appeared stunned by the remark. Mother whispered, "What's that mean, Ed?"

"No balls."

A damning assessment, but there was nothing Gruver could say. Handcuffed by concerns over China, the United States was essentially allowing North Korea to develop weapons of mass destruction with impunity.

"Hank," Gruver said to the American one-star, "get Don Kirby at the CIA's Korea desk. Kirby better have a damn good reason why he didn't pass this information along. If he tries to play it cute, tell him I'm going straight to the SECDEF."

"Let's go, Pete," the one-star said, pushing back from the table.

"Yes, sir," a colonel by the door replied.

"It's almost 0500 in Langley," the one star said to him. "We'll need to call Kirby at home. You got the number?"

"In my office, sir."

The two men left the room.

"Okay," Gruver said, focusing on Yee. "For now, I'm going to trust your information is reliable, General. Now tell me the rest of it. How does a possible war relate to the murder?"

Coffin edged forward to hear Yee's response.

Coffin's instincts proved right. But it took another five minutes before he realized it.

Yee's long-winded reply emphasized three key points: 1) ROK intelligence had confirmed that North Korean agents were attempting to slip into the country with greater frequency; 2) a spring attack would coincided with the rainy season, and cloud cover would shield the North Korean army's advance from satellite surveillance, but not from the U-2's advanced imaging radar; 3) at the western end of the base, a freshly cut hole had been discovered in the fence.

Yee finished his account without bothering to connect the dots. It wasn't necessary; the conclusion was obvious. An impending attack gave the North Koreans a motive to take out the U-2s, while the increased infiltration attempts and the hole in the fence provided means and opportunity for one of their spies to access the base and kill Olson.

Gruver sat with his chin to his chest, mulling everything over. General Cho lit a fresh cigarette and watched him through the smoke. Almost a minute passed; no one spoke.

"Other suspects," Coffin said softly to Mother.

"Except," she replied, "you still can't make a North Korean look like an American."

"Maybe they didn't have to."

"Huh?"

Abruptly, Gruver swung around and asked Mother, "You think a North Korean could have sabotaged the jet?"

"No, sir." She cautiously eyed Coffin before continuing. "U-2 maintenance ops run around the clock. Even if a North Korean operative breached the compound, he would have been noticed and challenged. Then there's the knowledge to pull the thing off. Even Chief Sessler couldn't tell me how it was done."

Gruver shifted his gaze to Coffin. "Any guesses, Ed?"

Using his first name. Something else that was out of character, and Coffin had an uneasy feeling about why. "Not yet, sir."

"And the North Korean angle?"

"I tend to agree with Mother . . ."

She reacted with surprise.

". . . and believe it's unlikely a North Korean sabotaged the plane. But if they paid a Westerner, perhaps a mercenary . . ."

"He wouldn't have stood out as much," Gruver finished. "So the North Koreans could be responsible, after all."

"There's another factor to consider, sir." Coffin said.

"Such as?"

"A bomb."

Gruver frowned, as did most of those who understood English, including General Cho.

The notable exception was General Yee. If anything, he seemed irritated by Coffin's remark.

"A bomb," Coffin repeated. "If we're talking about someone wanting to take out the U-2s, why not plant a bomb? It'd be a helluva lot easier than rigging up whatever they did. And if they attached explosives to all three of our U-2s, set them off simultaneously, they could have knocked out our operation completely. To me, that suggests it's probably not North Koreans."

"Got a point," Gruver said.

General Cho nodded his agreement. The other Korean officers took their cue and followed suit. All except Yee, who stood there, stone-faced. He didn't even blink.

"It appears," Gruver said, watching him, "you're still convinced the killer has to be North Korean."

"Yes."

Yee's response came out as a hiss, communicating his irritation. The man was a slow learner and Cho reeled him in with a look.

"You got anything else for us?" Gruver asked Yee.

"No."

"General Cho?" Gruver asked.

The old man shook his head.

"Lights," Gruver said.

As they came on, Gruver said to Mother and Coffin, "You two are dismissed. The political sensitivities on this investigation are obvious. The SECDEF will want answers, and fast. Your first priority is to rule the North Koreans in or out; second, find out how the hell Major Olson was killed. Anything you need, you let me know."

"Yes, sir," Coffin and Mother said, rising.

As they made their way out into the hallway, they heard Gruver say, "General Cho, I'm confused. If you believe the North Koreans are planning an attack, why aren't you increasing your armament and training? Why aren't you preparing your forces?"

"Wait, I want to hear this," Coffin said to Mother.

Before he could re-enter the room, Yee materialized and blocked the doorway.

"*I-geos-eul dawg-shin-e dae-han gyeong-go-ro sam-eu-shi-o,*" he whispered.

His tone was low, menacing, but Coffin was unfazed. He even smiled.

Yee angrily shut the door in his face.

★7★

Dee Dee was no longer in the hallway, but Lieutenant Colonel Kwan still stood guard. Even though he must have heard Yee's remark to Coffin, he gave no sign. But then he wouldn't.

Turning to go, Mother said, "So what did General Yee—Ed?"

Coffin crossed the hall to a door marked *Colonel Martin Bell, Commander.* He rapped once, paused, then entered, turning on the lights. Trailing, Mother asked him, "What was that all about back there? What did Yee say to you?"

"Close the door first. Lieutenant Colonel Kwan understands English."

Reaching back, she saw the Korean officer watching her. He gave her a little smile.

"Man," she said, pulling the door shut, "that guy gives me the creeps."

"He should."

"Why?"

Coffin didn't reply. He was scanning the office, which was spacious enough for a large desk and a small sitting area. Spotting a red lacquer Korean armoire, Coffin stepped over and opened the doors, revealing a TV and VCR. "You question Marty Bell yet?" He dug out the tape from his overcoat pocket and inserted it in the VCR.

"We're supposed to meet here at 2200 hours, but I'm not holding my breath. I've been trying to talk to him ever since I saw him at the hospital. Bell's one rattled individual, and not only because he lost a pilot."

He frowned at her.

"CYA," she said. "He's worried about his career and gave me a speech about why he can't be responsible for what his people do. This was right after he saw Olson's body." Mother made a face. "He's a real piece of work, that guy."

CYA was military speak for cover your ass. Coffin said, "You're judging Marty too harshly."

"Please. You notice the pictures?"

They were impossible to miss. One wall was literally covered with photographs of Bell, at varying stages of his military career. Another dozen or so smaller pictures were scattered throughout the room.

Coffin said, "A lot of people keep photos in their office."

"Of themselves?"

He hesitated. In the vast majority of pictures, Bell was alone, either posing heroically beside an aircraft or looking very John Wayne in a medaled uniform or spacesuit.

"Okay," Coffin said grudgingly, "Bell's a little into . . ."

He stiffened, noticing a photograph on the wall. He took a step toward it and stopped, a flicker of regret crossing his face.

Coming up beside him, Mother murmured, "Isn't that Bell's light bird promotion party?"

Coffin didn't reply; she knew it was. He sighed deeply and shook his head.

They both stared at the picture, which was a rare group shot. It depicted perhaps twenty-five casually dressed people standing near picnic tables, most holding beers. Martin Bell stood in the middle, grinning drunkenly, oversized silver oak leaves taped to his shoulders. But Mother and Coffin were looking to his right, at a smiling couple standing beside Chief Sessler and his wife and kids.

Facing him, Mother said, "That's all in the past, Ed."

"The past is who we are."

"It's who we *were*."

The finality of her words came through loud and clear. Coffin shrugged them off, hoping to give the impression that he, too, had no desire to relive the past. But from the way Mother was looking at him, he could tell she wasn't buying it.

"You're wrong," he heard himself say.

"Excuse me."

"You're misinterpreting my reaction. Don't. I am over you. I really am." He looked her in the eyes to convince her . . . and saw something that surprised him.

An expression of disappointment.

When Mother blinked, it was gone. She tapped her feet and seemed suddenly agitated. She said, "I'm glad for you, Ed. Thrilled in fact. It's been five years. It'd be damn pathetic if you *weren't* over me."

Her tone was harsh, resentful. Coffin didn't understand it. He said, "Hey, I thought that's what you wanted."

"It is, believe me."

"Then why are you upset?"

"I'm not upset. I don't give a damn either way. As far as I'm concerned we never *had* a relationship."

"Mother—"

"I don't want to talk about it, Ed. *Ever.*" She turned away and made an angry, stabbing gesture at the pictures on the wall. "What I *do* want to talk about is Colonel Bell. Are *all*

U-2 commanders like him? Immature narcissists who are their own biggest heroes?"

She couldn't resist slipping in a backhanded dig at him. But this time Coffin was ready for it. For five years, he'd done nothing but think about their relationship, wonder what he could have done differently. Now he knew.

"It won't work," he replied calmly.

She eyed him coldly. "I'm sure I don't know what you're talking about."

"Like hell. You're trying to get under my skin. It won't work. You can't tell me anything I haven't told myself. I *agree* with you, Mother. I *am* an ambitious, egotistical, self-serving prick."

Once again, he'd thrown her a curve. She regarded Coffin with something akin to shock.

This time he gave in to the smile.

The TV remote was on the desk. Walking over, Coffin picked it up and slid into the chair. Watching him, Mother demanded, "What's gotten into you?"

"Nothing. I've made a self evaluation and concluded I have faults."

"Why?"

"It's called growing up. Try it sometime."

"Cut the crap, Ed. You'd have sold your own mother to make rank."

"I don't know where my mother is. I'm adopted, remember?"

"Don't be a wise-ass."

"People can change. I changed."

"Not a chance."

Coffin gave up. It was like talking to a wall. He said irritably, "Don't you have pilots to question?"

But she made no move to leave. She just kept looking at him as if trying to understand.

He reached for the phone, then caught himself. Mother would wonder and he had no desire to explain. "Marty Bell," he said, turning on the TV with the remote. "I want the truth. I want to know why you're really dogging him." On the TV, an attractive army sergeant was giving the weather forecast; cold and clear for the next several days. Coffin thumbed the mute button and waited for Mother's reply.

She didn't seem to want to answer him. And when she finally did, he knew why.

She said, "I'm not sure we can trust him. In fact, I know we can't. I've investigated commanders like him before, guys who would do anything—"

"Enough, Mother—"

"Shut up and listen. I'm not saying he's involved in the murder; I'm talking about the *fallout*. Bell is sweating bullets it'll all come down on him. You should have seen him in the hospital. He didn't give a damn about Olson; he was worried about himself. And someone like him, someone that ambitious, you can't trust because he'll do whatever it takes to protect his career. You know I'm right about him. You *know*."

She put her hands on her hips. Waiting for his response.

To spite Mother, Coffin was tempted to stick up for Bell. But he held back because he had to accept an unpleasant truth. That Colonel Martin Bell was just like the person he'd once been.

Coffin shrugged and thumbed the remote. "Okay, we don't tell Bell too much."

An image of the U-2 appeared on the TV. Mother immediately stepped over and turned the VCR off.

"Dammit, Mother, I *said* I agree with you about Bell—"

"This isn't about him. You still need to answer my questions."

"What questions?"

Then Coffin remembered.

General Yee and Lieutenant Colonel Kwan.

Coffin told her about General Yee first, saying, "When I was the U-2 commander, Yee was the ROK intelligence chief assigned to the combined operations intelligence center here on base. He was a full colonel at the time, but already acted like a general. He thought he should be the one selecting the targets the U-2s imaged and would raise hell whenever his choices were preempted by higher level tasking. He couldn't accept that the U-2s were an American asset, not South Korean. The way he figured it, if the planes were flying to protect his country, they should be under Korean control.

"Now Yee's not a stupid guy. He knew he couldn't get away with complaining to a general, so he settled for ragging on me. I put up with him because I had no choice. Yee's well connected and not just in the military. His family owns one of the largest manufacturing companies in Korea and they shell out big bucks to the politicians. It's the reason he made rank so fast; his family essentially paid for it. Helluva system, huh? Your daddy's rich and you get to be a general. Anyway, that's why I couldn't tell him to pack sand. At least not for a while.

"Things came to a head right after we got the first intel that North Korea might be developing nuclear weapons. Everyone around here went a little crazy, especially Yee. He had this wild idea that the North might actually be on the verge of launching missiles at the South and came up with a list of targets, demanding they be imaged. When that didn't happen, I got a call that night from his exec, saying Yee was on his way to the squadron to see me. I knew what the problem was and took my time getting there, hoping he'd cool off. It was a mistake.

"When I arrived, I found Yee screaming at my admin clerk. I mean screaming at her. This girl was nineteen and six months pregnant, and he had her in tears. Not that the bastard gave a damn. I was so mad that I almost took a swing at him. Probably should have. Instead, I read him the riot act and had the SPs haul him from the compound. Then I got on the phone to General Krieger, the Seventh Air Force commander at the time, and told him what happened. Krieger was as pissed off as I was, and he contacted his ROK counterpart, another three-star, who called General Cho. Cho had just been appointed chief of staff, and I have to give the old guy credit. Because of Yee's family's influence, the easy thing for him to do would have been to blow off our complaints, but he didn't.

"The next day, Yee showed up in the squadron and personally apologized to my clerk. And it killed him. For a Korean officer, that's the ultimate humiliation. They don't apologize to enlisted; they sure as hell don't apologize to women.

"Anyway, that's it. That's why Yee hates me. Because I made him lose face."

Mother said, "And his comment tonight . . ."

"He said 'I'm warning you.' "

"Warning you about what?"

"He never said."

"You took it as a threat?"

"It *is* a threat. Yee will screw me the first chance he gets."

"You don't sound concerned."

"I'm not. I'm out of Korea as soon as the investigation is finished. As far as I'm concerned, he can kiss my ass."

"Okay," Mother said. "Now tell me about Kwan."

*

So Coffin repeated what he'd heard from a drunk Korean intel officer, that Kwan was a highly decorated special forces team leader who held the record for crossings into North Korea. During his last mission, Kwan had been captured in an ambush. Apparently, his interrogators realized who they had, because they weren't interested in getting him to talk; they just wanted him to suffer maximum pain before he died. But as they began cutting off body parts, they got careless and Kwan got the jump on them. After killing his captors, he put on one of their uniforms and escaped.

Coffin said, "In Korean intelligence circles, Kwan is a legend. They call him *shik-kal*. It means knife."

"Knife?"

"His preferred way of killing. It's why his captors used a knife on him, to give him a taste of his own medicine."

"So he's an assassin?"

"Yes. A very good one."

"And now he works for General Yee, a guy who hates you?"

"Right."

"And you're really not bothered by that?"

"No."

A squint; she was trying to decide if she believed him. Abruptly, she moved toward the door, saying. "Well, I'm glad Yee is pissed off at you and not me. At least now I know who to go after if something happens to you. Do me a favor, Ed. Lock your doors at night. I only want to work one murder at a time."

She walked out, grinning at her little joke. But Coffin wasn't smiling.

Through the open door, he could see Kwan was staring right at him. It was a piercing, unnerving gaze.

"Close the door, Mother," Coffin said, reaching for the phone.

A woman answered on the first ring, pulsing rock music blaring in the background. Coffin said a name and was told to wait.

After almost a minute, a man with a smoker's rasp came on. In Korean, Coffin explained he wouldn't make their meeting tonight. They briefly discussed a photograph Coffin had sent. He asked the man if he was certain about his identification, and he said he was.

Coffin asked for the address and the man immediately hissed disapprovingly, in the Korean way.

"Is there a problem?" Coffin asked.

"I want my money."

"You'll get it. I'd like the address now."

"The money first."

Coffin offered another hundred if he could have the address now, but the man insisted on being paid first. They bickered, but the Korean wouldn't budge. Hanging up, Coffin felt the frustration well up inside him. The pattern that had begun with Mother was continuing. Once again, he was going to have to be patient and wait.

Shaking his head, he picked up the remote and turned on the VCR, then settled back in the armchair to watch a friend die.

★8★

The taxiing U-2 reappeared on the TV, Major Olson's white helmet barely visible in the cockpit. A small box in the corner indicated the time and date: 2 Nov 93, 0657 hours. Turning up the sound, Coffin heard the soft hum of the jet's engine, then the audible click of a mike being keyed.

"Priority, Osan Tower. You are cleared for takeoff." Priority was the logic-based call sign reserved for U-2s, since they were regarded as priority aircraft.

"Cleared for takeoff," Major Olson's tinny voice repeated.

The U-2 rolled onto the runway and came to a stop. A pickup approached from behind, two men crouching in the back. Swinging to the ground, the men dashed to the ends of each wing and pulled the pins attached to the small orange wheels. Once the U-2 began its takeoff roll, the lift generated by the airflow over the wings would allow the wheels to fall free.

After the men hopped back into the pickup, a Ford Mustang came into view and made a slow 360 around the U-2. The final safety check.

The Mustang stopped abeam the cockpit. "All clear, Erik," a woman said. It was a voice Coffin knew well; it belonged to Major Caralyn Barlow, the female pilot.

"Copy."

"Look in the map holder after you level off."

"The map holder? Why?"

"Will you just look, Erik?"

Coffin heard the irritation in Barlow's voice. In the video, Olson's helmet could be seen swiveling back and forth, as if telling Barlow no. Gunning the Mustang almost angrily, she swung off to the side of the runway.

Olson gave a single, exaggerated nod, the signal he was adding power. Smoothly, the U-2's engine noise increased to a roar and the jet sat bucking and straining. Coffin glanced at the time on the TV screen. 0659:52.

The seconds counted down. At precisely 0700 hours, Olson simultaneously released the brakes and firewalled the throttle, and the jet shot forward, hurtling down the runway. Within moments, the long wings flexed upward and the orange wheels tumbled free. A beat later, the nose came up, paused fractionally, and the plane rose effortlessly into the air.

We know that he first displayed signs of distress within seconds of taking off.

Mother's words. Coffin stared at the TV and watched the seconds click by. Five, six, seven . . .

And then he saw it. Something that didn't fit.

The jet was climbing steeply when the nose inexplicably dipped.

Almost immediately, Barlow radioed, "Priority, pick up your nose."

No reply. The plane continued to drop.

Barlow, urgently: "Priority, raise your nose. Dammit, Erik, get your nose up."

A silence. The descent rate increased.

"Erik. Level off. *Level off!* Jesus, what's the matter with you?"

The image jostled as the cameraman tried to follow the U-2. The black jet slowly leveled off, but was waffling all over the sky. Barlow continued to talk to Olson, imploring him to respond. It seemed to take forever before he finally did.

His voice was slurred, almost incoherent. "Tired . . . sick . . . can't stay awake."

"Erik, return to base. Can you do that?"

There was a pause and the U-2 began a shallow turn. Olson: "I think . . . I can make it . . . I'm coming . . . back now. Jesus . . . what's wrong with me?"

Barlow: "Tower. Mobile is declaring an emergency for Priority."

"Trucks and EMTs are rolling," Tower replied.

Barlow: "Erik, you'll overshoot the field. Roll out. *Roll out.* You sure you can do this?"

The U-2 was abeam the field on downwind, positioning to roll out on final. But the wings still rocked constantly.

Olson: "I . . . I can make it."

The plane began a descending turn. But the control inputs remained dangerously sluggish and excessive.

Barlow: "Erik, break it off. I want you to climb and eject." No reply. The U-2 kept coming down.

Barlow: "Erik, did you hear me? Level off and eject. *Goddammit*, eject."

Another long silence. Then Olson: "Almost . . . down."

And he was. He was less than a quarter mile out, wings weaving all over the place. Barlow made one more attempt to tell Olson to eject, but it was pointless. Either Olson was too far gone to comprehend or he really believed he could land the plane. In any event, the U-2 screamed over the approach end of the runway, far too hot and high to make a safe landing.

Tires smoking, the Mustang peeled out after it. Over the

radio, Barlow began a nonstop chatter, saying, "Left rudder, raise your right wing. Keep it coming down. Too fast . . ."

Somehow Olson heard her commands and reacted. For a few moments, it seemed as if he would pull if off and salvage the landing.

But the U-2 is an unforgiving airplane, and Olson broke a cardinal rule. He touched down too fast, and when the tail dropped, the plane pitched up wildly and froze for just an instant.

Coffin heard Barlow scream.

It could have been a movie, but it wasn't.

Coffin saw the U-2 pancake to the runway and snap in two. He saw the wings break off and the fuel catch fire. He saw the Mustang roar up to the shattered cockpit as the flames closed around it. He saw Barlow jump out and frantically motion for Olson to eject. He saw the cockpit canopy fly off and the rocket-propelled seat explode high into the air. He saw the chute billow open and gently begin lowering Olson to the ground. He saw the firefighters arrive and spray foam on the burning plane. He sensed rather than saw the relieved looks on the faces of Barlow and an ambulance crew as they ran out to retrieve Olson.

The ejection had been successful and they were convinced Olson would survive. But of course, he didn't survive; he was already dying.

That singular fact bothered Coffin. If Mother was right and Olson had been *specifically* targeted, why would the killer choose such an elaborate way to kill him? Something of a party animal, Olson was a regular at the bars off base. Why not jump him in a dark alley and shoot or stab him?

Why drug him?

The images on the tape ended and Coffin continued to

stare blankly at the flickering screen. But the only thing he could come up with was that the drug was used for a reason.

When he turned his mind to understanding how it was administered, he hit another wall.

It was frustrating.

It made him angry.

No matter how many options he considered, there were two points he couldn't get around: those seven crucial seconds after takeoff when the drug took effect and the fact that isoflurane was a gas.

The latter suggested a contaminated oxygen supply, but the former made that impossible.

But dammit, Olson was completely enclosed in a spacesuit; there was nothing else he could have breathed during taxi out except the air in the tanks.

So there had to be another explanation, something he hadn't considered.

Coffin called the one man who might know.

Dr. Patrick O'Malley wasn't at the base hospital, but the physician on duty had his BOQ number. When O'Malley responded to his query, Coffin immediately noted the doctor's deep southern drawl and the conviction it contained.

"Isoflurane is a *gas*, Colonel. It has to be breathed."

"I understand, Doctor. But I'm wondering if it could have been cooled into a liquid, and either ingested through the mouth or absorbed in the skin?"

"Neither happened, sir."

"You sound pretty certain."

"I am. Liquefied isoflurane freezes skin on contact. In the autopsy, I would see some indication. I understand Olson made several radio calls when he tried to return to the field—"

"Right."

"You can forget about him swallowing isoflurane. If he had, his vocal cords would have been severely traumatized, making speech impossible."

That was clear enough. Coffin asked, "And the exact time before Olson would have displayed the effects of the isoflurane?"

"Within seconds of exposure."

Back to square one. "Thank you, Doctor."

"Sure. He breathed it, Colonel. Keep that in mind and you'll figure it out."

His tone had a patronizing quality, but Coffin didn't take offense. The truth was it shouldn't be difficult to understand how it was done.

But so far, it had been.

Ending the call, Coffin became aware of a commotion out in the hall. Loud voices and footsteps; the briefing was ending. As the sounds faded, he realized someone was saying his name. A woman.

"Colonel Coffin, sir. Are you in the building? Sir . . ."

"In here, Dee Dee."

She tentatively poked her head inside. "Line two, sir. It's the chief."

Coffin snared the phone. "Go, Chief."

"I pulled both tanks, sir. They survived the fire intact, don't ask me how. I already checked them. They're clean."

"Checked them how?"

"Shit's not supposed to be dangerous except in large amounts, right? So I did it the quickest way I could think of, sir."

"Chief, don't tell me . . ."

"Took a couple of deep breaths from each tank. Nothing. I feel completely fine."

A response Coffin never heard because he'd suddenly dropped the phone.

Coffin pitched forward, grabbing his head with both hands. It was all he could do not to cry out.

It felt as if a white-hot knife had been plunged into his brain. Coffin gritted his teeth, waiting for it to pass. He started to reach for his pain pills, but it was too soon. He had to keep a clear head, be able to think.

Stress will bring on more attacks, Colonel. You need to relax. A lot of my patients have success with yoga.

I'll give it a try, Doctor.

Ironically, this was an ability Coffin already possessed. A Buddhist monk at the orphanage had taught him the art of completely withdrawing into himself, to shut out a different kind of pain.

And that's the technique he used now. Closing his eyes, he slowed his breathing and willed the tension from his body. Gradually the pain ebbed and became tolerable. Within minutes, it was completely gone.

But the remedy was only temporary, because the trigger for the attack was always present. A sort of constant anxiety brought about by the uncertainty of not knowing. Not only about Olson, but all the other questions that gnawed at him.

Opening his eyes, Coffin became aware of Chief Sessler calling to him. When he picked up the receiver, he heard the chief barking orders, saying, ". . . get over to ops, Rudy. Take Jensen with you. Something's happened to Colonel Coffin . . ."

Coffin shouted to get the chief's attention. He said, "You can relax, Chief. I'm okay."

"Rudy, hold off." To Coffin, "Jeez, sir. You had me going. What the hell happened?"

"My hand slipped. Listen, I spoke to Doctor O'Malley. It's got to be the oxygen system."

"Well, the stuff sure as hell wasn't in the tanks."

"What about the lines?"

"Vaporized by the heat. But the brass connectors were still attached to the nozzles so we know they were hooked up. And I searched the Q-bay personally. There's nothing there that doesn't belong. Certainly nothing that would hold a gas."

The Q-bay was located in the belly of the fuselage and primarily housed the hydraulic reservoirs and oxygen tanks. Coffin said. "I'm coming over for a look. We're missing something."

"But that's what I'm telling you, sir. We've checked everything twice. *I've* checked everything twice."

He sounded defensive, but that was the chief. He hated being second-guessed.

"I still want to take a look, Chief."

The chief sighed unhappily. "You're the boss, sir. But take it from me, you're wasting your time." He hung up.

Coffin sighed, realizing Sessler was probably right. But the truth was, he couldn't think of anything else to do.

Heading for the door, he realized he'd left the videotape running and ejected it from the VCR. As he was about to turn off the television, he found himself staring at the screen. The news had ended and the Armed Forces Network was playing an old James Bond movie, one Coffin had seen about a dozen times. And an upcoming scene flashed in his mind.

"Son of a bitch," he murmured.

Spinning for the desk, he grabbed the phone and punched in Dr. O'Malley's number.

★9★

*S*hit.

Coming down the walkway, Coffin tensed at the sight of a lone staff car still in the parking lot. A Hyundai, and he had a suspicion why it had remained. When he saw the fluttering two-star flag, he knew.

A master at intimidation, Yee intended to send Coffin another message by jacking him up in the lot and chewing him out. And Coffin would have to take it because two-stars, even Korean ones, outranked an American colonel's eagles.

Of course, Coffin could have avoided a confrontation by circling to the right and taking the long way to the hangars. But then Yee would conclude Coffin was afraid of him, and that was something Coffin couldn't accept.

When Coffin had told Mother he wasn't worried about Yee, he'd meant it. As part of his self-evaluation, he'd prioritized what was important in his life and a pissed-off Korean two-star wasn't anywhere on the list. And that's what he was determined to prove to Yee, that there was nothing the bastard could do to rattle him.

Coffin calmly walked toward the staff car and stopped. Waiting.

But nothing happened.

He leaned over and stared into the darkened windows, daring Yee to emerge.

The car continued to sit silently.

Coffin upped the ante by saying loudly in Korean that he wanted to settle his differences with Yee. He used the diminutive pronoun in addressing the general, essentially insulting him. He knew Yee was too arrogant to allow the slight to pass.

But he did. Even though Coffin detected movement in the backseat, no one emerged. He was perplexed. If Yee *wasn't* waiting for him, then why was he still here?

Shaking his head, he continued toward the hangars. In front of the one housing the U-2 wreckage, two security policemen were in the process of setting up a semicircle of red cones to control access. After Coffin went through the drill of exchanging salutes with the cops, he turned to look back at Yee's car.

Still there.

"Men," he said, "I need a favor."

The hangar was a swirl of activity. The wreckage filled most of the floor space, and a small army of maintenance troops, aided by forklifts and dollies, were arranging the pieces into a loosely formed jigsaw puzzle. Their methodology was obvious. Guided by an oversized chalk outline of the U-2, they were placing anything that could be identified in its proper relative position; the rest, they deposited on pallets for later analysis.

Except for the horizontal and vertical stabilizers, the entire fuselage had been assembled on an intricate grid of raised steel beams, the latter to allow access into the belly bays. Compared to the prolonged timetable of most aircraft accident reconstructions, the progress of this one was startling. But then again, most planes don't crash relatively intact on an airfield, where the wreckage can be instantly recovered.

They'd gotten lucky and Coffin was counting on their luck to hold.

Upon entering the hangar, he found himself pausing to survey the scene. It was something he felt compelled to do. Despite the grimness of his task, he had a sudden sense of belonging, of coming home. He'd always been happiest flying and hadn't realized how much he'd missed it—not only the physical act of being in the air, but the environment and the people and the unambiguous nature of the job.

In the staff world, everyone has his own agenda: It's all about political maneuvering and making that next promotion and looking good. But in a flying squadron, people work for the common goal and there's a natural camaraderie that develops, one that crosses the boundaries of position and rank. A young airman can be even more crucial to the mission's success than the commander, and that reality has a leveling effect that reduces the petty jealousies and bullshit conflicts and ultimately strengthens the organization's bond.

Watching the maintenance troops in action, Coffin saw evidence of that bond. As they worked, their faces were somber and respectful. While it was clear their thoughts were on Olson, Coffin suspected many were second-guessing themselves, wondering if there was anything they could have done to prevent what had happened. And until he uncovered the answer, they would continue to wonder.

As he moved forward, people noticed him and threw up a hand or called out. Among the faces, Coffin didn't see the chief, but spotted Sam Hardy crouched by the open Q-bay hatch, located under the fuselage below the cockpit. Because this section was reinforced to protect the pilot, it had survived the impact with little structural damage. It was yet another bit of luck, and while it hadn't mattered to Olson, it was crucial to their investigation, since the Q-bay housed the oxygen tanks.

And as he came up behind Hardy, that's what Coffin was looking at.

Specifically, he was fixated on two beach-ball-sized metallic spheres sitting on a dolly. The normally green-painted surfaces were charred black and flecked with dried fire-suppressing foam. A fresh-faced female sergeant was bent over one of the spheres, unscrewing a hose attached to an oxygen mask.

Seeing him approach, she came to attention. The effect of a full colonel. Coffin smiled disarmingly, glancing at her nametag. "Easy, Sergeant Morton. I don't bite."

She relaxed only slightly.

He nodded to the tanks. "So the chief really was crazy enough to test them on himself?"

"Yes, sir. Twice."

"Twice?"

"The second time," Hardy said, rising from the hatchway, "was right after he spoke to you on the phone. Says you believe someone tampered with the oxygen lines."

"I don't see another option, Sam."

"I'm inclined to agree with you even if the chief doesn't."

"Oh?"

"Thank our oxygen system expert here," he said, looking at Sergeant Morton. "She mentioned something real interesting. Apparently, this bird recently arrived from the Lockheed depot in Palmdale with a brand spanking new modification. One even Chief Sessler didn't know about. No one did except Morton. Tell him, Sergeant."

Morton appeared hesitant about talking to Coffin, but when she spoke, she possessed the self-assurance of someone who knew her field. "Sir, you know how the oxygen system normally feeds out of tank number one first. And when that empties to a liter, number two kicks in."

"Right."

"That design never made sense to us because the oxygen in number two was rarely used. Frankly, it was a real hassle for us in maintenance because we had to swap the tanks every other flight."

"And now?" Coffin asked.

"Lockheed finally got around to addressing our complaints. In the latest mod, they've added a diverter valve upline of the tanks, to make them feed evenly. Now we only have to top off the tanks for flights, not waste a couple of hours pulling them."

But Coffin wasn't listening to her. Not since she'd said the words "feed evenly." At that instant, everything became clear.

Still, he had to be certain. So he took his time, thinking through the new oxygen system. How it had to work.

Morton had lapsed into silence and she and Hardy were frowning at Coffin. "You okay, Ed?" Hardy asked.

Coffin slowly blinked. "Fine, Sam. Never better."

And he flashed a smile to prove it.

"Ah, hell." Hardy grinned. "I know that look. You figured it out, didn't you? Someone *did* rig the oxygen lines."

"Yes."

"But that's the part that threw me. If the system feeds evenly, that still doesn't explain why it too so long for Olson to feel—"

"It's a diverter valve, Sam."

"I understand, but—"

The answer finally hit him. Hardy sighed, looking a little sheepish. "Christ, I must be more tired than I thought. The damn thing *cycles*."

"Right, Sam."

But the theory wasn't a slam-dunk. Not until they had the answer to the final question, which Coffin posed to Morton now.

"How often did the diverter valve shift between tanks?" That was what Coffin had to know.

"Every tenth of a liter sir," Morton answered.

"In minutes?" Coffin said. "Assuming an average rate for a pilot to process oxygen?"

"Fifteen to twenty, sir."

"That cinches it," Hardy said excitedly. "That explains the time delay. Now all we have to do is find the canister with the gas."

At the sound of muffled swearing, everyone turned toward the wreckage. Legs were dangling out of the Q-bay hatch. Stepping over, Hardy said, "Hey, Chief. Good news. We now know how—"

That was as far as he got before Sessler cut him off.

"I *heard*, sir," he said. "And you're flat wrong."

As Chief Sessler extricated his bulk from the confines of the Q-bay, he was not a happy man. His face and BDU uniform were streaked with soot and sweat, and when he came up to Coffin, he made no attempt to hide his annoyance.

"Three times," he said, glowering at him. "I've crawled into that thing three times for nothing, sir."

As if Coffin were responsible. "So you didn't find anything?"

"I told you we wouldn't, sir. You ask me, that proves it *wasn't* the oxygen system."

"It has to be, Chief."

"Then where the hell is the canister or tank or whatever the hell the gas was stored in, Colonel? We pulled every damn thing in the Q-bay. The accumulators, the hydraulic reservoirs, you name it, it's gone. There's nothing left inside. I mean *nothing*."

He locked Coffin with a scowl; he was tired and frustrated and looking for a fight. Coffin sighed. When the chief got like this, there was no reasoning with him. With a shrug, he said, "I still want to take a look, Chief."

"Didn't you hear me, sir? There's nothing *there*."

"I understand, Chief, but humor me, huh? Now, I'll need to borrow a set of coveralls and a flash—"

Coffin didn't finish; there wasn't any need. Because the chief had thrown up his hands and was stalking away.

Sergeant Morton jogged toward the double doors leading to the maintenance offices, to get the overalls. Over by the water fountain, the chief was wetting a rag and wiping his face. He paused to glower at Coffin.

"What got the burr up his ass?" Hardy asked.

"Guess."

"You're infringing on his turf?"

"That's part of it. The chief also can't bring himself to accept that someone actually sabotaged a jet on his watch."

"Who's to say he isn't right about that? I mean, nothing suspicious has been found."

"It's there. The chief didn't know what to look for."

"And you do?"

"I think so. Dr. O'Malley said the isoflurane could have been in a highly concentrated form, which means the container could have been very small."

"How small?"

"Hard to say. There's a Bond movie where Sean Connery uses a small breathing apparatus in a pool . . ."

"You're serious?"

"Why not? We were all spring-loaded to believe the container was fairly large, but it doesn't have to be. It could be the size of one of the chief's cigars or even smaller—"

"Sessler would still have found it."

"Not necessarily. That was another erroneous assumption we made— Ah, thank you, Sergeant Morton." Taking the coveralls she offered, Coffin started to don them.

Sounding puzzled, Hardy said to him, " 'Not necessarily'? Ed, either the container is inside the Q-bay or it isn't."

"Obviously, it isn't."

Now Hardy appeared completely confused. "Huh? You're talking out of both sides of your mouth."

Coffin was tempted to say "not necessarily" again. But it was quicker to explain.

"Where's a flashlight?" he asked, looking around.

Coffin crawled through the hatch.

The Q-bay was a cramped space about three feet high and five feet deep, and ended at the bulkhead directly aft of the plane's nose. The smell of jet fuel was overpowering, and Coffin tried not to gag. Splaying the flashlight beam, he essentially saw the interior of a large, empty box, the walls and floor covered with a mixture of soot and fire-suppressing foam residue. The brackets for the oxygen cylinders were bolted to the forward bulkhead, and he crawled forward until he butted up to them.

Training the light on the roof, he located the clips for the two oxygen lines, which would have run from the tanks to the cockpit above. Mentally marking a section of floor, he slowly crawled backward, methodically probing the layer of ash with his fingers.

Midway down the bay, he jerked his hand up and swore.

"What is it?" Hardy said. "What's the problem?"

"Give me a sec."

Focusing the flashlight, Coffin carefully brushed away the ash. At least he attempted to. But most of it remained stuck to the floor in a definite pattern, as if glued. Leaning close, Coffin noticed a glint. He touched it and felt a point. A needle.

"I need a knife, Sam," he shouted out.

★ 10 ★

Down the hall, a clock faintly chimed ten. In the break room next door, someone turned on a radio and a pulsing hip-hop number began playing. Without looking up, Chief Sessler rapped on the wall. He didn't say anything; he didn't have to. The music immediately stopped and it was quiet again.

The chief was seated at his desk in his private office, Coffin and Hardy camped on chairs across from him. None of the men spoke. They were concentrating on the object in Sessler's hand, the one Coffin had pried off the floor of the Q-bay.

It was a rigid, circular mass, perhaps a foot in diameter and no more than an eighth of an inch thick. Mottled by bits of ash, it resembled a charred long-playing record, but of course it wasn't.

Sessler chewed thoughtfully on his cigar. "The original shape was probably a sphere before it melted."

Nods from Coffin and Hardy; a given because of the disk-like shape.

"Feels like some kind of plastic," the chief said.

"Or a structurally strong polymer," Coffin said. "It would have to be strong to override the pressure in the cylinders. Try to bend it, Chief."

The chief attempted to, but couldn't. Setting the disk down, he spoke slowly, thinking aloud. "So it was attached to one of the oxygen lines. To whatever system Olson wasn't breathing out of during taxi out. After takeoff, the diverter valve on the tanks switched and Olson began sucking in the isoflurane contained in this thing. And it killed him."

More nods from Coffin and Hardy. Another given.

Squinting at Coffin, the chief seemed on the verge of adding something, but instead produced two sets of keys from his pocket and tossed them to Coffin.

"Six B was open, sir," he said. "It's the duplex across from Colonel Bell's. Your bags are in the bedroom. The car keys there are for a red Tempo. Motor pool dropped it by your quarters."

"Thanks, Chief."

"Command Post also wants you on the net ASAP." Reaching behind, he grabbed a portable radio from a charger and gave it to Coffin. "You're Rescue One."

Coffin went through the drill of checking in. When he finished, another voice came on. It was Mother, wanting to know where he was. After he told her, she said, "Don't leave for a few minutes, Rescue One."

"Why?"

"Something has come up."

"What?"

"Give me the chief's office number, Rescue One."

"You can't tell me what the problem is now?"

A pause. Then: "The chief's number, Rescue One."

Coffin took the hint; Mother wasn't about to discuss this over the net. As the chief called out his number, Coffin relayed it.

"You ask her about backing off, sir?" the chief asked, watching Coffin clip the radio to his belt.

"Yes."

"And?"

Coffin shook his head.

"Oh, for—" He almost spat up his cigar. "Sir, you've got to get her to back off. We can't do our jobs if this keeps up."

"Why not?" Hardy asked mildly.

The chief blinked.

"You're only talking a couple of people at a time," Hardy said. "Out of what, sixty or seventy troops. It doesn't seem that big a deal."

"It is a big deal, sir. Most of my troops are young kids. All her questions are messing with their minds."

"Only *their* minds?"

He carefully placed the cigar in an ashtray, eyeing Hardy. "You trying to tell me something, sir?"

"Only this. You been harping about the OSI from the beginning. It seems you're the one who's really bothered by them. Why?"

"I told you, sir. I've got a timeline to keep and if they keep interfering—"

"Your turf? Is that it, Chief? You don't like the OSI infringing on your turf?"

Coffin had concluded this was what really irked the chief and nodded his agreement. It was a mistake. The chief caught the movement and jerked around to him. "Hey, what is this, sir? You think I'm making this up, too? I'm telling you the OSI bastards are way out of line on their questioning. They've got a good cop, bad cop thing going. A couple of my kids left their sessions thinking they were suspects. It ain't fucking right."

Coffin said, "Chief, forget it—"

"Hell no, *sir.* You guys act like I'm lying about this. If you think I've got something to hide—"

"We don't," Coffin said sharply. "So you can calm down. No one's accusing you of anything."

"Sure sounded like it." He gazed sullenly at Hardy.

Hardy smiled apologetically. "Didn't mean any harm, Chief."

The chief didn't reply. Hardy shrugged; he'd tried. Stretching out, he picked up the needle from the chief's desk. Earlier, Coffin had removed it from the circular mass with pliers. As Hardy inspected the needle, the chief's irritation faded to the point where he appeared embarrassed. He turned to Coffin as if to tell him something. But as before, nothing came out.

Pride, Coffin thought.

They watched Hardy roll the needle between his fingers. It was over an inch long and much thicker than one found on a typical syringe. "Damn sharp," Hardy murmured.

Coffin absently rubbed his finger where he'd been stuck.

"Have to be to pierce the line," the chief said.

Once again, he looked to Coffin as if to speak. And this time, he finally got out what was troubling him. "It was a good call, sir. I should've considered the container wasn't made of metal."

"Don't beat yourself up, Chief," Coffin said. "You had no way of knowing."

"You did, sir."

It came out as an accusation, but the chief's body language indicated the words weren't targeted at Coffin. As the maintenance head, the chief believed he should have been the one to figure out what had happened. Whether that was true was debatable; anyone could have missed the ash-covered disk. What wasn't debatable was the chief's ignorance of the oxygen system mod; it was annotated in the plane's paperwork, which he should have read.

And when he'd worked for Coffin, he would have read it. Back then, the chief stayed on top of everything. It had been a compulsion; it was what made him so good at his job.

So why was he slipping now? Was he stretched thin because of his business interests? Was the job finally burning him out?

Watching the chief under the harshness of the ceiling lights, Coffin decided it was the latter. The chief was growing old fast. His once-brown hair had gone completely gray, his heavy face was pale and haggard, and his sunken eyes gazed out with the unfocused look of someone who hadn't slept in days.

The chief was not a man at peace with himself.

As if sensing Coffin's thoughts, the chief said quietly, "I'm thinking about retiring, sir."

Hardy reacted with surprise, but Coffin merely nodded. He said, "Be the air force's loss, Chief." It was the thing to say.

"Yeah . . ." The chief's eyes drifted to the photograph on his desk. A pretty Korean woman wearing a colorful *hanbok*, the traditional kimonolike gown, her arms around two small boys. His family. Staring at them, he got a strange expression. Unsettled.

Coffin said, "Good-looking kids. Don't you have a few more?"

A vague nod. The chief was still preoccupied by the picture. He said, "My wife had two girls from a previous marriage. You've met them, sir."

Coffin tried to recall. Since he'd never been to the chief's home, it must have been at one of the squadron social gatherings—

The chief faced him, saying, "Soon-yee has been bugging me to quit, sir. She wants me to be more involved with our businesses. And the kids are getting to the age where they need me around."

"Sounds like you've already made your decision, Chief," Coffin said.

"I have, but . . ." He shook his head. "I mean it's the smart call. Hell, another year or two won't matter much for retirement. Besides, it's not like we need the money. I'm not even sure why I stayed on this long."

"I am," Coffin said, looking at him. "So are you."

The chief smiled ruefully. "Who am I fooling, right, sir? I enlisted at seventeen; the military is all I know. I like coming here to the base, being around my own kind. Once I retire, I won't have my security clearance anymore, so I won't be able to come around much. Another couple years, I'll be lucky if I remember what's it's like to be an American."

Coffin and Hardy frowned at the remark. Returning the needle to the desk, Hardy said, "You've already been here, what, fifteen years, twenty years? You live downtown, speak Korean . . ."

"Not as good as the colonel here."

"The point is," Hardy said, "I'd think the change wouldn't be that traumatic. It seems you're half Korean as it is."

"That's the problem, Colonel. I'm too Korean."

"Oh?"

Instead clarifying his comment, the chief said something in Korean to Coffin. Another curious remark.

"*Neo neun da-haeng-i ae-yo.*" You were lucky to leave, sir.

"*Hal-su-eopt-da?*" And you can't?

"*Ga-jok.*" Family.

He gave Coffin a knowing look, as if that single word said it all. In Korea, it did.

Americans can never appreciate the importance of the family unit in Korean society, not unless they've lived it as the chief had. It's more than blood bond or a relationship; it's essentially a way of life. Every member is expected to subjugate individual needs and desires to the good of the unit. Those who don't play ball are considered disloyal troublemakers who can expect to face criticism, banishment, or worse. In feudal times, death was the ultimate punishment, and while Westerners might consider that barbaric, they need to understand that maintaining the family unit in an agrarian society was a matter of survival. Everyone had to do his part, and those who wouldn't were viewed as bad seeds who might influence others. So the family did what they had to do; they weeded them out to prevent them from blooming.

And that's what the chief was telling Coffin, that he'd been assimilated by his wife's family so completely that he couldn't bring himself to counter their wishes, become a *tam-tak-chi-ant-da*. A bad seed.

The chief was right. He had become "too Korean."

"*Al-a-seo*," Coffin said sympathetically.

But the chief was no longer looking at him. Instead, he was staring down at the needle and the disk on his desk with a sudden interest. He slowly picked the items up. "I wonder if . . ."

He trailed off, his brow furrowed. Thinking hard.

Hardy gave Coffin a questioning look. Coffin relayed it to the chief, asking, "Wonder what?"

A silence. The chief was locked in concentration. His eyes shifted between the needle and the disk. He turned and stared at a schematic of the U-2 hanging on the wall. Then back at the items he was holding.

And then he reacted in a dramatic fashion, slamming his hands to the desk. "Son of a bitch, that's it. *That's it.*" He excitedly focused on Coffin, speaking in a rush. "This whole thing's been driving me crazy. What you said on our way in

here, sir. That wild stuff about North Korea maybe being involved and all the rest of it. Especially the part about why they
would kill Olson this way instead of using a bomb? You're
right about that. It makes no fucking sense. I mean it didn't,
not until now. Jesus, those bastards were smart. They almost
got away with it. If it hadn't been for the mod—"

He was all over the place. Hardy couldn't take it anymore
and said, "Chief. Slow down. Take a deep breath."

The chief did. And started coughing.

"Back up," Hardy said. "You're telling us you know *why*
they drugged Olson?"

"They had to, sir. That's why they didn't plant a bomb. *Because they didn't want anyone to know.*"

Hardy exhaled slowly as he started to understand.

"We're listening, Chief," he said.

After the chief finished his explanation, he kept grinning. In
his mind, he'd atoned for not finding the remnants of the oxygen container because he'd done something Hardy and Coffin had been unable to do. He'd put everything together in a
way that made sense.

According to the chief, the *unmodified* oxygen system was
the key. The fact that no one knew about it except Sergeant
Morton.

"You're the killer," the chief had said. "Maybe you know a
lot about the U-2 and maybe you don't. But you probably
know airplanes and logic tells you the oxygen system must
feed out of tank number one first. So when you rig the canister, you hook it up to the line leading out to tank *two* because
you don't want Olson to get drugged right away. You want it
to happen sometime late in the flight. When he's boring
holes in the sky off the North Korean coast, over the water.
Since you don't want anyone to be suspicious of Olson's

death, a bomb was out. As soon as it went off, the radar controllers would see the plane disappear from the scope and know there was an explosion. And that's not what our boy wanted, no, sir.

"So the bastard went with a drug. He knew if Olson were unconscious or dead, the plane would keep flying on autopilot until it ran out of gas and spiraled into the water. The radar controllers would track his descent and we'd all end up believing that Olson had some kind of physiological incident, maybe a heart attack, or went hypoxic. With the plane under a thousand feet of water, who's to say different? Gotta hand it to this guy, he had a helluva plan. If it had worked, no one would ever have known how Olson died.

"But it didn't work because he never knew about the mod. He never figured the drug would kick in so soon. And because it did, we know. We fucking know how it happened."

At this point, the chief started grinning. And soon after he did, Hardy and Coffin realized he wasn't reacting this way only because he'd solved a crucial piece of the puzzle.

"You know what this also proves?" he said.

Hardy hesitated.

"I think so," Coffin said. "The killer can't be from the squadron."

"You got that right, sir," the chief said.

But Hardy had a blank look. Until Coffin reminded him what Sergeant Morton had said about why the oxygen system had been modified.

"Right, sure," he said. "During a flight, the system hardly ever bleeds out of tank two. So if the drug had been hooked up to an unmodified plane, it never would have kicked in. Since people in the squadron probably knew that—"

"They'd never rig it that way in a million years," the chief finished. "Be damn stupid to."

Hardy had to nod.

"And another thing," the chief went on. "This also proves the killer ain't a North Korean. Why the hell would they care whether or not we knew Olson was murdered? I mean, it's not like we could prove they were involved, and even if we could, so what? Remember when they hacked those choppers pilots to death along the DMZ. The North loves pissing off Uncle Sam."

Coffin and Hardy shared a look. While the chief had a valid point, neither of them could accept it completely. Hardy said, "Aren't you forgetting the complexity, Chief?"

The chief frowned.

"Think about it," Hardy said. "Someone had to obtain the drug, which is usually only found in hospitals, design and build a canister to hold it, and rig it to the plane without being spotted. That's far too complicated for your average military member or an individual acting on his own. For one thing, they wouldn't have the resources. And that's what all this took, someone or some organization with significant resources." He gave the chief a knowing look.

The chief deflected it with a shrug. In this case, he had no problem with being second-guessed. "Hey, so maybe it is the North Koreans. Or maybe it's some group of crazies with a hard-on for U-2 pilots. The important thing is it ain't one of us. I mean it can't be, am I right?"

A rhetorical question, but Coffin and Hardy nodded anyway. It was one thing in this case they were certain about. Perhaps the only thing.

Sitting up, Coffin motioned for the chief to hand him the phone so he could brief General Gruver on their discovery. But as the chief reached for it, it rang. Picking up, he immediately nodded to Coffin, saying, "Yes, ma'am, he's still here, Agent Hubbard."

Coffin held out his hand.

The chief ignored him and continued to talk to Mother. From his excessively polite tone, his intentions were obvious, and Coffin told him he was crazy to even try. The chief ignored the advice; he was determined to make his pitch. Hardy and Coffin traded frowns; neither understood why the chief wouldn't let this matter drop.

Coffin shook his head. "Screw him. It's his funeral."

"Funeral?"

"Just watch, Sam."

★ 11 ★

A minute.

Coffin figured the chief had a minute until Mother buried him; his estimate wasn't even close. All the chief got out was, "Ma'am, I got me a problem. My people can't do their jobs because your agents—"

By then Mother had heard enough and let him have it with a tirade that was loud enough for Coffin and Hardy to hear. The chief jerked the phone from his ear, stunned by her high-volume assault. He attempted to defend himself by talking over her, but she wouldn't let him get a word in. As he persisted, his voice rose until he was practically shouting at her.

"Ma'am, I can prove none of our people was the killer. Talk to the colonel, he'll tell you. We uncovered evidence—"

Once again she brutally cut him off. The chief looked furious enough to throw the phone against the wall.

"Uh, Ed." Hardy leaned close to Coffin. "Was Mother like this when you dated? So . . . confrontational?"

"She had her moments."

"And it didn't bother you?"

"You kidding?"

Hardy looked at him as if he was certifiable, and maybe

Coffin was. Who knows why someone is attracted to someone else; you just are.

"What the—" Hardy suddenly squinted at the chief. "You catch what Mother said to him just now, Ed?"

"No."

But whatever it was had knocked the chief for a loop. He'd gone slack-jawed, his eyes darting to Coffin with a suggestion of panic. Into the phone, he said, "No, ma'am, I didn't mean to tell you how to do your job. Yes, ma'am. I'll put him on now."

Cupping the mouthpiece, the chief held out the phone to Coffin with a shell-shocked expression. "Sir, I don't care what she says, sir. It's not one of us. It can't be."

Coffin and Hardy stared at him.

The chief nodded.

Shaking his head, Coffin took the phone.

A suspect.

Mother confirmed she had a suspect who was from the squadron. But she played it cute and wouldn't identify the person to Coffin. Not until he made two promises to her, beginning with his assurance that he wouldn't overreact. Her insinuation irritated Coffin; it was completely baseless. You don't get to be a four-star general's exec unless you can keep your cool.

"No dice, Mother. We're on the same team, remember?"

"All I want is your word you'll stay calm, Ed."

"I'm *always* calm."

"You don't sound calm."

"I said I'm calm, Mother."

"Your *word*, Ed. Just promise me."

Hardy had his ear close to the phone, listening in. He mouthed, tell her no. Coffin resisted the urge to do so because he had to know the name of the suspect.

"Fine," he relented. "I give you my word. Happy?"

A pause. "I'm not sure I trust you."

Hardy reacted the way Coffin felt by throwing up his hands and making a derisively sucking noise. "Adult," Mother snapped. "Real fucking adult, Ed."

Encouraged by her irritation, Hardy pursed his lips to repeat the sound. He looked disappointed when Coffin shook him off.

"Mother," Coffin said, "if you can't trust me, then why are we even talking?"

Another pause. "I need your help. This person is a good friend of yours . . ."

Coffin tensed. "Who is it?"

". . . which is why I'm calling. If you talk to him, gain his trust, he might admit the truth."

Her words suddenly clued Coffin to the suspect's identity. There weren't many people on Osan who qualified as good friends. And only one who had previously attracted Mother's suspicion. "Christ," he said, "don't tell me you still think Marty Bell is involved?"

Hardy's eyebrows went up. The chief reacted as if he'd been slapped.

"If he is," Mother said cautiously, "will you promise to behave?"

"I thought I just did."

"I mean it, Ed. No getting in my face or throwing a fit. You just come here and talk to him. Find out anything I can use."

"You're making a mistake, Mother. Marty Bell isn't a killer."

"Oh, so now you're a homicide cop? Tell me, how many cases have you solved, Ed?"

"Chill out, huh. I'm only trying to—"

"*You* chill out. This is what I was worried about, Ed. I

knew you couldn't keep from interfering. Remember what *we* talked about? What *you* promised?"

She was getting revved up again. Coffin said quickly, "Mother, will you relax—"

Too late.

She went off, reminding him that she was in charge, all the rest of it. There was no use fighting it, so Coffin didn't try. But after a minute, she was still talking. She wouldn't stop. Hardy looked right at Coffin as if to say, *So, you just going to take it, buddy?*

Maybe that's why Coffin finally reacted. Or maybe it was his years of pent-up anger coming out. Or maybe he decided it was finally time to lose his cool.

Whatever the reason, Coffin exploded into the mouthpiece, ordering Mother to shut the hell up. Somewhat to his surprise, she actually did. Hardy and the chief sprouted big grins. The chief pumped a fist, score one for the guys. On the other end of the line, Coffin detected faint breathing. He waited for Mother to hang up on him, but her breathing continued. He considered this a good sign; she really did need his help.

Finally: "So talk, Ed." Her voice was ice.

"I'm only trying to keep you from making a big mistake. The chief wasn't blowing smoke when he said the killer isn't from the unit. We've uncovered evidence. Conclusive proof."

"That's pretty high-standard, Mr. Detective."

"I'm not a detective."

"Then quit acting like one."

Coffin sighed. He'd walked into that one. He started to tell her what they'd found, but she cut him off. "Not over the phone. I'll be in Colonel Bell's office. Tell me something, Ed. Do you think I'd classify someone a suspect without a reason?"

"Well . . ."

"This person got into a screaming match with Olson. Made threats against him. Was seen crawling around Olson's U-2 last night at one in the morning. But hey, you're right. There's nothing there and I should take your word for it that you have proof he couldn't be involved in the murder. So you're that sure, huh? You know he didn't do it? Even with what I've told you. *You fucking know?*"

Coffin hesitated.

"Yeah," Mother said, her voice hard and sarcastic. "I thought so. Nice work, Kojak."

Hardy shook his head gloomily, realizing there was nothing Coffin could say. Because what they'd uncovered only made it unlikely that someone from the squadron was a killer, not impossible.

"You said two promises?" Coffin reminded Mother.

"Hmm. Oh, right. Bring back the picture, huh. Your buddy Colonel Bell raised a stink when he saw it was gone."

"Picture?"

"C'mon, Ed. It had to be you. You had an emotional experience looking at it."

"Emotional experience—"

He finally caught on. "Marty's promotion photo is *missing?*"

"Like you don't know. I don't have time for this, Ed. Just bring it with you. Bell's a pain in the ass as it is and he's whining to have it back."

"It wasn't me. I didn't take—"

A dial tone.

Ten minutes later, Coffin left the hangar, his head spinning over a second puzzling phone conversation, this one with General Gruver.

"Good work, Ed," Gruver had said. "So we understand how Olson was murdered."

Using his first name again. "Yes, sir."

"But not the who or why?"

"No, sir. But Mother has a suspect."

"She told me."

"I don't see one person pulling this off, sir."

"I understand this individual could."

"Oh?"

There was a pause as if the general seemed to consider whether to reveal the suspect's name. When he terminated their conversation without doing so, Coffin knew it was because Mother had asked him not to.

As Coffin cut across the concrete tarmac, it was this fact that nagged at him. Mother's obsessive secrecy over the suspect, even though Coffin had already guessed his identity.

Or had he?

If anyone was tuned to the squadron grapevine, it was the chief. But he didn't know anything about a conflict between Colonel Martin Bell and Major Olson.

"Hell, they were friends, sir."

"And you weren't aware of an argument they had recently?"

"No."

"Or if anyone spotted Colonel Bell here last night, poking around the U-2 Olson flew?"

"He wasn't here. I'd have known about it, if he was."

"Oh?"

"I was working until about 0200, give or take. That's why my ass is dragging. We were replacing an engine on another bird. If Colonel Bell had shown up, someone would have said something to me."

"Sounds like Mother has bad information," Hardy said.

"Maybe," Coffin said.

But the reality was that Mother was too good a cop to implicate a full colonel without confirming her facts. So he had to at least consider the possibility that Mother had thrown up a smoke screen. Made him think she suspected Bell when—

A voice called out, "It left, Colonel."

The two cops manning the security perimeter stood at attention, waiting for him. Looking at them, it suddenly came to Coffin. How he might be able to clear out the smoke.

Walking up, Coffin returned their spring-loaded salutes, his eyes on the parking area in front of ops. No Hyundai staff car.

"It drove off about forty minutes ago, sir," the taller of the two cops said. "We think they must have been watching you."

His muscular buddy bobbed his agreement. Coffin said, "Because . . ."

"As soon as you went into the hangar, a couple guys got out and went into ops, sir. The whole time, they kept looking over here. Kinda like they expected to see you."

"Describe the men."

"Jimmy got a closer look, sir."

"Sure did, sir," Jimmy said to Coffin. "I was hanging around outside ops when they came back out. Couldn't have stayed inside more'n five minutes. One guy was a Korean lieutenant colonel with thick glasses and a messed-up ear . . ."

Coffin nodded. Kwan.

". . . and the second man was real young looking. I think he was a lieutenant, sir."

The officer who ran the audiovisual equipment. Coffin asked whether General Yee had ever left the car; he hadn't. Pointing across to the guard shack by the compound's gate, he said, "I want to know who was working at around 0100 hours last night."

"Janet, sir," the tall cop said. "Airman Janet Morgan. She comes on at midnight."

"Contact her in the dorms. I need you to ask her a question . . ."

After explaining what he wanted, Coffin thanked the SPs for their help and started to leave. "Uh, sir," Jimmy said, "you want to know about the package?"

"A package?"

"Yes, sir. The one those two Koreans were carrying when they left ops. Guess that's why they went back inside. They must have forgotten it."

But as Jimmy described the package, Coffin realized the package hadn't been forgotten.

Why would General Yee want the picture?

★ 12 ★

"Yo, Ed, over here!"

Coffin stopped on the walkway in front of operations, squinting toward the rasping voice. In the shadows, he could make out two shapes at the end of the barbecue pit, sitting on the picnic table.

A cigarette glowed bright. As Coffin moved toward it, the voice said, "So where the hell is it, Ed?"

Coffin came up to the table. Mother sat across from a blond full colonel wearing a flight suit. Neither appeared pleased to see him. Par for the course for Mother, but the colonel—

Coffin eased out a breath, staring at Colonel Martin Bell. And wondering if maybe, just maybe, Mother was right after all.

A beefy man with rugged features, Bell shared not only Coffin's reputation as a fast burner, but also his fanaticism for maintaining his appearance. In all the years Coffin had known Bell, he'd never seen him with a hair out of place or needing a shave. Now Coffin was confronted with both.

Bell looked as if he'd just rolled out of bed. His hair was a wild mass and his jaw was peppered with stubble. He also swayed as he sat and there was the distinctive odor of—

"Yeah, yeah," Bell grunted sourly. "I'm drunk, all right. What the hell do you expect? I got a busted twenty-million-dollar airplane and a dead pilot. A *murdered* pilot. I talked to a general I know and he fucking confirmed it. I'm toast, Eddie boy. Everything I've worked for is down the crapper, because I was in command. It's my responsibility. Well, they can kiss my ass. How was I supposed to know this was gonna happen? Tell me, Ed. *How the fuck was I supposed to know?*"

His speech was sloppy and overly loud. He sucked hard on his cigarette, staring up at Coffin with unfocused eyes.

"You couldn't have known, Marty," Coffin said.

"Goddamn right." He jabbed at Mother with the cigarette, almost burning her with a flying ash. "So tell her, huh? Tell her none of this is my fucking fault. *Tell her.*"

Coffin humored him by doing so. Mother patiently nodded.

"And no more questions," Bell said to her. "I don't know shit about shit. If I did, you think I would have let anything happen?"

Mother yawned.

"No, Marty," Coffin said. "You wouldn't."

"Fuckin' A, I wouldn't. I'd a' killed the bastard who tried it. I *protect* my people. Jesus, I need a drink. C'mon, Eddie boy. Let's have a drink. I'll buy and you can tell me all about making general. 'Cause it ain't gonna happen to me."

Bell fired his cigarette into the dark and started to rise. Coffin had reached down to prevent him from doing so when Mother said, "It's okay, Ed. We'll take him to his BOQ. My car is out front."

Coffin tried not to smile as he checked the smokescreen column. Mother had just confirmed that she'd known all along that Bell was too drunk to be questioned.

Bell stood unsteadily, shaking his head. "No BOQ. I want to go to the club. I want a *drink*."

"Club will close soon, Marty."

"We'll go downtown. Be like old times. We'll shell out for a couple of mama-sans. Helluva lot cheaper than paying for two ex-wives, that's for damn sure."

"You would know," Coffin said.

"And how," Bell said. "You know, when Jean left me, she cleaned out the house and took every dime I had. And now she's pushing for a chunk of my retirement. Twenty-three years and I ain't got a pot to piss in."

"I'm sorry to hear that, Marty."

"Yeah, well." He got quiet, staring at the ground. "Take my advice. Never get married. Women fuck up your life."

Coffin was silent. Aware that Mother was watching him.

"So, whaddya say?" Bell suddenly grinned at him. "Let's get us those mama-sans, Eddie boy. You still like mama-sans, right?"

"Sure, I like mama-sans."

"So I've heard."

This remark came from Mother. Coffin assumed she was joking, but her glare suggested otherwise. It was yet another baseless allegation, and Coffin was fed up enough to call her on it.

As she turned for the walkway, he said sharply, "Let's get one thing straight, Mother. I don't troll bars and sure as hell don't—"

"Stop right there."

Coffin frowned.

Mother said, "You don't want to get into this, believe me."

"Is that some kind of threat?"

"That's up to you. It depends on—"

A sudden cry from Bell. Mother and Coffin turned just in

time to see him sprawl face first on the snowy ground; he'd tripped stepping away from the picnic table. Rolling over, he began to laugh as if hurting yourself was really funny. In his condition, it probably was.

As they went over to him, Mother made a comment to Coffin, completing her earlier response.

"Your reputation," she said. "It depends on whether you give a damn about your reputation, Ed."

With Mother's help, Coffin lifted Bell to his feet and guided him up the walkway. The front of his uniform was wet and dirty, and he reeked of booze. Two young mechanics approached and made head-snapping double-takes. "Jesus, sir," one said, "is Colonel Bell—"

"He's sick," Coffin said, putting an edge in his voice. "Do I make myself clear?"

They nodded numbly and hurried past.

Bell smiled crookedly at Coffin. "Thanks, Eddie boy. But it don't matter. I'm fucked."

"Maybe not, Marty."

"I am. The general told me. I'm fucked, fucked, fucked." He giggled. "The general also told me a secret."

"What secret?"

His voice dropped conspiratorially. "I'm not supposed to tell."

"So don't."

Mother's car was a government-issued Crown Victoria, complete with a radio, rear doors with no handles, and a bar in the back for attaching handcuffs. It was a perk for being the head of the base OSI, assuming you considered arresting people a perk. Walking up to it, Bell suddenly jerked away from Coffin. "Hey, why'd you take my picture anyway?"

"I didn't take it, Marty."

Bell looked accusingly at Mother, who was opening the back door. "She says you did."

"Why would I take it? I have one. At your promotion party, I asked you for a print. Remember?" Coffin watched Mother as he spoke, knowing she'd put two and two together. But her expression never changed.

"Hey, that's right." Bell's face lit up. "You fuckin' already got one. It couldn't be you."

"No."

They helped Bell into the backseat and strapped him in. As Coffin was about to shut the door, Bell gave him a sloppy wink. "You want to know the secret? It's about the list."

"What list?"

He pressed a finger to his lips. "Shhh. No one can know. Promise me."

"Okay. I promise."

Bell motioned Coffin closer, then jerked away, noticing Mother. "Tell her to move back. She's got to move back."

"Marty, does it really matter—"

"*It's a secret.*"

Coffin sighed, eyeing Mother. "You mind?"

Silly question; she obviously did. Folding her arms, she stared coolly at Coffin, sending him an unstated message. *You better tell me.*

He said, "It doesn't sound as if this has anything to do with the murder."

"Murder?" Bell said. "Shit, no. This isn't about any murder. This is *personal.*"

But Mother wasn't about to leave until she got the assurance she wanted. So Coffin nodded, indicating he'd pass along what Bell said. No sooner had she moved away than Coffin realized he'd made an agreement he couldn't keep.

Because Bell suddenly whispered his secret and Coffin's knees buckled from the shock.

A person has few genuine surprises in life, and this was one.

Bell's revelation had the effect of physically overwhelming Coffin. He literally stood trembling, unable to speak or even breathe. He was paralyzed by the conflicting emotions surging through his body. He didn't know whether to laugh or cry or slap Bell a high-five. Not that any of those responses was a luxury he could afford.

Because of Mother.

She was sliding behind the wheel. Any moment, she would notice him. And when she did, the cop in her would read his face and know—

She pulled the door shut and suddenly looked back. He gave her a big, friendly smile.

She frowned, puzzled by it. His stomach churned, but he held the smile.

Until she finally turned away.

"It was killing me, Eddie boy," Bell said, grinning up at Coffin. "Shit, I almost fell over when I heard. And I was *sober*. But hey, it shows what busting your ass can do. Let me be the first."

He stuck out a meaty hand and seemed mystified when he couldn't keep it still. After they shook, Bell pressed his finger to his mouth again. "No one fucking knows, right? It's our little secret."

"Mum's the word, Marty."

"Man, I'm drunk. I haven't been drunk in years. Too damn scared. Worried about a fucking DWI. But now it don't matter anymore. I can get a DWI and they can't do shit to me. Fucking air force."

He slumped heavily against the seat and closed his eyes.

Coffin shut the door and started to get into the passenger seat.

"Colonel Coffin! Sir!"

Glancing toward the guard shack, Coffin saw two security cops standing out front. One he didn't know; the second was Jimmy.

Waving his arms, Jimmy broke into a jog. "Hold it. sir! got what you wanted!"

"What's he got?" Mother asked.

"Something you already know," Coffin replied.

She frowned up at him.

Coffin closed the door and walked over to Jimmy.

A lie.

The name printed on the paper Jimmy gave Coffin confirmed Mother had lied to him. Staring at it, Coffin felt no anger toward her because in her position, he might have acted similarly. It came down to what she said to him over the phone, her fear that he would overreact.

Slowly folding the paper, Coffin fought the impulse to do just that. Part of him wanted to spin around, run over to her, and scream that she was way off base on this. But as a child, he'd survived by suppressing his emotions, and that's what he forced himself to do now. Disconnect from his feelings and appraise the situation objectively

The name on the paper and what it meant.

Mother's assertion that there had been an argument.

General Gruver's remark that this person had the ability to single-handedly orchestrate the sabotage.

This was the most damning point. Could an individual . . . this individual . . . actually pull off something so complex?

He grimaced at the answer.

"Problem, sir?" Jimmy said.

"Hmm. No, no. This is exactly what I wanted. Do the gate guards know to contact me if General Yee returns?"

"Yes, sir. I posted a note in the shack with the number to your quarters."

"Appreciate it, Jimmy. Good night."

"Good night, sir."

Turning for the car, Coffin saw Mother standing by the driver's door, watching him. As he headed over, her eyes never left him. It was another unspoken message; she was telling him she knew he knew. She added to the message by placing her hands on her hips. Coffin thought it an unnecessary gesture.

Of course she didn't give a damn.

Mother's hands remained on her hips as Coffin approached the car. She said, "I didn't think you'd agree to help if you knew the truth."

"Probably not."

"I never actually said it was Bell. You assumed it."

"Relax, it's okay. It's not a problem."

"Look at it from my position, Ed. I knew you two were close. To me, it made more sense to tell you in person—"

"You don't have to explain, Mother. I understand."

She was still unconvinced. She was on edge, waiting for him erupt. When he didn't, she said, "You're really not upset with me?"

"Why? You've got to follow the evidence. Let's do this before I change my mind." He reached for the passenger door.

She stared at him. "You still intend to go through with the questioning?"

"If you'll agree to a couple of conditions . . ."

She was instantly cautious. "Such as . . ."

"Don't bug me about what Marty told me. It's a personal matter and has nothing to do with your investigation."

"And your second condition?"

"I want us to be civil. I'm not asking us to be friends, but it seems silly that two mature adults who once loved each other can't act civilly. How about it, Mother? Can we cut out the bickering and get along?"

Mother weighed her reply, watching Coffin over the roof of the car. As the seconds passed, Coffin felt a growing frustration. Even now she apparently couldn't get past her resentment—

"Don't," she said, speaking up at last. "Don't do this, Ed. I can't deal with it."

"Deal with what? All I want is for us to—"

She turned away, looking out across the runway. Coffin couldn't understand why this decision was so difficult for her. He'd only suggested a truce, not a relationship. "Look, if I said something wrong—"

"You didn't." She faced him. "You said something very right. It's . . . confusing."

"Confusing?"

"You said we loved each other . . ."

"I thought we did. You don't think so?"

She was shaking her head at him. "In the beginning, I did. But people who love each other don't do certain things . . . and when trust is gone, it's difficult to . . . impossible really . . ."

She trailed off, lost in the past. Remembering.

Coffin was stung by her inference. He almost protested his innocence, but realized it wouldn't do any good. She'd long ago judged him guilty of a crime that he didn't know he'd committed. Her willingness to believe the worst without hearing his side bothered him. Why hadn't she confronted him, given him a chance to explain?

It came to him in a rush. A possible reason. It depended on whether Mother really had loved him. Because if she didn't . . .

Abruptly, Mother resumed speaking, hesitantly voicing her thoughts. "In the end . . . right before I left . . . I didn't believe you loved me. I couldn't. Maybe . . . that wasn't fair. Perhaps you did feel . . . something." She gave him a little smile. "You asked Colonel Bell for a copy of his promotion picture. That was because of me, wasn't it?"

"We never took any pictures. I wanted something . . ." Coffin shrugged; he'd said enough.

For a long moment, Mother didn't say anything. She just gazed at Coffin searchingly.

"Doubt, Ed," she said, with a trace of sadness. "When you say things like that, you make me doubt myself. Part of me still wants to believe we had something special."

"Believe it. I went through hell when you took off."

Her eyes held his again. "You have no idea why I left? Not even a suspicion?"

"I never violated our commitment or trust."

"Oh, Ed . . ." She shook her head. "Ed . . ."

"It's the truth."

"Please. I'm a cop, remember? I *work* with the security police. Didn't you consider that one of them would tell me?"

"There was nothing to tell."

"Stop it, Ed. Stop the lies—"

"How? I don't even know what I'm supposed to be lying about. You're something, Mother. If I were a suspect in one of your cases, I'd know what I was supposed to have done. But that's not a courtesy you'll extend to me. For the life of me, I couldn't understand why you were being so damned close-mouthed, but now I finally figured it out. You want to know what I've come up with? You're not going to like it."

"I'm not really interested—"

"*You're* the one who is lying. You made up all this stuff about— Let me finish." Coffin spoke rapidly to prevent her from interrupting. "You thought our relationship was moving too fast and you got cold feet. You didn't have the guts to tell me to my face, so you took off. You never counted on seeing me again, but that's the problem with the military. You can never say never and after five years, your worst nightmare was about to happen. You were going to work with the boyfriend you screwed over."

"Ed, this is ridiculous—"

"You telling me you *weren't* worried what I might do? C'mon. I'm somebody now. I'm a colonel with the ear of a four-star general. One word from me and you could kiss your career good-bye. That was a chance you couldn't take. You figured your best defense was an offense, so you decided to lay a guilt trip on me."

Coffin shook his head at her. "It was a helluva plan, lady. Except you overplayed it. You tried to make me think I was some kind of oversexed bar-crawling scuzzball, but I'm not even close. You know how many women I slept with in Korea? One. Guess who?"

"You're insane, you know that? A raving lunatic."

Coffin grinned. "I must be crazy, because I should be plenty ticked off at you, but I'm not. The truth is, things *were* moving too fast between us. Hell, we barely knew each other, and if we'd gotten married, it would have been a disaster. You did us both a favor by leaving."

"You trying to tell me you're *glad* I walked out on you?"

"All I'm saying is I'm okay with what you did. We had a relationship that didn't work out. If you'll admit neither of us was to blame, we can drop this matter for good."

"I'm a liar. Is that it?"

"Mother, I'm only trying to—"

"*Lied.* You want me to admit I *lied.*"

Her back was up. Mea culpas didn't come easy to her. Coffin said, "I only want the truth. I'll settle for a nod. Just nod and that'll be end of it."

He watched her closely, waiting for any movement that would pass for an admission. Instead, Mother she threw him a curve he never saw coming.

She smiled.

A disconnect.

Mother shouldn't be smiling. She couldn't think this was funny. But apparently, she did, because she chuckled, indicating she was genuinely amused.

"Ed," she said, "you're living in a fantasy world. You're delusional. My God, you honestly think I left because we were getting too serious?" Still smiling.

Coffin felt off balance, trying to figure it. When he did, he said, "Jesus, you never give up. You're still trying to shift this back to me—"

"We broke up because of *you.* You couldn't keep your primal fucking urges to yourself."

"I don't have primal urges."

"Oh, right. Now you're suddenly a monk. Brother Coffin."

"Mother, give it a rest. You can't tell me what I'm supposed to have done because I didn't do anything. You made everything up. It's all a crock—"

"Okay. Fine."

He looked at her.

"You win, Ed. You boxed me into a corner. You want to know so damned badly, I'll tell you."

The words Coffin had waited so long to hear. Then came Mother's qualifier that told him she was only buying time.

"But after," she said. "After we wrap up the case. You're the one who wants to be so all-fired civil, so we're going to be civil. We talk about this now, we'll only end up fighting. Besides, I have no desire to humiliate you. I truly don't." She opened the driver's door, gazing at him coolly. "Don't look at me like that, Ed. Despite what you think, this isn't a stall. The investigation has to come first. When it's over, I show you the evidence I have. Yeah, you heard me. I said *evidence*. You're the wannabe detective; you can figure out what that means. Now do me a favor and get in the damn car. We've wasted enough time and we still have a killer to find."

She climbed inside and shut the door with a bang. Coffin shook his head, feeling his balance slipping again.

Evidence?

★ 13 ★

As major military bases go, Osan was unusually compact, less than four square miles, with much of that land occupied by the golf course and runway. During the eighties defense boom, many of the buildings had been renovated to comply with stateside standards. Driving around, a visitor would have difficulty determining he was at an overseas installation unless he happened to notice that the more strategically significant facilities—the intelligence and command centers and the hospital—were hardened to survive bomb blasts. Two more telltale differences were the Korean military compound tucked into the northwest corner and the lack of private vehicles on the base roads. Most of the assigned personnel were on unaccompanied tours and had no need for a car; everything was within walking distance and few had any desire to risk fighting post traffic.

The BOQs—the two story bachelor officers' quarters buildings—resembled dominos as they tiered up the steep hillside adjacent to the sprawling Officers' Club. The rising elevation roughly correlated to an increase in rank, with full colonels and generals residing in duplexes or houses at the very top.

As Coffin and Mother drove from the U-2 compound,

Colonel Bell began nodding off. By the time they reached the three-way stop at the hill's summit, he was slumped sideways, snoring loud enough to rattle the windows.

During the short ride, Mother provided Coffin a synopsis of the evidence implicating the suspect. There was nothing new except for the motive. As Coffin had anticipated, it was related to the argument; what he hadn't anticipated was that it would be so compelling.

And yet . . .

"You do realize," he pointed out, "motive doesn't prove murder. All you really have is innuendo and suspicion. You have no smoking gun."

"Thank you, Mr. Detective."

"I thought I was a monk."

"What you are is extremely annoying."

"That's not very civil."

"Did I say *fucking* annoying?"

Trading barbs with Mother was a losing proposition and Coffin decided to quit while he was behind. As they turned down a quiet street lined with single-story duplexes, he told her about the melted container he'd found and the chief's theory about why a gas had been used to kill Olson. She listened without interruption until he mentioned Sam Hardy's conclusion that the sabotage was too complex for the average person to arrange.

"We're not talking about an average person," Mother said.

"No, we're not."

In the end, this was why he hadn't confronted her over the suspect. This person had capabilities far beyond average.

Even though the duplexes were identical, Bell's place stood out because the motor pool had been as good as its word. Spotting the red Ford Tempo he'd been issued, Coffin waved Mother to the driveway across the street. After she pulled in, she left the engine running, figuring this would be a touch and go. Not quite.

Bell had completely passed out. They couldn't awaken him. Coffin shrugged. "We'll have to carry him."

"I'm not busting my ass. He's a big boy and they haven't shoveled the walkway."

So after patting Bell's pockets for his keys, they settled for half dragging him to the door. By the time they deposited Bell on his bed, they were panting as if they'd run a race.

As they started to leave, Coffin did a double take. "Hang on a sec."

As with Bell's office, an entire wall was filled with photographs. Coffin went over and squinted at one. "It's identical."

"Big surprise," Mother said. "Bell probably likes to go to sleep looking at himself. *What are you doing?* Son of a bitch. You did take the other one."

Coffin had unhooked the photograph. "It wasn't me. General Yee took it. Or rather he had two of his men grab it."

In two strides, Mother was on him. "Put it back, Ed."

"A security cop saw Colonel Kwan and that Korean lieutenant leave ops with it."

"This cop must have had damn good eyes to recognize this picture in the dark."

"He didn't actually see it—"

"Ah . . ."

"It was wrapped in newspaper. But the timing fits and from the cop's description—"

"Nice try, Ed. Now put it back."

He tried to walk around her. She sidestepped and cut him off. He said, "Out of my way, Mother."

"Why the hell would General Yee want Bell's promotion picture?"

"Move and maybe I can find out."

She set her jaw stubbornly. Coffin said, "Mother, use your head. You honestly believe I'm so hung up on you that I would steal this picture? A picture I already have?"

"You tell me."

"Now who's being delusional? Christ, after all these years I can't believe you'd seriously think— Hey, *hey!*"

She'd lunged forward and latched on to the picture with both hands. They tugged like kids fighting over a toy. *Screw her.* Coffin adjusted his grip on the frame and was about to jerk it free.

"You'll break it," Mother said.

"Then let go."

"You let go."

"All I need is a few minutes—"

"I'll haul you in for attempted burglary."

"Like hell you will."

"Try me."

A tense impasse followed. Logic told him she wouldn't dare arrest him. But her coldly determined gaze suggested she just might.

He slowly let go. And hated himself for it.

She grinned at him. "When you're right, you're right, Ed. It's so much better if we settle our differences civilly."

As if she knew what the word meant.

He moved aside so she could rehang the picture. But instead of doing so, Mother looked over the bedroom. "Let's try the kitchen table. The light's probably better."

"The kitchen table? Why are— Hold it." His squinted at her suspiciously. "Are you saying you *believe* Yee's men took the photograph?"

"Sure. That admin clerk Dee Dee mentioned seeing Colonel Kwan and the ROK lieutenant come back into operations. She told her they'd forgotten something. I didn't put together why until you mentioned it."

Coffin was beside himself. He demanded, "Then what was this all about just now? Why the hell did you insist on—"

He stopped. Her reason was obvious.

"A lesson." He glowered at her. "You were teaching me a lesson."

She winked. "You got it. I'm the detective, not you. Oh, come on. Don't sulk. We don't have time. We've got to figure out whatever it is General Yee doesn't want us to see."

As she left the room, Coffin gnawed his tongue to keep from firing off a caustic remark. If Mother wanted to play I'm-the-cop-and-you're-not, she could have at it. He had a helluva lot better things to do, like driving downtown to find out what he'd come to Korea to learn.

Walking into the living room, that was the decision Coffin reached. To leave Mother and her considerable ego on their own. But instead of continuing to the door, he found himself drawn toward the kitchen.

Damn.

For the next several minutes, Coffin and Mother stood over the dining table and scanned the photograph. looking for something, anything that might have tweaked General Yee's interest. But nothing peered back at them except familiar smiling faces.

U-2 pilots like Bell and Coffin.

And maintenance personnel like the chief.

And wives and children.

And girlfriends like Mother.

That was it. There was nothing suspicious and no one who didn't belong. It made no sense. They had to be missing something. There had to be a reason General Yee wanted this photograph.

But they couldn't see it.

Coffin rubbed his face hard, looking at Mother. Her frustrated expression mirrored his. When he suggested they wait to question Bell in the morning, she shook him off. Her curiosity meter was pegged; she wanted answers now.

"Besides," she said, "Bell probably wouldn't have a clue; you don't. You sure you recognize everyone?"

He shrugged. "Except for the kids."

"All the Korean women wives?"

"Mostly."

"What about the two standing behind the group? The ones with glasses? They look more like college kids."

He squinted, but their faces were grainy and a little out of focus. "Not sure—wait." He recalled the chief's earlier comment. "They're the chief's stepdaughters."

She pointed. "That must be his wife there. She's pretty." She frowned as if puzzled by something. Then shrugged as if it wasn't important.

"There are a couple other possibilities," Coffin said. "One is the picture frame itself. Something might have been hidden in it—"

"Then why steal it and draw our interest? Why not just remove the item?"

Coffin nodded. He'd considered this. "So that leaves the background."

They studied the image again. It had been taken on the grassy area near the barbecue pit, looking out toward the compound gate and the runway.

"Ed . . ."

"I see them."

★

Mother and Coffin took turns, peering closely.

At the right edge of the photograph, they could make out the nose of a U-2, a group standing beside it. They were far too small to identify.

"Can't tell if they're Korean," Mother murmured. "We'll need a magnifying glass."

"I doubt that would even work. Better take it to the pros."

"Pros?"

Since Mother wasn't familiar with the U-2 operation, this option of taking the picture to photo imagery analysts wouldn't occur to her. Once Coffin explained the unit was manned around the clock, she nodded her approval. But with a caveat.

She said, "We don't let on why we're interested. We can't go around accusing a Korean two-star of being a thief unless we have absolute proof."

"What about General Gruver?"

"Especially not Gruver. He won't want to embarrass the ROKs. He'll order us to drop it."

"Then maybe we should."

She stared at him.

He shrugged. "Our focus is the murder. We can't afford to get sidetracked."

Her head bobbed as if she agreed; she didn't.

"Jesus," she said. "What's with you? You're the one who wanted to know about the picture in the first place. Now you want to cut and run. Why?"

"I told you—"

"A load of crap. It's General Gruver. You're backpedaling because you're afraid of getting on his bad side. Man, don't your lips ever get tired? Hell, they must."

A less-than-subtle way of calling him a kiss-ass. He said irritably, "That was out of line."

"No, no, I really want to know. What's your secret? You keep the lips limbered up with Chapstick? Maybe a little Vaseline?"

"Fine. Play it your way. But if you blindside General Gruver, he'll have your ass."

"Repeat after me, Ed. Stealing is a *crime*."

As if that was the only consideration. To Mother, it probably was.

She'd always viewed the world through her own ethical prism. If she judged something wrong, she felt duty-bound to address it, the repercussions be damned. When working a case, she made no allowances for rank or political considerations and was openly critical of those who did. Tactless and stubborn, she regularly butted heads with her superiors and rarely backed down even when ordered to do so. For anyone else in the military, this kind of in-your-face independence was a one-way path toward career oblivion, but Mother had not only survived, but flourished.

And Coffin had a pretty good idea why.

He said, "You really aren't worried about upsetting Gruver, huh?"

"I'm the OSI chief; it's my call." She shrugged and started for the door.

"Hang on," Coffin said. "You mind answering a personal question?"

"How personal?"

She seemed puzzled by Coffin's query. "Why else do you think I get promoted? Because I'm good at my job."

"But you do have a sponsor, right?"

When she hesitated, Coffin had his answer. Someone with stars was looking out for her. Protecting her. Despite her hypocritical kiss-ass remark, he wasn't surprised. Mother knew how the military worked. She knew that in order to make the higher ranks, she had to latch on to an influential general and go along for the ride.

"Let's just say I know someone," she admitted finally.

"How many stars?"

This time, she answered without hesitation. "Two."

"Then do the math. Three stars trump two. If General Gruver hammers you, your boy won't be able to offer cover."

She just looked at him; she still didn't give a damn. Coffin gave up; he'd tried. Trailing her out of the kitchen, he said, "You're forgetting something."

"Not me."

She went into the living room, her heels clicking on the wooden floor. Shaking his head, Coffin returned to the photograph on the table. But he couldn't bring himself to pick it up. It was a little thing, but it bugged him. Earlier, they'd almost come to blows over the damn thing. Now Mother expected him to lug it around, treating him like a gofer.

You're overreacting, Ed. Just pick it up.

No good; he couldn't. It was a matter of respect. Mother wouldn't treat any other full colonel this way.

In his best command voice, he ordered her to return and retrieve the photo. Her heels continued to click and he heard her open the front door. "Mother, I'm not kidding."

Silence. She was blowing him off. Then unexpectedly, "Ed, you need to see this. There's something screwy going on."

I'll bet. "Okay, but I'm leaving the photograph."

"Shit, I saw it again. You're in the duplex across the street, right? The unit on the left?"

"Yeah—6B."

"Should anyone be there?"

"No. My bags are already inside."

"Then you got company. Hurry up and get out here. And bring the photograph with you."

Nice try. He saw through her ruse. She was coming on like Chicken Little in order to entice him into carrying the picture outside. When he did, she'd have a laugh at his expense—

Coffin glanced down. A voice was coming over his radio. As he listened, his body tensed when he realized he'd misread the situation. Mother wasn't trying to trick him. She couldn't be.

Because she was on the command net, requesting police backup.

★ 14 ★

A panic.

Coffin felt a growing panic at the realization that someone was in his room. If that person was a burglar—

He snatched up the photograph and raced for the front door. It was wide open. Mother stood on the stoop, looking across the street, a radio wedged against her ear.

"Right," she was saying to the command post controller. "Notify the SPs we have a possible intruder. No, I only saw a light. I'm going over to check it out now. Out."

She shoved the radio into her coat, glancing back at Coffin as he came up. "Give me the picture. You wait here and give our suspect a heads-up we'll be late." She gave him the four-digit phone extension.

"I'm coming with you," Coffin said.

"We went through this. This is my job." Pivoting on her heel, she walked toward the driveway. He followed, saying, "There's something in my suitcase. It's important to me."

"Sorry."

"I'm coming."

"Read my lips. *No.*"

They arrived at her car. As Mother stopped to place the picture in the backseat, Coffin continued toward the street.

"Stop, Ed. I mean it."

Still walking.

She swore at him. Then in exasperation: "Okay. *Okay.*"

He looked back and smiled.

"*You,*" she said, "I'm starting not to like."

"Only starting?"

"Keep out of my hair. Understand?"

He saluted mockingly. She stepped around to the front passenger door, muttering. As she dug out a flashlight from the glove box, Coffin kept his eyes on his duplex. Both units were completely darkened. When Mother joined him, he mentioned it.

"I caught a couple of flashes from there." She pointed to a corner window. "The guy might have seen me. You know if you have a neighbor? No? Stay behind me and try not to be a hero."

She clicked on her flashlight and they crossed the street, pausing to study the walkway. In the snow, Mother's beam revealed several sets of footprints, going and coming.

"Airman Jensen dropped off my bags."

Mother nodded, leading him across the tiny lawn toward the door. There were more footprints on the stoop. Avoiding them, Mother removed her pistol and tried the knob. Locked. She and Coffin peered in through the living room window: blackness.

Mother pointed to the left, then motioned downward with her palm. Coffin nodded. They ducked under the front bedroom window, circling to the rear. The backyard was much larger than the front and descended toward a heavily treed park, the BOQ buildings visible beyond it.

Approaching the back door, Mother abruptly stopped and holstered her gun. "I'll stay here, Ed. Go through the front door and check out your stuff. Keep your gloves on and touch only what you need to. We might call in a print team. Probably will."

"What if the guy is still inside?"

In response, she focused her flashlight on the back door. "It's not closed all the way. Our friend left in a hurry." She ran the light down the hill; two distinct lines of footprints glistened back, one set going, the second coming.

"One person," Coffin said, commenting on the obvious. "He came up from below to avoid being spotted."

Mother scanned the darkened park. "Probably a teen. We've had a couple of break-ins recently. High school kids out for kicks and cash."

Reassuring remarks. As Coffin retraced his steps to the front door, he heard approaching sirens. Then a shouted question from Mother, one he wasn't about to answer.

"By the way, Ed, what have you got that's so valuable?"

He quickened his pace.

As he opened the front door, Coffin half expected someone to rush at him. But the interior remained quiet and still.

When he clicked on the living room light, he saw moisture on the wooden floor. The trail led from the back door to the master bedroom, the one where Mother had detected the flashlight beam. He went over to it, expecting to find his bags. But they weren't anywhere to be seen. The panic feeling returned. He rushed over to the closet and threw open the doors.

He relaxed.

His luggage, apparently untouched. He quickly unzipped his suitcase and dug out a leather portfolio. Tucked inside the back cover was a dog-eared red envelope encased in a protective plastic sleeve. He gazed at it almost reverently before closing the portfolio and returning it to the suitcase. By now, blaring sirens and squealing tires had announced the arrival of the cavalry. Out front, he heard shouts and footsteps, then Mother's calm voice from somewhere out back, directing them.

A brief search of Coffin's belongings confirmed what he now knew, that nothing had been taken. Leaving the bedroom, he saw Mother standing by the open back door, briefing three male cops. In the living room, a fourth SP, a female master sergeant, was speaking into the phone. Hanging up, she thumbed in another number, announcing, "He says he didn't, Agent Hubbard."

Mother nodded, continuing to talk to the male cops. She pointed toward the park and they took off, fanning out down the hill. The master sergeant's radio crackled; a unit reported it was beginning a search of the park from below. Seconds later, someone else radioed that the cars along the street were being checked. Coffin tried to make sense of the response. The excessiveness of it. Joining Mother, he asked her about it.

"I don't like things I can't understand, Ed."

"What's not to understand? It was an attempted burglary. We scared the kid off before he could take anything."

"Wrong on both counts."

"Oh?"

"For starters, I was mistaken about your visitor being a kid. Take a look. Notice anything?" Moving aside, she waved her flashlight at the back door.

"It's a door."

She looked at him.

"It's also white."

"You do realize you're not amusing."

"Not even a little?"

"Do I look amused?"

She had him there. "I was just trying to lighten things up."

"Don't."

She shifted her light from the lock mechanism to the doorjamb. Coffin saw the problem at once. He said, "No damage. It wasn't jimmied."

"Neither were the windows or the front door. And Master Sergeant Kathy Baker over there contacted Airman Jensen. When he dropped off your bags, he said he didn't go anywhere near this door."

Coffin nodded. This was why she'd concluded the intruder wasn't a high school kid. Because the person apparently had entered using—

"A key," Sergeant Baker said loudly from the living room phone. "We're trying to find out if anyone stole a key. How long? An hour?"

She looked to Mother, caught her head shake. "We need you to check at once, Mr. Larson. I understand you're busy, but— Mr. Larson, don't be rude. Mr. Larson— Let me talk to the night manager. I don't care. Interrupt his dinner. Mr. Larson, I'm not going to argue with you."

"Then don't," Mother said sharply.

Baker glanced over in surprise.

"Lean on this asshole, Kathy," Mother said. She gave her a knowing look.

Baker responded with an almost predatory smile.

And proceeded to do precisely that.

Baker flipped some kind of internal switch. One moment, she was smiling at Mother; the next, she was snarling into the phone, saying, "*Mr. Larson, I've had it with you.* By not cooperating, *you* are committing a criminal act. *You* are withholding evidence and obstructing an official investigation. Unless *you* change your attitude, I will arrest you. I want to talk to the manager. *Now.*"

Baker appeared to be genuinely furious. Watching her, Mother said, "Kathy's good, isn't she?" She sounded like a proud parent.

"Can she do that?" Coffin asked. "Actually arrest the guy?"

"Hell, no. But Larson doesn't know that."

Cupping the mouthpiece, Baker tossed Mother a grin. "You should hear him. He's suddenly Mr. Cooperation."

Mother nodded, pleased. "You understand now, Ed?"

It took Coffin a moment to realize she wasn't asking about the verbal strong-arm tactics. "About?"

"The key." Mother nodded to the back door. "You clear about its significance?"

"Somewhat. A high school kid wouldn't have used one. I'm still not sure how that rules out burglary as a motive."

"If you were a detective, you would." Her tone was anti-septically light, a facade of civility while she reminded him of his place.

"Just tell me, Mother."

"Giving up already?" She sounded disappointed. "Put yourself in the perp's shoes. Pretend you're a burglar." She waited. "C'mon, at least *try*."

Coffin wasn't about to beg and turned away. Felt a tug his arm. "Not so easy, is it, Ed?"

"I never said it was."

"You thought it." Her eyes narrowed, her civility fading fast. "That crack about why I keep getting promoted. Like it's some big surprise to you. You don't think I'm any good, do you?"

Still on hold, Baker tensed; she knew it was a loaded question.

Play it smart, Ed.

Instead, he found himself saying, "Mother, if that thing gets any bigger, you're going to fall over."

"Excuse me?"

"The chip on your shoulder."

She reddened, realizing she'd walked into that one. Baker sprouted a grin. Not smart. Noticing, Mother blistered her with a glare and Baker wisely became fascinated with the wall.

"Listen," Mother growled at Coffin, "you need to respect my abilities. I've *earned* your respect. I've solved a lot of big cases, impressed a lot of people. *Important* people. Twice I was the OSI investigator of the year. I'm good at my job. Damn good. Hell, I may even be the best."

Miss Modesty. "I'm sure you're—"

She poked him in the chest. "Remember that murder in D.C., the colonel's wife? The one that took a dive off a balcony? Everyone thought it was suicide, but I knew better. I was the one who solved it. *Me.* And that's not the half of it."

Another poke as she told him about a second high-profile case. Listening to her, Coffin confirmed a suspicion he'd long held. That Mother's hard-nosed image was all an act, a shell she'd created to hide the insecurities she felt at having to compete in a male world.

He pictured her reaction if he actually told her this. Talk about throwing a fit—

Mother poked his chest *hard.* He coughed. "Dammit, will you cut that out?"

"What are you smiling about?"

Coffin hadn't realized he was. "It's . . . nothing."

"You find murder funny?"

Christ. "If you must know, I was thinking of you."

"*I'm* funny?"

He couldn't win. Out of the corner of his eye, he noticed Baker grin again. This time she was smart enough to shield her mouth with the phone.

Mother puffed up, waiting for an explanation. Coffin yawned and scratched his ear. Stalling. If anything, this annoyed her even more. Which was precisely his intent.

"If I were you, Ed," she said finally, "I sure as hell wouldn't be smiling. I'd be damned worried."

Coffin was grateful for the subject change. "About?"

"A guy broke into your place. Since he wasn't a thief, I'd be wondering why he really came here." She punctuated the remark with an ominous look.

Baker's face went blank. Coffin was similarly mystified. And then it came to him. "Oh, hell," he said to Mother. "You can forget about that possibility."

"No. It's something we have to consider."

"Not me. What I said about General— Oww."

Another painful poke to keep him from saying the name. Taking him by the elbow, she drew him into the kitchen, out of earshot of Baker. "Ed, we've got to keep this *quiet*."

He jerked free. "Why? No one in their right mind would believe—"

"Yee hates you."

"Hate's an exaggeration."

"I was *there*. I saw the way he looked at you. The man *hates* you. He hasn't forgotten how you humiliated him. You don't think he'd pass up the opportunity to get even?"

"He sent a goon to rough me up? Please. He's a military officer, not some mob boss."

They went back and forth. It was a futile exercise, and Coffin decided to end it by walking out of the kitchen. But as he started to leave, something in Mother's eyes made him pause.

It was concern. She was genuinely worried for him. He said, "My God, you really believe what you're saying?"

She swallowed hard, nodded.

As they gazed at each other, the tension between them crumbled away. And in its place, something else appeared. An inexplicable feeling of attraction. Coffin felt it and knew Mother did also.

"Sometimes," he said quietly, "I wish things had turned out differently."

"So do I." She smiled at him. It was a nice smile.

"Whatever I did, I never meant to hurt you."

"I know that . . . now." She reached out and held his hand. Caressed it. Then suddenly pulled back as if shocked by what she was doing.

"It's okay," Coffin said gently. "It's no big deal."

But to Mother, it was. For an instant, she'd let down her guard, allowed Coffin to breach her protective shell. And that was something she couldn't accept.

Before his eyes, her face went blank, devoid of all emotion. Once again, her barrier was in place, the moment they shared was forgotten. All business now, she addressed Coffin in a clipped, formal voice—a cop's voice—and asked if he had any other enemies besides General Yee.

"No."

"Think. This is important. Was there another Korean officer you had a run-in with? Possibly even an American?"

"There's no one."

"Then it's got to be General Yee. He must be behind the break-in."

"Back up. You still haven't told me why you're so certain robbery wasn't the motive."

"It can't be. No burglar in his right mind would ever—"

They heard a polite cough. Master Sergeant Baker stood in the doorway.

"The answer is no," she said to Mother.

★ 15 ★

The "no" was the billeting manager's response to the question about missing keys. According to Baker, the manager had personally checked the keys for Coffin's duplex, including the master. Only one was gone—the one in Coffin's pocket.

"You ask about the maids' keys, Kathy?" Mother asked Baker.

"Yes, ma'am. They turn them in at the end of their shifts."

"So someone could have gotten to one of them? Made a copy?"

A nod.

"Was this unit reserved for Colonel Coffin ahead of time?"

"No, ma'am. They didn't know he was staying here."

Mother glanced at Coffin.

"I was planning to stay in a hotel off base."

Her expression never changed. But Coffin sensed she wasn't happy at his answer.

Taking out her notepad, Mother asked Baker if the unit next door was occupied; it was. "A Colonel Stefanski," Baker said, spelling the name. "He's on leave in the States."

Mother made a note. "He a permanent party?"

"Yes, ma'am. Been here for almost a year."

Mother looked at Coffin as if this were a significant revelation. He nodded. At last, he understood why Mother was so troubled by the break-in. It came down to choices a thief would make.

Or more specifically, wouldn't make.

The unit next door was filled with items worth stealing, its occupant gone. More duplexes lined the street, similarly furnished. Yet the intruder had bypassed them and chosen to break into this unit. A unit that had been empty until an hour ago and still appeared unoccupied from the outside.

Mother had called it; robbery wasn't the motive, it was Coffin. The intruder had come here for some reason related to him.

Still, Coffin wasn't ready to sign on to her second premise, that General Yee was responsible. But the intruder's use of a key was troubling. To obtain an original and copy it so quickly—within minutes—took someone with influence and connections.

Like a general officer.

I-geos-eul dang-shin-e dae-han gyeong-go-ro sam-eu-shi-o.

That had been General Yee's warning to him tonight. He'd expected to rattle Coffin with it.

Instead, Coffin had smiled in his face. An obsequious, fuck-you smile. And later, insulted him in his car.

For an egomaniac like Yee, such blatant disrespect from a *mi-gook*—an uncultured American—was bad enough. But to have it come from a *chosiyo*, an impure half-breed like Coffin, would have been intolerable.

Yee hates you.

Hate's an exaggeration.

I was there. The man hates you.

"Oh, hell," Coffin said. "You're right."

Baker and Mother had been talking. They abruptly fell silent, looking at him. "Right about what?" Mother mildly asked Coffin.

"I was thinking about Gen—" He almost said Yee's name. "Anyway, you might be on to something."

"So how'd he arrange to copy the key? It doesn't seem possible with what Baker said about the maids."

"The maids?"

But Mother was pocketing her notepad and looking at her watch. "It's almost midnight. We've got to roll, Ed. But first, I need to make a couple quick calls. Good work, Kathy." She squeezed past Baker into the living room.

Trailing, Coffin again asked about the maids. But Mother was already placing her first call.

"They go home at five, Colonel," Baker said.

"I see."

And Coffin did. The maids would have turned in their keys hours ago. Long before anyone knew which duplex he'd been assigned.

Mother was right; it seemed impossible for someone to have copied his key. Unless they had a crystal ball.

Mother's first call was to arrange for a print team to go over his duplex. Coffin thought it was a waste of time; the intruder would have worn gloves. But Mother was insistent; her people might uncover hair or fiber evidence.

"They'll be here first thing in the morning," Mother said. "You'll have to sleep in the second bedroom tonight."

"Whatever." He was yawning again, this time for real.

"An SP will also be posted outside around the clock."

He swallowed the yawn. "No. Absolutely not."

Mother and Baker reacted with surprise.

Coffin said. "I'm a big boy. I can take after myself."

"Ed," Mother said, "the visitor might return."

"That's his problem. I'm a black belt, remember?" Tae Kwon Do—Korean karate—had been a necessity at the orphanage. To protect himself from bullies.

"And if the guy has a gun?"

Coffin shrugged.

Mother sighed. "You can't bullshit a bullshitter. What's the real reason you don't want a guard?"

"I told you. I've been practicing martial arts for thirty years."

"Yeah, yeah. You're a regular Jackie Chan. Now tell me the rest of it."

"There's nothing else to tell."

"Uh-huh."

She shook her head, but elected not to press him. Since the transforming moment they had shared earlier, she seemed to be trying to get along. Still, Mother was Mother, and she couldn't resist making a sarcastic remark as she placed her second call. "Macho fucking bastard," she said.

Another grin from Baker. She seemed to enjoy grinning.

"We used to date," Coffin said to her.

Baker nodded as if she understood; she couldn't possibly.

Mother ended her call moments later, appearing puzzled. She announced, "Not there."

The suspect.

She hit the redial. After a dozen rings, she slammed down the receiver. "Dammit, I *said* to wait. I *said* we were coming by tonight. Let's go, Ed."

But a step later, they pirouetted back around at the sound of Mother's name, except it wasn't Baker who said it, but a male voice on her radio. A security cop major named Sutter was requesting Mother's immediate assistance and the reason he gave was jarring.

They now understood why Mother's call had gone unanswered.

"Still think I'm wrong, Ed?" Mother asked.

A reference to the suspect's guilt. Before Coffin had a chance to reply, Mother strode to the door, telling Baker to radio that she was on the way.

★ 16 ★

Mother's short legs were really motoring across lawn. She smelled blood and wanted a quick kill. Shifting into high to catch up to her, Coffin told her not to jump to conclusions. She didn't reply; she just kept walking.

"Mother . . ."

"Your *friend* assaulted someone." She made friend sound like a dirty word.

"Allegedly. And since when is assault murder?"

"We're talking about a capacity for violence. And that's something I can't ignore. I *won't* ignore it."

"Maybe you should."

Though Coffin kept his tone casual, his remark had an instant effect on Mother. Approaching the curb, she hit the brakes and eyed him. "Let me get this straight. Are you *asking* me to ignore the assault?"

"I might."

"And the motive? And the rest of the evidence implicating your friend?"

"I might."

"You're playing with fire, Ed. You're a senior officer. You could be charged with using your influence to interfere with an official investigation. Do you understand what I'm saying to you?"

"I . . . might."

"Listen, smart guy, I'm trying to keep you out of trouble. This is a big case and everybody from the SECDEF on down is watching. You can't be seen as trying to influence it. So don't stick your nose where it doesn't belong. Okay?"

"Since when did you suddenly start playing by the rules?"

"I don't cut corners in murder cases."

"*Right.*"

She stepped back with a frustrated grimace. "I said my piece. You want to kiss off your star, be my guest. But leave me out of it."

"I thought you didn't care about your career."

"Ed—"

"Okay, okay. We never had this conversation." Coffin started to add something, reeled it in.

"Now what? Spill it."

He wished he could. "Relax. I know what I'm doing."

"Now *that's* reassuring."

As they crossed the street, that's precisely what Coffin had almost explained to her, absent the sarcasm. That she should be reassured because fate had dealt him a hand that made him professionally bulletproof. No matter how much trouble he got into or whom he pissed off, his chances for further promotion would be unaffected.

Because the outcome was preordained.

As they went up Bell's driveway, Mother said, "Explain something to me, Ed. I thought you wanted to be a general."

"I did."

It took a step for the tense to register. "*Did?*"

"It's too much of a crapshoot. I'd be crazy to count on it." He shrugged.

"Come off it. You're a lock. You've got a four-star sponsor and made colonel what, five years early?"

"Six."

"And now you're ready throw away all that away?" She shook her head. "All I got to say is you two must be damn tight."

The suspect again.

They came to Mother's car. She angled toward the driver's side, looking at him. "Change of plans, Ed. You stay here. I don't think it's a good idea for you to handle the questioning."

He froze, his hand on the passenger door. "Aren't you overreacting?"

"Am I? You're the one who's risking his career for a potential killer."

He exhaled slowly to check his emotions. "So I was right. Your mind *is* made up. Without knowing the facts, you've concluded—"

"I said *potential* killer. And here's a news flash; your friend might actually be a killer. That's not me talking, but the *evidence*. Right now I got one suspect and I need someone who'll help me get at the truth and fast. What I don't need is a defense lawyer. You understand my position, right?"

Coffin didn't trust himself to respond.

She dismissed his irritation, saying, "Don't blame me. You brought this on yourself. If I were you, I'd go practice my karate moves. Something tells me you might need them." She smiled sardonically and opened her car door.

"Aren't you forgetting something?"

She frowned at him.

"Erik Olson," Coffin said with feeling, "was also my friend. And I want the son of a bitch who killed him."

"You'd have to make a choice. How could I be sure you'd make the right one?"

"You know damn well I would." Coffin tapped his chest. "In here, you know I wouldn't cover for a killer."

"No can do. Too much is riding on—"

Coffin slapped the roof of the car. The flat crack sounded like a rifle shot in the quiet. Mother jumped back, startled. "*Jesus.* What's your fucking problem?"

"You. You're making excuses. You know you can trust me."

"You're too *close*. It's too risky for me to—"

"You know me, Mother!"

It was another calculated outburst and this time it had the desired effect. Mother grudgingly nodded, indicating that she believed him, at least at some level. But what Coffin sought was her complete trust. And to achieve that, he had to answer a question they'd both been avoiding. One that went to the heart of his relationship with the suspect.

He did so now, beginning with the answer. A flat denial.

"What's the question?" she asked.

"You know what it is."

"Do I?"

"Yes. It's been bothering you from the beginning."

But Mother played it coy, insisting he state the question. When he finally did, she showed no reaction and he thought he'd been mistaken. Then he saw her relieved smile.

"Get in the damn car, Ed," she said.

As Mother strapped on her seatbelt and started the car, she glanced at Coffin, still wearing that relieved smile. All along, she'd been telling herself that he'd never compromise his integrity to protect a friend. He certainly wouldn't protect a murderer. And yet . . .

And yet a grain of doubt lingered because she also realized

friendships were unique. In Coffin's case, he and the suspect went back to his college ROTC years and had lived together. That kind of history implied a bond that would be difficult to break, especially if an additional factor were considered. One far too important to be settled by a generic denial.

Initially, she had been puzzled by Coffin's resistance to stating the question. Then, as she continued to press him, it finally dawned on her why.

"Why Ed, you're actually embarrassed to talk about this."

"I'd . . . rather not. That's all."

"That's not an option. You either tell me now or I'm gone. Well?"

"Okay, okay. The question is: Did I sleep with Major Caralyn Barlow? The answer is no, never. Her dad was my ROTC commander and I've known her since she was a kid. I never thought about Caralyn that way. None of us ROTC students did. Ask Sam, he'll tell you."

"Sam wasn't around when you and Caralyn lived together. She's an attractive girl and I find it hard to believe two heterosexual adults could—"

"It'd be like screwing my sister! Jesus, I can't believe I said that. I hope you're happy."

Mother was, but not exclusively for the reason Coffin assumed. Rather, it was because she was starting to question something she believed. If Coffin *hadn't* slept with Caralyn Barlow, then perhaps he didn't—

"Hold it," Coffin said to her. "Sergeant Baker is waving to us."

Baker came over to Coffin's window, leaning down as he lowered it.

"Sir, you have a phone call. A woman. She insisted it was urgent she talk to you immediately."

"What woman?"

"She wouldn't say and I kept asking her, sir." Baker hesitated.

"Yes, Sergeant?"

"Well, sir, when we were talking, I heard a man call out, 'Major.' Yelled it. He had to, on account of all the loud music in the background. The woman cupped the phone for a few seconds. You know, like she was answering the guy and didn't want me to hear."

"My, my," Mother said, "I wonder who she could be," her tone sarcastic because she knew precisely who the female major was, as did Coffin.

"Tell Major Barlow I'll see her in five minutes," he said to Baker.

"What the hell—"

Coffin sat up fast. So did Mother.

Turning down the hill, they were stunned to see an armada of emergency vehicles a quarter mile ahead. Coffin counted over a dozen—mostly security police Humvees and pickups—all with colored strobes pulsing blindingly. Mother jammed on the brakes to keep from blowing through them.

"Houston," she murmured, "we have a problem."

A given. The vehicles were ominously parked across from the first BOQ on the right—their destination. While an SP presence had been expected, one of this magnitude wasn't.

Coffin's stomach lurched at a realization. When he voiced it, Mother grimly confirmed that the SPs wouldn't respond in force for a simple assault case. Coffin said, "So that means the victim must have . . ."

"Don't go there."

He looked over.

"You're thinking too much. The radio call said your friend was arrested for assault."

"If the victim died—"

"In the last five minutes?"

They drove past the small park. More lights could be seen coming from it. Moving lights. "Okay," Coffin said, sitting back. "That's what this is about. They're still looking for the burglar."

"Not so fast."

She pointed down the hill. Shadowy figures with flashlights could be seen darting between the remaining BOQ buildings. "They wouldn't be searching over there for your guy."

"Then who are they looking for?"

Mother shook her head. They were almost to the vehicles. A cop setting out red cones for a roadblock ordered them to stop. Mother swerved right by him, pulling into a space beside an ambulance. The cop stalked over, angrily gesturing and shouting, then underwent an instant attitude adjustment at the sight of Coffin and Mother emerging from the car.

He came to a sudden stop, his mouth open. Winching it closed, he reluctantly continued forward.

Saluting Coffin, he said to Mother, "Jeez, Agent Hubbard. I'm sorry. I didn't know it was your car. If I had—"

"My fault, Airman Collins," she said. "I should have put on my flashers."

"Yes, ma'am." But this was the military and Collins waited for a sign from the colonel. Only when Coffin nodded did he allow himself to relax.

Mother said to him, "Major Sutter requested me."

"Yes, ma'am. He'll return in a few minutes. He said you can question Major Barlow in the victim's room—4G."

"That where the assault took place?"

"Yes, ma'am. The med techs are still treating the victim. A major named Steiner."

Mother's eyebrows crept up at the name, but it meant nothing to Coffin.

Coffin gave a suggestive cough, but Mother was already asking how serious Steiner's injuries were.

"The word on the radio is she'll be okay. Sure didn't look that way at first, I can tell you—"

"Why not?" Coffin asked.

Collins seemed surprised he had actually spoken. "On account of all the blood, sir. But Major Sutter said that's because Major Steiner got hit in the head and the scalp can really bleed."

He tensed slightly, anticipating a follow-up. But Coffin had what he wanted and returned the ball to Mother with a glance.

"Where is Major Sutter now?" she asked Collins.

Collins waved toward the park. "Searching for Jeanne, ma'am."

"Jeanne?"

"Airman Jeanne Roche." He nodded to the nearest Humvee. "That's her vehicle there. She was first one on the scene, looking for that burglar. Now we can't find her and she's not answering her radio. We think she might have fallen in the park, maybe got knocked out."

"That's probably it," Mother said.

But as she and Coffin went up the walkway, her troubled expression suggested another possibility.

So much for following her own advice about not thinking, Coffin thought.

"Hold it, Ed," Mother said.

They'd just entered the ground floor of the two-story building. Room 4G was four doors down on the right, a cop the size of a house parked outside it. Past him, a small group in bathrobes had gathered, talking in hushed tones. They squinted at Coffin, trying to place the unfamiliar colonel, then went blank when they couldn't.

Lowering her voice, Mother said to Coffin, "You know what I'm going to say?"

Coming up the walk, she'd been sneaking glances as if she wanted to tell him something he didn't want to hear. "I can guess. You probably want to assign a guard to watch my place."

"Yes."

"Don't. If one shows up, I'll order him away."

"A cop is *missing*. If your intruder is responsible—"

"Then a guard won't help. Not if Yee sent him. This is his home turf, and if he wants me roughed up, he's got the clout to make it happen."

"So you're going to make it easy for him? Call me crazy, but I'm starting to think you *want* Yee to make a try for you."

"It's not that. I'm just not going to lose sleep over it." He shrugged.

"That still doesn't explain your stud karate man act. You trying to impress me? Because if you are— Oh, you're impossible."

Coffin was chuckling. He couldn't help it. "I've been accused of being a lot of things, but never a stud." He winked at her. "So what do you find particularly studly about me? My body? You notice I've been working out?"

She was doing her best to ignore him, unlike the crowd. Coffin's remarks had carried down the hall, generating embarrassed titters from the women and grins from the men, including the cop. By tomorrow morning, the base grapevine would be buzzing about the studly colonel, and Coffin realized he was okay with it.

Not so with Mother. She was glaring at the amused faces, but with no apparent effect.

"Look at me, Ed," she whispered tersely.

He casually did.

"My eyes. Look into my eyes. This isn't some kind of macho act for my benefit, is it? You really aren't worried about Yee at all?"

"I told you I wasn't."

"But this isn't like you. You never came off as a tough guy before. Certainly not physically. And the Ed I knew was too smart to look for a fight with a guy like Yee or one of his goons. What's gotten into you, Ed?"

"I told you I've changed."

"No one changes that much. Why did you really come to Korea? Is it Yee? You got an old score to settle with him? *Why are you here?*"

Once again, Coffin resisted the urge to confide in her. "Mother, I don't want to talk about it. Besides, you'll know soon enough."

"It *is* Yee. You're in trouble with him. What? Tell me."

"Patience. It won't be long."

She stiffened at something in his voice. A profound sense of weary inevitability. "Ed, it can't be that bad. Talk to me. Whatever is wrong, I can help."

"You can't. No one can. I have to do this alone."

His shoulders dropping, he slowly continued down the hall.

★ 17 ★

The door to room 4G was closed, muffled voices coming from behind it. As Mother and Coffin approached, the big cop came to attention. He was no longer smiling and neither were the people in the crowd. They'd picked up on the sudden somberness in Coffin's mood.

The cop reached out to open the door. Just then, they heard a muffled voice say, "You've got nothing on me, so I'm leaving. If Agent Hubbard shows, you can tell her— Hey, what are you doing? *Stop touching me.*"

The sound of a commotion and a grunt of pain. "Oh, hell." The big cop flung open the door, attempting to rush inside. Lunging forward, Coffin grabbed his arm and the cop spun angrily. He tried to wrench free, seemed surprised when he couldn't. Mother shouted at Coffin, "*What are you doing? Let him go.*" But Coffin clung to the cop, saying, "He'll only make things worse. I can handle the situation." There were more shouts from the room, followed by the sound of something heavy falling. Coffin tried to see what was going on, but the cop was in the way. "Move, Sergeant. *Move.*"

Instead of doing so, the cop emphatically pointed to the doorjamb, saying, "Colonel, I wouldn't go in. She can be dangerous. She did that earlier. It's not safe."

Coffin and Mother saw only splintered wood where the metal deadbolt plate had once been. "By *herself?*" Mother said.

"Yes, ma'am. You and the colonel better stay here until I can stabilize—"

"It's stabilized," Coffin said. "Listen."

Mother and the cop did. But there was only silence now. Releasing his grip, Coffin jerked a thumb and the cop finally stepped aside. As he did, he glanced over his shoulder into the room, his eyes widening. "That's impossible. She couldn't have— Damn. *Damn.*" He reached for his gun and again moved toward the door. Coffin blocked his path and told him to put the weapon away. The cop looked to him as if he'd lost his mind.

"Sir, she's *dangerous.*"

"Put the gun away, Sergeant."

"Sir, can't you see—"

"Put the damn thing away."

The cop reluctantly complied. Mother said to Coffin, "You better be able to handle her. Because if you can't—"

"I can."

Mother stared past him into the room, shaking her head. "I suppose you taught her how to do that?"

"I was her first instructor."

"And you didn't tell me because . . ."

Coffin didn't respond; she knew the answer. The crowd was creeping closer and Mother froze them with a look, Then transferred it to Coffin, saying irritably, "It'd serve you right if I let the sergeant here jack her up."

"It'd be a mistake."

"Maybe. Maybe not."

Mother placed a hand on her weapon, eyeing Coffin. A less-than-veiled threat. From the room, they heard the faint sounds of running water, as if someone had turned on a shower, then a soft moan, and Mother's hand tightened on the gun butt.

Coffin sighed. "Aren't you overdoing it a little?"

"That depends on Major Barlow's emotional state. There's something I didn't tell you earlier. The woman who Barlow saw with Erik at the club last night was . . ."

At that instant Coffin knew. "It was Major Steiner," he finished.

It was a typical field-grade officer's BOQ, which meant it qualified as a one-bedroom apartment. There was a one-size-fits-all combination kitchen, living, and dining area toward the front and a bedroom at the very back. The furnishings were low-bidder faux-wood and included a television set with rabbit ears, since Uncle Sam didn't shell out for cable. The decor could be described as motel bland, the only color coming from a picture that looked as if someone had kicked over a bucket of red paint onto the canvas.

There were five occupants in the room. None even noticed Mother and Coffin as they walked in.

The two female med techs huddled by the bedroom door were fixated worriedly on a couple of male cops, sprawled out on the living room floor. Both were grimacing in pain and had their guns out, pointing them up with shaky hands. And standing over them was a diminutive blonde woman in a flight suit, combing her hair as if she didn't have a care in the world. It was Mother's favorite murder suspect, Major Caralyn Barlow.

"She's a cool one," Mother murmured.

But since the two cops obviously weren't, Coffin ordered them to put their guns away.

*

A woman taking out two large men had to be a first for Osan Air Base and possibly even for the air force, but that was par for the course for Caralyn Barlow, her martial arts background notwithstanding.

Caralyn regarded *everything* in life as a competition; she was all about winning, and anything less, she judged a failure. Up to now, this philosophy—this uncompromising drive to be first—had served Caralyn spectacularly. At the Air Force Academy, she achieved a number of distinctions: the first woman to graduate at the top of her class; the first woman to major in three separate science/engineering disciplines; and the first cadet to win an NCAA karate title. After a stint at MIT where she received two advanced degrees, she traded academia for pilot training and another first. By finishing the year-long course as the top pilot, she'd earned the right to fly any jet in the air force fleet, including fighters. But this was the early eighties and Caralyn had a problem; women still weren't allowed to fly combat aircraft. Since every previous female pilot had accepted this policy as a given, no one expected Caralyn to raise a stink.

But she did, big-time.

For someone as ambitious as Caralyn, it was a risky decision: Air force officers who bucked the status quo rarely were rewarded with promotions or long careers. But as Caralyn saw it, she had no choice. Filling in the fighter pilot square on her résumé was crucial to attaining her goal of becoming the first female Shuttle pilot. If that meant actively lobbying for her cause and stepping on a few high-ranking toes, so be it. America's attitude toward female warriors was evolving and she was convinced all she had to do was stare down the brass and Congress, and eventually they would all collectively blink. The only question was when.

She figured a year, tops. In Coffin's view, she was being

wildly optimistic, and he counseled her not to get her hopes up. He needn't have bothered.

Nine months later, Congress passed a landmark bill allowing women to fly in combat, opening the door for Caralyn to experience another of her trademark firsts. Only when it happened, it wasn't the one she anticipated.

For the first time in her professional life, Caralyn experienced failure.

When the initial cadre of women fighter pilot trainees was released, she read the names again and again, but it didn't matter. Hers wasn't on it and never would be. She didn't understand it. She'd spent years molding herself into the perfect, most highly qualified candidate. How could she not be selected?

How, Ed? It can't only be because I made waves.

That's part of it, sure.

Part? What do you mean, "part"?

Forget it. You really don't want to know.

Like hell, I don't. I have to know.

So Coffin told her the truth. That while being qualified was important in the selection process, there was an even more crucial criterion. One in which she was lacking.

Self-control. A fighter pilot has to have it and you don't. When you get mad, you give in to your temper and fly off the handle. It scares people, makes them question you. That's why your father wanted me to teach you Tae Kwon Do. He thought it would help you develop emotional self-discipline. But it obviously didn't work. Like now. You don't like what I'm saying and you're getting upset.

Hell, yes, I'm upset. This is all a crock. I don't have a self-control problem.

Look in the mirror, Caralyn.

I thought you were my friend.

I am your friend. That's why I'm telling you this. I want you to get counseling. Please.

Get out of my house, Ed. Get out.

Caralyn—

Get out. You hear me. I never want to see you again. Get out.

So Coffin got out. And after giving her some time to cool off, he gave her a call. Said he had another option for her. One that might be a stepping-stone to the Shuttle because it was kind of like being an astronaut.

I can get you an interview for the U-2 program, but it's a boys' club and you'll be the first woman candidate. They'll be looking for a reason to reject you, so don't piss anyone off.

You know me, Ed.

And Coffin did know Caralyn then, and knew her even better now. He knew she'd undergone counseling to control her anger. He knew she rarely flew off the handle anymore, and when she did, the episodes weren't explosive and they certainly weren't violent. And as he gazed down on the bruised and battered cops, his faith in Caralyn—the new Caralyn—didn't waver. Not even when Mother asked what had happened and one of the SPs rose to his feet, saying, "The major is *nuts.* She jumped us for no reason." And his buddy stood, voicing his support and painting a picture of Caralyn as some crazed Rambo wannabe. Not even then did Coffin harbor doubts, because of the confident look Caralyn was giving him. That's when he knew she had a card up her sleeve, something that trumped their accusations. What it was, Coffin couldn't even begin to guess, not that it mattered.

He simply asked her to play it now.

"I was provoked," Caralyn announced, pocketing her comb and eyeing the first cop who'd stood. "By Sergeant Carlotti. He touched me in the chest."

"You were trying to leave, Major," Carlotti said sourly. "I was only trying to stop you."

The second cop said to Mother, "Our orders were to keep Major Barlow here, ma'am."

"Sergeant Carlotti," Mother said, slowly measuring him, "did you touch Major Barlow inappropriately?"

Carlotti grudgingly nodded, his face sullen. "It was an accident, ma'am. Major Barlow turned, just when I reached out."

The admission drew a smile from Caralyn. She had her get-out-of-jail-free card.

Mother sighed, jerking her head to the door. "Take off, guys."

"Ma'am," Carlotti said, "you're not going to let her get away with assaulting us?"

Mother gave him a hard look. Grumbling, Carlotti headed for the door. His partner started to follow, then suddenly reached into his jacket and said to Mother, "Ma'am, my notes from the interview with Major Steiner. Major Sutter said you'd want them."

The cop tore several pages from his notepad and passed them to Mother. Scanning the notes, Mother's eyes flickered in surprise. She looked at Caralyn and seemed on the verge of saying something to her. Instead, she nodded to the cop. "Thank you, Sergeant."

"Yes, ma'am."

As Caralyn watched the cop leave the room, she couldn't keep from grinning. So Mother decided to help her.

"You do realize, Major Barlow," she snapped, "that I can still arrest you for assaulting two security policemen."

"Assault," Caralyn coolly countered, "is defined as unwelcome or improper physical contact perpetrated by one or more persons on another. It seems to me that's precisely what Carlotti did to me."

Her tone superior and patronizing, Caralyn was reminding Mother who had the five degrees and by extension, the lead in the brain cell department. From across the room, the young med techs held their breaths; they couldn't believe a suspect—a murder suspect—would dare imply that the chief of the OSI was somehow stupid.

But Coffin could. Euphemistically, Caralyn had balls and possessed the innate arrogance of the cerebrally blessed. The way she figured it, it was worth a shot to slip in her academic pedigree on the off chance that Mother might shy away from a battle of wits, knowing she might lose.

It was flawed logic, proving intelligence didn't equate to common sense. Unless maybe Caralyn's real goal was to get her figurative ass handed to her.

"Behave, Caralyn," Coffin said.

She turned to him innocently. "Colonel?" She always called him by rank in public.

"You heard me. Agent Hubbard's running a murder investigation. When she questions you, I expect you to treat her with—"

"It's okay, Ed," Mother said.

But Coffin kept lecturing Caralyn, determined to nip this in the bud. "It's *okay*, Ed," Mother persisted

And looking over to her, he saw that it was.

Instead of being angry at Caralyn's dig at her intelligence, Mother appeared amused by it. "It's not a problem. Really. You two stay here while I talk with the med techs."

"Sure. Okay."

But Coffin wasn't buying Mother's act for a minute. If Miss-Sensitive-to-Any-Slight was curtailing her impulse to come down hard on Caralyn, she had a reason. And seeing Mother smile at Caralyn as she moved away, he realized what it was. Mother was setting Caralyn up for a future grilling, if it came to that. And the instant Caralyn relaxed her guard, Mother would launch into her—

". . . to see you. You on some kind of diet; you've lost weight. Earth to Colonel Coffin. *Come in, Colonel.*"

Coffin's eyes snapped into focus. Caralyn was standing beside him. Sounding upbeat, she said, "Man, it creeps me out the way you do that mind-trip thing. Dad told me he never knew anyone who could concentrate like that. He says it's your defensive mechanism. Where you go to get away from the world. Me, I'd rather go to mountains or the beach. By the way, I like your girlfriend. I didn't think I would, considering what you said about her— Oh, oh, I know that look. You're still upset with me. Look, I know I shouldn't have roughed up those cops but, Jesus, when the guy grabbed me, I snapped. Anyway, everything worked out in the end and I don't see a problem. Do you?"

She had to be kidding.

Taking Caralyn by the arm, Coffin led her to the opposite end of the living room and spoke rapidly, his voice low. "You out of your mind? You're a murder suspect and you just beat up two policemen. What are you trying to do? Get thrown in jail?"

Caralyn blinked slowly. "I'm not in jail, am I?"

"Only because Mother is giving you a break."

Another slow blink. "Is she giving me a break?"

"You know damn well she is."

"Do I?"

"Stop answering everything with a question. This is serious. You could be in a lot of trouble."

"Could I?"

"Oh, for—"

Coffin checked himself; he couldn't give in to frustration.

In this respect, Caralyn was a lot like Mother. If you revealed they'd gotten to you, they'd won.

"Caralyn," Coffin said calmly, "we both know that your temper almost got you thrown in jail tonight. We both know that if you give in to it again, you could find yourself facing a murder charge. We both also know that I'm telling you this because I care about you. You do know that, don't you? I *care*."

The magic word.

Within seconds, it took effect, and her defensive shell began to crumble. There was the usual slow blink, but no smart-ass query. Dropping her eyes, Caralyn contemplated her shoes. "Yeah. I know. I'm . . . sorry, Ed." She was using his first name because no one could overhear.

"Sorry's not good enough. An arrest would have blown any chance you have of being an astronaut. You want to throw that away?"

A silence. She kicked at her flight boots. Thirty-four going on sixteen.

"Ed!"

Coffin looked at Mother, still beside the med techs. In her eyes, he saw a heavy dose of suspicion. She curtly nodded toward the sitting area, signaling it was time.

Coffin hesitated, glancing at Caralyn. And as he did, the years fell away and all he saw was the dimpled young girl he'd once trained.

"*Now*, Ed," Mother said impatiently.

His impulse was to flip her off. But that wasn't a right granted to full colonels. "In a minute."

"It's late and I need to know whether—"

"In a minute, Mother."

But in his heart, Coffin knew he couldn't go through with it. Bracing himself for Mother's reaction, he started to walk over and break the news to her. Then Caralyn said something that made him pause.

"What was that again?" he asked.

"I said, 'Go ahead and question me.' It's why you're here, right? To get me to confess?"

"You . . . *knew?*"

"Give me some credit. You waltz in out of the blue with Mrs. Kojak and I'm not supposed to wonder why?"

Coffin felt his face flush. He couldn't look at her.

"We'd better get started," Caralyn said. "Your old squeeze is giving us the evil eye. It must have been some reunion, you and her. You'll have to tell me about it sometime." Her tone was breezy, as if what they were about to do wasn't any big deal.

But Coffin knew better, and as she started to walk away, he said, "Caralyn, I'd like to explain—"

She continued toward the sofa.

Sitting down, she looked back expectantly. When Coffin didn't follow, she said, "You can relax, Colonel. I didn't kill Erik."

He didn't move.

"I can *prove* I didn't kill him, Colonel."

The conviction in her voice filled the room, and Coffin felt the tension leave his body. Walking over, he tossed Mother an "I told you so" look. She promptly countered with a subtle yet unmistakable middle-finger salute. Apparently, the rules of etiquette for colonels didn't apply to OSI chiefs.

Suppressing a smile, he eased down beside Caralyn on the couch.

★ 18 ★

Coffin and Caralyn shifted so their backs were to Mother. He whispered, "If we talk normally, she'll hear us."

"Isn't that why she wanted you to question me out here?"

"Probably. She doesn't trust me."

"That's obvious, since she just learned I wasn't the one who hit Charlotte . . . Major Steiner . . . and she didn't tell you."

It took Coffin a moment. "The cop's notes."

"Right. It's all there. Charlotte screamed because the guy said something right before he slugged her. She's not sure what he said, but she's certain it was a man's voice."

That explained Mother's surprised look, when she'd scanned the notes. Coffin said, "Caralyn, if you'd rather go somewhere private—"

"Hell, no. When I get through, Agent Hubbard will know I had nothing to do with Erik's death."

The answer he wanted. "For the record, I only agreed to do this because—"

"No explanations."

"I'd feel a whole lot better if—"

"I *know* you don't think I'm a killer. But with my temper, you couldn't be sure. Especially not with the way Erik was killed. That took someone with serious technical expertise. Word is he was killed by a gas. What'd the killer do, splice it into his oxygen line with some kind of pressurized container? Why the surprise? Any engineer would tell you that's the simplest way. Could I have rigged something up? You bet. But you knew that, which is why, at the back of your mind, you had to wonder. Don't shake your head. If the situation were reversed, I'd wonder about you. Could he? Did he? Well, it's all right here." She produced a folded paper from a flight suit pocket and handed it over.

"And this is . . ."

"Questions I know you'll have to ask. Figured it'd save time. Go ahead and follow along. The points are generally chronological. Get ready, because I'm going to do this fast." She glanced over her shoulder to Mother, checking if she was watching.

She was.

Abruptly, Caralyn began speaking so quickly that Coffin had to work to keep up. She said, "Yes, Erik broke a date with me last night and I later saw him having a drink with Charlotte at the O-Club. And yes, I made a scene and said things I shouldn't have, but one look at Charlotte and you'll understand. And yes, I went to the squadron late last night and crawled into his airplane. And yes, I did slip something into the cockpit, but it was only a note, apologizing for getting mad, because Charlotte explained it was an intelligence matter . . . Charlotte's an intel officer . . . and I believed her. And no, I didn't kill Erik and I can prove it when your girlfriend hooks me up to a lie detector and they find the note in the cockpit wreckage, verifying my story about why I went to the plane. And no, I didn't jump Charlotte, because she was slugged when she came out of her bathroom by someone who'd crawled in through the window. And yes, if you look out the window, you can see footprints, which I'm betting won't match mine. And yes, even if that's not definitive enough, I can still prove I couldn't have been the intruder because I was the one who was coming down the hall when Charlotte screamed. And yes, I broke down the door and saved her by scaring the guy off. And no, I didn't see the assailant, because he must have heard me knocking and took off. And no, there wasn't anyone else in the hall when Charlotte screamed, but someone probably heard her. And yes, Charlotte will tell you that she didn't get a good look at the guy either, but she's convinced it was a man. And yes, the last part is what I told those cops when I tried to leave. And no, I didn't write that on the note, which is why you look confused. I just thought of it. Oh, and one more thing. A freebie for your girlfriend: Tell her Charlotte and I have bonded; I really like her and sure as hell had no motive for hurting her. So? How'd I do, Ed? I think that pretty much covers everything. Don't you?"

Coffin paused, his eyes seeking out Mother. But she had resumed her conversation with the med techs, a sign she no longer considered Caralyn the primary suspect. It was also a sign that even an experienced detective like herself could miss a crucial, investigation-altering revelation.

"Not quite, Caralyn," Coffin said.

Caralyn appeared startled by Coffin's remark. It had never occurred to her that there was a question she might have missed.

"Relax," Coffin said. "I'm only bothered by one point, but it could be important, depending on your answer. Your comment about the way Erik was—"

"I'll bet I can guess."

Her competitive streak again. "Caralyn, it's easier if—"

"Give me a minute."

"No."

"Why not? What's a minute, Ed?"

Coffin relented, checking his watch. "All right. You've got exactly a minute."

Leaning against the couch back, he became aware of the pain in his head. He closed his eyes, attempting to focus it away. No dice this time, and he patted a pocket for his pills, hoping to head off an attack. If he only took a half dose, he might still be lucid enough to—

He sat up, twisting toward Mother. Struck by a question she'd just posed to the medical technicians.

In response, one said, "We don't know why Major Steiner refuses to go to hospital, ma'am."

Mother pointed to the cop's interview notes. "It says here she was *ordered* to the hospital by the doctor and refused."

"Yes, ma'am," the second tech said. "Dr. Blaney is worried about a concussion. Major Steiner was out for several minutes. Worse case, she might have an internal hemorrhage. Sometimes symptoms don't show up for several hours, and when they do, it's often too late."

Mother said, "You told Major Steiner this specifically? That she's risking death?"

"Oh, yes, ma'am," the same tech said. "Dr. Blaney made it clear he only wanted to run tests and observe her overnight. But Major Steiner still refused. Doesn't make much sense to us. I mean, it's almost 0100 hours. All she's going to do is sleep anyway."

At this remark, Mother contemplated the bedroom door. She went over to it and rapped sharply. "Charlotte, it's Mother. I need to talk to you. Why are you refusing to get checked out?"

Coffin felt a tug on his sleeve and turned, anticipating a

triumphant grin. Instead, Caralyn met him with a grimace.

"Give me a hint, Ed."

"This is ridiculous."

"If I can't guess, you tell me. Okay?"

"The *gas*."

He waited a beat, but she still didn't make the connection. He said, "How you knew that Erik was killed by a gas."

"Well, because . . ."

The significance registered and her eyes widened. "Hang on. Are you suggesting that I shouldn't have known about the gas?"

"I'm *telling* you it's closely held information. Only a handful of people in the chain of command know about it. I suppose that security cop major . . ." He went blank.

"Sutter."

"Sutter could have told you, but I'm not even sure he's in the loop. So if you didn't get it from him, I've got to consider—"

"Whoa, whoa. She's no killer, believe me."

A female source. For some reason, this surprised Coffin. "Who is she?"

"Ed, you're barking up the wrong tree. For starters, she wouldn't have the knowledge or ability to kill Erik."

"So now you're suddenly a detective?"

"Are you?"

Logic he couldn't counter. Behind them, Mother had begun talking to Major Steiner, who'd opened the bedroom door. "Charlotte, I want you to go to the hospital. It's for your own good and I can't understand why— Don't change the subject. Of course, I want to investigate your assault, but from these notes I already know—well, not everything. There are a couple questions: You're sure the perp was a man? Yes? Where did he hit you exactly? Show me."

"I saw the bump," Caralyn said to Coffin. "Once the med techs cleaned it up, it didn't look too serious. The cut didn't even need stitches, so I don't know why Mother's making an issue out of it."

"So now you're also a doctor?"

A smile that was amused and sarcastic. This was the difference between her and Mother. Not only could Caralyn dish it out, she could take it . . . sort of. He again asked for the woman's name.

"I'm telling you she's no killer. Promise me you'll go easy on her."

"The *name*, Caralyn."

"Okay, okay. Remember when I said if you got one look, you'd understand why I reacted so angrily at the club last night?"

"Your source. We're talking about your source."

"Turn around and look, Ed." She sounded amused.

"Look? Why should I—"

The light came on and Coffin was on his feet, looking toward the bedroom. And as he did, he found himself shaking his head, convinced he was seeing things. Because the woman framed in the doorway and talking to Mother had one of the most famous faces in the world.

"Wait," he said. "It can't be her. There's no mole."

"Congratulations, Ed. You must have her poster on your wall."

Caralyn still sounded amused.

★ 19 ★

Cindy Crawford.

Seeing Major Charlotte Steiner framed in the doorway, that was the first name . . . the only name . . . that popped into Coffin's mind. Other than the missing mole and perhaps softer facial features, Steiner was identical to the famous model in every way. She possessed the same willowy frame and wholesome girl-next-door sensuality. Her robe was cinched tight, accentuating her figure, and her eyes were big and dark, her skin flawless. No bandage was visible on her still-damp head, supporting Caralyn's assertion that her injury wasn't particularly serious.

Listening to Mother, Steiner absently toweled off handfuls of her luxurious brown hair. It was a functional act and not intended to be erotic, but Coffin thought it was the most erotic thing he'd ever seen. Steiner acknowledged Caralyn with a nod and tired smile, and greeted Coffin with a perfunctory, "Good evening, Colonel." When Mother identified Coffin by name, Steiner studied him with sudden interest and seemed on the verge of saying something. But before she could, Mother again tried to coax Steiner into accompanying the med techs to the hospital.

Caralyn said, "I thought you didn't know Charlotte, Ed."

"I don't."

"She was married to some big-shot DOD civilian. Could be you met them at a function with the general."

"I didn't." Someone who looked like Steiner, you don't forget.

The conversation between Mother and Steiner continued, but went nowhere. Steiner wouldn't budge from her decision to remain in her quarters. Her frustration growing, Mother said, "So return here after Doc Blaney runs his tests. For Christ's sake, at least get checked out, Charlotte."

"He'll insist I stay."

"And that's a problem because . . ."

"It's unnecessary. I have a lot of work to do in the morning. I'm fine."

"Getting into a pissing contest with Blaney isn't worth it. He could charge you with disobeying a direct order."

"The victim of an assault? I rather doubt it."

And on it went.

"Number six, Ed," Caralyn counted softly.

Tracking the glances Steiner had tossed Coffin. Normally, he would be flattered by a beautiful woman's interest, but Steiner's looks were curiously furtive, anxious gestures. And as they continued, Coffin began to get the feeling that she was—

"Frightened," Caralyn murmured. "You ask me, she looks a little frightened."

"It's the intruder. She's worried he'll come back."

"So why remain here instead of going to the hospital?"

A rhetorical question, which they both began to ponder.

Her brow knitted, Caralyn cycled through various explanations, only to shake them off. When Coffin mentioned a possibility, she immediately dismissed it.

"But she knew about the gas," Coffin countered. "And if she is involved in Erik's killing, that might explain her behavior."

"Why would she be interested in you?"

She had him there.

Sighing, she said, "I give up," and started to cross the room.

"Wait, Caralyn."

"For what? Mother's not getting anywhere and Charlotte might talk to me. Besides, we haven't told Mother that she knew about the gas."

"Wait. You'll want to hear this first."

Because Mother had finally lost her patience with Steiner and was now demanding an answer to the question everyone wanted to know: What was Charlotte's *real* reason for not wanting to leave?

"So what is it, Charlotte? Tell me."

"Mother, we've gone through this. I've already explained—"

"You're hiding something. What is it? You meeting some guy for a little late-night R&R? Someone on the late shift? Who is he? Is he the one who struck you? A lovers' quarrel, maybe? Hey, don't get upset with me. You won't tell me and I've got to figure out something that makes sense. Yeah, yeah, I see the wedding ring. Listen, you know how many people come to Korea and screw around—don't turn away. Are you crying? *Why are you crying?*"

Steiner didn't answer; she couldn't. She lovingly caressed her wedding ring, tears welling in her beautiful eyes. Watching her, Mother reddened and looked away. Confronted by open emotion, she had no idea what to say or do. It wasn't surprising. One reason the name Mother had stuck was that no one could be less nurturing.

Hurrying over, Caralyn put her arms around Steiner, glaring at Mother. "You insensitive bitch."

"Now listen, Major—"

"Her husband's *dead*. He died a few months ago."

Mother visibly deflated. "But her ring. I naturally assumed—"

"Proof. You want proof she wouldn't screw around. *Look*."

Caralyn made an angry motion at the bedroom.

Mother turned toward the open door, with a puzzled expression. Hesitantly, she walked toward it, Coffin slowly following. As they entered, they immediately noticed a large red stain in the carpet roughly a body length from the bathroom—Steiner's resting place after she'd been struck. And several feet to the right, they saw the evidence Caralyn had been referring to.

"Jesus," Mother said.

A literal remark.

Her Catholic faith and her husband.

Those were the two most revered things in Major Steiner's life, not necessarily in that order.

One corner of the room was a shrine to both. Framed paintings of Jesus Christ and of a handsome, graying man in a suit—her husband—hung midway up their respective walls, angled toward each other, a gilded cross above each, vases of freshly cut flowers arrayed on the carpet below. Over the bed, there was another smaller cross draped with rosary beads and a framed photograph of Charlotte and her husband, standing arm in arm and smiling.

More photographs of her husband were strategically placed throughout the room, as if Charlotte always wanted to view him, regardless of the way she faced.

"Caralyn called it," Coffin said quietly, voicing the obvious. "Major Steiner's not staying to meet some lover."

"But there must be a reason. Nothing else makes sense."

"Neither does the possibility that she might be involved in the killing. Not someone who's this religious."

She slowly faced him. "Start talking, Ed."

No more good cop/bad cop.

Mother didn't have time; she needed answers fast. After summoning Steiner to the bedroom, Mother sat her on the bed, so Steiner could view the testaments to her faith and be reminded of her obligation to be truthful. Betting on this psychological assist, Mother intended to pepper Steiner with questions about the gas until she cracked.

The operative word was intended.

Mother never got a chance to grill Steiner, because of a knock on the bedroom door and the appearance of Airman Collins, the security cop from the parking lot. He was sweating as if he'd been running, and his anguished face suggested why.

"My God," Mother said, "Don't tell me . . ."

"Major Sutter needs you ASAP, ma'am," Collins panted. "They found her dead."

The missing security policewoman.

When Collins said she'd been discovered in the park with her throat cut, he was met with surprised gasps and stricken expressions. Afterward, Mother became eerily still, lost in a private rage. "Does anyone know who she was?" Caralyn asked quietly. "Did she ever guard the U-2 compound?"

But Mother was too angry to speak and Collins had wheeled toward the door, motioning the stunned med techs to follow. That left Coffin to identify the SP to Caralyn.

When he did, her buckling knees confirmed the name was familiar.

"Jeanne was just a kid," she said dully. "Who the hell kills a kid?"

A silence. She wasn't asking for a response.

Coffin became aware of Major Steiner again staring at him. When he faced her, she looked away, but unlike before, quickly refocused on him. And in her eyes, he noticed her earlier anxiety had been replaced by a resolute coldness. Almost a hate.

Twice more, she swiveled away only to look back. Realizing she was still torn about talking to him, Coffin decided not to push her. He just waited for her to make up her mind.

Apparently she settled on a no because her silence continued.

Coffin had had enough and threw out, "What's on your mind, Major?"

He said it casually, attempting to allay her concerns. Instead, Steiner appeared startled that he'd actually spoken. By now, Mother and Caralyn were watching her with interest, and noticing them, Steiner blinked nervously, her anxiety returning.

"Major," Coffin said. "What's the problem? What's wrong?"

She was shaking her head, even as he spoke. "Nothing's wrong, sir. It's just the assault. What happened?"

"You're lying, Charlotte," Mother said quietly.

Coffin shot her a look, to tell her to back off. But Mother's arms remained crossed; indicating she understood the situation and wouldn't interfere . . . much. Steiner said, "It *is* the assault. I was attacked. The guy really scared me. Why would you think I'd lie about that?"

Silence. Three faces skeptically gazed back.

"Oh, this is ridiculous." Steiner sounded suddenly angry. "I was *assaulted*."

"No one is denying that, Major," Coffin said. "But it's obvious that you're holding back something and we want to know— Where are you going? We're not through."

Rising from the bed, Steiner went over to a lacquer Korean desk. Coffin told her to sit down; she ignored him and reached for a drawer. Stepping around her, Coffin held it shut. "I said sit, Major."

"Sir, if you'll let me—"

"That's an order."

She hesitated; she didn't want to do so. Reluctantly, she let go of the drawer and returned to the bed.

"What's in it, Colonel?" Caralyn asked Coffin.

A reference to the drawer. He was already opening it. Caralyn and Mother came over, watching as he rummaged through the contents. It didn't take long.

Caralyn said, "All I see is typing paper and a few pens and pencils."

"What did you want in here?" Mother asked Steiner.

Steiner just looked at her sullenly.

"Charlotte," Caralyn said, "why won't you trust us? Can't you see we want to help?"

"You can help by leaving me alone."

"Charlotte, please—"

"Leave. I'm tired. I have nothing to say to you."

"What about to Colonel Coffin?" Mother asked her.

Steiner hesitated; that was enough. "She's all yours, Ed," Mother said.

★ 20 ★

Coffin took a page from Mother's book, but it wasn't easy. It wasn't that he'd never come down hard on a subordinate before; he had, on many occasions.

But never someone as beautiful as Steiner.

Twisting his face into a passable glare, he forced himself to speak in a low, menacing tone. He explained that whatever she had to say to him, this was her chance. Perhaps her only chance.

"So start talking, Major, and I want all of it. And it had better be the truth. Now let's have it."

He waited.

Nothing. She sat with her knees pressed together, eyes on the floor.

"Major, do you understand that this is a murder investigation? And the person who attacked you could be the killer?"

A shrug. "I don't know anything about that, Colonel."

"But you know something. Something you're afraid to—"

Her head shot up. "But *I don't*, sir. I don't know anything. Why won't you believe me?" Her voice was overly loud; she was practically shouting at him.

Caralyn said, "Charlotte, take it easy."

"How can I? I'm the victim and you're acting as if I'm guilty of something."

Another high-volume denial. Steiner perched on the edge of the bed, glaring at them with the outrage of the wronged. Mother caught Coffin's eye and nodded. He understood.

Steiner had made a mistake and given them an opening.

"Are you guilty of something, Major?" he demanded suddenly.

She flinched, staring up at him. It was another mistake; he caught a flicker of fear in her eyes.

"Sir, I don't know what you're talking about. I haven't done anything to—"

Coffin interrupted her harshly. "Stop the lies, Major. You're in trouble. We know you're withholding information from us. And if you continue to do so, you will be arrested."

"On what evidence, sir? Suspicion? The UCMJ requires more justification than that. So unless you can prove I'm guilty of something—"

"Major Olson's death."

She looked to him in shock.

Coffin spoke rapidly, keeping her off balance. "We know you had crucial details about his death. Details you couldn't have known about unless you were either directly involved or learned them from someone— *Hey! Get back here, Major. Stop her.*"

Because Steiner had sprung from the bed, shoved him back, and was now rushing into the bathroom. She slammed the door shut and clicked the lock. Coffin was dumbfounded. He whirled to Caralyn, demanding an explanation. But she was already striding to the bathroom. Banging on the door, she called out, "Charlotte, open up. What the hell do you think you're doing? Charlotte, talk to me. I'm your friend . . ."

"I think I know," a whispered voice from behind Coffin said.

He slowly turned.

It was Mother. She looked uneasy.

"The paper," she murmured. "She wanted the damned paper."

"From the drawer? Why?"

She hesitated. "We'll talk outside."

"Why not in here?"

"Let's go outside, Ed."

That came through loud and clear. She had a specific reason for not wanting to talk in the bedroom.

Shaking his head, Coffin went outside.

"Fine," he said. "We're outside. Now you mind telling me why it was necessary—"

He broke off. Mother wasn't behind him.

From the bedroom, Caralyn continued to pound on the bathroom door. Then came the sound of blaring rock music. Poking his head through the doorway, Coffin saw Mother standing by a clock radio on the dresser. He said, "What? You suddenly want to listen to—"

Coffin inhaled the remaining words because it became obvious what Mother was up to. And if she was right . . .

"I'll be damned," he murmured.

Mother motioned Caralyn away from the bathroom. The two women spoke in hushed voices. Caralyn glanced to the phone on an end table and shook her head emphatically. At another remark from Mother, she stared at the radio, her eyes widening.

Mother whispered in her ear and Caralyn rushed over to the computer desk, opened the drawer Steiner had been reaching for earlier, and removed a single sheet of bond paper. Coffin stared at it, searching for some kind of writing. When he saw it was blank, he knew Mother's hunch was right.

Caralyn handed the paper to Mother, who wrote something on it. Stepping over to the bathroom, she slid the paper under the door.

It instantly disappeared.

Mother placed her hand on the knob, expecting the door to open. Instead, the paper reappeared through the crack at the bottom. Snatching it up, Caralyn scanned it and gave it to Mother.

"Do we have a deal?" Steiner's voice asked through the door.

"Yes." But Mother was scowling at the paper as she said it.

"Give me a few minutes to get dressed."

"All right."

Caralyn murmured something to Mother. She nodded and, still holding the paper, turned and walked determinedly toward Coffin, thrusting up the paper. On it, Coffin saw a neatly printed statement that confirmed what he now knew.

Charlotte, if you believe your room is bugged, we'll talk outside.

And below, a response scrawled in what looked like an eyeliner pencil:

I can only talk to Colonel Coffin.

Mother pointed to the front door and they left.

Mother wasn't taking any chances.

After exiting the building, she continued down the walkway for a full ten paces before feeling secure enough to speak. Coffin was glad for her caution; as they stepped into the shadows, he managed to pop a pill without her noticing.

"Caralyn will notify you when Steiner is ready," Mother

said to Coffin. "It's your call, but Caralyn thinks it'll be okay to use her room to interview Steiner."

"Fine. Caralyn's place won't be bugged."

She watched him in the semidarkness. "So you're buying Steiner's story?"

Coffin shrugged. "She obviously believes what she's saying. Besides, it wouldn't be the first time North Korean operatives targeted an intel officer." With hundreds of Korean workers on base, spies were a constant worry.

"But a listening device suggests the North is behind her assault and Olson's murder." Mother gave him a long look. "So your buddy General Yee's theory could be right after all."

"Assuming both events are connected."

"They have to be, Ed. We got Steiner and Olson meeting in the bar last night. And thirty hours later, he's dead and she's almost killed. Toss in Steiner's fear and the fact that she won't reveal what she and Olson discussed, and it all adds up to—"

Coffin shook his head. He understood her logic, but she was ignoring . . .

"What? You don't agree? You can't possibly believe it's all a coincidence, Ed."

"Exactly. It *all* can't be coincidence. There are two other incidents you're discounting. What about the break-in at my quarters and the photograph Yee had taken from Marty Bell's office?"

This time it was her turn to shake her head. "I see what the problem is. You still can't get over your bias against Yee. Now maybe he is a ruthless son of a bitch and an all-round scuzzball—"

"*Maybe?*"

"Deep down, you know he wouldn't have anything to do

with Olson's death. He'd have no reason to. Yee's on our side, remember?"

"Yee's on nobody's side. He has his own agenda."

"Which includes killing a pilot and destroying an intelligence asset he himself uses? Get a reality check, Ed. The ROKs are pissing in their pants over the possibility that North Korea might have nukes. You think Yee, as their intelligence chief, would sabotage his most effective surveillance platform?"

"Look, I know it doesn't seem logical—"

"You bet it doesn't. Not unless you're suggesting Yee is a traitor. You honestly believe a guy worth a zillion bucks could be enticed into selling out his country?"

Coffin was getting annoyed. She knew he didn't have all the answers. "Yee is capable of anything. He sent a goon after me tonight."

"Correction. *Someone* sent a goon."

"C'mon, Mother. Back at the BOQ, you said—"

"I said a lot of things. But you haven't been playing it straight with me. How do I know that your visitor isn't connected to the reason you came to Korea?"

"For Pete's sake—"

"You're getting a guard assigned to your quarters. And if you buck me, I'll go straight to General Gruver."

Her determined gaze told him there was no use fighting it. "You're making a mistake assuming the North Koreans are behind what's been happening. Take Major Steiner: Aren't you wondering why she won't tell what she knows?"

"She's willing to tell you. In fact, she's been hot to talk to you since . . ." She illuminated her watch. ". . . 0115 hours, give or take."

"And you know this because—" The time she'd stated suddenly clicked. "Wait a second. That call to my quarters. The one Sergeant Baker told us about. Are you saying it was made by *Steiner*?"

"Caralyn swore it wasn't her. She also confirmed Steiner was alone in her bedroom for several minutes, with the radio playing." Mother's eyes narrowed suspiciously. "Damn curious. That Steiner is so anxious to confide in someone she supposedly doesn't know."

Coffin sighed. "Mother, I've never met her."

"So you've said."

"Ask yourself why I would lie about knowing her."

"Oh, I'm asking, believe me."

He shook his head and turned away. But when he glanced back, he still saw her suspicion.

"Look," he said, "I'm a colonel. Steiner might want to talk to someone with rank."

Mother's suspicion remained. "There are other colonels, Ed. And three generals on base."

"That could be it, then. She could be interested in my boss, General Ford."

She measured him with sudden interest "Go on . . ."

He shrugged. "Think about it. If Steiner knows I work for General Ford, then talking to me makes sense. My guess is she wants me to approach Ford with whatever—"

"Got it, Ed."

And apparently, she did.

Mother's suspicion was replaced by a vague look of approval. It was her way of apologizing for questioning his veracity.

"You do realize," Coffin said, eyeing her, "that Steiner's reluctance to reveal what she knows doesn't fit your theory of North Korean involvement."

"Sure it does. Olson's dead and Steiner is afraid that if she comes forward, the same thing will happen to her."

"Then your people wouldn't be doing your jobs."

"Our jobs?"

And then she understood. "Right, right. If Steiner was in protective custody, the North Koreans couldn't get to her. Since Steiner would know that . . ."

"She's afraid of someone else," Coffin finished.

A slam-dunk conclusion. Then Coffin saw the ball pop out from the rim when Mother shook it off.

She said, "Nice try, Ed. You're still trying to implicate Yee, but you're forgetting a crucial point."

"Okay . . ."

"We could protect Steiner from *anyone*. And until you talk to her, we'd only be guessing at who she thinks is after her. As screwy as she's been acting, there's no guarantee that she'll tell you the truth. So let's get a warm and fuzzy about her first. It'll only take a minute."

As she keyed her radio to make a call, Coffin took a shot at guessing her intentions. Once again, the ball rimmed out.

★21★

Instead of requesting someone with a lie detector—the nearest technician was a member of an army criminal investigative unit, based at the Yongsan army garrison in Seoul—Mother asked the command post to mobilize a signal intel team to sweep Steiner's room. In Mother's mind, the presence of a bug would go a long way toward enhancing Steiner's credibility.

"Team will be here in twenty minutes," Mother announced, putting away her radio.

"And to clear her room?"

"A half hour, give or take." Noting Coffin's scowl, she added, "You don't wait to question Steiner, if that's what you're wondering."

It was.

"We got company," she said, pointing.

They watched a staff car pull into the parking area. Coffin anticipated seeing one of the base's heavy hitters, but instead a stocky man emerged carrying a medical bag.

"Doc Humphrey," Mother said. "Hospital pathologist."

The reason for Humphrey's presence was twofold; he would officially certify the latest death and aid Mother in her forensic analysis. As two SPs led him up the slope toward the park, Coffin pictured the horror that awaited them. Something burned within him and he knew it was fueled by hate.

"I want the bastards," a bitter voice said.

A beat later, Coffin realized the voice was his.

"So you think there's more than one?" Mother asked quietly.

"A lot more."

She pensively nodded. While one person might have managed Olson's murder, they both realized that Steiner's attack, coupled with her inexplicable fear and the probable presence of a listening device in her room, indicated something of a much larger scope.

As Humphrey disappeared around the building, Mother expanded on what they were both thinking.

"A conspiracy," she said, facing Coffin. "Assuming we're talking about a well-organized conspiracy, that brings us back to either North Korean operatives or South Korean sympathizers, or both. If so, we haven't got much of a chance of getting them. The ROKs will circle the wagons if it looks like we're targeting one of their own because of what you talked about earlier. Saving face. No way will they admit they have a spy working for them. Or a traitor.

"Normally that wouldn't be a problem for me, because the ROKs would take care of the guy on their own. Fit him with cement shoes and take him for a one-way boat ride. Now, you're the Korea expert, but I'm thinking that solution won't work this time because we're talking a conspiracy. If a lot of people turn up missing, that would be damned hard to cover up, even for them. Am I right?"

"Especially now." With the recent election of a former dissident to the presidency, the South Korean government had implemented a series of feel-good democratic reforms, including a much freer press.

"And arresting the bastards would also seem to be out," Mother went on. "Because that would mean publicity and a trial and a scandal. I'm hoping I'm wrong, but—"

"You're not." This was a reflection of the collective Korean psyche—anything that dishonored one's family name or organization was to be avoided at all costs.

She shook her head. "Well, that cinches it. We're caught between a rock and a hard place. The only way to get a line on the killer is to get the ROKs to admit they've got a spy in their ranks. But as soon as we try, they'll demand we back off. And guess what? If they holler loud enough, Uncle Sam will."

"Our military would never drop a case with two murders."

"I said 'back off,' Ed. Officially, the case will still be open, but we won't be allowed to go anywhere near the ROKs. Quit shaking your head. I've danced to this tune and know what I'm talking about. A couple months back, a ROK major raped one of our lieutenants. When we tried to arrange to get a DNA sample from him, we hit a wall. The old guy we met tonight, their chairman—"

"General Cho."

"Cho made it damn clear he wasn't about to cooperate and our generals sure as hell weren't about to pressure them." She gave a resigned shrug. "This is Korea and the ROKs set the rules."

"It sounds like you're ready to give up."

Her face tightened. "You know me better than that, Ed. I just want you to understand what we're up against."

"What I understand is that we do whatever it takes to solve the case."

"You deaf? I just told you that if General Gruver orders us to stay away—"

"Screw Gruver. They killed Erik."

"Oh, Ed . . ." She shook her head at him. "Ed . . ."

"What?"

"You. Your tough-guy act is getting old. We both know you'd never disobey a direct order."

"In a heartbeat."

"Let me guess." She stepped back, running her eyes over him. "This is the new and improved Ed Coffin. The kind of stand-up guy who'd risk a court-martial to avenge a friend."

"Hell yes. If it's the only option."

"I don't buy it. Sorry."

"So don't. I'll go it alone."

"Listen, big talker." She appraised him coolly. "You haven't changed nearly as much as you think."

"Whatever."

"Look at your uniform. It's *perfect*. So is your hair. You're a *striver*, Ed. Yes, sir, yes, sir, three bags full, sir, and all the rest. Unh-unh. When push comes to shove, you won't fall on your sword. It's just not in you."

"It is now. I told you I don't care about a star."

"Oh, please." She pointed to his chest. "In there, you still care big-time. Brigadier General Ed Coffin sounds damned good to you."

He hesitated.

"Now, now, the truth, Ed." She had the beginnings of a smile. "You know I'm right. Admit it."

He sighed. "Fine. Okay."

"Ah . . ."

"But that didn't stop me from resigning as General Ford's exec."

A delayed reaction from Mother. She looked momentarily perplexed, as if she'd misunderstood. Then her mouth fell open, when she realized she hadn't.

"You *quit*?"

"Last week. I realized making rank wasn't worth it. The long hours . . . having no life of my own . . ." He shrugged. "Anyway, I'd had enough."

Mother still appeared shell-shocked. She stared at him as if she was seeing him for the first time.

"So all that stuff you've been telling me . . ."

"Is true."

Mother seemed embarrassed. She tried to speak but didn't seem to know what to say. "Look," she managed awkwardly, "if I was wrong about you . . . God knows, I want to be wrong . . . I'm sorry."

Conditional or not, it was an apology Coffin had never expected to hear. And when Mother's eyes remained on his, Coffin realized she might not stop there.

He watched her, allowing himself to hope. But taking this last step—revealing why she'd left him—wasn't easy for Mother. As the seconds passed, her silence continued. Coffin knew he couldn't push her; he had to let her make up her mind.

But the waiting was slow.

It was agonizing.

And finally, he saw it. Her sudden, determined nod. She began, "Ed, I was told that you were seen—"

She turned away. "You hear something?"

"Him."

The security policeman jogged up to Mother, holding out his radio. Like most, he was a fresh-faced young airman; unlike most, he had red hair and wore black-rimmed glasses. Peering myopically through thick lenses, he panted at Mother, "Agent Hubbard. Major Sutter wants to talk to you."

"Tell him I'm on the way."

The cop relayed the message between breaths, then

promptly extended the radio to her. "He needs to talk to you, ma'am."

A required translation because the volume was turned low.

"Ask him why," Mother said.

The face behind the lenses went blank. Sighing, Mother took the radio and after asking Major Sutter this question, rolled her eyes at his answer.

"Relax, Fred," she said. "It'll be okay. So let him ask. We can't tell him what we don't know. What do you mean it might not matter? Of course it—" She appeared stunned. "He *told* you that? It's definitive? I see. Well, at least we have twenty-four hours."

An ominous remark, and Coffin tossed her a questioning glance.

But an approaching siren drew Mother's attention down the hill, toward an intersection near the flight line. A car with flashing lights was turning the corner at a high speed. Even though it was a half mile away, they could see it was a dark sedan topped by a telltale white roof.

"In sight, Fred," she said. "It's General Gruver's car, all right. I'll escort him up. I'm sorry as hell, too."

Returning the radio to the cop, she dismissed him with a curt nod, her face heavy with disappointment. While Coffin realized what had happened, he knew the ROKs weren't to blame; they didn't have the clout.

"Who did it?" he asked. "Who had you dropped from the case?"

Mother didn't seem to hear. She was watching General Gruver's car, lost in her thoughts. "Bastards," she murmured. "They think I'm only a military cop and out of my league. But if they'd checked my record, they would have known I was qualified. But maybe that wouldn't have mattered because . . ."

She trailed off, shaking her head. Looking at Coffin, she said angrily, "They have no guts, Ed. They're running scared."

"Who's running scared? General Gruver?"

"This came straight from the top. The Pentagon. General Gruver's exec showed up at the crime scene and told Fred that the SECAF called in the FBI. A team is flying out from Quantico to take over."

"It's no reflection on you, Mother. This is a high-vis case, and the FBI are the pros from Dover."

"But dammit, I'm a pro, too. It's not right."

"No, but it's politics and the Pentagon brass are covering their asses."

General Gruver's car blew through a four-way stop by the BX. Watching it, Mother's jaw hardened perceptibly.

"Well, screw them," she said. "I still have twenty-four hours."

"Let it go, Mother. You said yourself there's not much chance of the case being solved. You ask me, the brass is doing you a favor. This is the FBI's problem now."

Her head jerked around as if to argue. Then she gave another little jerk, this time in surprise. She said, "You're my one chance to end this quickly. Whether I succeed depends on you. What you know."

"Me? I don't know any more . . ."

Coffin fell silent, realizing her eyes were focused toward the entrance to the BOQ. Turning, he saw a woman in civilian clothes standing behind him. From her height, he concluded who she had to be, though it wasn't easy to tell.

"Going for the Unabomber look," Coffin said dryly.

★ 22 ★

Only Major Steiner didn't stop at the hooded sweatsuit and sunglasses. To further obscure her appearance, she'd wrapped her lower face with a scarf, covering her mouth. Her need to so thoroughly disguise herself puzzled Coffin and he asked her about it.

"I didn't want to be seen talking with you, sir."

"How? I don't see anyone with night vision goggles."

The dark glasses just looked at him.

"Listen, Major," Coffin said, "if you're so worried, then why didn't you send Caralyn out to get me?" He glanced past her. "Where is Caralyn, anyway?"

"Our discussion is . . . private, sir."

"We're sure not going to talk out here. Didn't Caralyn tell you we'd probably use her room?"

"No, sir."

An unexpected hesitation preceded her answer, and Coffin slid Mother a look. But she was digging out a notepad and pen from her jacket, her eyes on General Gruver's car. As it approached the hill, she wedged the light under her chin and hurriedly scribbled notes. By then, Coffin had noticed something else odd about Steiner's appearance.

She wore a heavy coat over her sweatsuit. And looking down, he saw gloves and boots.

"You wearing long johns, Major?" Coffin asked.

"Sir?"

He gave her a flat smile. "Planning on going somewhere?"

Another pause and Coffin anticipated a denial. Instead: "Okay, sir."

"Okay, what?"

She moved farther up the walkway, away from Mother. Coffin took the hint and followed. Leaning close, Steiner tersely whispered what she wanted him to do. As he listened, Coffin knew he couldn't possibly agree to her proposal. Then she hit him with the punch line, and it took all his willpower to keep from reacting.

"Sir," Steiner said. "You don't seem surprised."

Coffin slowly unclenched his teeth to reply. When he spoke, he managed to sound calm.

"I'm not, Major," he said. "But I'm angry."

An understatement.

Coffin was quietly seething. And the more he thought about Major Olson and the dead female cop, the more furious he became. He took a ragged breath to calm himself. Then another. Watching him, Steiner asked, "Sir, can I count on you?" and when he didn't answer, she began an impatient two-step, knowing she had made him an offer he couldn't possibly refuse.

But lesson number one for a four-star's exec officer was to never to make a decision without considering all the angles. And that's what Coffin was doing now. Weighing the odds of success against the risks—

Steiner stopped dancing and looked to the street. "Sir, please, I need your answer."

"Not until I clear up a few points, Major."

"Sir, there's no time. The general's almost here."

Coffin took a look; Gruver's staff car was perhaps twenty seconds out. "Then you'd better talk fast, Major. Your source, do you trust him?"

"Completely, sir. Absolutely." She was now watching Mother, as if worried she might suddenly stop writing and come over. "He warned me about the bug in my room and said I was in danger."

"And he's helping you because . . ."

"We're friends. It's the only way he knows to keep me safe."

"Why would a ROK national risk his life for— Scratch that." For a woman as beautiful as Steiner, it was an unnecessary question. "His name, Major?"

"I can't tell you, sir. If it comes out he's cooperating, he'll be killed."

"Major, I'm going to meet him—"

"I can't. He made me swear to tell no one. And I gave my word."

Coffin didn't push it. He would learn the man's identity soon enough. "Okay, I'm on board as long—"

"Thank God."

"—as we keep Mother in the loop."

Steiner looked shocked. "No, sir. No one else can know about this."

"This is ridiculous."

"She'll want to come with us. And my friend was specific that I can only bring you."

"But why? Why does he only want to talk to me?"

"He has his reasons. I don't have time to explain, sir."

And this time, she really didn't.

A squeal of tires announced General Gruver's arrival. As if

on cue, Mother materialized beside them, tossing a question at Steiner and shoving her penlight into Coffin's hand.

"Hold it over the pad so I can see, Ed."

"I'm trying. Quit moving."

"I'm not moving."

"You did it again."

Because she'd turned to glance at Gruver's car. Cops had surrounded it and were hurriedly opening the doors. "Quick, Charlotte," Mother said to Steiner. "I've got to know if you have a problem with me telling General Gruver that you'll provide a break in the case. Because it seems to me—"

"I'd wait."

Mother got big-eyed. "*Wait?* You either know who is behind the killings or you don't."

"It's better if you wait," Steiner said.

"Hang on. Do you *know* who is responsible?

"I have . . . suspicions."

"What are they? Tell me."

A stubborn silence. Mother made two more attempts with the same result.

After being dissed by Caralyn earlier, Steiner's act of defiance was almost too much for Mother. She stood with her pen poised, on the brink of an eruption. But the sound of slamming car doors forced her to close her notepad and settle for an anticlimactic glare.

"Ah, shit." She squinted down at the parking lot. "What's *he* doing here?"

Voicing precisely what Coffin was wondering. Because this was strictly an American matter and there was no official reason for his presence. Yet standing beside General Gruver and looking up at them was the familiar figure of Major General Yee.

At a regal motion from Gruver, Mother headed down the

walkway. A stride later, she angrily pulled up, reacting to a remark from Coffin.

"Knock it off, Ed. I mean it."

"And I'm telling you that Yee is here to find out what you know. So watch what you say to him."

"He's an *ally*. He could just be offering his support."

"Don't trust him, Mother."

This response came from Steiner, and Mother and Coffin looked to her in surprise. Except, she wasn't there.

She'd hopped a bush and was pressed against a building, trying to hide. Coupled with her remark, this reaction was more than suggestive.

"Yee," Mother said to Steiner, "you telling me he *is* involved?"

"Turn away. Don't look at me."

"Now see here—"

"*Don't look.*"

Mother shook her head disgustedly and pivoted away from Steiner. From below, General Gruver's baritone sounded out, ordering her to come down. But three-star edict or not, Mother wasn't about to leave yet.

With her back to Steiner, she growled, "Charlotte, if you're not afraid of Yee, then why that remark and who are you hiding from?"

"We've had run-ins. He likes to belittle female officers."

"Cut the crap. You think Yee is involved. Why?"

"You're putting words in my mouth."

"Charlotte, so help me—"

"Try a different question, Mother," Coffin said.

"What the hell for? She's not going to say shit."

"Major," Coffin said, over his shoulder, "will you go with Mother to talk to the generals?"

A pause. Coffin could almost feel Steiner's eyes boring

into his back. But she had to realize they had to give Mother something.

"No, sir," Steiner said finally.

"Even if I order you?" Coffin said.

"No, sir."

Coffin gave Mother a knowing look; he'd gotten her a backhanded confirmation. She licked her lips, appeared slightly dazed. "Oh, fuck," she murmured.

"Agent Hubbard!" Gruver roared. "Front and center. *Now*."

"Yes, General. Right away, sir." She hurried down the walkway.

"Colonel Coffin," Steiner said, her voice strained. "If Mother says anything to General Gruver about her suspicions . . ."

"She won't. Not without proof. Your source *does* have proof, doesn't he?"

"He said he knows where to get it."

"Meaning . . ."

"I don't know, sir. We only met for a few minutes today. In the break room, after work. He was too afraid to come to my office. Anyway, that's when he told me . . . you know . . . about Major Olson's murder and that I might be next."

"You should have come forward, Major. We could have protected you."

She sounded tired. "Believe me, I wanted to, sir, but it wasn't an option. Even if I didn't reveal his name, it would be obvious he was my source. I'm not close to any other ROK officers. Certainly none who would take this kind of chance for me. Yet knowing what would happen to him . . . what they would do . . . I still . . . I almost . . ."

She left the statement hanging, her guilt loud in the silence. Coffin said nothing. He watched Mother cross the sidewalk toward Gruver and his entourage. Her notepad was out and she kept glancing at it.

Steiner resumed speaking, her voice soft and regretful. "It was the attack. It terrified me. And I made up my mind to tell what I know. I even picked up the phone to call Colonel Farris, my supervisor. You know what stopped me? It was the bug in my room. Ironic, huh? But it gave me time to think. And as I did, I kept looking at the picture of Bill. My husband. And suddenly I wasn't afraid to see this through. I know it doesn't make much sense, but I realized that the worst thing that could happen to me is—"

She stopped, realizing what she was about to say. The implication of it.

"Colonel Coffin," she added quickly, "don't misunderstand. As much as I loved my husband, I assure you that I have no desire to—"

"Join the club, Major."

"Sir?"

"The ultimate unknown. I don't fear it either. Why should we? Death is an extension of life's journey, the final destination."

A silence.

Coffin sighed, knowing his remarks had thrown her. He was tempted to explain, but figured he'd said too much already. Switching gears, he asked if she had noticed anything peculiar about Mother's briefing.

"Peculiar, sir? Not really. General Gruver is understandably upset . . ."

"Look at General Yee."

★ 23 ★

Standing in the quiet and the dark, Coffin and Steiner watched Mother hold court with a quorum of the Osan base brass. In addition to the two generals, her audience consisted of three full bull colonels, two air force and one army. Per military decorum, Mother directed her remarks at General Gruver, who gestured animatedly and often, making his three-star displeasure apparent. By contrast, Yee was restrained and aloof, showing little interest.

"Smart," Steiner concluded quietly. "He's playing it smart, sir. He doesn't want to seem too eager."

"I agree," Coffin replied.

"Do you have a car, sir?"

"At my BOQ. They'll see us if we get it. We could get a ride from an SP—"

"They might tell Mother where we've gone, sir."

Secrecy at all costs. Shrugging, Coffin said, "Then we walk."

"But we have to be there by 0215 hours. We won't make it, if we don't leave soon."

A time limit?

Before Coffin could ask about it, Steiner said, "Never mind, sir. They're going."

They watched Gruver and Mother stride purposefully across the sidewalk toward the darkened hillside, the remaining officers wheeling around to follow. All except—

"Wait, wait," Steiner said. "General Yee. Why isn't he leaving, Colonel?"

As if Coffin would know.

Yee had stopped under a lamppost and was lighting a cigarette. The army colonel said something to him. Pointing to his cigarette, Yee motioned the colonel to go on. The man did, but kept glancing back suspiciously.

Steiner said, "Colonel Holland acts as if he thinks Yee is staying behind for a reason, sir."

"Yee always has a reason, Major."

"Could it be . . . me, sir?" Her voice had gone tense.

"He can't see you, Major. No, there's some other—"

Coffin broke off. *Of course.* This was related to their one-sided confrontation at Yee's car. When Coffin had insulted him.

"But, sir," Steiner said, sounding increasingly panicked, "if he knows I'm here. If he saw me earlier—"

"It's not you, Major. It's *me.* He's waiting for the others to leave. As soon as— *There. Look.*"

With a sudden, dramatic movement, Yee pivoted in their direction, his face contorting into a maniacal expression that didn't appear quite human. Even across a distance of twenty yards, Coffin could feel the rage flowing toward him. And because he was only visible to Yee in silhouette, he had to stand there and take it.

Or did he?

He glanced down at his hand . . . and smiled.

"Jesus," Steiner breathed. "I've heard the rumors and they're true. He really is insane."

"He's not the only one, Major."

"Sir?"

In one motion, Coffin clicked on Mother's penlight, splaying the beam on his face. And grinned broadly.

"Colonel, what are you doing?"

"Sending a message."

At first, Yee didn't react. So Coffin upped the ante, making exaggerated faces and pretending to laugh. That did it, and Yee suddenly bolted forward, as if to rush up the walkway at Coffin. But Yee hadn't gotten to be a two-star general by surrendering to his emotions. At least not completely.

Hitting the brakes, Yee fired his cigarette toward Coffin as hard as he could, then turned and stormed up the hill, disappearing in the dark.

Coffin calmly lowered the light. From the parking area, Airman Collins was staring at him in astonishment. When he glanced back at Steiner, her sunglasses were fixated on him, suggesting she was similarly wide-eyed.

He waited, but she didn't move.

"Uh, we can go, Major. General Yee is gone."

No response. She just stared at him.

Coffin sighed. "I was just giving Yee a taste of his own medicine. I'm not crazy."

When she still didn't move, he gave her his sanest smile to prove it.

The smile worked.

Hesitantly, Steiner left the safety of her wall and drifted toward Coffin. She said, "So it's true. Yee hates you, sir. I mean he *hates* you."

"Yee hates a lot of people, Major."

"Not like that, sir. Just now, he'd have killed you, if he could."

Coffin passed on a response. But he couldn't help but

wonder whether she'd come to this conclusion solely based on what she'd witnessed.

Steiner continued past him, removing her sunglasses and scarf. He started to follow, but she'd paused to look at her watch. She said, "There's no hurry, sir. We still have time."

"For?"

She nervously peered in the direction Yee had gone. Coffin sighed, "Major, you're safe. General Yee won't return any time soon."

"He'll see us leave, if he turns around, sir. And what about the officer who's helping him?"

Coffin stiffened. This was a very real worry. "What officer? I haven't noticed anyone— You *see* him? Where? Can you tell if he's wearing glasses?"

Because Steiner was staring toward the parking area with sudden interest. Coming up beside her, Coffin followed her gaze, staring intently. But the only person he saw *wasn't* wearing a ROK uniform.

"That's Airman Collins, Major."

"Exactly, sir. You think he'll tell Mother that we've gone?"

"Not until she returns. She'll be at the crime scene for quite a while."

She nodded, scanning the nearby buildings. At first, Coffin assumed she was again searching for the second Korean officer. But then she voiced an entirely different concern.

"Crossing the O-Club parking lot will be a problem," she said. "It's well lit, which means they'll be able to see us from the park. We'll have to walk quickly, keep our exposure to a minimum. Once we reach the club, we should be okay the rest of the way."

She looked back at him.

"Got it. We're going to play hide and seek with Yee. But right now I'm more interested in this other officer. Who is he?"

"I don't know, sir, but he works for General Yee and could have accompanied him tonight."

"Accompanied him? Those were all staff officers, working for General Gruver."

"Yes, sir."

"*American* staff officers. Yee's key aide is a Colonel Kwan. You know Kwan? One ear? Yes? Well, unless your eyes are better than mine, he wasn't here. Neither were any other ROKs. Go. What is it, Major?"

She was spring-loaded to say something. "Sir," she said, "you misunderstand. I'm not *talking* about a ROK."

Coffin blinked. "Not a ROK. But who—"

He went slack-jawed. His mind felt as if it was packed in mud. It was the pill; it had to be. Not that it mattered. Her inference was obvious.

"My God . . ."

She nodded grimly.

"You're wrong. You have to be wrong."

"I wish I was, sir. But the main reason my friend is frightened about trusting anyone is that there is at least one American officer working with Yee. And that person was the one who actually murdered Major Olson."

"My God," Coffin said again.

A cold wind touched Coffin's face. From somewhere on the flight line, he heard the whine of a jet engine being tested. Then Steiner's voice, talking to him. But her words didn't register because all he could think about was the possibility . . . just the possibility . . . that what she was saying was true. That an American officer had colluded with Yee, to kill one of his own. Coffin couldn't believe it. He didn't want to believe it.

But a little voice reminded him of his own words from the briefing, when he'd told General Gruver a Korean national couldn't sabotage the U-2 without being noticed. And that the person must have been a Westerner, perhaps a mercenary.

The voice in his head kept talking. Coffin tried to ignore it, but it wouldn't stop.

All the U-2 officers are pilots. It must be one of them.

No. As junior pilots, it was unlikely they'd even meet General Yee.

You're forgetting the squadron commander, Ed. He regularly briefed Yee.

Coffin's stomach knotted at the possibility. He told himself that Marty Bell would never kill one of his own pilots.

He said he was broke and didn't have a pot to piss in.

I don't care.

He was also drunk on his ass. Maybe it's the guilt.

You're wrong. It's not him.

Marty only cares about himself. If he got desperate enough—

"Oh, hell," Coffin said.

"Sir, are you okay?" Steiner was frowning at him. "You look a little strange."

He forced a smile. "Your friend has no clue who this American officer is?"

"Only Yee and a few key people on his staff know. My friend did answer the phone once, when the man called. He said he sounded older. I say something wrong?"

Coffin was shaking his head. "No," he lied.

Steiner pointed to her watch. "Sir, we really need to go. We have less than ten minutes."

"Not just yet. We might have a problem."

"Problem, sir?"

Coffin didn't explain. It was a feeling of unease brought about by her revelation. And if he was right—

He again gazed out across the parking area. It was empty except for a handful of cars. Most were official military vehicles—

He paused, squinting. Then casually resumed his panning.

"Sir," Steiner said. "General Yee might come back."

"Yes. Okay."

Coffin was thinking hard. What he had to do was obvious; the question was whether it was viable. He addressed Steiner, speaking fast, asking her why her ROK friend insisted on talking only with him.

"Sir, we can talk on the way."

"*Now*, Major."

She was flustered by his tone. Recovering, she said, "I think he mentioned two . . . no . . . three reasons, sir. First, you work for a four-star general and are in a position to use the information; second, your hatred for Yee means you won't let political pressure stop you from bringing him down; and third, you are someone he can talk to."

"Talk to?"

And then Coffin realized she meant it literally. "Right. I speak Korean."

A nod. She was frowning, trying to understand.

"Will he talk to me alone, Major?"

"Alone? Why would—" Her eyes widened. "Sir, you want me to *stay*?"

"I'm considering it. So? Will he talk to me?"

She hesitated. "Sir, I wish I could say yes—" She shook her head. "But he won't. He's young and confused and scared out of his mind. He says Yee is known to kill people who cross him. He told me about a guy who'd been killed recently. Now, whether it's true or just a rumor isn't important. The thing is my friend believes it and if I'm not there, he'll back out."

"I might be able to reassure him."

"I doubt it, sir." She paused, sounding embarrassed. "You see, he's . . . infatuated with me. I've never encouraged him; I wouldn't. In fact, I've even tried to tell him as nicely as I . . ." She shrugged. "That's not important. What *is* important is for you to understand that without me, there's no guarantee he'll cooperate. But if you want me to stay, I'll stay. I never wanted to get involved. Well, sir?"

"It'll have to be your call, Major."

He told her about the problem.

It was too dark to see the blood drain from Steiner's face, not that it mattered. Her stricken expression told Coffin that her earlier remarks about not being afraid were precisely that: talk. But still she insisted on going. Major Steiner, it seemed, was much more than a pretty face.

"So what do we do, sir?" she asked.

"Let me worry about that, Major. With your get-up, there's every chance nothing will happen. But if it does and I tell you to do something, you do it. And remember, walk fast and don't look over. Okay?"

"But you don't think it's . . . him, sir?" she asked quietly.

"If I did, you wouldn't be going."

"So the man who attacked me . . ."

"Was him."

"You sound sure, sir."

"I am." He quickly explained.

Afterward, she bit her lip. He saw her fear.

They left.

★ 24 ★

They kept up a brutal pace over the snow-crusted ground, more a jog than a walk. Neither spoke; they were breathing too hard from the exertion. Once they cleared the danger zone of the open parking lot, their pace slowed, but only slightly. Keeping to the shadows, they hugged the massive stone wall by the Officers' Club entrance, following it toward a service road. At two in the morning, the base resembled a ghost town, the only visible souls a group of young men trekking unsteadily along the main street, having closed down the bars. One bent over and threw up. His buddies laughed drunkenly and cheered him on.

Not that Steiner and Coffin took much notice. With a fantasy land of bars and girls located a stone's throw from the main gate, it was a scene played out nightly.

They swung down the service road; it was dimly lit and snaked past the club. A block ahead was a cross street, a darkened hill looming beyond it. As they walked, the laughter faded and it grew quiet again.

"Think we made it, sir?" Steiner asked.

"We'll see."

They stepped onto the sidewalk. For the first time, Coffin looked back.

"Stop, Major," he said.

Steiner's head snapped around.

Coffin was completely still for a moment. Then he grabbed her hand, pulling her farther down the street, to a line of dumpsters. She said, "Colonel, did you see someone?"

"No."

"No? Then why are we—"

"*Listen.*"

They hunkered behind the closest dumpster, ears straining. The metal door creaked in the wind. Then they heard something else. Familiar crunching sounds. The footsteps came closer, slowly at first, then more rapidly.

Coffin pushed Steiner behind him. As she clung to his arm, he felt her tremble. The footsteps stopped.

Silence.

A second passed. Then two.

Coffin took a peek. The shadowy figure of a man stood no more than five feet away. He was slowly turning, searching. As he did, Coffin studied his profile and felt a twinge of satisfaction; empty hands and no eyeglasses.

The man's head tilted to the ground. He squatted, studying the footprints on the snow. Slowly his head turned toward them, a hand reaching under his jacket.

Coffin acted.

In two steps, he was on the man; saw his look of surprise. A second later, it was over, and the man was toppling backward, unconscious, something falling from his hand. Coffin touched the man's head with a shoe; it tilted limply to the side.

"Colonel," Steiner said, sounding awed as she came over. "Did you even *hit* him?"

Coffin didn't reply. Using Mother's penlight, he knelt to

verify what he'd concluded moments earlier. That the man was an unfamiliar Korean.

Keeping the beam on the man's face, he gave Steiner a questioning look; she shook her head. She'd never seem him before either.

"Sir, how did you know," she asked, "that he wasn't Colonel Kwan?"

"His cigarette. That's how I knew someone was in the car. Kwan wouldn't have made that mistake."

A vague nod. She was staring at the prostrate man and seemed puzzled by something.

"Your height," Coffin said.

She looked at him.

Coffin said, "Why he followed us. He knew you were very tall and when he saw you covered up, he put two and two together."

Another vague nod; she still appeared confused. Noticing the object the man had dropped, she stepped over and picked it up.

A black automatic pistol. Her only reaction was to give a little shiver. She was working hard to keep it together.

Wordlessly, she wiped the snow from the pistol and handed it to Coffin. After slipping it in his waistband, he patted down the Korean, who was dressed in black clothing. Finding two items of interest, Coffin rose and passed the first—a billfold—to Steiner. He shone the light down as she opened it.

"Looks new," she said.

"Probably is."

Steiner removed a few thousand-won bills and a single laminated ID card, written in Korean and English, identifying the man as a base worker.

"Fake," she said.

A conclusion rather than a question. Coffin nodded anyway.

"What else do you have there, sir?"

Coffin hesitated, uncertain whether to show it. Slowly he extended a hand, revealing what appeared to be a short metal tube. But, of course, it was much more than that.

"A silencer," Steiner murmured.

Instead of being shaken by it, she again appeared puzzled. Glancing at the unconscious Korean, she said, "Now, I really don't understand, sir. You said you believe the man who attacked me was Colonel Kwan and not him . . ."

Coffin nodded. He knew where she was going.

". . . because Kwan is the trained assassin," Steiner said. "The one General Yee would choose to kill someone . . ."

"Yes."

"Yet this man is trying to kill me now. Someone obviously not very proficient. Why? What happened to Kwan? Where is he?"

"That," Coffin said quietly, "is what worries me, Major."

Coffin checked the time. They'd wasted almost five minutes; they would be late.

"Your friend," Coffin said to Steiner, "you said he wouldn't wait."

"I don't know, sir."

"He might?"

"He's scared, Colonel. I don't know."

So this could be for nothing. Shaking his head, Coffin took off down the street.

"Wait, sir. What about him?"

Steiner was looking at the Korean. She said, "Shouldn't we have him picked up?"

"Why? He'll just be turned into ROK custody and Yee will get him released."

"He tried to kill me, sir."

"We can't prove that, Major. His only actual crime was to carry a gun, and I'm willing to bet Yee will produce paperwork showing he was authorized."

"So we just let him go, so he can try to kill me again?"

Coffin had to admit she had a point.

Stepping over to the Korean, he waved Steiner down the street. "Go over there, Major."

She froze. "Why? What are you going to do, sir?

"You don't want to know. Now go."

Her eyes widened in horror. "Sir, please. You can't just—"

"I'm not going to kill him. Now *go*."

She slowly backed away, her big eyes locked on his, wanting to believe him, but not being able to.

Looking down at the Korean, Coffin knew he should feel a flicker of remorse. Some kind of emotion. But the reality was, he felt nothing at all. Not when he felt bones of the man's hands crack under the force of his heel. Or even when the man regained consciousness and screamed and Coffin knocked him out again.

Calmly, he strolled over to Steiner. Once again, she was looking at him in horror.

Coffin said, "Right now, it's you and me and your unnamed friend. And he'd better come through. Now, when we first talked, you said you didn't know why General Yee had Major Olson killed. And this friend wouldn't tell you because he wants to protect you."

She nodded numbly, still rattled.

"But surely you must have some idea."

It took her several swallows to find her voice. "I believe it's related to a flight Major Olson took in the U-2. A test flight to check out a new radar imaging system: Why else would the tapes be missing?"

She was referring to a videotape record of the transmitted radar images from Olson's mission. "By missing, you mean . . ."

"Stolen, sir. We're going there now. I'll show you."

They resumed walking. Offering her the pistol, Coffin said, "Major, until this is over, I want you to take this."

She hesitated. "Sir, if it's all the same to you . . ."

"It's not. You *do* know how to use it?"

"I'm required to fire annually, sir."

"Hit anything?"

Ignoring the dig, she reluctantly slipped the pistol in her coat. They turned down the narrow cross street, the darkened hill looming before them.

They walked toward it.

★ 25 ★

*E*on-doek-i a-ni-ya.

Korean slang for their destination. In English, it loosely meant the hill that wasn't a hill. But from a distance, that's precisely what it looked like—just a hill. Until you got close enough to pick out the concrete berms and the barbed-wire fence and the armed guards.

Any rational person knows it's impossible to build a structure to survive a nuclear blast, but the designers of the top secret Korean Combined Operational Intelligence Center (K-COIC) still tried. They carved out a chunk of the hillside, crafted a massive four-story concrete-and-steel facility supported by giant springs, and equipped it to operate completely self-contained for two weeks. For anyone assigned there, the natural follow-up question was what would they do once the two weeks were up and the outside world was still glowing. Rumor has it that a ballsy major once asked a general precisely this question at a party and actually got a response. "Go outside and take a deep breath, son," the general said. It turned out the general was half in the bag at the time, but if you really thought about it, his advice was pretty sound.

"I'd get it over with and breathe," Coffin said.

"Breathe, sir?"

"Just thinking aloud, Major." Steiner obviously hadn't heard the story.

It took them three minutes to work their way up the hill. On the way, they passed several groups of ROK officers coming off shift, but no one gave them a second look. Even though they were headed for the K-COIC, they bypassed the facility and continued toward the boxlike Hardened Tactical Air Control Center building, several hundred yards away.

The reason was the guards. At the K-COIC, the ROKs provided security; at the HTACC, Uncle Sam's finest. While it was unlikely that General Yee would have briefed the ROK guards to watch for Steiner, Coffin was paranoid enough to think he just might have.

The HTACC was the nerve center for military flight operations—South Korean and American. Upon entering, they flashed IDs to a pretty boy security cop who grinned at Steiner, signed in and received badges, and finally stepped through a floor-to-ceiling turnstile, all under the watchful eye of a TV camera.

"I forgot about them," Coffin said.

"When we get there, I'll put my hood up, sir," Steiner said.

They entered a gleaming half-moon foyer with massive wooden double doors at the opposite end, a bored guard camped outside. On one door, gilded letters read *Air Battle Room*, and on the other, the Korean translation.

Steiner smiled at the guard. He suddenly didn't appear bored anymore.

"This way, sir," Steiner said.

Coffin nodded; he remembered. They followed a corridor past an elevator to a stairwell, then went down two flights to a door stamped *Tunnel Access*. They pushed through into a dank hallway that smelled of mildew. They were well below ground and could hear the whine of machinery above them.

To the right was a large circular passageway with embedded steel tracks running crossways across the floor. A two-foot wide opening was cut into the wall directly above the tracks, the edge of a massive steel plate peeking out. On either side of the opening were palm-sized red actuators encased in glass, each with a sign reading *Danger. Hydraulic Blast Door. Actuate only in bio, chemical or nuclear emergency.*

"When did they make the doors operational?" Coffin asked.

"Three, four months ago, sir. When they realized the North Koreans might really have nukes." Steiner pointed to the closest actuator. "Just make sure you're well clear before you push that. The door weighs five tons and closes in a little over a second. When they first powered up the door at the other end, there was some kind of an electrical short and a maintenance man lost his leg. It was a real mess."

That was more than Coffin wanted to know, and he practically jumped over the rails. Watching him, Steiner smiled. "I know, sir. It creeps me out, too."

"So should that," Coffin said, looking at the TV camera over their heads. "Get ready."

She put up her hood and donned her sunglasses. As they went down the tunnel, the security camera followed their progress, whirring softly.

Walking the length of the hundred-yard tunnel, they passed three more cameras, the last two manned by ROK security. Even though Coffin knew Yee wouldn't try anything in here, he still halfway expected a welcoming committee. But when they entered the bowels of the K-COIC, they were alone.

Major Steiner's office was on the fourth floor. Instead of taking the stairs, they continued down a long hallway to the far end of the basement, stopping at a steel door equipped with a cipher lock. A placard across the front said: *U-2 Imagery Collection Center—authorized personnel only.*

Steiner dialed the combo. At a click, they stepped out onto a metal staircase that overlooked an enormous open bay fully two stories deep. Scattered over the expansive floor space were partitioned desks and banks of high-tech workstations, reminiscent of NASA mission control. Along the back wall were two silver Airstream trailers, each painted with a U-2 logo.

"You've updated your equipment," Coffin said.

Steiner nodded, removing her hood and sunglasses. "Most of it is telemetry-oriented, sir, so we can receive all the imaging data the U-2 collects in real time." She went down the steps, glancing back at Coffin. "That's one of the things Major Olson was doing for us on that flight I mentioned. He was testing a radar sensor called CARSON. It's essentially a more powerful version of ASARS."

ASARS stood for advanced synthetic aperture radar system, and was to regular radar what a laser beam was to light—more concentrated and focused. Coffin said, "By more powerful, you mean . . ."

"Increased wattage and a shorter, more penetrating wavelength, sir. The CARSON beam can burn through porous materials like wood, canvas, even sand or dirt several feet deep. It also can be pointed by a joystick in the cockpit, giving us much more flexibility in targeting."

They came to the bottom of the stairs, headed out across the floor. Whenever a U-2 was flying, the room was a hub of activity. But since the planes were grounded, it had become a tomb.

Coffin said, "And everything Major Olson imaged was relayed to you and recorded on videotape?"

"Yes, sir."

"You reviewed the tape?"

"Completely, sir."

At ground level, the patchwork of partitions gave the impression they were walking in a maze. They wove past sections reserved for the linguist and threat analysts. Angled toward the comm station.

Coffin said, "And you saw nothing suspicious or incriminating to General Yee?"

"Not a thing, sir. Most of Major Olson's flight was conducted over the Sea of Japan. We were testing the CARSON's ability to track ships."

"Maybe there was something on one of the ships."

"Only fish, sir. In the area we were flying, all that was out were fishing trawlers. Major Olson did fly over an island with several large buildings. But they were empty."

"Define empty."

"Zilch. Nada. There was absolutely nothing in the buildings." She shook her head. "That's what's got me so stumped, sir. There wasn't anything damning on those tapes. Why would anyone take them?"

"Could they have been misplaced?"

"One, possibly. But we're talking four tapes, two originals and two copies. And I personally secured them in this trailer. Since we never lock the door, anyone with access to the room could have taken them, including the ROK linguists. Anyway, that's the cabinet the tapes were stored in, sir. The one on the right. And you can see how the drawer has been forced open."

She'd opened the trailer door and was gesturing inside it.

Stepping around her, Coffin peered inside. He saw the cabinet drawer she'd mentioned with the sprung lock. He saw a wall lined with video recording equipment and a bank of TV monitors. He saw a large mainframe computer that hummed quietly and a control console that could launch the shuttle. He saw a mounted map of Korea, topped by a plastic overlay marked with U-2 flight tracks. He saw all this, but what he didn't see was—

He turned angrily to Steiner. "Your friend bailed out on us."

"Sir, we don't know that for sure."

"You honestly believe he'll return? After he's already left?"

"Sir, what are you talking about? He was never here."

He stared at her. Saw her nod.

"Major." Coffin was incredulous. "You told me he was too frightened to come to your office. That's why we were coming here. You said I could talk to him—"

"Exactly, sir."

Coffin frowned.

"Talk," Steiner said. "I said you could talk to him. And my guess is you still might be able to because—"

She broke off, looking into the trailer.

A phone was ringing.

"Oh, hell," Coffin said.

"Excuse me, sir." Steiner motioned him from the doorway. "He'll want to talk to me."

"Tell me his name, first."

Lieutenant Sun. It was a name Coffin didn't expect to recognize and didn't.

Standing at the console with the phone to her ear, Steiner spoke to Sun in reassuring, almost motherly tones. "Yes, the colonel is with me, Lieutenant," she said, looking at Coffin. "Yes, yes, he's agreed to help. Whatever terms you want. What was that?"

Her eyes were still on Coffin. Only now, they looked alarmed.

She said, "Perhaps you're imagining it. Of course, I didn't

identify you. Calm down, Lieutenant. If you'll calm down—"
Suddenly, her voice turned severe. Rebuking him like an ex-asperated parent.

"*Excuses*, Lieutenant," Steiner said. "You are making ex-cuses. You are frightened and no longer want to keep your promise to me. But there has been another death tonight. A young American girl. And I want you to know that I blame you for her death. *You* could have prevented it by talking to my superiors. But *you* are a coward, Lieutenant. Do you un-derstand me? A *coward*."

She fell silent, looking as disgusted as she sounded. On the other end of the line, Coffin heard a male voice stammer out a response.

Apparently, it wasn't what Steiner wanted to hear, because she cut in, "I said no more excuses. My life is in danger and you promised to help. Will you keep your word? Will you help us get General Yee? *Will you*, Lieutenant?"

She pressed the phone to her ear, anticipating an answer. But for several long seconds, it didn't come.

Steiner shook her head, thinking she'd overplayed her hand. But at last, Coffin heard a faint reply. One that initially relieved, then excited Steiner.

"You have it now?" Steiner asked. "What's the name on—It's not? Of course we still want it. Yes, tonight. Meet where? I remember. We will be there, Lieutenant. But first, I want you to tell Colonel Coffin what you just told me. And any-thing else you know. No, there will be no more delays. You are afraid and I do not trust you, Lieutenant. So you will talk to the colonel. *Now*."

She cupped the phone and held it out to Coffin. As she did, her shoulders sagged and he saw her guilt.

Gently, Coffin said, "Major, it's okay. You had to treat him roughly."

"If so, sir," she said sadly, "then why do I feel so ashamed?"

Coffin had no response to that. So he just took the phone from her and as he raised it, he heard what sounded like a whispered chant. He was about to interrupt when he realized the lieutenant was repeating a Korean phrase.

"*Bi-geop ha-ji-ant-da,*" the lieutenant kept saying.

Telling himself he wasn't a coward.

The chanting stopped, replaced by faint breathing. Coffin waited a beat before speaking; he had no desire to embarrass the lieutenant further.

When he identified himself, the lieutenant immediately responded in accented, somewhat broken English.

"Colonel Coffin," he said formally. "I am Lieutenant Sun Yon-kee. I see you at briefing."

"You did?"

And then Coffin realized who he was. "The projector? You ran the slides, Lieutenant."

"Yes, Colonel. I am new officer. Two months now. I assign for . . . I assign *to* General Yee—" He abruptly switched to Korean. "*Han-guk mal mal-ham-yeon cho-a-yo?*" Is it okay to speak Korean, sir?

"*Cheon-cheon-he mal-hae-yo.*" As long as you don't speak too fast, Lieutenant.

Sun gave a tight, nervous laugh, then choked it off, realizing that Coffin wasn't making a joke. Speaking slowly, Sun said, "*Yee so-jang cheuk-geun-ja i-e-yo. Il-jae-mi.*" Telling Coffin he was General Yee's aide. But in actuality, he was a *il-jae-mi*, a worker ant. Sun specifically used this term—a common Korean colloquialism—so Coffin would understand that he was too insignificant to have been told of Olson's murder.

"*Al-ass-eo-yo,*" Coffin said. But you did know.

"*U-yeon-he-yo deul-eoss-eo-yo.*" Only by accident, Colonel.

According to Sun, he'd returned to the office late one night and overheard Yee and Colonel Kwan talking. Initially, Sun couldn't believe they were serious. He didn't want to believe it. But that had all changed this morning, when he learned of Olson's death.

Sounding bitter, he added, "*Steiner so-ryeong maj-a-yo. Eol-saen nim-i juk-eun-i yu-neun ne ga chim-muk-eul haet-gi-dae-mun-im-ni-da.*" So Major Steiner is correct. I am to blame for Major's Olson death because I said nothing.

"*Dae-ui—*" Coffin corrected himself; it was the wrong word. "*So-ui chaek-im-I-an-i-da.*"

"*A-nim-ni-da. Na neun chaek-im-i-eoss-eum—*"

Coffin interrupted Sun, explaining to the lieutenant that he'd been in an untenable position, and that his conscience should be clear, because he was doing the right thing now.

Sun's only response was to suck air through his teeth—the Korean way of expressing disapproval. Regardless of what Coffin said, he would continue to beat himself up.

Coffin picked up a curious sound in the background. "*So-ui, a-gi iss-eo-yo?*" You have a baby, Lieutenant?

"*Eo-ni ui i-e-yo. U-ri neun gat-eun jib e-seo sal-at-da. Jeon-hwa reul sseuss-eo-yo.*" The baby is my sister's, Colonel. She lives in my building. I am using her phone.

At the implication, alarm flickered across Coffin's face. Watching him, Steiner asked what was wrong. Instead of answering her directly, Coffin shifted back to English and asked Lieutenant Sun the obvious follow-up: Did he think his phone was tapped?

Steiner murmured, "Oh, Lord. But how . . ."

"I think maybe, sir," Sun replied. "A man is across street. In alley. It possible I make mistake when I copy tape."

"What tape, Lieutenant?"

"It's a cassette from Yee's office," Steiner said. "Apparently, Yee is so paranoid that he records all calls to his office."

This matched what Sun was attempting to say in English. Switching to Korean, the lieutenant went on to explain that he'd snuck into Yee's office tonight, to make a copy of the cassette. And just as he was replacing the original, Colonel Kwan interrupted him.

"Gi-ge reul go-chin-da-go het-ji-man gu nam-ja neun na reul ui-shim eul het-da." I told him I was repairing the machine, sir. But he was suspicious.

Sun paused, expecting Coffin to reply. When he remained silent, Sun said in English, "I speak too fast, Colonel? You understand mistake I make?"

Coffin did, but for a moment he was unable to speak. Because it finally had dawned on him precisely what the lieutenant was telling him and why Steiner had been excited earlier.

Swallowing hard, he said, "I understand, Lieutenant Sun. You're telling me this American officer's voice is on the cassette."

"Yes, Colonel," Sun replied.

"But not his name," Steiner added.

Coffin stared at her, wide-eyed. Steiner nodded an angry confirmation. By then, Lieutenant Sun was revealing why the officer's name wasn't on the cassette.

Though the man was a traitor and a murderer, he wasn't stupid. And knowing General Yee recorded his conversations, the man always spoke in a whisper, kept the conversation brief, and never used his name.

When Coffin asked, Lieutenant Sun recounted the American's conversation with Yee in its entirety. Not that that was difficult to do, since it was only five cryptic sentences.

The American: "He's flying tomorrow, General."

Yee: "What time?"

"Oh-seven-hundred takeoff."

"The plane will be in hangar?"

"Until 0500."

That was it.

Only eight words were spoken by the American, and none that could be considered expressly incriminating.

But at least they had the bastard's whispered voice on a tape. And it gave them a start. A place to begin looking.

Just like what Lieutenant Sun revealed next.

He mentioned seeing a top secret file in General Yee's safe. He had only made the connection because of what Steiner had told him today, when she'd mentioned the missing videotapes.

"And you have no idea if there's a connection to the tapes?" Coffin asked Sun.

"No, Colonel."

"But you're sure about the name you saw? There is no mistake?"

"No, sir. Title say 'Chong Do.' "

The same name as the island Major Erik Olson had flown over.

★26★

Thirty seconds later, Coffin ended the call after adjusting their meeting plans. Again, he spoke English, so Steiner could follow along.

"So we go to his apartment," Steiner said, "if Sun doesn't think he can slip out the back way without being spotted?"

"Right," Coffin said. "He'll leave me a message with billeting."

She tugged on her ear. "Am I missing something, sir? That must mean there are at least two guys watching his apartment. Won't one of them see us go in?"

"I doubt it."

She blinked quizzically, curious about what Coffin had up his sleeve. But rather than go into details, Coffin related Lieutenant Sun's second revelation. At which point Steiner became understandably defensive.

Standing at the wall map of the Korean Peninsula, she jabbed a manicured finger at a black dot in the Sea of Japan, saying, "Then there must be two Chong Dos, sir. Because I'm telling you there was nothing on that island."

"You only imaged the buildings, Major. Something could be buried— Why not?"

A vehement headshake. She said, "Because we did image

the island; we couldn't help it. It's *small*, the size of maybe three football fields, and made of solid rock, sir. And that's something else we can tell from the CARSON returns, the density of material. The land around the buildings reflected the beams to a factor of nine point six on the TORK scale. Concrete registers only eight point four."

Coffin nodded, as if he understood; he didn't. The CARSON's capabilities far exceeded those of the ASARS he was familiar with.

Glancing at the map, he guesstimated Chong Do Island was roughly ten miles off the South Korean coast. He asked Steiner if she knew who owned it.

"Since it's in territorial waters, I assumed the ROK government. I suppose it could be private. Daewoo and Hyundai bought several islands for operations requiring toxic chemicals. They're well south of Pusan, near Cheju Island."

But Coffin wasn't listening to her any longer. Not since she had said the word private.

She frowned at him. "Colonel, you're . . . smiling."

"Am I?"

"Sir, you're on to something. Wait. Isn't General Yee wealthy?"

"Extremely."

"And you think he bought the island?"

"I know he did."

"But why, sir? It's completely uninhabitable. And why would he put up empty buildings on it?"

"You have the most recent satellite photos?"

"On microfiche. They're in this file cabinet. We use them to plot our targets."

"And the nearest light table is . . ."

"In the next trailer, sir. We only have a few minutes to do this."

"What I'm looking for won't take long. Need me to read out the coordinates?"

Steiner had already yanked open a drawer. "Please."

Since the microfiche strips were catalogued according to latitude and longitude coordinates, Steiner located the appropriate one in seconds. A minute later, they were in the next trailer, powering up the light table, which was typically operated by highly trained military photo interpreters. The light table included a complicated microscope apparatus that was attached to a slide bar to enhance precision.

Watching Coffin attempt to slide the microscope over the microfiche, Steiner gave a little cough. "Uh, sir. Have you actually ever *used* a light table?"

"I've seen PIs do it."

"I was trained as a PI, sir."

Translation: Get out of the way, Colonel. Coffin took the hint and promptly moved.

After positioning the microscope, Steiner peered into it, asking, "What am I looking for, sir?"

"A name, logo, flag. Anything on the buildings or island that might identify the owner."

Steiner adjusted several knobs. Scowled. Increased the intensity of the table light and scowled again.

"No markings anywhere," she murmured. "But that's curious."

"What?"

Her fingers moved constantly, working the knobs in minute increments. "The buildings are huge. Much bigger than I realized from the CARSON images. And on the roofs, there seems to be— Hard to tell for sure."

She straightened, glancing at Coffin. "Have a look and tell me if you notice anything peculiar about the roofs, sir."

They switched positions.

Steiner said, "I backed off the magnification so you'll know what you're looking at, sir." She pointed to two knobs. "These focus and magnify. And the ones over here adjust your axis horizontally and laterally. Small movements go a long way."

"Got it."

Looking through the microscope, Coffin saw an image of a very small and very rocky island with three enormous, flat-roofed rectangular buildings arrayed in a rough triangle, two smaller structures in the center. He gave a soft whistle. Though it was difficult to calculate the dimensions of the larger buildings, the compound covered almost the entire island. And if that was the case—

"Major," he said, "you said the island is the size of three football fields."

"Actually, when I measured the length of CARSON returns, I calculated it was a little bigger. Almost a thousand feet at its widest."

Coffin whistled again. "That means the largest buildings are over three hundred feet long."

"Yes, sir. And if you'll zoom in on the roofs of the ones at two and seven o'clock . . . that's it, sir."

Coffin twisted the magnification knob.

"Focus in and tell me what you see, sir."

One roof filled the viewfinder; it was blurred. Coffin twisted the second knob. The image sharpened.

"A line," he said. "I see a line of shiny . . . almost like—" He glanced at Steiner. "Are those *hinges?*"

"Be my guess, sir."

Coffin shook his head. "Hinged roofs on empty buildings. Doesn't make sense."

"And if we assume one of the smaller buildings is a power

plant," Steiner said, "then something else makes even less sense, sir."

She looked at him in a knowing way.

Again, Steiner was referring to an anomaly on the buildings, but this time, she was pointing out something that was absent.

"You're right," Coffin said, standing back from the microscope. "There are no power lines or external lights anywhere."

Steiner nodded. "To me, that indicates the construction phase isn't completed, sir."

"Unless the lines were buried to shield them from the elements."

"Still need lights, sir." She shook her head. "No. I think it's evident Yee hasn't finished the building process. And until he does, we can't reach any conclusions about his intentions."

"Except for one, Major."

She looked at him.

"Whatever Yee's intention," Coffin said quietly, "he's willing to kill to keep it secret."

Steiner and Coffin retraced their steps because they had no choice; they had to swing by Coffin's BOQ to pick up his car and for him to change into civilian clothes.

Approaching the O-Club service road, Coffin had Steiner stop and hand over the pistol. Holding the weapon against his leg, he eased ahead just far enough for a clear view. A glance confirmed the Korean was gone, but Coffin carefully scanned the shadows before signaling to Steiner.

They continued down the cross street, eventually zigzagging their way up the hill they'd left earlier. As they crested it from the backside, they had a view of the darkened park and a brightly lit perimeter in the middle of it, courtesy of three portable light generators. Silhouetted figures could be seen milling around, two bending over what was obviously a body. Coffin thought he spotted Mother's small frame and immediately looked at the parking area. General Gruver's white-topped staff car was gone, but Mother's sedan was still there.

"Looks like they don't know we've gone, sir," Steiner said.

"This will give us a better idea," Coffin said.

Resuming their trek toward his BOQ, he took out his radio and turned up the volume.

At first, there was only silence. Then someone asked the command post to notify the hospital to prepare for receiving the body. It was a man's voice, probably that of the doctor, who was doubling as the ME. A minute later, the CP relayed that the morgue was ready and asked for an ETA. The man said thirty minutes.

That was the extent of the radio traffic. There were no panicked calls, asking for the whereabouts of Coffin and Steiner.

Clicking off the radio, Coffin again had Steiner stop. He indicated his quarters, a half block ahead, and they surveyed the area out front. Nothing moved, and the only vehicle on the street other than Coffin's car was a blue air force pickup that hadn't been there earlier.

Steiner said, "It could be an SP vehicle, but I don't see anyone inside, sir."

He'd mentioned his intruder and Mother's intention to assign him a guard. Shrugging, Coffin said, "Mother probably hasn't gotten around to it."

"So for all we know," Steiner said, looking at him uneasily, "someone could be waiting for us with another silenced gun."

"Iffy. Even if the Korean who followed us has contacted

Yee, the general wouldn't have had time to set anything up yet. Remember, he's been in the park, looking at the body."

"What about Colonel Kwan?"

A question Coffin hadn't wanted to bring up. "Kwan wouldn't use a gun; he prefers a knife."

"Gee," Steiner said. "Now I feel a lot better, sir. As long as we outrun him, we should be okay."

Coffin met her sarcasm with a tight smile. "You could always wait here, Major."

Steiner looked at him as if he was out of his mind. As Coffin went forward, she tucked in right behind him.

Smart move.

There were no lights on in his BOQ, inside or out. Coffin put his ear to the door, but heard only silence. He tried the knob. Locked.

"Here." Coffin gave the pistol to Steiner and took out the door key. "When I go in, I'll leave the door open and reach for the lights. If anyone jumps me, shoot him."

Again she looked at him as if he'd lost his mind.

But she nodded anyway.

Inserting the key, Coffin pushed open the door and waited, coiled. But there was nothing. Stepping inside, he felt for the light. And that's when it happened.

He caught movement in the dark. Spinning toward it, Coffin called a warning to Steiner and threw up a hand to fend off the attack he knew was coming.

Too late.

But instead of the searing pain from a knife, Coffin felt a powerful grip latch on to his arm while another hand grabbed him by the seat of the pants. The next thing he knew, he was off his feet and flying across the room. At that fractional instant, time seemed to compress. He clearly heard

Steiner behind him, screaming at someone to back off or she would shoot. He heard a man give a surprised grunt and swear. By then, another man was also shouting and swearing. Instantly, Coffin's mind processed their voices and concluded they were familiar. But before he could say anything, he landed hard and his world turned black.

★27★

Voices in the fog. Worried voices.

"Jesus, he could be dead. He hit the wall hard."

"He's not dead. He's breathing."

"A concussion. He might have a concussion."

"He's coming to. Thank God. Sir, how do you feel? Sir?"

Coffin's eyelids fluttered open. He winced at the brightness of the light. He was lying on the living room floor, Steiner bent over him, her beautiful face knitted in concern. Behind her, Chief Sessler and Lieutenant Colonel Sam Hardy anxiously peered down.

"Say something, Ed," Hardy said. "You going to be okay?"

Coffin just looked at him.

"How's your head, sir?" the chief asked. "You want us to take you to the hospital?"

Ignoring him, Coffin glowered at Hardy. "Smooth move, asshole."

Hardy bristled. "Hey, I didn't know it was you. We were told you were conducting an interview and wouldn't be back for at least an hour."

Coffin sat up with the help of Steiner. He felt a pulsing pain at the crown of his head. He gingerly touched it and grimaced.

"That's a pretty good bump, sir," Steiner said, peering closely at him. "If you think you'd better get checked out—"

She fell silent at Coffin's sharp look. They both knew that wasn't an option. Hardy and the chief pulled him to his feet. Eyeing them, he said, "Let me guess. You're the protection Mother arranged."

Two somewhat guilty head bobs. The chief said, "Some SP master sergeant came by the squadron—"

"Baker," Hardy said.

"Right," the chief said. "Baker told us about the break-in, sir. Said you were all fired up about not wanting security cops around and would probably order them away if they showed. So Agent Hubbard had the bright idea that if maybe the colonel here or me or someone you knew kept an eye on you, that maybe you'd be okay with it."

"And you both volunteered?" Coffin said.

"Why not?" Hardy answered, shrugging. "We were done for the night and had to be back at 0600 anyway. Might as well sleep here as anywhere."

Coffin felt himself smile. There was no way he could keep his irritation meter pegged, not with what they'd just told him.

"Thanks, Sam," he said, "but I really don't need you here."

"I'm starting to see that," Hardy said.

And he looked right at Steiner, who reddened.

Coffin sighed. "Mind out of the gutter, Sam."

Hardy's face went blank, innocent.

"Sir," Steiner said to Coffin, "I can check your messages while you change."

"Fine." He watched her go over to the phone and pick up.

"Change?" Hardy frowned at Coffin. "You're changing clothes. Why?"

"We're going downtown."

The chief and Hardy blinked. The chief said, "*Now*, sir? It's almost three in the morning. The bars are closed."

"This doesn't have anything to do with the bars," Coffin said.

"Then what *does* it have to do with?" Hardy asked.

Coffin hesitated.

"No messages, sir," Steiner announced, cradling the phone.

"Ed," Hardy said, "if this is a personal matter, fine. Don't tell us. But if this has anything to do with your investigation, we've got a right to know. Eighteen hours of busting our asses gives us that right."

The chief grimly nodded his agreement. Coffin said, "Look, it isn't that cut and dried."

"What you're really saying," Hardy said quietly, "is you don't trust us."

Christ. "That's not it at all, Sam. We gave our word that no one else would be involved."

A silence. Hardy and the chief just stared at him.

Coffin sighed, tugging on his cheek.

"Nuts," he muttered.

Coffin spoke rapidly, hitting the highlights about Yee and the unnamed American officer's roles in Olson's killing and how the motive behind it almost certainly involved some secret about Chong Do Island. He also told them about Lieutenant Sun and the audiotape he supposedly possessed, and how there was a good chance that Yee was on to him. He revealed everything except his nagging suspicion about the identity of the American officer. That was something Coffin couldn't bring himself to admit publicly. Until he heard the tape.

When Coffin finished, Hardy and the chief were too stunned to respond. That was fine with Coffin. There wasn't time for any discussion.

As he headed into the bedroom to change, Coffin glanced at Steiner, expecting her to be angry with him. Instead, she had a resigned expression, and when she saw him looking, she simply shrugged. Like Coffin, she realized keeping Sun's identity secret didn't matter anymore, since his cover was probably blown.

In five minutes Coffin had traded his uniform for civilian clothing. As he was throwing on a ski jacket over a bulky sweater, there was a knock at the door and Hardy entered the bedroom. "I'm coming with you, Ed," he said.

"I told you we can't spook Lieutenant Sun."

"General Yee's not stupid. If he is on to Sun, he'll expect you to meet with him. You could be walking into a trap."

"We're not. Sun would have left us a message."

"Only if he couldn't get away. Someone could be trailing him to get at you."

They bickered back and forth. Hardy was determined to go. While Coffin appreciated the gesture, he couldn't allow it for Sam's own good.

"Listen to me, Sam," he said, "you don't want to get caught up in this. By keeping Mother and General Gruver in the dark, I'm breaking about a dozen regs. Even if I succeed in getting the tape, I'll have my ass handed to me. And you have your career to think of."

"If you think I'm going to sit here—"

"I don't think; I know. In fact, you don't know a damn thing about it."

"Ed—"

"No."

"Fine," Hardy said sullenly. "But at least reconsider taking Steiner. There have been two attempts on her life tonight. And that's on base. Downtown, you'll be on Yee's turf."

"I'd have her stay if I could. But without her, Sun might reconsider handing over the tape."

"What if something happens to her, Ed? You going to be able to live with it?"

Coffin didn't reply.

"Yeah," Hardy grunted. "I didn't think so. Take my advice and leave her."

"We need that tape, Sam."

"For Christ's sake—"

Coffin held up a hand. "Let me finish. You're right; it is too much of a risk for Steiner without taking additional precautions."

"Such as . . ."

After Coffin explained, Hardy grinned. "Now you're talking."

"Not so fast," Coffin said. "We only do this is if you agree to my conditions."

"Got it. No playing hero unless you give the okay." Hardy threw up a mocking salute and started toward the door. Then stopped when he noticed Coffin slip two items into his jacket.

"Say," he said, "isn't that the letter you had at school?"

Coffin was silent; Hardy knew it was.

Hardy's face softened. "That's why, isn't it?" he said. "That's why you came to Korea?"

"That's why."

"And the magnifying glass . . ." Hardy looked at one of Coffin's pockets. "You must be close."

"I have . . . hopes."

Coffin gave no further explanation and Hardy didn't expect one. Both men realized that this was something Coffin needed to do alone.

"Sir," Steiner called out, "we've got ten minutes."

"Coming, Major," Coffin said.

They went into the living room to brief Steiner and the chief on the change of plans.

Visualize a Mexican border town with an Asian theme and more flashing neon, and you get an idea what the Ville looks like before the military-mandated 0200 curfew. Since it was after 3:00 A.M. when Coffin and Steiner drove out of the Osan main gate, the Ville's streets were dark and silent, the only people out an occasional bar girl walking home after a night of pushing drinks, or a young airman, hustling to base after visiting a whorehouse.

Glancing at Coffin, who was driving, Steiner said, "I've never seen the Ville shut down before. Not at night anyway. It's so . . . *dark.*"

She was alluding to the fact that many of the signs and all the streetlights had been turned off. "Beats driving around in traffic, Major," Coffin said. "Anyone who follows us will stand out."

"Like now, sir?"

Coffin checked the rearview mirror. He slowly nodded.

A dark sedan had suddenly appeared from an alley and was closing rapidly. Squinting through the brightness of its headlights, Steiner said, "Looks like only one guy. Maybe he'll just go on by."

The car immediately slowed and rode their bumper.

Reacting to a furtive look from Steiner, Coffin said, "The Ville ends in a mile. Chances are he'll turn off."

Five blocks later, the car was still there. Coffin thought hard, weighing his options, then realized Steiner had already settled on one.

Sighing, he said, "Major, put the gun down until you have a reason to use it." Glancing behind, he added, "And for now, you keep out of sight."

Reluctantly, Steiner lowered her pistol, complying with Coffin's first command, since that was the one addressed to her. Whirring down his window, Coffin waved the car by. It remained right behind them.

After another block, Steiner again eased up her pistol and pointed it at the car. This time, Coffin didn't say anything. At the next cross street, he made a sudden right and hit the brakes, looking back.

The car went by.

They waited; it never reappeared.

With a relieved smile, Steiner pocketed the pistol, saying, "The guy weaved a couple times. Maybe he was drunk."

"Maybe."

They rolled down the street. Steiner said, "It's the next left, sir. Past the fish market."

"I know the way, Major," Coffin said. "I grew up here."

She looked over in surprise. "You mean the Ville?"

"Until I was seven and was sent to an orphanage." He pointed to a building with a tattered awning. "Lived there for several years."

Steiner contemplated a response, but nothing came out. They cruised past the boarded-up stalls of the outdoor fish market and turned down a narrow street lined with seedy rooming houses used by the bar girls.

"We're getting close," Coffin said.

"Less than two blocks, sir," Steiner replied.

Coffin pulled over to a particular darkened section of the curb. As Steiner got out, Coffin hung back, issuing cryptic instructions and adjusting the volume on the radio clipped to his belt. After two distinct hisses, the radio went silent; they were beyond the range of base transmissions.

"I don't see anyone, sir," Steiner said, when he joined her on the sidewalk.

Coffin nodded, briefly searching for the car that had followed them. The problem: There were dozens of dark sedans lining the dimly lit street.

As they walked forward, Steiner glanced behind and nodded. "Good choice, sir," she said. "From ten feet away, no one can see inside the car—"

Her head snapped to the front.

"Easy, Major," Coffin said. "It could be another false alarm. Hold on to that gun in your pocket and be ready."

They continued toward the voices.

★28★

Males. Talking loudly, their words slurred.

Coffin and Steiner slowed their pace, focusing on the two thirty-something Korean men coming toward them, arms linked in a common display of close friendship.

Spotting Coffin and Steiner, the smaller of the men—the one on the right—sang out drunkenly and his friend laughed.

Coffin resisted the urge to reply. He and Steiner kept walking.

The same man made another comment, generating more laughter.

"What's he saying, sir?" Steiner asked Coffin.

"You don't want to know."

As the men approached, Coffin's radio hissed twice. He keyed the transmit button once. The Koreans leered at Steiner as she strolled past. Turning to admire her, the talker called out another remark.

It was too much. Spinning, Coffin fired off a harsh response in Korean.

The men looked shocked.

Coffin spoke again and they took off running.

"Sir," Steiner said, "I don't suppose you're going to tell me what that was all about."

"Can't you guess?"

"Sir, I'd rather know. Despite what you think, I'm not a prude."

"And despite what you think, I am."

She glanced over in surprise. When Coffin nodded unapologetically, Steiner suppressed a smile.

A block later, they arrived at a worn-out building fronted by a dilapidated neon marquee identifying it as a soju bar. Soju bars were ubiquitous, after-hours drinking establishments specializing in soju—the rice-based alcohol popular with Korean men, since it afforded a quick and cheap drunk.

A short staircase led to a front door that seemed ready to fall off its hinges. Going up, Coffin said to Steiner, "You've met Lieutenant Sun's uncle?"

"Once. He was insulted when I wouldn't drink soju. But I didn't feel like going blind."

She was only half joking. Soju gave new meaning to the term "blind drunk," since imbibing too much of it occasionally led to temporary paralysis of the optic nerve.

Pausing before the door, Coffin keyed his radio. When it hissed back twice, he reached for the knob, then abruptly jerked his hand away.

"Something the matter, sir?" Steiner asked, alarmed.

Coffin was unprepared for the emotion he felt. Gathering himself, he said, "No, Major. It's just that this was another place I visited as a child. Before it was a soju bar."

"What was it back then, sir?"

Coffin considered telling her in order to prove he was ready to accept his past. But in the end, the shame won out.

"I don't recall," he said vaguely. "It was a long time ago and I was pretty young—"

"Was it a hotel?"

"A hotel?"

"Yes, sir. When Lieutenant Sun's uncle showed me his living quarters upstairs, I was curious why there were so many little rooms. When I mentioned it to Sun, he never really answered me. In fact, he seemed upset that I'd asked the question, and I never understood—"

She broke off, her eyes widening.

She shook her head, looking suddenly embarrassed. She struggled to speak, but couldn't get out the words. Coffin felt his face get hot, and for several seconds, they stood in an awkward silence. Lowering her eyes, Steiner murmured something under her breath. It was an apology.

"Major," he said softly, "I'd appreciate it if you didn't say anything."

A nod. She wouldn't look at him.

Déjà vu.

Coffin sighed, realizing Steiner's reaction mirrored Hardy's, when Coffin had first told him the truth.

Standing there, Coffin waited for the shame to return. When it didn't appear, he felt encouraged. Maybe . . . just maybe . . . he was ready to accept his past after all.

But just as he was about to enter the bar to find out, Steiner spoke up, making a remark that confused him.

She told him to talk to Mother.

"Talk to her about what?" Coffin asked, frowning.

"This." Steiner nodded to the building. "Your past."

"Why? Did she say something to you? What did she say?"

"Not to me, sir. A mutual girlfriend named Tanya Bently, who heard it from— Never mind. The point is: you *were* the guy Mother was almost engaged to, right? About five or six years ago?"

"Yes, but—"

"Sir, I know this isn't any of my business. But just now, your reaction to the obnoxious drunk. That wasn't some act. You were really bothered by what he said to me."

"Major, I don't see how—"

"So bothered that you couldn't bring yourself to repeat what he said. Sir, I've got to tell you that makes you unique. A lot of guys would have wanted me to know what the drunk said, so I could appreciate what they had done for me. Don't shake your head, sir. It's true. Men are always looking for ways to impress me, so they can get into my pants. But not you, which is why I'm telling you this. It can't be true, what I heard about you. You're just not that kind of guy, sir."

"And that kind of guy is . . ."

When she told him, both relief and anger overcame Coffin. And a crushing emptiness for the years senselessly wasted.

"For what it's worth," Coffin said, "I had a good reason for going to those places—"

"Sir, don't tell me. Tell Mother."

The memories flooded back.

The bar's interior still resembled a cramped, dimly lit box, with the same peeling gold wallpaper and warped pine floor. Only instead of the table in the middle where the old woman sat with her strongbox full of money, there were a few rickety tables and chairs. And along the mirrored wall at the back—where Coffin used to practice making scary faces—there was now a narrow wooden bar topped by bottles of soju and rows of grimy glasses.

And, of course, the stooped old man standing behind the bar and blinking nervously hadn't been there thirty-five years ago.

"Not here," Steiner whispered.

A reference to Lieutenant Sun, who was obviously absent since the old man was the bar's lone occupant.

Coffin glanced to a door in the corner. "Sun could be waiting for us upstairs."

Steiner bit her lip, allowing herself to hope. As she trailed Coffin to the bar, the old man watched her with no sign of recognition. Not even when she flashed him a tiny smile.

At that moment, Coffin knew.

Still, he went through the drill of asking the old man if his nephew Sun Yon-kee was here or had visited earlier tonight. The old man shook his head even before Coffin finished the question.

His nephew hadn't been here. In fact, he hadn't seen him in over a month.

Coffin didn't bother to pressure him; it would have been a waste of time. The old man's voice quivered as he spoke and his bent frame seemed ready to buckle at any moment.

He wasn't merely scared; he was terrified.

The implication sickened Coffin. Turning, he motioned Steiner to go.

But she shook him off, saying, "Sir, we should wait. Sun didn't leave a message, which means he still intends to—"

He cut her off, voicing what she knew in her heart but was unwilling to accept—that Sun had either changed his mind about cooperating or, far more likely, had been intercepted by Yee's men. Either way, the result was the same.

Lieutenant Sun wasn't coming.

"Sir, *don't*—"

Steiner grabbed Coffin's arm to prevent him from exiting

the bar. Through anguished eyes, she glanced at Sun's uncle, saying, "Sir, the only reason he's so afraid is that someone came here. Threatened him . . ."

"Right."

"Then they could be waiting for us outside."

"I'm sure they are, Major."

She was incredulous. "And you're just going to walk out of here? Sir, that makes no sense."

"Actually," Coffin said, "it makes perfect sense. Without Sun and his tape, we're no longer a threat to Yee."

"Sir, you can't know that. What if you're wrong?"

"They let us walk in here, didn't they?"

"So what? You saw General Yee tonight. He's crazy. He's capable of anything."

Logic Coffin couldn't ignore.

Removing the radio from his belt, he keyed it once and gave it to Steiner. "If I'm not back in five minutes, you call on the radio, and if no one answers, you phone the base. And don't pull the pistol until you need it. No sense in scaring the old man."

"Sir, don't do it. Please. Let's phone the base now and—"

With a polite nod to the old man, Coffin stepped into the night.

Even though Coffin knew he was right, he braced himself for the sound of a gunshot. Or at least a confrontation.

But the street remained silent and empty.

Retracing his steps, Coffin felt eyes watching from the shadows and purposefully kept his gait slow and unhurried. While Yee's men had won the round, he wasn't going to give them the satisfaction of seeing him sweat.

Approaching his car, he caught movement. If it disturbed him, he gave no sign.

Calmly unlocking the door, Coffin slid behind the wheel and placed the key in the ignition.

"I counted two," a deep voice from behind said. "When I saw you leave the bar, I tried to radio. Steiner told me about Sun. Damn shame about him."

Coffin carefully adjusted the rearview mirror so he could see the big man crouched in the backseat.

"Where are they, Sam?"

★29★

A rock and a hard place.
     If they waited for help, odds were they would be too late to save Sun. And if they acted on their own, they were breaking Korean law and risking an international incident.

No choice; they had to try. Now the question was whether Sun was in the custody of the two men. While Coffin concluded that was unlikely, he realized the men would at least know where the lieutenant was.

Coffin quickly briefed Hardy on his plan, then added the disclaimer: "Sam, I only wanted you to watch our back. I didn't intend involve you."

Hardy grinned. "You kidding? I'm going to enjoy this. We're talking *payback*." He pounded his chest hard. Then did it several more times. Pumping himself up the way he did before football games.

"Easy, Rambo," Coffin said. "If one of them is Colonel Kwan, you could have your hands full."

"You talking about Yee's four-eyed exec?" Hardy shrugged. "Well, if that's what's worrying you, you can relax. Neither of those guys is Kwan."

"You got close enough to tell?" This surprised Coffin.

"Sure." Hardy sounded amused by the question. "And I never even left the car."

"You didn't? Then how—"

The light came on. Coffin sighed, mentally kicking himself for ignoring the obvious. "You're sure they're involved? There's no mistake?"

Hardy had popped out the cover of the ceiling light and was unscrewing the bulb. Pocketing it, he said, "Not unless they had another reason for doubling back after you went into the bar. Here, you'll need this." Handing Coffin his radio, he cracked open the door nearest the curb, anxious to get started.

"Remember, Sam," Coffin said, "I want them healthy enough to talk."

Hardy winked. "You know me, Ed."

Which was precisely the problem.

Softly, the door clicked shut, and as Coffin radioed Steiner, he felt the beginnings of yet another headache. A little over an hour since the last one. The frequency was disturbing but expected. Fumbling for his pills, he watched Hardy crawl to the nearest building and slide along it, disappearing into an alley.

"Thank God, sir," Steiner said. "I was getting worried—"

"Just listen, Major," Coffin said. "In five minutes, we'll create a diversion . . ."

It was time.

Starting the car, Coffin looked up from the clock on the dash and saw Steiner emerge from the bar and look over. Flashing his high beams, Coffin eased on the gas and drove toward her. As he approached, Steiner motioned for him to pull over and he slowed, indicating he intended to do so.

And then at the last instant, he gunned the engine and, with tires squealing, angled toward a black Hyundai sedan parked some distance up the street. As he closed on it, he blared the horn until two heads popped up in the front seats. For a moment, the figures sat completely transfixed. When it became obvious that Coffin intended to plow into them, the doors flew open and the men bailed out.

It was a mistake.

Hardy had hidden in a nearby alley, and when he saw the occupants' attention fixed on Coffin, he crept toward their car and in a blur of movement, dropped the passenger with one swing, then dove over the car's hood and tackled the driver.

Slamming on the brakes, Coffin wildly fishtailed to a stop, inches from a collision. As he leaped from the car, he saw Hardy pin the driver with a knee and wrench a pistol from his grip. "Sam, the passenger!" The man was groggily sitting up, reaching into his jacket. Hardy sprang up, swinging the automatic pistol around.

"Freeze!"

Looking into the barrel, the passenger made the smart choice and froze. Rushing over, Coffin recognized him as the foul-mouthed Korean who had insulted Steiner. Snatching away his weapon, Coffin hurriedly frisked him for additional surprises, then hauled him to his feet. As he and Hardy piled the Koreans into the backseat of Coffin's car, Steiner ran up, saying excitedly, "My God. It worked. It worked. Where are their car keys? I need their car keys."

"Catch."

After Hardy tossed them to her, Steiner rushed over to the Hyundai and opened the trunk.

"He's not in here," she shouted. "What about the tape?"

Coffin looked at Hardy, who shook his head. "It's not on the men," Coffin said.

Steiner began a frantic search of the Hyundai's interior. Coffin questioned the Koreans about the tape and Sun. The talker suddenly became mute and the men glared back sullenly. By now, lights were coming on in the surrounding buildings and they heard angry voices. Someone threw a bottle, which shattered near Coffin's door.

That settled it and Coffin ordered Steiner to the car.

"Sir, I haven't found—"

"The tape will be with whoever has Sun. Now get in. *Move.*"

Steiner jogged over and jumped in. As they sped away, people spilled onto the streets. Several pumped fists, shouting obscenities.

"That went well," Hardy said dryly.

Reality has limits; imagination doesn't.

After another round of questions and continued silence from the Koreans, Coffin drove from town without saying anything more. He just set the stage by whispering to Hardy and watched in the rearview mirror, waiting for cracks to appear in the men's armor.

It didn't take long.

Hardy's size was naturally intimidating. And once he settled back with a menacing smile and leveled his pistol at the men's heads, the talker immediately began wetting his lips and tugging on his collar. Moments later, his partner joined in with big swallows and furtive blinks. Both men kept glancing at Coffin, expecting him to say something. They desperately wanted a hint about their fate.

But Coffin never said a word.

The drive took ten minutes. It was enough.

By the time Coffin turned down an isolated farm road at the edge of the frozen rice fields, the men were visibly shaking. And when Coffin abruptly pulled over to a drainage ditch and ordered them from the car, they were practically crying.

The men resisted moving and Hardy and Coffin had to drag them. As they forced the Koreans to their knees, the men pleaded to be spared. They swore they were only following orders and it wasn't their fault. That they weren't responsible.

"*U-ri neun ha-go-ship-ji-an-a-yo. Maeng-se-han-da.*" We didn't want to do it. I swear.

"*Me-eut ham-ni-ka? Mu-eut hess-eo-yo?*" Do what? What did you do?

The men hesitated. Even now, they didn't want to make this admission. But finally the talker answered Coffin, telling him what he'd expected.

And then the man revealed something completely unforeseen.

Jesus—

For several minutes, Coffin brutally questioned the Koreans, hoping to pry an admission of Yee's involvement or at least a clarification about motive. But the men hid behind a "hear no evil, see no evil" defense, claiming they were strictly hired muscle working for a middleman, a person who, even now, they were too afraid to identify by name.

"Let's go, Sam," Coffin said, backing away in frustration.

"Hang on. What'd they say?"

Coffin told him, saving the shocker for last. Afterward, Hardy's big frame shook with rage. "They were *warned* we were coming. That's impossible. They have to be lying."

"They're not. That's why they showed up at the bar. Because Sun did manage to slip away from his apartment without being seen."

"This American working for Yee. He couldn't have tipped them off because he couldn't have known . . ."

"No."

"So it has to be a bug. The guy who broke into your quarters must have bugged it."

"Probably."

"Lieutenant Sun. Where is he now, sir?" asked Steiner, who was now walking over from the car. As he faced her, Coffin wasn't sure how he could possibly find the words to tell her. But somehow, he did.

It would have been cruel to allow Steiner to hope, so Coffin went with the truth. That after the men had dragged Sun from the bar, they turned him over to the man who'd hired them.

"They wouldn't identify him because they're afraid for their families," Coffin said. "But I got them to admit the man had a missing ear and wore glasses."

"An ear?" Steiner said.

Then the tears came.

Coffin did his best to comfort Steiner, but she continued to cry softly, thinking about Lieutenant Sun and blaming herself. Confronted by her grief, Coffin realized there was nothing he could say, so he just hugged her until she pulled away, dabbing her eyes with a handkerchief Hardy had given her.

"Fucking assholes." Hardy glared at the Koreans with hate. "They knew what they were doing when they handed over Sun. You ask me, we should blow them away."

He placed the gun barrel against the forehead of the talkative Korean. The man began to tremble, babbling nonsensically at Coffin. Hardy told him to shut up, but the Korean continued to talk. He seemed on the verge of hysterics.

"I said, *shut the fuck up.*"

The Korean bowed low, cowering.

"Take it easy, Sam," Coffin said.

"Screw easy. I say an eye for an eye. Who's gonna know?"

"You're no killer, Sam."

"Always a first time." He sounded as if he meant it.

Steiner appeared suddenly uneasy, but Coffin wasn't concerned. Hardy had always possessed a flair for the dramatic. He said, "Sam, put the gun down. We both know you're not going to shoot them."

The pistol didn't move.

"Sam . . ."

Hardy slowly looked over. "This is bullshit, Ed. We should be taking these guys to jail. For all we know, they had something to do with Olson's death."

"I explained all that—"

"Yeah, yeah. We got no proof and once they're in custody, they'll deny everything. Well, I say we turn them in to the ROK authorities anyway."

"We do and we'll be the ones locked up. Technically, we're kidnapers, remember?"

"Fine. We do it my way. Better take Major Steiner over to the car, Ed. Now."

Hardy's tone was cold, dead. Both Koreans picked up on it, their eyes widening in terror. For the first time, Coffin felt a twinge of alarm that Hardy might actually be serious. But that was ludicrous.

"Sam," he said, "this has gone far enough and I want you to give me the— What are you doing? *Let him go.*"

In a sudden, violent movement, Hardy had snatched the talker upright and was worming the pistol into his mouth. The Korean struggled, but Hardy was too big and strong. The man gagged and choked on the barrel. The second Korean sprang to his feet and tried to run. With one hand, Hardy grabbed him by the neck and slammed him to the ground. Steiner shouted at Coffin, "My God, he's going to kill him. For God's sake do something." But for an instant, Coffin was too stunned to react. And that brief delay was all the time Hardy needed. Because when Coffin finally rushed him to knock the gun away, Hardy had pulled the trigger and Steiner was screaming.

★ 30 ★

It was a little after 4:00 A.M. and Coffin was behind the wheel, winding his way through the sleeping Ville, toward the base. Despite the hour, the area stirred with the first signs of life. In the darkened streets and alleys, garbage men shouted animatedly to one another, as they heaved trash into the back of a moving truck. By contrast, the car's occupants sat in weary silence, too physically and emotionally spent to attempt conversation. With slumped shoulders and sagging heads, they dully watched the buildings roll past, lost in their thoughts. In their efforts to uncover the truth, they'd succeeded only in getting a man killed. And now had no option except to come clean with Mother and General Gruver and face their wrath.

It wouldn't be pretty.

By acting on their own and ignoring their chain of command, they had violated one of the prime military tenets. As the senior officer, Coffin would take the biggest hit, which was what he wanted. The question was whether he could absolve Steiner and Hardy and salvage their careers.

In Coffin's view, it came down to whether their actions could be judged reasonable under the circumstances. After viewing everything with the clarity of twenty-twenty hindsight—including Hardy's homicidal antics and his own maiming of a South Korean national—Coffin still decided they were.

Especially considering what they'd witnessed only minutes earlier.

Steiner had insisted on the detour. One way or another, she had to know Sun's fate. As she said, miracles happen, and maybe Sun had somehow managed to escape.

But approaching Sun's neighborhood, they saw the towering flames and realized there would be no miracle. And as they turned onto Sun's street, they spotted two firemen carrying a charred body from a burning apartment building. Though the face was blackened beyond recognition, the corpse's identity became apparent when a young woman clutching a baby collapsed to her knees, shrieking out the Korean word for brother.

"Roll down your windows," Coffin said.

Steiner and Hardy did so, and as Coffin made a U-turn at the police barricade, they clearly heard the woman scream out Sun's name.

Several policemen rushed over to comfort her. The woman was inconsolable. It was a wrenching scene and Steiner turned away, unable to watch. But she shed no tears; she was cried out.

As they left the scene, the woman's screams followed them. It seemed a long time before they couldn't hear her anymore.

"Bastards," Hardy growled from the backseat. "I should have killed those bastards."

Coffin and Steiner could only nod. Of course, Hardy hadn't actually shot the Korean, because he'd removed the bullet from the chamber before pulling the trigger. A fact that Coffin had been slow to realize until Hardy erupted in laughter and called out, "Better get back, Ed. He's pissing all over himself. Some tough guy, huh? Come on, let's get out of here. If we're lucky, maybe they'll freeze to death before they can walk back."

Riding back to town, Hardy's mood remained upbeat. It wasn't that he'd deluded himself that the punishment he'd administered had fit the crime. It was simply that he had done something, made them pay in some small way. And for a while, that was enough to satisfy his need for justice. Until he saw the flames.

The tires hummed over the road. Coffin rubbed his eyes and tried to ignore his fatigue. Ahead, he could make out the glow of Osan's main gate and turned right.

"Uh, Ed . . ."

Coffin's eyes crawled up to the rearview mirror. Hardy was frowning at him. In the passenger seat, Steiner also seemed puzzled.

Sighing, Coffin said, "You're wondering why I'm not going to the base."

Two heads bobbed.

"Another detour," Coffin said. "It's personal."

The sign above the shuttered windows said it was a photography studio. Coffin rang the bell and banged on the door. After perhaps a minute, lights come on upstairs. An irritated male voice shouted down and he shouted back.

"Ed Coffin?" the man said in accented English. "Colonel Ed Coffin?"

Switching to Korean, the man said he would be right down. Seemingly within seconds, the door flung open and a fat man in a silk bathrobe ushered Coffin inside, grinning as if they were old friends.

The studio was small and cluttered with photography

equipment. They remained just inside the door, standing by a display case filled with portraits of U.S. service personnel in their uniforms. The man got right to business and tantalizingly held up a manila folder. When Coffin reached for it, he pulled it back.

"*Mi-an-he-yo*," he said apologetically.

Coffin produced his wallet and handed over ten one-hundred-dollar bills. The man's pudgy finger curled; he wanted more. "*Don-i deu neun il. Geun-mu hal-su-eopt-da. Gwang-ju e gas-eo-ya-man-da.*" Expenses. I lost work. I had to travel to Kwang-ju.

Coffin passed him another hundred. The fleshy face wrinkled in an exaggerated show of disappointment. Sighing, Coffin gave him another hundred and finally saw a smile.

The Korean passed over the folder, then waited for Coffin to open it.

Coffin said, "*Hon-ja it-gi-rul won-han-da.*" I'd like privacy.

The man smiled in understanding. Crossing the small room, he disappeared through a door.

Coffin laid out the folder's contents on a table. There was a packet of photographs and a folded piece of paper. Reaching for the photos, he abruptly selected the paper.

Handwriting doesn't lie.

On the paper, Coffin saw a brief, hand-scrawled note, written in Korean. Coffin felt a flicker of disappointment, when he noticed the signature at the bottom. It was an unfamiliar woman's name.

For someone like her, marriage would be unlikely. But if she'd changed her name to avoid humiliation . . .

Coffin focused on the body of the note. In it, the woman was notifying her *gwan-li-in*—supervisor or boss—that she was ill and wouldn't be able to work for a few days. She asked for the boss's understanding and hoped he would not fire her.

Reading the words, Coffin felt a stir of emotion. A sadness.

Digging out the magnifying glass and the old letter he'd brought, Coffin compared the letter's writing against the note's. As he did, his disappointment returned. Korean writing was based on alphabet construction similar to English, only with symbols instead of letters. And as Coffin studied the few common words, he realized that while they appeared similar enough to have been written by the same hand, only an expert could reach a definitive conclusion.

Shaking his head, he set down the letters and the magnifying glass. For several long beats, he stared at the photographs, hesitant to pick them up. Closing his eyes, he took his mind back, trying to form an image. When it appeared, it was dull and unfocused, diffused by time.

His eyes opened. He took a deep breath, staring at the packet.

Then slowly picked it up and opened it.

At least a full roll of photos. Sorting through them, Coffin saw they were all of the same subject, taken at the same time and place. An old, stooped woman in a threadbare coat, tending pigs in a pen layered with snow. The day was bright and sunny, and as was typical for female laborers, she wore a *miljip mo-ja*—a traditional wide-brimmed hat—to shield her face.

Roughly half the photos were close-ups, taken with a zoom. In those, Coffin saw a weathered, wrinkled face that was old beyond its years. Studying the woman, Coffin desperately wanted something, anything to register. But to him, it was just an old woman's face and nothing more.

Then he came to a picture near the end of the stack. A frontal shot of the woman, slightly bent at the waist. Something dangled from her neck, glinting. A charm of some kind.

Coffin stared at the photograph. As he did, his hands

began to shake. Snatching up the magnifying glass, he focused on the charm.

And saw what looked like a single gilded Korean word. He tried to read it but couldn't. Then he moved toward the center of the room, under the light.

Coffin suddenly lowered the photo, his heart pounding through his chest. The room seemed to spin and he couldn't breathe. At the creak of a door, he looked up. The fat man in the robe was watching him.

Coffin struggled to sound calm. "*Bon-jeok pil-yo-he-yo.*" I need her address.

The man pointed to the manila folder. "*Yeo-gi iss-eo-yo.*"

Coffin turned the folder over. In the upper left corner, he saw neat Korean printing.

The man said, "*Al-gess-um-ni-ka?*" Okay?

"*Al-gess-um-ni-da.*"

As Coffin left, he wiped the wetness from his eyes.

The silent treatment.

When Coffin returned to the car, Steiner and Hardy didn't say a word to him. In fact, they went out of their way to avoid even eye contact. Driving to the base, Coffin figured their curiosity would win out and they'd eventually say something, but they never did. To Coffin, it was apparent they were making a concession to his sensibilities; they didn't want to bring up his past and risk offending him.

While it was a gesture Coffin appreciated, he was tempted to tell them it wasn't necessary. Not anymore.

Looking at those photographs, really seeing them, had been a singularly transforming moment. It was more than the questions he'd finally answered or an understanding of what his life might have been like. It was the appreciation of the gift he'd been given—the selflessness of it—by someone who had nothing to give. It was all that and more. It was also the realization that he'd once been truly loved and probably still was.

No, Coffin wasn't ashamed of his past; he was proud of it.

And that's just what he would have told Steiner and Hardy . . . if they'd asked.

★31★

"That settles it," Hardy announced. "We talk to Mother first."

They were coming up to the gate. Coffin shook his head. "No. General Gruver will be upset as it is. If he finds out we briefed Mother before—"

"Better look, Ed," Hardy said.

His arm slid past Coffin's ear, pointing. By then, Coffin had focused on the three figures, standing in front of the guard shack. Two were security cops and the third was a woman in civilian clothes.

Mother.

"Sir," Steiner murmured, "I don't think I like this."

A reaction to an apparent disconnect.

Cops working a murder investigation don't waste time hanging out at a gate. And the only possible reason for Mother to do so was that she was furious at Coffin for taking off with Steiner and couldn't wait to chew him out. But on her face, they saw no sign of anger or even irritation. If anything, she appeared relieved to see them.

"How'd she know you went off base, Ed?" Hardy asked.

"She's a cop." Coffin shrugged. "She probably saw my car was gone."

"The chief could have told her."

"He wouldn't."

They zigzagged through the concrete security barriers. One of the cops stuck out his hand and Coffin braked, lowering his window. Mother immediately stepped over and as she leaned down, Coffin found himself confronted by another disconnect. One that alarmed him.

Mother's eyes were filled with worry. He said, "Mother, what is it? What's wrong?"

"Follow me, Ed." Her voice oddly strained.

"First tell me—"

"No questions. Follow me."

Pivoting, she hurried to her car, parked behind the guard shack. Watching her pull out, Steiner shook her head uneasily.

"Now I *know* I don't like this," she said.

Three minutes later, they were even more confused. Instead of turning toward General Gruver's hilltop residence or his headquarters building, Mother kept to the main road, bypassing even her own OSI offices.

"The First," Hardy concluded. "We're going to the First."

But at the intersection adjacent to the flight line, Mother headed west, driving farther from the U-2 squadron.

They rode past the NCO Club and the rows of large dormitories. Then the buildings ended, replaced by expanses of snow.

Sighing, Hardy said, "Ed, I think your girlfriend's taking us on a wild goose chase. There's nothing out this way except for— I'll be damned. She *is* taking us there. But why? It's closed for the winter."

Mother had turned down the winding drive, toward the golf course clubhouse.

★

"*Now* what's she doing?" Hardy asked.

They were slowly circling the empty clubhouse parking lot. Instead of pulling over, Mother led them to the rear of the sprawling building. Finally stopping behind a metal carport adjacent to the pro shop, where the golf carts were stored.

As Coffin rolled in beside her, Mother hopped from her car and motioned him to lower his window.

"Leave the engine running, but kill the headlights, Ed. Be back in a minute."

"A minute? Where are—"

Mother took off, hurrying in the direction they'd just come from. Looking over, she hit the brakes. "Ed, your *lights*."

She waited until Coffin clicked them off before continuing. "What," Hardy asked, "was that all about?"

"Mother has a thing about wasting electricity," Coffin said.

"Huh? You kidding?"

Nearing the front of the club, Mother stopped and peered in the direction of the main part of the base.

"She seems to be looking for something," Steiner said.

Hardy said dryly, "And your first clue was . . ."

After a glance back at them, Mother resumed walking.

"Enough's enough," Hardy muttered. Opening his door, he hollered to Mother, demanding to know what she was doing.

"Making sure we're okay."

"Okay for what?"

She again stopped, her head cycling between their car and the base. Abruptly, she nodded as if satisfied and started back toward them.

Slumping against his seat, Hardy said sourly, "About time. She's acting like she's afraid someone's watching us."

"Or could," Coffin said.

Steiner and Hardy looked at him.

"Mother," Coffin said, "wants to be sure that we can't be seen from the base."

"*Hiding* us, sir?" Steiner said. "You think she brought us here to hide us?"

"She had us kill the headlights." Coffin shrugged.

"All I know," Hardy said, "is that it's five in the morning and we're sitting at a fucking golf course. And if Mother doesn't have a damn good reason for wasting our time, I'm going to be plenty pissed—"

He broke off at the sound of footsteps. He'd left his door open and as he turned, he saw Mother peering down at him.

Her arms were folded, an unmistakable sign of what was coming unless Hardy apologized. But Hardy remained silent; he had no intention of doing so.

Coffin sighed. A blowup between Hardy and Mother was the last thing they needed. "Listen, Mother. Sam didn't mean anything by—"

"It's okay, Ed."

Her arms slowly unfolded. In a calm voice, she said, "My fault. I should have explained beforehand. Hello, Charlotte. You mind moving over, Colonel Hardy? Thank you."

Watching Mother slide in beside Hardy, Coffin could only shake his head. More than anything this third disconnect—Mother's uncharacteristic restraint—indicated that whatever reason she had for bringing them to the golf course had trumped her natural impulse to react angrily to any slight, real or imagined.

"That bad?" Coffin asked.

"Worse, Ed."

★

Mother spoke hesitantly, with long pauses, as if what she was saying was hard for her. She prefaced her remarks by stating she didn't have much time, and insisted there be no interruptions.

Focusing on Coffin, she continued, "Frankly, I'm not sure where to begin. So much has happened in the past few hours . . . a situation came up that places you and Charlotte in . . . an awkward position. For now, I want you and Charlotte to remain . . . unavailable. That's why I brought you here. No one will look for you here until I can figure out where to take you. Some place more permanent. I'm trying to keep our options open without involving General Gruver. Or anyone else up the chain of command. Because of their positions and the politics involved, their hands would be tied and . . . well . . . that's primarily the reason, the politics of it and . . . there was something else . . ." She trailed off, searching for what to say next. Sounding frustrated, she said, "Look, bear with me. I know none of this makes any sense yet. But it will."

She spent a few moments organizing her thoughts. No one said anything. She was scaring the hell out of them and they wanted her to get to the punch line.

Abruptly, Mother resumed speaking, her voice turning bitter. "It's that bastard Yee, Ed. You were right about him. He's ruthless as hell and he outsmarted us. He's turning the situation into a political quagmire, taking it out of the military's hands. That's why we have to keep Gruver out of the loop. It won't be his call; he'll have to follow orders. Now, I'm not saying a decision has been made; it hasn't. That's why I brought this." Filtering moonlight revealed a microcassette recorder in her hand. "I need you and Charlotte to provide accounts of your actions, since I last saw you. Something I can use for a rebuttal, though I doubt it will do much good. When I left his office, Gruver and Yee and Chief Yung, the local provincial police chief—he's bought and paid for by Yee—were having a conference call with higher-ups in the ROK and U.S. governments. I mean *serious* higher-ups: our SECDEF and his ROK counterpart, Ambassador Solvin from the embassy, General Cho, a couple of State Department undersecretaries; you name it." Reacting to the stunned faces, Mother added, "Yeah, this has become political as hell. General Yee and the police are making accusations against Ed and Charlotte. Accusations that are supported by eyewitness accounts—"

Steiner was squirming, struggling to contain herself. But the implication of Mother's last statement was too much.

"A crime?" she exploded. "We're accused of a crime?"

Mother nodded grimly.

"What a crock," Hardy said. "It's a fucking frame. They didn't do anything. I was with them and will swear on a stack of— Wait, am *I* accused of anything?"

"Only Ed and Charlotte."

"Yee wouldn't have known about you, Sam," Coffin said.

"The *crime?*" Steiner said, still squirming. "What's the crime?"

Everyone looked at Mother. Waiting.

Even now, she was reluctant to tell them. And as the seconds passed, everyone's anxiety grew, sensing what was coming. Still, when Mother finally spoke, her words came as a shock. While those in the car had prepared themselves to hear a specific crime, they hadn't considered a victim.

"Lieutenant Sun," Mother said. "The ROKs are accusing Ed and Charlotte of murdering a ROK lieutenant named Sun."

A delayed reaction.

For several seconds, everyone stared at Mother, unable to

process what she'd just said. Then Steiner and Hardy erupted, voicing incredulity and denials.

"*Evidence.*" Steiner came out of her seat. "*What evidence?* We never saw Lieutenant Sun. At least not alive."

"Damn right," Hardy said, pounding his hand with a fist. "And I'm a *witness.* I was with them the entire time we were downtown. This is a fucking *frame.*"

Mother told them to calm down; they couldn't. If anything they spoke even louder, protesting the absurdity of the charge. Mother shot Coffin a look, wanting him to intervene. But Coffin had gone into crisis mode, closing his eyes and retreating inward to think. In the end, Mother resorted to shouting Hardy and Steiner down. It took her several attempts, but the car was again quiet.

Coffin's eyes remained closed; his breathing was deep and regular. He could have been asleep, but of course, he wasn't.

With a sudden clarity, it hit him what they had to do, and he wondered whether they could pull it off. The problem was what Mother was saying; if the murder charge stuck, they would never get official approval. And acting on their own ensured almost certain failure, because too many people had to become involved—

He opened his eyes.

Mother was talking again, confirming his worst fears.

★32★

"What you two don't understand," Mother said to Steiner and Hardy, "is that this is a *perfect* frame. General Yee did his homework. He has five witnesses who'll swear Ed and Charlotte went to Sun's apartment tonight and when they left, the fire began."

"Shit," Hardy said.

"You bet it's shit," Mother fired back. "With those odds, no one will give a damn about your testimony. And don't forget, we're talking about a trial in a civilian Korean court where Ed and Charlotte's guilt will be determined by a judge, not a jury. Anyone want to take odds that his honor won't be in Yee's pocket?" Her eyes flowed over the three faces. "Didn't think so. And it gets better. Yee also told General Gruver that he could link the murder weapon—a knife—to Ed. With the probable cause Yee presented and at General Cho's insistence, General Gruver had to okay a search of Ed's quarters."

Steiner caught her breath and Hardy got a sick look.

Coffin rarely swore, but did so now.

"It's not as bad as you think, Ed," Mother said. "My agents are conducting the search, with two ROK cops observing. Still, I've got to tell you I'm worried. Yee sounded confident we'd find the weapon. Too confident. Any guesses why?"

"The break-in." Coffin's voice was almost a whisper.

"The break-in," Mother repeated. "Whoever broke into your place probably planted a knife— I'm getting to that." Coffin and Hardy had spoken up, pointing out a discrepancy in logic.

"You're right," Mother said to them. "The timeline doesn't fit. Sun was murdered *after* the break-in, which means any knife found in Coffin's quarters couldn't be the murder weapon. Now, before you get the idea that's good news, it isn't. Remember what I said about Yee doing his homework . . ."

Cautious nods all around.

"Well," Mother said, "the type of knife used in Sun's killing was part of it. It has a distinctive curved blade. Like one of those Mediterranean scimitars, only smaller. Very rare in Korea. If we find a similar one, that's all the ROKs will need to charge Ed and Charlotte and . . . and have them remanded into their custody."

Mother forced out her last remark. And as it sank in, it became clear why.

"Huh?" Hardy said. "ROK custody?"

Coffin said, "Mother, we can't be turned over to the ROKs."

"Jail?" Steiner said. "We're going to a Korean *jail*?" She sounded close to hysterics.

"No, Major," Coffin said. "No one's going to jail."

"But sir, Mother just said—"

"She's wrong, Charlotte," Hardy said flatly. "Turning you over before you're found guilty in a trial is a violation of the SOFA. Tell her, Mother." SOFA stood for the Status of Forces Agreement, which detailed jurisdictional requirements and legalities for all U.S. military personnel in Korea.

Mother was silent, her expression pained.

Steiner said, "Mother, please. If you have some reason . . ."

"I do, Charlotte," Mother said quietly. "The ROKs are asking Ambassador Solvin for a waiver to the SOFA."

"Can they do that?" Steiner looked around fearfully. "Can they get a waiver?"

"Hell, no," Hardy said. He glared at Mother. "Why are you doing this? Scaring her. There's never been a waiver to the SOFA. Ever. Right, Ed?"

Coffin watched Mother, thinking that she knew this better than they did. Knew that waivers weren't granted. And yet, she was apparently convinced—

"Mother," he said suddenly. "There's something you're not telling us."

She eased out a breath, nodding. Instead of answering Coffin, she checked her watch and said, "It's a little after five. Turn on the radio, Ed."

"The radio?"

"A Korean news station. It won't matter which one."

Steiner and Hardy were shaking their heads. Like Coffin, they were mystified by Mother's request. But its meaning became dramatically clear when Coffin tuned in a station and in the stream of Korean, two recognizable words were heard.

Coffin's and Steiner's names.

The news account was intended to inflame passions and generate hate. Liberally employing words like butchering and bloodbath, the Korean talking head, who spoke with a slight lisp, discussed the murder in grisly detail, then spent two full minutes describing the horror of Sun's charred body and the gut-wrenching anguish of his sister. Shifting into outright fantasy, the newscaster stated that the motive for the killing was a sexual liaison between Sun and Steiner. And that when Coffin, a jealous former lover of Steiner's, learned of the affair and confronted her, Steiner tearfully accused Sun of raping her. That revelation sent Coffin over the edge and, accompanied by Steiner, he went to Sun's apartment and in a fit of rage, brutally murdered him.

The expected character assassinations followed: Steiner was portrayed as a seductive, oversexed vixen—a *yu-hok ha-nun yeo-ja*—who preyed on men to get what she wanted. And Coffin was portrayed as a ruthlessly ambitious officer who'd gained his promotions on the backs of his peers and his subordinates.

At this point, the commentator dropped a teaser about knowing a bombshell about Coffin, then paused to let the anticipation build. When he abruptly began speaking, Coffin realized what the man intended to say and tried to turn off the radio, so he wouldn't have to hear it. But he was too late.

"*Dae-ryeong eo-meo-nim un gal-bo yeot-da*," the lisping voice said.

The colonel's mother was a whore.

Somehow Yee found out your secret. And now the world knows.
    I don't care.
    You say that, but you do care. Your mother was a whore.
    I don't care. She was my mother and she loved me.
    C'mon, Ed. Admit Yee got to you. Admit he shamed you.
    You're wrong. I'm okay with people knowing. It's a relief.
    And sitting back in his seat, Coffin had an affirmation

that he wasn't in denial; he couldn't be, because of the way he felt. A quiet sense of ambivalence.

"Ed," Mother said. "You don't seem too . . . upset."

Coffin shifted around. Three puzzled faces looked back at him.

"What gives?" Hardy asked. "The newscast wasn't that bad?"

"No, it's . . . bad." Coffin recited all the inflammatory rhetoric except for the commentator's final comment. That item he felt obliged to reveal to Mother . . . privately.

When he finished, everyone appeared shell-shocked. In the States, this newscast would be damning enough. But here in Korea—

"Riots," Hardy said suddenly. "There must have been talk about riots."

He was looking at Mother. She nodded. "Perhaps as soon as tomorrow. The concern is the anti-American movement will use this incident to mobilize more than their usual student base. If they're successful and the general populace takes to the streets . . ." She trailed off, not bothering to point out what everyone knew—that a riot six months earlier had turned the neighborhood outside the Yongsan garrison in Seoul into a battleground, leaving dozens dead and entire blocks in flames, all because a GI blew through a crosswalk, killing three young girls.

"Anyway," Mother added, "that's why I said what I did about the waiver. The United States can't afford to be seen as . . . obstructing."

Hardy had no reply. For once, he was at a loss for words.

Another silence fell upon the car as everyone digested Mother's grim assessment. It came down to a numbers game—two lives balanced against the possible loss of hundreds. Factor in the increased South Korean outrage and almost certain worldwide condemnation if the United States didn't grant a waiver and the result was inevitable. Coffin and Steiner would be turned over to the ROKs and interned in a Korean prison.

Exactly, Coffin thought, as Yee had planned.

Steiner hugged herself and rocked slowly. Watching her, Coffin was torn: Should he tell her why Yee had gone to the trouble to frame them? What his true purpose was?

A moment later, Steiner spared him a decision.

"Sir," she said dully, looking at him, "we'll never leave that prison, will we? General Yee will have us killed."

She deserved to know what he believed. But instead, he opted for: "Only me, Major. Two deaths would be hard to explain, and I'm the one he hates."

A vague nod. Steiner stared into the dark.

"I couldn't take a Korean prison," she whispered. "I'd rather die."

Mother placed a hand on her shoulder. "It's not over yet, Charlotte. We still have a chance."

"Chance?" Steiner said bitterly. "What chance? You said yourself we'll be handed over."

"You're forgetting something, Charlotte," Hardy said. "Mother brought you here."

Steiner turned to him, her expression confused.

"Mother brought you here," Hardy repeated.

Steiner's eyebrows crawled up. She stared at Mother. "You mean . . ."

Mother nodded.

"They'll *court-martial* you." Steiner was dumbfounded. "You'll get in a lot of trouble. You'll be arrested. Why would you—"

She broke off; her question had been answered. Mother was now fixated on Coffin. And she was smiling.

"I'm not the only one, Ed," Mother said softly. "Cara-lyn . . . the chief. Probably others from your squadron; the chief says all we have to do is ask."

Coffin didn't trust himself to speak. Once again, he was being given a selfless gift, one he didn't want to accept. And if it was just him, he wouldn't have accepted it: Why have people ruin their lives and careers merely to delay the inevitable?

But of course, it wasn't just him. And Mother's remark about others altered the equation. She was right; they now had a chance.

"Tell everyone thank you," he said.

After that, Mother got back to work with a sudden energy. Digging out her radio, she hurriedly briefed them on her game plan, which centered on the chief. He'd gone downtown to scope out locations—possibly properties belonging to his in-laws—where Coffin and Steiner could safely be hidden.

"Once he gives me the word," Mother said, "we'll smuggle you out in my car; no one will search me. And before you ask, the answers are yes and not a clue. Yes, we have to stash you downtown because the base will be turned inside out to find you two, and no, I haven't got a clue what we'll do next. Right now, I'm only focused on keeping you out of ROK hands, assuming it comes to that. Let's hope it doesn't."

She turned up the volume on the radio, then keyed it, saying, "Colonel Bradley? Agent Hubbard. Sir, I was won-dering . . ."

"General Gruver's chief of staff," Hardy said.

Coffin nodded. Responding to Mother's query, Colonel Bradley reported that no decision had been reached regard-

ing a waiver to the SOFA; political considerations notwithstanding, the Americans were concerned over the prece-
dent that a waiver would set, as well as a secondary issue.

"What issue, sir?" Mother asked.

"That's the problem; the ROKs are keeping us in the
dark. General Yee's handling the negotiations and all he'll
say is that their government is about to make a major an-
nouncement with respect to North Korea. And they don't
want public unrest to detract from it."

Mother looked to Coffin. *Something there?*

"Maybe," he whispered.

Mother told Bradley she would be there with information
that might influence a decision. Probably in thirty minutes.

"Better make it twenty. The ROKs are pushing hard, so
there's no telling." Bradley paused as if to add something.

"Sir?"

"It's General Yee. He dug up some dirt on Coffin and
we'll need you to check it out."

"What kind of dirt, sir?"

"Not over the net, Hubbard. We'll talk when you get
here."

A hiss; he was gone.

Lowering the radio, Mother looked at Coffin. Waiting.

"Mother," Coffin said quietly, "it's not what you're thinking."

"I see." Her eyes measured him. "And exactly what am I
thinking . . ."

Coffin felt Steiner squeeze his arm. *Tell her.*

But Coffin couldn't. Not here.

Mother turned away, her face tight with disappointment.
She said, "You heard the man. I've got twenty minutes,
which means you've each got five. So talk fast, but don't
leave out anything important. Ed, you first."

She slapped the recorder into his hand hard enough to sting.

They read it on Mother's face; it was killing her not to interrupt. But she continued to gnaw on her tongue, waiting for Coffin and Charlotte to finish their accounts. And the instant Charlotte turned off the recorder, Mother snatched it away, throwing out questions, desperately searching for something that wasn't there.

Evidence. She wanted something, anything that would support the charges Charlotte and Coffin had made.

But Sun was dead.

His tape implicating an American officer was gone.

And the Korean talker and his partner would never testify.

"Nothing," Mother finally said, surrendering to the obvious. "You got a big fat nothing. I play the tape without supporting evidence and the ROKs will laugh me out of the room. They'll say it's a desperate attempt to save Ed's skin by implicating Yee, a man Ed is known to hate. Jesus, you've got to give me *something*."

Her eyes pleaded with Steiner and Coffin. Even sought out Hardy.

"What about the picture?" Coffin said. "The copy of the one in Marty Bell's office; you were going to have it analyzed . . ."

"C'mon, Ed," Mother said. "That the best you can do?"

"Yee wanted it for a reason. It could be evidence . . ."

". . . which is why I had a PI look at it. Those two people by the U-2 were airmen from the squadron. Satisfied?"

"Get me an enlarged copy."

"Ed—"

"There's something in it. There has to be."

She sighed. "Fine. Okay." Sounding exasperated, she added, "You do understand we need something now. Not tomorrow or in an hour. *Now.* Once Yee gets his waiver, he wins. The brass won't have the balls to rescind it unless they can hold up evidence to the cameras, conclusively proving someone else killed Sun. Now *think.* There must be something you haven't told me."

She looked at Steiner and Hardy. Returned to Coffin. "Three items," he said. "None is a smoking gun . . ."

Mother rolled her eyes.

". . . but they do support our assertions."

"Make it quick."

"First, did you find a bug in Major Steiner's room?"

"Yeah, but you're barking up the wrong tree. Charlotte's an intel officer and the ROKs will say it isn't unusual—"

"I'm not in intelligence. And two bugs bolster our story that we were targeted—"

Mother slowly blinked. "*Two* bugs."

"Oops," Hardy said. "You missed one, Ed."

A given. In Coffin's cryptic account, he'd neglected to mention their suspicion about a listening device in his room.

"Jesus, Ed," Mother said, after Coffin filled her in. "Didn't I say not to leave out anything important?"

"It wasn't intentional."

"Uh-huh."

Shaking her head, she got on her radio and contacted one of her agents searching Coffin's BOQ. No weapon had been found yet and neither had a listening device.

"CP?" Mother said. "You monitoring?"

"Yes, ma'am," the command post controller replied. "We're sending a team to sweep Colonel Coffin's quarters."

Ending the call, Mother said impatiently to Coffin, "Go. Let's have the rest of it."

"It's only a suspicion. It's about the identity of the American officer . . ."

Coffin tried to ignore the guilt as he told her about Marty Bell. His drinking and money problems and his presence at the U-2 compound the night Olson's plane was sabotaged. And, of course, he reminded her that Bell's position as a commander required him to regularly meet with Yee.

"You know Bell," Mother pressed. "You think he could be bought?"

"It's . . . possible. Marty's also . . . upset at not making general."

"So we're talking a twofer. He's pissed at the world and has money problems." She had the scent and was getting excited.

"Better get going, Mother," Hardy said, tapping his watch.

"What? Oh, right, right." Unlocking her door, she said to Coffin, "Checking out Bell will take a few days. Still, if I say we've got a suspect, it might influence the decision about a waiver. At least delay it. As soon as I know something, I'll be back. Until then, sit tight— What's this?"

Hardy had given her a slip of paper. "My office number," he said.

Mother looked at him quizzically

"My detachment worked all night on the wreckage and are on telephone standby in their quarters."

Mother slowly nodded, realizing what he was asking. "If someone sees Ed or Charlotte—"

"They won't. We'll keep the doors locked and the only two other people with keys are asleep. Okay?"

Hardy slipped Coffin a knowing glance, tacitly hinting he had a reason for wanting to go to his unit.

Mother hesitated.

"Look," Hardy said, "it's not any riskier than staying here. And it's a helluva lot more comfortable."

Grudgingly, Mother nodded her assent. As she slid out the door, she suddenly bent and peered in at Coffin. "Wait a minute. You had *three* items to tell me."

"I'll walk you to your car," Coffin said.

★ 33 ★

The cold night air smelled faintly of burning charcoal from the nearby farms. The chill felt good on Coffin's skin. Mother led him to the driver's side of her car, pivoted. "It's your dime."

"It's about us. Why you left."

Her jaw tightened. "I don't have time for this, Ed. Unless you have anything related to this case—"

"This goes to the heart of it. It concerns my character. You walked out because you thought I was immoral—"

"I don't give a damn about your morality." Her voice was like ice.

"No? You deny that cops patrolling the Ville told you that I went to—"

"Not *now*." She yanked open the car door. "I specifically told you we'd deal with this after— *Let go*."

Coffin grabbed her hands, pulled her from the car. She fought him, struggling to wrench free. "Ed, I'm warning you. If you don't let me—"

Coffin talked over her, the words pouring from him. For him, it was a cathartic release; the more he spoke, the better he felt. And as she listened, the impact on Mother was equally transforming. Almost immediately, her struggles ceased and she rapidly progressed from tight-lipped anger to cautious suspicion and finally settled on an expression of sadness and regret.

Falling silent, Coffin released her hands. For several moments, they gazed at each other, neither knowing what to say. What was there to say for years of hurt brought about because of a misunderstanding?

"Ed," Mother said, her voice tight, "this better be the truth. Because if it isn't . . ."

"Those whorehouses; I only visited them hoping to find someone who remembered my mother. It's why I returned to Korea. A man I'd hired located her. I can prove it. Look."

Since the manila folder containing the photos was in his car, Coffin settled for showing her his old letter, intending only to allude to its significance. But as he spoke, he found himself sharing his mother's last words to him. For some reason, it was important to him that she know.

So he told her that he'd received the letter shortly before he left the States, after being adopted. In it, his mother expressed her love for him and apologized for giving him up. She also asked for his understanding and pleaded with him not to hate her. She ended the letter by telling him that his new family deserved his love and she wanted him to do something that might seem difficult now, but was for the best—she asked him to forget about her.

When Coffin finished, Mother's eyes glistened and he was pretty emotional himself.

"It couldn't have been easy for her to write that," Mother said.

"No . . ."

Coffin and Mother were quiet, looking at the letter. As he slowly tucked it away, she asked what his mother was like and Coffin revealed the little he still remembered. That she was young and beautiful and could never bring herself to spank him, even when he was bad. That remark generated a smile from Mother, and after that, there didn't seem to be anything left for either of them to say. For Coffin, there was satisfaction in having achieved a measure of redemption. It wasn't only that he'd convinced Mother she'd been wrong about him, it was also that she now knew he'd been deserving of her love . . . at least for a while.

"Funny," Mother murmured, wiping the wetness from her eyes. "In some ways, knowing the truth makes it all the more . . . difficult."

Coffin nodded; he knew what she meant.

She turned away, signaling she was ready to go. But rather than leave, she suddenly began explaining why she'd left him. As if under some obligation to do so.

Coffin told her it wasn't necessary. He said, "I'm the one who's to blame. I should have trusted you enough to tell you about my mother."

She contemplated him sadly. "This for me, Ed. You have to know how difficult it was for me to leave. Even when I learned you visited those places, I almost didn't go. But in the end, the thought of you . . . the man I loved . . . being with those women. *Paying* to be with them . . ." Her mouth trembled; she couldn't finish.

"Loved," Coffin said softly. "I'm not sure I ever truly believed you loved me."

She sighed. "If I didn't, it wouldn't have hurt so much."

"What about now?"

Mother was taken aback by the question. She shook her head. "Ed, don't do this. Too much has happened. We can't suddenly pick up where we left off."

It wasn't a no.

Coffin moved toward her and Mother began backpedaling. He said, "Why not? If we still love each other, why not?"

"No, Ed. I'm not ready. That was over five years ago. I can't handle this now."

"Tell me you don't love me and I'll drop it. Just tell me."

She backed up to the car. He continued to press her for an answer. She said, "This is crazy. You understand this is completely crazy."

Placing his hands on her shoulders, he felt her resistance leave. "So do something crazy. For once in your life, do something crazy."

Coffin drew her close and she collapsed into his arms with a force that surprised him. As they clung to each other, she finally whispered the words he desperately wanted to hear, telling him she still loved him and always had. Afterward, Mother tilted her head and Coffin kissed her gently, then with increasing passion. Breaking away, she said, "For the rest of our lives, promise me we'll never have another misunderstanding," and even as Coffin promised, he felt himself jarred back to reality. It wasn't the troubles with General Yee or the possible murder indictment that worried him, but something else entirely unrelated.

The rest of their lives, Mother had said. And Coffin knew he had to tell her what those words really meant and soon.

If he could.

A twinge in his head; to Coffin, it was a reminder of the preciousness of time.

So he chose to stand in the dark and wave to Mother as she drove away, only lowering his hand when she was completely out of sight.

Returning to his car, he knew there wasn't any need to explain to Steiner and Hardy what had transpired. Even in the dim light, they would have seen enough to guess most of it; the rest, they would have overheard, because Hardy's window, now whirring up, had been discreetly lowered earlier.

As Coffin climbed behind the wheel, Steiner and Hardy again gave him the silent treatment, this time accompanied by a smile and a grin, respectively.

"Enjoy the show?" Coffin said dryly.

"You bet," Hardy said. "Never figured Mother for such a good kisser."

A couple of caustic responses came to Coffin. Instead, he casually gave Hardy the finger, breaking his rule about bird flipping. Hardy responded by making kissing noises.

"Knock it off, Sam."

As Coffin drove toward the flight line, Hardy's kissing noises only became louder.

With only three helicopters and twenty-six assigned personnel, Hardy's Jolly Green rescue detachment rated little more than an oversized concrete box to serve as its operations building, but at least it had His and Hers restrooms, which Steiner and Coffin used to clean up before settling into easy chairs in Hardy's surprisingly spacious office.

Neither felt like eating the prepackaged sandwiches Hardy appropriated from a battered refrigerator and none of the three thought they could relax enough to sleep, as they waited for Mother's phone call.

So they watched an old Cary Grant comedy on the

Armed Forces TV station. Just to take their mind off the tension. But as Cary traded barbs with Katharine Hepburn, Coffin felt the pull of fatigue and closed his eyes to rest them. Hardy said something about going into the hangar next door and there was the sound of a door opening and closing. Then Coffin heard the ringing of an alarm clock and wondered why Hardy had set one. The ringing ended and he dimly became aware of voices, but they sounded far away.

Coffin felt someone shake him. A woman said, "Colonel, get up. We're getting the call now." After more shaking, Coffin realized it was Steiner who was talking to him.

"Give me a minute." Coffin cracked his eyelids and struggled to sit up. Steiner was standing over him. Past her, the television was off and daylight peeked through the window blinds.

"Jesus . . ." Coffin rubbed his face and smoothed his hair. "What time is it?"

"A little after eight, sir," Steiner replied. "Colonel Hardy is talking with Mother; they found the knife in your quarters."

Coffin looked toward the desk, suddenly awake. Hardy was gripping the phone hard enough to break it.

"I'll let you know what we decide, Mother," he said.

Cradling the phone, he eyed Coffin and Steiner. His grim expression said it all but he told them anyway.

"As you probably guessed," he said, "the waiver was granted. The United States didn't want to give in, but their hand was forced and finding the murder weapon was only part of it. What really swung the decision was what we discussed in the car, the response of the Korean public. Everybody knew it could be bad, but nothing like this. And the word is that it's happening outside every American installation, even the ones along the DMZ. The Korean media were showing scenes from Seoul earlier, while you two were asleep. It made me sick to watch it. We've spent billions of dollars and almost fifty thousand lives in a war to protect these people and they're still ready to believe the worst." Picking up a remote control, he reluctantly trained it on the TV, saying, "Anyway, if you want to know why the United States caved, take a look. It's pretty damned disillusioning."

The screen flared and a video appeared, showing an enormous crowd moving along a narrow street, many holding up signs with anti-American slogans, written in Korean and English. In the background, a Korean commentator's staccato rant could be heard. Hardy wearily hit the mute button, cutting him off.

They watched in silence. It was chilling.

The sea of humanity numbered in the thousands. And while the crowd walked peacefully, the promise of violence became apparent when the camera focused on a knife wielding group, stabbing away at an effigy of the American president, as onlookers cheered.

"You notice a lot of people are older?" Hardy asked quietly.

Steiner and Coffin nodded.

The camera continually shifted, focusing on segments of the crowd. Everyone looked grim and angry. As they watched, Hardy mentioned an incident that had prevented the technicians from sweeping Coffin's BOQ for the suspected bug. Coffin only half listened because the presence of a bug seemed of little importance now. Then Hardy said the words, ". . . by a ROK cop."

"The techs are sure, Sam?"

"They're sure. When they left to get more stuff from their van, a ROK cop was hanging around their equipment. Coming back, both guys saw the ROK cop sitting on the couch, giving them a shit-eating grin. That's how they knew it was him: the grin. As soon as they got everything set up and applied power, it was spark city—it turned out that someone had shorted out the power supply. And get this: When the techs looked over at the ROK, he still had that damn grin. Ballsy bastard, huh? Fucks with their stuff and dares them to prove it was him."

Hardy paused, anticipating a response. But Steiner was still worriedly fixated on the TV and Coffin was frowning hard.

"Anyway," Hardy said, fighting a yawn, "Mother blames herself; she said she should have considered that Yee might try to keep them from finding a bug and verifying your story. And if you're wondering, she still intends to sweep your quarters, once the replacement power unit arrives. What was that, Ed?"

Coffin gave him a blank look. "Sorry."

"Just now you said something about Yee."

"Did I? Well, I was wondering how Yee knew we would search for the bug. If he didn't, that suggests the cop acted on his own . . ."

"That's the way Mother figures it. The ROK cop is obviously a Yee stooge. And when he saw the techs arrive, he realized he had to do something fast."

Coffin nodded, as if he agreed. But he still felt uneasy, thinking that it was possible Yee did know of the search beforehand. And if so . . .

Steiner murmured, "No, no . . ."

Her beautiful eyes were locked on the TV, watching in horror as the camera homed in on signs emblazoned with her name and Coffin's. The words murderer and killer scrawled in blood red lettering below them.

No one spoke. One by one, they turned away, unable to watch.

"Anyone know . . . where this is taking place?" Steiner asked haltingly.

"Yes," Hardy said.

He didn't expand on his response. She looked at him.

Sighing, Hardy said, "It's why Mother said her plan to hide you downtown is out the window. The gate is closed and no one can leave because—"

Steiner's head snapped to the TV screen. "My God, it's *Osan.*"

Hardy grimly nodded. "Mother says we need to come up with a game plan. She was leaving to escort the ROK cops to your BOQs, for the arrests. Once they realize you're both gone, they'll mount a search of the entire base, but it will take them a while to get around to looking here. That's the good news; we have time. The bad news is that the ROKs won't be the only ones doing the looking, so you'll have to avoid everyone, including Americans. Mother spoke to Chief Sessler and he told her he'd found a safe location. Since I'm restricted on where I can take you, we won't know if it will be accessible to us. At the very least, we'll need to pre-position a car."

There it was. From his remarks, it was now obvious why Hardy had insisted on coming here. To Coffin, Hardy's foresight wasn't surprising; he never took anything for granted and always planned for worst-case scenarios. Did he know the Koreans would mobilize this rapidly, resulting in a base lockdown? Of course not.

But he thought they just might.

Steiner smiled her appreciation for what Hardy was offering. But she still needed reassurance and requested it now.

"Believe me, Charlotte," he said, "there won't be a problem. The only thing that could gum up the works is if we're surprised before we're ready. But Mother assured me that she'd steer the search away from the flight line—

Just then, they heard banging from the front of the building. "Open up," a man shouted. "I know you're in there. *Open up.*"

★ 34 ★

"God, oh, God . . ."

Steiner twirled like a top, desperately searching for an escape. "We have to get out of here. Is there a back door? *Where's the back door?*"

Coffin and Hardy told her to relax, realizing there was nothing to worry about. But Steiner was too frantic to listen. The banging from the front of the building continued, only now there were two voices calling out—a man's and a woman's. Steiner rushed to the window, peering through the drawn blinds. "I don't see anyone. Where are they? We're probably surround— *You're letting them in?*"

She'd jerked around, reacting to a remark Coffin had just made to Hardy.

"Listen to the voices, Major," Coffin said.

Steiner just looked at him.

"Charlotte," the woman shouted. "If you're in there, let us in, dammit."

A flicker of recognition crossed Steiner's face. She calmly stepped away from the window, flashing an embarrassed smile.

"Want me to get it, Ed?" Hardy asked.

"I'll take care of it."

Coffin left the office, to unlock the front door for the chief and Caralyn.

Coffin had barely cracked the door before Chief Sessler burst through, almost bowling him over. The chief rarely appeared excited, but he did so now.

"Jeez, Colonel," he said, talking a mile a minute with the cigar clenched between his teeth, "you had me and the major worried. We thought maybe you guys took a powder. Good thing you didn't. That goddamn protest threw me for a loop and I had to scramble to find a new place. They're expecting twenty thousand protestors. *Twenty thousand*. Agent Hubbard said General Yee was behind the frame job on you. I knew he was a real sick son of a bitch, the first time I met him. Anyway, you can count on me, sir. If the air force wants to hammer me, fuck 'em. I'm retiring; what are they going to do? Did I tell you the place I found is perfect? Ask Major Barlow here, she'll tell you. Hey, Colonel Hardy. You got a map? You won't believe it until I show you. I mean this place is fucking *perfect*."

The chief lumbered toward Hardy, who stood in his office doorway. The chief's heavy footsteps faded; it grew quiet in the hallway.

"Oh, Ed . . ."

Caralyn's eyes crawled up to Coffin's, her face vulnerable and sad. Sounding lost, she said, "I can't believe any of this. I just . . . can't."

"Then don't." Coffin squeezed her hand. "Yee hasn't won. I have an idea how to get out of this."

She stared at him, hope creeping into her eyes. "You're . . . serious?"

"Very. And I'll need your help and the chief's and maybe a few others'."

"Anything. Tell me what you want us to do."

"As soon as we're inside." Coffin guided her toward the office. "Now about this location the chief found. Is it secure?"

"Absolutely. He drove there this morning. You could be there for weeks and no one would think to look for you there."

As she described it, Coffin felt the beginnings of a smile. For the first time he began to believe he might . . . just might . . . survive long enough to uncover the secret behind Olson's murder. But as he followed Caralyn into Hardy's office, she stopped so suddenly that he bumped into her. And looking past her, he saw the problem at once.

Portrayed in vivid images on the television was yet another shocking twist manufactured by Yee. One that finally and brutally wrenched from Coffin any hope of salvation. But as he stared disbelievingly at the screen, Steiner made a remark that suddenly crystallized what he was really seeing.

"Impossible," she said. "This is impossible."

Chong Do Island.

The video was an overhead shot of the island, taken from a hovering helicopter. Unlike the satellite images that Coffin and Steiner had analyzed earlier, here figures could be seen milling around, most dressed in drab green ROK Army uniforms. Several looked up, showing no concern over the helicopter's presence, and rigid armed sentries guarded the compound, rifles pressed menacingly to their chests, as if posing. Not that anyone in the room gave the island's personnel more than a passing notice, if even that.

Because what held everyone's attention were the three large buildings. More specifically, the buildings' hinged roofs, each of which was folded back to reveal a single white tube. But, of course, they were far more ominous than mere tubes. And as the camera zoomed in on one, everyone recognized the distinctive pointed nose and the fins at the back, as well as the massive articulated arm of—

"A launcher," the chief breathed. "Son of a bitch, the ROKs got missiles ready to launch."

That remark broke the ice and Caralyn and Hardy joined in, voicing their thoughts.

"Nukes? You think the warheads are nukes?"

"Wouldn't make sense otherwise. And you can bet they're pointed right at North Korea."

"I guess this shouldn't be a surprise. We all knew the ROKs were desperate to do something."

"Where'd they get nuclear missiles? Can't be from the United States."

"My guess is Russia, Chief. After the breakup of the Soviet Union, the Russian mafia reportedly smuggled out warheads, to sell on the open market."

"Could be, sir. Those missiles look like Russian Scuds."

And on the theories continued. The blind leading the blind. Until Hardy finally bucked the trend by concluding what he believed was an undeniable certainty.

"Well," he said, "at least we know why Olson was killed. He must have seen these damn nukes on his flight over the island."

He glanced around, anticipating nods of support. He got two, as well as an emphatic negative response from Steiner.

"You're wrong, Colonel," she said flatly. "Major Olson wasn't killed because he saw missiles."

Hardy's surprised expression matched the chief's and Caralyn's. Jabbing at the television, Hardy said, "The hell he wasn't, Charlotte. What do you think those are?"

"Sir, they might look like missiles—"

He snorted. "*Might?* Oh, come on . . ."

"Sam," Coffin said. "What Major Steiner is trying to say is that Erik Olson wasn't killed because of what he saw, but what he didn't see."

"Exactly," Steiner said. "He was killed for nothing."

Now Hardy, the chief, and Caralyn appeared completely lost. It was understandable.

"Better explain, Major," Coffin said.

Anger.

That was the unifying expression on everyone's faces as Steiner described the CARSON returns from Olson's flight over the island. How nothing in the buildings reflected a radar image. "Jesus," Caralyn said, staring at the TV. "If what you're saying is true, Charlotte . . ."

"It is."

"But they look so . . . *real.*"

Steiner shrugged. "They're intended to look real. But since they don't show up on radar, we know they can't be metallic—"

"Wood," the chief said. "The ROKs are bluffing the North with wooden mockups. Go to hell, you lying son of a bitch. *Go to hell.*"

The chief's outburst caught everyone by surprise. Then they saw his eyes focus on the TV and understood.

The image had changed and now showed a ROK general standing at a podium, soundlessly talking into the camera. It was everybody's favorite megalomaniac—Yee.

The chief's hands balled into fists and he looked homicidal. Hardy appeared similarly enraged and snatched up the remote, snarling, "So long, asshole."

The screen went black. Coldly eyeing Coffin, Hardy said, "Whatever it takes, we've got to get that son of a bitch."

Everyone looked at Coffin, waiting for his response.

"It won't be easy, Sam," Coffin began cautiously. "We have to realize we can't expose the ROK deception. Like it or not, they're doing this for survival. Those fake missiles are their only insurance against a pre-emptive North Korean attack— Sam, you don't mean that; you're just upset." Hardy had muttered a disparaging remark about the South Koreans.

"Hell, yes, I'm upset." He puffed up defiantly. "But what I said still goes: The Koreans can go fuck themselves, for all I care. Every chance they get, they scream 'Yankee go home' and treat us like dirt. And these are the same people who kiss the ass of a murdering bastard like Yee and call him a hero. Let me ask you something, Ed. You think if it got out he had Olson killed, your average Korean would give a damn?"

"Sam—"

"Shit, no. Olson's an American. An occupier. The only reason they put up with us GIs is it's in their self-interest. Well, I say we do what's in our self-interest. If the North calls the South Korean bluff, that's too damned bad. The truth is, I got no use for—"

"I'm Korean, Sam," Coffin said.

Hardy stared at Coffin in astonishment. He tried to formulate a response, saying, "I never think of you as Korean, Ed. Not like the rest of . . ."

He trailed off, sensing he was only digging a bigger hole. Shaking his head unhappily, he contemplated the floor. An uncomfortable silence fell upon the room. Steiner and Caralyn turned away from Coffin, as if embarrassed. In contrast, the chief had withdrawn into himself and was looking into space. His face was very red and he was obviously still angry.

"I got a big mouth," Hardy said, finally looking up. "You know I didn't mean anything by it . . ."

"I know."

Hardy sighed, waving to the TV. "It's just . . . Yee. If we can't reveal what we know about the island, I don't see how we get him. I mean, that's what this is all about. That damned island and what's on it."

"There *is* a way, Sam," Coffin said.

"Oh? I thought you said—"

"—it wouldn't be easy. And believe me, it won't. It depends on two things: First, did Yee seek permission before taking out Olson? My hunch is he didn't. Despite the risk Olson posed to the ROK deception plan—" His eyes flickered to Steiner. "And Major Steiner, no one in the South Korean government would dare sanction the murder of an American officer, much less two. They couldn't afford to; they need American support too much— You got something, Major?"

Steiner was pensively nodding.

"It was something Lieutenant Sun once told me, sir," she said. "He mentioned General Yee often expressed disdain over the timidity of senior Korean generals. Particularly General Cho."

Coffin felt the beginnings of another smile. The second piece was sliding into place.

Caralyn said, "You said two things, Ed?"

"Right. This is the hard part. It involves blackmail."

"Blackmail?" the chief said. He tossed his soggy cigar into the trash and peered over with interest, again following the conversation.

"Have a seat, everyone," Coffin said. "This will take a while."

An hour and twelve minutes.

That's how long it took Coffin to explain his plan. To say

that it was met with skepticism would have been an understatement. "Sir, there's no way," or, "Ed, you haven't got a chance in hell," were typical responses, but eventually everyone signed on because the reality was this was the only way to procure evidence for blackmail and, by extension, bring General Yee to justice.

Once the details were worked out, everyone moved swiftly. While Coffin and Steiner clicked away on keyboards and Hardy readied for their eventual departure, the chief checked the dimensions of the hangar next door, then announced, "Plenty of room," and left for the U-2 squadron. Caralyn rode with him but returned an hour later with a flight suit and jacket large enough for Steiner, as well as a bag of burgers and drinks, blankets and toiletries, and other items purchased from the BX. Hardy was impatient to get started and asked the women how long they would need. When they said thirty minutes, he paced for twenty and change, then hurried off, carrying Caralyn's purchases in a duffel bag.

Of course, the women took much longer. When they reappeared, Coffin saw at once the wait was worth it.

"My God," was all he could say.

Steiner had cut and dyed her hair to match Caralyn's. Aided by the skillful application of makeup, they could pass for sisters . . . sort of.

"You got the envelope, Ed?" Caralyn asked.

Coffin passed her two. Caralyn frowned at the second one; it was actually a manila folder with Korean writing on one side, and on the other—

"Huh?" Caralyn said. "This is addressed to Mother and me?"

"Inside are pictures of the woman who I believe is my mother, as well as three letters—one for her, the others for you and Mother. I only want them read if something happens to me."

Caralyn swallowed hard, looking at him. "Jesus, Ed. First Erik and now if something happens to you . . ."

"Now don't bury me yet. What'd I always tell you? If you believe you'll succeed . . ."

"You will," she whispered.

"That's my girl. You ready to do this? Good. Tell Sam we'll make our move five minutes after you drive away— Not yet, there are some items we need to cover." She'd started to leave.

Speaking rapidly, Coffin said, "If you have any trouble finding General Cho's itinerary, talk to Mother. She'll know someone who can probably get it. She'll also help you with the new ID card. That should be your priority, so get it first. If you need to contact us, the chief will have the number. It goes through a ROK military switch, so only use it in an emergency. Getting through the protestors might be a problem, but they should be gone by tonight. My concern is roadblocks; it's a good bet the provincial police will cordon off the area around the base, hoping we might return. So whatever you do, make sure Mother is with you. Let's see, there was something else . . ."

His face went blank.

"The photo," Caralyn said softly.

"Right," Coffin said. "Remind Mother to bring it with her. Now, you'd better get going. You don't want to be around when the fireworks start."

Caralyn nodded numbly. On cue, they heard the faint whine of a turbine engine starting up.

"Come on," Coffin said, putting his arm around her. "I'll walk you out."

As Caralyn left the building, she turned to look back at him. And wave good-bye.

★

Coffin watched Caralyn drive away, noting the time. Five minutes later, he took out one of the pistols he'd taken from the two Koreans, then nodded to Steiner, waiting beside Hardy's desk, her hand on the phone.

"Okay," he said.

She hesitated, her eyes frightened. "You're . . . sure?"

"No choice. It's the only way to focus the search off base."

"If something goes wrong—"

"It won't. It will take them at least a minute to respond. Make the call."

She reluctantly picked up the receiver and punched in a number. As she did, her hand shook, but when she spoke, her voice was calm. "Security Police. Those people you're looking for . . ."

She hung up seconds later. The point of no return.

"All right," Coffin said. "Let's go."

But as he headed for the door, he saw her reach down to pick something off the floor. He was dumbfounded. "Dammit, there's no time for that. *Hurry.*"

★ 35 ★

The Blackhawk helicopter sat on a pad fifty yards away, its rotors spinning. As Coffin and Steiner ran toward it, they kept looking back down the flight line. No cars with flashing lights . . . yet.

The helicopter's cargo door stood open and they scrambled inside. Normally, three crewmembers operated a Blackhawk; today, there was only one. Hardy sat in the right cockpit seat—the aircraft commander's seat—a headset over his ears. He gestured to Steiner, who quickly slid into a rear passenger seat and strapped in. Crouching behind Hardy, Coffin leveled the gun at his friend's head, keeping far enough back to ensure he could be viewed through the open cargo door. The men gazed expectantly down the flight line, waiting.

The seconds ticked by. Despite the cold, Coffin felt a trickle of sweat.

At last, he saw a security police Humvee race around a corner and speed toward them. As it closed, more vehicles appeared, including Mother's sedan and a Korean provincial police cruiser.

"Ed," Hardy shouted. "How long you going to wait?"

"Until they get a good look."

The first Humvee was down to four hundred yards, then three . . . two . . . one . . .

"You're cutting it too close!"

At that instant, Coffin made out two distinct faces in the Humvee. He swung the pistol around, saw their expressions of panic.

"Go, Sam! Go!"

As the Humvee swerved wildly to the side, the helicopter rose into the air.

For the initial portion of the flight, Hardy cruised high enough to be painted by radar. Then when he reached the mountainous terrain to the east, he dipped to treetop level and flew a circuitous route to a rural area, setting down on a road intersection.

By now, Coffin occupied the second pilot seat and wore a headset. Both men gazed out their windows, watching for the car they'd seen as they descended.

"There he is," Sam said.

Cresting a rise, the car drove up to the helicopter, stopping no more than five feet away. The driver was a Korean male, and he eyed the spinning rotors nervously, throwing up a little wave.

Hardy waved back. "Chief's nephew?"

"Brother-in-law."

From a distant farmhouse, they dimly saw people watching them. After a few seconds, Hardy signaled the driver to go. "That should do it. When the provincial cops check, those witnesses will confirm my story about a car meeting the helicopter."

"Except they won't actually see us get inside it."

Hardy shrugged. "From where they were standing, they couldn't swear you didn't."

"Even so—"

"*Quit* worrying. After your Jesse James act, I'll be in the clear."

"What about the radio? They'll want to know why you didn't call in a description of the car."

The Korean was driving away and Hardy had been about to lift off. Sitting back, he said wearily, "Fine. Give me your gun."

"My gun?"

"Just hand it over and tell Charlotte not to get excited."

She still jumped when Hardy pulled the trigger. The smell of burned gunpowder filled the cockpit. "No radio, no problem," Hardy said, grinning at Coffin. "Now quit worrying."

After a short flight, Hardy eased the helicopter into a hover, scant feet off the ground. As he and Coffin scanned the area, Hardy made a slow, 360-degree turn.

"The chief's right," he grunted. "It's a ghost town."

"Make another turn, Sam."

"Oh, for—"

"Yeah, yeah. I worry too much. Humor me."

Coffin couldn't help feeling that this was too easy. But no matter how hard he looked, the only movement he saw was branches swaying with the wind.

After the second turn, Hardy flew to a building that was isolated from the rest. Perhaps forty yards from it was a steel-mesh fence topped by barbed wire, a two-lane road on the other side. Approaching the building, Hardy climbed slightly to view the road in both directions.

"No traffic," he grunted.

"It's only an access road."

The Blackhawk descended in a swirl of white.

*

A perfect place to hide. The chief's words and it looked like it.

After Hardy lifted off, Steiner and Coffin surveyed the snow-covered tarmac of the former U.S. military airfield, half expecting someone to challenge them. But once the chatter of Hardy's rotors faded, the only sound that greeted them was silence.

"Spooky," Steiner murmured.

They stood at the very edge of the airfield, a small brick building just ahead. In air force–ese, these facilities were commonly termed alert shacks, since their purpose was to house fighter pilots near their jets, facilitating a rapid response to airborne threats.

They headed off toward the shack, Coffin lugging the duffel bag, Steiner carrying the burgers and drinks. She said, "Sir, you mentioned you've been here before . . ."

"Right. When Osan's runway was renovated, we staged U-2 operations out of here for several months. This shack is where our pilots stayed. Over there is the hangar we used."

"And it's now a ROK airfield?"

He heard her apprehension and smiled it away. "You can relax. They only use it for quarterly exercises."

She gazed around, still appearing skeptical. "But everything looks like it's maintained. Surely someone keeps it up, sir."

"Maintenance crews inspect the facilities before the exercise. The chief checked; no one is scheduled here for several weeks. Now relax. Those look like one set to you?"

They stopped, peering at a line of footprints in the snow. The prints went from the front door of the building and circled around to the back.

"Definitely one set, sir," Steiner concluded. "It must be the chief."

Coffin eyed a gate in the perimeter fence that was a little farther away than he'd originally estimated. Tire tracks led from the gate to the rear of the building.

Squinting, Steiner said, "There's a lock on the gate." She sounded surprised.

"The chief," Coffin said. "He had to replace the one he busted off."

They went up to the shack's front door. As anticipated, it showed signs of having been forced, a folded wedge of paper jamming it closed. Coffin pushed on the door and it swung open, the paper falling free.

Entering, they felt the warmth. "Chief turned on the heat," Coffin said. He flipped the light switch and the ceiling light came on.

They were essentially in a small apartment, complete with a living/dining area and dime-sized kitchen, two bedrooms, and a bath off to the left. Coffin checked the dial tone on the wall phone by the door, then pulled the drapes on the window facing the fence and the road beyond it. "At night, we need to keep the lights off in here."

Steiner nodded.

They set their supplies down on a rickety dining table. After each claimed one of the windowless, cell-sized bedrooms, they unpacked.

"Pretty dusty," Steiner said, looking around. "Maybe I should clean up a little."

"We won't be here long. Hungry?" He offered her a burger.

A head shake. She looked as tired as he felt. Grabbing a blanket and toiletry items, she said, "Sleep is what I need now. They'll be here when it gets dark, which is what— 1715?"

"About."

"I'll set my watch alarm for 1615."

"Make sure I'm awake." He sat down and unwrapped his food. Steiner watched him, her face becoming troubled.

"It's okay to sleep," Coffin said, smiling. "We're safe for now."

"It's not that, sir."

Coffin picked up something in her tone. "Okay . . ."

"Those pills you take," she said suddenly. "You mind telling me what they're for, sir?"

Coffin managed to hide his surprise. "Major, I don't think that's any of your—"

"Headaches," she said. "Tell me you don't get headaches."

Her tone pleading. Again Coffin checked his surprise . . . barely. "Major, I have no intention of telling—"

He clammed up.

She had a mortified expression, her shoulders sagging. "It's true," she murmured. "You won't deny it because it's true. God, I'm so sorry for you."

Coffin was silent. He told himself she was guessing and couldn't possibly know. But then Steiner hesitantly extended her hand. And lying in her palm, he saw two pill bottles.

His hand went to a pocket.

"They're yours," Steiner said dully. "They were what I picked up in Colonel Hardy's office. When you took out the pistol, you must have dropped them."

Coffin eased out a breath, taking the containers. Steiner watched him, sadness etching her beautiful face. Slowly, Coffin began to understand.

"Your husband?" he said softly.

A vague nod. "Bill took the same medications." She added, "And don't worry, sir; I won't tell anyone."

"I appreciate it, Major. I think it's best that we keep this between us."

"Actually, it isn't, sir."

"Oh?"

She spoke quickly, her tone apologetic. "Sir, I know why you're determined to maintain your secret, but it's entirely the wrong approach. You're not doing anyone a favor by keeping it from them. You really aren't. Having experienced this firsthand, I can tell you that those who love and care for you would rather know—"

She was actually lecturing him? On something this personal? Coffin couldn't believe it. "Major," he snapped, "I think I can make my own decisions."

Steiner was shocked by his tone. "Sir, I didn't mean it like that. Whatever you decide, it's up to you. I was only sharing my experience, so you wouldn't regret—"

"Good night, Major."

She blinked. "Yes, sir. Good night, sir."

She hurried toward her bedroom, looking flustered and hurt. Coffin sighed, watching her. *Ed, you're a jerk.*

"Wait, Major—"

Steiner paused, tentatively looking back.

"Look," Coffin began, searching for the right words, "I didn't mean to cut you off. It's just that I'm not good at this kind of thing. Sharing my problems. Since my parents passed away, I've gotten used to handling things on my own."

A silence.

Coffin offered her an olive branch in the form of a smile. Still no reaction. He said, "Major, I do appreciate your advice. But frankly, I have a hard time believing that it's better for loved ones to know. It will only cause them needless pain."

Her expression thawed. "Sir, that's what I was trying to tell you; the alternative is far worse. In situations like this, the outcome is easier to accept when you're emotionally prepared. Look at the way you're handling it. You told me you weren't afraid any longer. But I'm betting you were in the beginning."

"Point taken, Major. Thanks for the advice."

"Sir, if I might add something else . . ."

Coffin nodded.

"You're going to have questions. I'm not saying I have all the answers, but I have some of them. So if you ever feel like talking . . ."

She trailed off, letting the offer float toward Coffin. He accepted it with another smile. "Thank you . . . Charlotte."

She returned the smile. "You're welcome . . . Ed."

Her response signaled an acceptance of his counter offer; she felt comfortable enough to address him by his first name.

Withdrawing, Steiner softly closed her bedroom door. Afterward, Coffin tried to eat, but couldn't manage more than a few bites. For a long time, he sat at the table, his mind torn by conflicting thoughts. He tried to concentrate on the task at hand, go over his mental checklist so he would avoid a crucial mistake. But all he could think about was what Steiner had said and the irony of his situation. If he failed in his attempt tonight, there was nothing to be gained by telling Mother, because the end result would be the same.

No choice; he had to wait.

"It's after six, Ed," Steiner said, glancing at her watch. "They're late."

"They'll be here, Charlotte," Coffin replied.

"If something happened? If they couldn't get through the protestors—"

"We would have gotten a call; they'll be here."

They were standing in darkness, bracketing the window, eyes fixed on the gate. In the past twenty minutes, they hadn't seen a single vehicle. With the base in hibernation, no one had a reason to come here.

Another minute passed. Steiner fidgeted with her newly cut hair. She wore the flight suit Caralyn had given her and looked every inch a military aviator. But of course, she wasn't.

"Lights," Steiner said. "*Finally.*"

Through a fence of bare trees, they watched flickering headlights approach.

"Definitely a car," Steiner murmured.

As opposed to a truck or a van.

Nearing the darkened turnoff, the car didn't slow, and Coffin began to worry the driver would miss it. But moments later, he saw brake lights and after a slight fishtail on the snowy road, the driver successfully negotiated the turn, stopping at the gate. For several long beats, the vehicle just sat there, the engine running.

"What's she doing?" Steiner said. "That is Mother's car, isn't it?"

"Looks like it."

Finally, the high beams flashed on and off, twice.

"Stay here," Coffin said, stepping away. "I'll help Mother unlock the gate."

"That might be a problem, sir," Steiner said.

Frowning, Coffin took another peek out the window. Under the moonlight, two people were visible, emerging from the car. Though they were fifty yards away, Coffin saw enough of their silhouettes to know only one of them was expected.

Steiner had called it; they had a problem.

★ 36 ★

Since she was OSI chief, Mother's presence guaranteed safe passage to the base without the car being searched. But as Coffin jogged toward the gate, he was met by the familiar faces of Caralyn and Chief Sessler.

He bent down, looking into the car. Empty. Caralyn and the chief greeted him with tired smiles; Coffin was in no mood to reciprocate. "Why isn't Mother here?" he demanded. "Don't the provincial police have roadblocks up?"

"Only in the last couple hours, sir," the chief said, inserting a key into the lock. "They had to wait until the army cleared out the protestors."

Coffin clenched his teeth. For a moment, he was too angry to speak.

"Ed," Caralyn said hastily, "Mother got called out to investigate an assault case. It was something she had to respond to—"

"An *assault* case?" Coffin finally erupted. "She put us at risk because of an assault case? What was Mother thinking? She knew we needed her—"

He instantly deflated, looking at Caralyn in astonishment. Because she'd just spoken over him, answering his question.

"My God," Coffin said. "Marty Bell was the person who was assaulted?"

"More like attempted murder, sir," the chief offered up, pocketing the lock. "Colonel Bell was strangled with a rope until he lost consciousness and is damn lucky to be alive. Whoever attacked him wanted to make it look like suicide."

"Suicide?" Coffin said.

The chief shrugged. "Agent Hubbard found a bag the guy dropped. It had rope and some kind of metal gizmo with a hook on the end. You know, to string the rope through." He motioned Coffin aside, walking open the gate.

"His attacker?" Coffin said. "Can Marty identify him?"

Matching head shakes. Caralyn said, "The problem was that Colonel Bell was asleep in his bed—"

"Drunk," the chief sang out, "he was passed out, drunk."

"—and woke up in the middle of being strangled," Caralyn went on. "The guy straddled him from behind and Colonel Bell never saw his face before losing consciousness again."

Reading Coffin's frown, she added, "Colonel Bell *survived* because someone shot his assailant before the guy could finish him off, Ed. According to Mother, this is the really puzzling part. She found indications that the shooter hid in Colonel Bell's bedroom closet. If true, he obviously knew beforehand an attempt would be made on Bell's life. But how and who is he?"

On those points, Coffin couldn't even venture a guess. But as to why . . .

"Marty," he said. "He must have been Yee's accomplice, and Yee decided he was too dangerous to live."

Two heads nodded back.

Coffin followed the thread, saying, "Even if Marty doesn't confess, it doesn't matter. The attempt on his life bolsters Charlotte's and my story. Only Yee had a reason to—"

He fell silent. The nods had turned into head shakes.

"You have two major hurdles to overcome, Ed," Caralyn said quietly. "First, the evidence against you: Mother says the big boys have decided it's just too damning for them to consider withdrawing the waiver until they get slam-dunk proof of your innocence, independently verified by the FBI."

Coffin had forgotten they were about to take over the case. "That could take weeks."

"At least."

Coffin sighed. But it wasn't as if Mother hadn't warned him. "And the second hurdle?"

"Those missiles," Caralyn said. "They've made Yee untouchable, Ed. The Korean public regards him as some kind of savior, for installing them on his private island and protecting the country. Mother said if he ran for president now, he'd win in a landslide—Ed? You okay?"

Coffin was smiling oddly, as he internally kicked himself. "Jesus, I should have seen it. You're absolutely right, Caralyn. That's what this was all about from the beginning. Yee doesn't care about protecting South Korea; he wants to be president."

"Fuckin' A he wants to be president," the chief said. "All that bastard wants is *power*. He is one evil son of a bitch. You hear me. He is fucking *evil*."

Another angry outburst that came out of nowhere. Noticing Coffin and Steiner watching him, the chief inhaled raggedly, calming himself. Forcing a smile, he said, "Sorry, but when I think about Major Olson. What that bastard did to him . . ."

"We'll get Yee, Chief," Coffin said softly.

"You really think it's possible now, Ed?" Caralyn asked. Coffin looked at her.

"Mother and I were talking," she said, "and we're worried. Yee's popularity changes the equation. It's given him power. Real power. Even General Cho might not have the balls to cross him."

Their eyes met. She was really asking if the blackmail card was still on the table.

Coffin took his time before replying. He had to be absolutely sure. He recalled what he could about Cho's reputation and his own impressions at their few meetings.

"We're okay," Coffin said finally. "In the end, it's still an offer Cho can't refuse."

Caralyn got in the car and drove through the gate. As the chief pulled it closed, he verified a suspicion voiced by Coffin, regarding Colonel Bell's assailant.

"Mother figures it must have been Kwan," the chief said. "A lady colonel up the street heard the shot, but by the time she went outside, the guy was jumping into a car. She said he might have been Korean."

"Could she tell if he wore glasses?"

"Mother never said, sir." The chief shrugged.

"But she's sure he was wounded?"

"Oh, he was wounded, all right. There was a blood trail."

When Coffin went with the obvious follow-up, the chief said the witness never saw the second man because he'd snuck out the back—a fact confirmed by footprints.

Locking the gate, the chief eyed Coffin, adding, "You know, sir, if he did shoot Kwan, he did us a helluva favor. No way Kwan can mess with us, not with a bullet in him. Hell, the bastard might even be dead by now."

Coffin nodded, concluding the same thing. Caralyn had

driven to the opposite side of the building, out of view of the road. Since she would have the car unloaded by the time they arrived, the chief and Coffin headed for the alert shack. As they walked, Coffin decided to go over the more crucial aspects of his personal checklist with the chief. But first, he needed to confirm another suspicion.

"Chief," he said, "you don't seem concerned about getting past the police roadblocks."

"Oh, I'm not, sir. I got a sure-fire way to keep them from hassling us. It's why we were late. We had to swing by clothing sales. Get me a new Class A uniform." He reached into his coat pocket.

"I'll bite," Coffin said. "Why do you need new Class As?"

"'Cause stripes wouldn't go with these, sir."

Grinning triumphantly, the chief thrust up a small plastic envelope to Coffin. Looking at it, Coffin couldn't see well enough in the moonlight to tell what was inside. But once he felt the contents, he knew.

"Jesus, Chief," he said. "You're actually *serious?*"

"Like a heart attack. We even picked up the DV plates from Motor Pool. Why, you don't you think it'll work, sir?" He sounded disappointed.

"It'll work. I'm just picturing you wearing those."

As he said it, he recalled what Bell had told him and was amused by the irony of the situation. And despite everything, Coffin had to laugh.

During the remainder of the short walk, Coffin rapidly cycled through his plan. Mentally checking off each item, as the chief responded.

"All the equipment in place?" Coffin asked.

"Yes, sir."

"Encounter any problems?"

"Not a one, sir. Everyone knew we needed extra hangar space on account of all the wreckage we're storing."

"What about additional personnel?"

"Not worth the risk, sir. Major Barlow, Colonel Hardy, and me can handle everything." He shrugged.

"So Colonel Hardy's in the clear?"

"Yes, sir. Agent Hubbard handled his questioning and kept the ROKs off him."

"Did he say when we could expect a call?"

"Maybe an hour. Still too many people around. The runway is back open and the fighters are night flying."

"Are the protestors expected back?"

"Not if they're smart. When they started tearing up the town, the ROK Army busted serious heads to clear them out. Shot a few, too."

"So the base is still in lockdown?"

"Yes, sir, but it's no problem. Agent Hubbard cleared everything with the gate guards."

"And the letter Caralyn gave you . . ."

"Will be delivered as soon as I make the call."

They came to the front door. Pushed through. "Anything I'm missing, Chief?"

"Nothing important, sir. Oh, we brought subs. Best we could do."

But as they bypassed the darkened living area and went into Steiner's bedroom, where the two women had gathered, Coffin realized at once that something important had been forgotten. Only not by him.

"The photograph was *stolen*?"

Steiner and Caralyn sat cross-legged on the cot, eating subs. Caralyn nodded energetically at Coffin, trying to answer him and chew at the same time.

"Fom da bath-theet of da ca."

"It was taken from the backseat of her car," the chief translated.

"Da ca wath wocked."

"The car was locked, sir," the chief added.

"I got all that, but—" Coffin grimaced at Caralyn in frustration. "I don't understand how Yee knew you had it. He *couldn't* have known."

Caralyn took an enormous swallow and replied in lucid English, "A provincial cop lieutenant was hanging out in Mother's office right before she gave it to me. We thought he'd gone, but maybe he hadn't."

"A bug," Steiner tossed out. "Yee could have bugged Mother's office."

Nods all around. Except for Coffin, who'd gone still, staring into space. No one said anything. They let him have his time, to think.

The seconds passed. Steiner and Caralyn resumed eating. Everyone continued to watch Coffin. But he never moved.

Finally, his eyes flickered. "No," he murmured.

The chief frowned. "No, on the bug angle, or— What, sir?"

Coffin was shaking his head. He said, "Yee had *no* reason to take the photo, because he gains nothing except time. Not if Mother still has the original."

"She does," Caralyn said, putting down her sandwich. "I saw it in her safe."

"Then all Yee has accomplished is to draw attention to it. Ensures Mother will scrutinize the photo until she *does* find something."

"Time," Steiner said, shrugging. "Maybe all Yee was interested in was buying time."

"How long does it take to have a photo enlarged?" Coffin countered. "An hour? What's the point?"

Steiner was silent. So was everyone else.

Coffin said, "What makes this so confusing is that Yee *is* the logical choice to have arranged this theft. He had Kwan steal Marty Bell's copy from his office; there's obviously something in the photo he doesn't want us to see. But since Mother still has her original, we know it wasn't Yee. He wouldn't have left it behind; he isn't stupid and he certainly isn't sloppy. And that's what we're talking about here. Someone who is sloppy and stupid, or maybe for his own reasons wants to implicate— Oh, hell."

Just like that it hit Coffin. What he was about to say and what it implied. And from the growing excitement on the faces of the others, it was apparent that they'd made the connection also.

"The same guy," Steiner said. "It must be the same guy."

"Sure he's the same guy," the chief said. "He's out to get Yee, just like us."

"But who is he?" Caralyn said. "Who could he possibly be?"

The million-dollar question. But at least they now realized that the person who had saved Marty's life and later stolen the photo from Caralyn's car were likely one and the same.

The chief gave a little cough. "Uh, boss . . ."

"I hear it, Chief."

All eyes turned uneasily to the closed bedroom door. The wall phone in the other room was ringing. And it shouldn't be.

"Kill the lights," Coffin ordered.

Coffin opened the bedroom door. Moonlight filtered through the window, bathing the room in a soft glow.

He went toward the ringing phone, the others filing behind. "Sir, it can't be Hardy," the chief said. "The fighters are still night flying."

"Quiet. How many rings is that?"

"Four," Caralyn said. "Now five."

Coffin said, "If it stops anywhere after eight, we'll know it's Hardy."

To preclude any chance that someone might eavesdrop on their conversation, Hardy would communicate their arrival time by hanging up after the appropriate number of rings.

They all circled the phone. Caralyn said, "There's seven. Eight . . ."

"He should hang up soon," Steiner said.

But the rings continued. Midnight came and went. And still the phone rang. Until it mercifully stopped.

"Well," the chief said. "We know it's not Colonel Hardy, sir."

"No . . ."

"It's General Yee," Steiner said, her voice shaking. "He was checking on us. Somehow he knows we're here."

No one responded. She'd only voiced what they were thinking.

Coffin and the chief went to the window, looked toward the gate. Everything was still and quiet.

"Be better to take a look outside, sir."

Coffin nodded, taking out his pistol and following the chief to the door. But before they could leave, the phone began to ring again.

"Whoever it is," Caralyn said, "obviously knows we're—" She cut Coffin a look. "An emergency?"

"One way to find out," Coffin said.

He picked up the phone.

★

Recognizing Mother's voice, Coffin repeated her name, generating expressions of relief. Looks of irritation soon followed because of what Coffin relayed next.

"You gotta be kidding me, Ed," Caralyn said. "Mother wants a *private* conversation with you?"

"She's insisting on it," Coffin said. "She says it's important."

"What are we supposed to do?" the chief asked irritably. "Plug our damn ears?"

"Mother suggested you go the bedrooms," Coffin offered.

"Sir, with all due respect—"

"Five minutes, Chief. That's all."

The chief rolled his eyes in disgust. But he turned and headed toward the bedrooms. Steiner obediently followed him.

But not Caralyn.

"Tell Mother I'm not going," she snapped.

"Caralyn . . ."

"No. I know you two just got back together and are hot for each other, but this is ridiculous. And dangerous. Who knows what phone she's calling from. If it's her office, we discussed the possibility that Yee might have bugged—"

"It's not her office."

"I don't care. That call goes through the ROK Army switchboard. You said we could be compromised—"

"This is an emergency. There's a break in the case she wants to tell me about."

Coffin had mistakenly thought the admission would settle the argument. It had the opposite effect. Now Caralyn appeared really put out.

"A break in the case?" she flung back. "And Mother doesn't want us to know to about it?"

"Caralyn, go to the—"

"No. No."

She puffed up stubbornly and Coffin knew better than to ask again. Sighing, he said to Mother, "You got two out of three."

"Who stayed?"

When he told her, Mother said, "That's okay, Ed. She's not the problem."

It was a disconcerting remark. So was the pregnant pause that followed it.

"Mother?"

An audible sigh. "Still here, Ed. I'm not sure how I can even tell you this. To be honest, I can't believe it myself. I must have listened to the tape twenty times. And with that damn whisper—"

Coffin squeezed the phone hard. "Tape? You have *Sun's* tape?"

Caralyn appeared startled. A giant step later, she'd wedged her head close to the phone, listening in.

"Yeah," Mother said. "It turned out he'd made a second copy and given it to his sister. If it weren't for the riots, she would have gotten it to us earlier. Ed, this is going to come as a shock. You should know that there's a chance I'm wrong, but I don't think so—"

Caralyn stepped away, looking over her shoulder. Then she went tense, murmuring, "Lord . . ."

Coffin turned, then did a double-take that almost snapped his neck. He fought to keep his cool, to think. In his ear, Mother continued to speak, saying, "—even in a whisper, there was something familiar about the voice. I'm almost convinced it belongs to—"

"It's not the chief," Coffin said loudly.

Caralyn jerked around at the remark. Mother said, "Not

the chief? You haven't heard the tape. I'm telling you it's his voice."

"You're wrong, Mother. The chief is innocent.

"Ed, I've got the cassette right here. Let me play it for you—"

"Later. Right now, I don't have time. But take my word for it, you're on the wrong track. It's definitely not the chief's voice."

And he hung up on her.

★ 37 ★

Seconds earlier, a palpable fear had permeated the room. Now, confusion reigned.

Standing near the bedrooms, the chief and Steiner had gone slack-jawed over Coffin's remarks. And Caralyn was giving him a bug-eyed look, as if he'd lost his mind.

And perhaps he had.

But in the shock of the moment—at the precise instant he'd turned around while on the phone—his mind had kicked into high speed like a processor on full compute. Trying to bridge a logic gap between what he was witnessing—the validity of it—and what he believed he already knew.

—*The chief's recent outbursts against Yee—those weren't theatrical displays; they were real.*

—*His genuine shock and subsequent anger, when Steiner concluded the missiles were fake.*

—*The appearance of the two Koreans outside the bar, the ones who'd been warned that Coffin and Steiner were en route to talk to Sun.*

—*The chief's presence at the U-2 squadron the night Olson's plane was sabotaged.*

—*The photo that was stolen from Caralyn, one that Yee*

would have no apparent interest in, but someone who was in it—someone from the squadron—would.

And there was more: There was the person who had saved Bell and stolen the photo from Caralyn's car.

And, of course, there was the gun. The one that the chief was brandishing now, as he stood beside a very frightened Major Steiner.

As well as the fact that Coffin had a history with the chief and knew him well.

"Okay," Coffin suddenly said to Steiner. "We're okay."

She just looked at him. The chief started to respond, but he was interrupted by Caralyn's icy: "*Okay?* You actually think we're okay, Ed?"

"Yes. There's nothing to worry about."

Caralyn really torched off then, furiously gesturing at the chief. "*Nothing to worry about?* He's got a gun. He rushed out here with it when he realized Mother had found Sun's tape. That proves it was his voice. He's the sellout. He's the person who helped Yee kill Olson."

Coffin said, "Caralyn . . ."

"On top of that, you just defended him to Mother. Said he was innocent. And now you're saying we've got nothing to worry about. It's like you two are somehow involved in this thing together." She sounded completely disgusted.

"You know me better than that," Coffin replied calmly.

"Then why, sir?"

This remark came from the chief. Coffin briefly contemplated him, seeing what he wanted. A mixture of shame and regret.

Coffin eased toward him. Instantly, the barrel locked on his chest.

"That's far enough, sir."

Coffin cautiously took another step. The chief's finger

tightened on the trigger. "For God's sake, listen to him, Ed," Steiner said. "What are you trying to prove?"

"He won't shoot," Coffin said, walking slowly.

"The hell I won't," the chief said roughly. "You're trying to get close enough to use your Tae Kwon Do."

Coffin continued walking. By now, Caralyn had joined the chorus with Steiner, telling him to stop. The chief drifted back, jabbing the pistol menacingly. He said, "Sir, this is your last warning. If you take another fucking step—"

Coffin calmly took two more, backing the chief into the bedroom doorway. He held out his hand.

"Give me the gun, Chief."

The chief glared at him. "You loco? Why the hell would I do that?"

"Because," Coffin said quietly, "Yee isn't here."

The chief's eyes flickered in surprise. He sighed heavily, comprehension crossing his face. Steiner and Caralyn watched him in growing amazement. "Jesus," Steiner said, "that's *right*."

In a resigned voice, the chief said to Coffin, "I'd never have called him, sir. I hated the bastard. He lied to me from the start. When he first approached me, he said he only wanted information. That's all. Just a little information. No one was supposed to get hurt."

Coffin didn't say anything. He just stood there, with his hand extended. Waiting.

The seconds ticked by. The chief continued to point the gun at him.

"It's over, Chief," Caralyn said softly. "Unless you're willing to kill us all to get out of here."

The chief's eyelid twitched. He said nothing.

Caralyn came forward and stood beside Coffin.

Moments later, Steiner followed suit.

The message was clear; it was three against one and they knew he wouldn't shoot.

Even now, surrender wasn't easy for the chief. For what seemed a long time, he stood there shaking his head, agonizing over the decision. At one point, he even turned on the bedroom light to consult a picture in his wallet, becoming visibly emotional. Finally, with a hesitant hand, he placed the gun in Coffin's palm, murmuring a Korean word, as if in explanation.

Coffin nodded, signaling he understood.

Caralyn said to him, "*Ga-jok* means . . ."

"Family," Coffin replied. To the chief, he said, "You told me the same thing yesterday."

The chief nodded dully. "I wanted to tell you the truth then, sir. But I couldn't bring myself to do it."

"Your involvement with Yee," Coffin said quietly. "Your Korean in-laws must have business dealings with him and pressured you to cooperate—"

"No," the chief said. "They had nothing to do with it. I did it for revenge. I did it for her."

He held out the picture in the wallet to Coffin. It was a family portrait and Coffin automatically focused on the chief's wife. Then the chief pointed out a different face and Coffin froze, staring. Taking the wallet, he tilted the picture toward the light. His hand started to tremble.

"Ed," Caralyn said, "what's the matter? You look like you've seen a ghost."

"He has," the chief replied.

The chief sat on the edge of the bed, talking in a somber voice filled with pain—a father's pain. "You saw her . . . how beautiful she was. She was that way as a child . . . both girls were . . . so beautiful and sweet. From the first . . . they accepted me as their father . . . always wanted to hang around me. You know, like kids do when they're young . . . before they get too old . . ." He took a big swallow, fighting his emotions. "But the funny thing was they never stopped wanting to be with me . . . even when they were teens . . . Oh, Jesus . . ."

He blinked rapidly, almost losing it. "Man, this is hard."

Coffin, Steiner, and Caralyn stood before him, nodding sympathetically. "Take your time, Chief," Coffin said gently.

The chief fortified himself with several deep breaths. When he spoke, his voice was still subdued but contained a hint of anger. "I blame myself for her death. I told her . . . told both my girls . . . that they didn't have to settle for what Korean society was telling them . . . could do anything they wanted. If I hadn't pushed them . . . if I'd kept my mouth shut . . ." He trailed off, shaking his head. "The oldest girl, Yong-chee . . . wanted to be a reporter . . . become a TV anchor . . . but knew she could never crack the good ole boys club here in Korea. So she went to the States. Got hired by a station in Seattle. I encouraged my youngest . . . my baby . . . to join her sister. You know . . . for the opportunities.

"But she didn't want to be away from her mother and me. Didn't even want to go up to Seoul. She went to college there . . . didn't like it. So she hunted for jobs around town. Clerks and sales. Jobs that were beneath her. So . . . I suggested the base. I had contacts, figured I could get her a job as a secretary or maybe even one of the junior management positions at the NCO Club. Anyway, I made some calls and a guy I know at the personnel office said I might try the ROKs. They were always looking for people fluent in English. So I did, and that's where I made my mistake.

"The next day I got a call at work and it's Yee himself on the line. And he's telling me that he wants to hire my little girl as a translator. Right then, I should have realized something was up. I didn't think he knew me from Adam and he's talking like we're old friends. Going on about how he'd seen my daughter with me and even talked to her a couple times." The chief looked up at Coffin. "Sir, you know Yee came to the squadron the day of Bell's promotion party. He spoke to her then, right after we had the picture taken."

Coffin faintly remembered. "So that's how he knew she was in it."

"Yes, sir. After he showed her photo in the briefing last night, he was all in a panic, thinking you might spot the picture in Colonel Bell's office and make the connection to me."

Coffin nodded. While he and Mother probably should have noticed the resemblance, they'd been thrown off by the glasses and long hair, which the chief's youngest daughter had worn in the promotion photograph, but not in the one at the briefing.

"She was a beautiful girl," Coffin said gently.

"Yeah . . ."

The chief got quiet, looking at his big hands. Shaking his head, he said, "It turns out that's why Yee recruited her. Because of her beauty. And I encouraged her to take the job. Hell, I practically forced her. Of course, the son of a bitch never told me he was going to turn her into a spy. If he had, I'd a' never allowed her to do it. She was my baby girl and I was supposed to protect her. But I didn't and that's something I have to live with.

"It damn near killed my wife and me, when we learned she was dead. And when Yee told me how it was done . . . my wife still doesn't know . . . I couldn't tell her. Jesus, the North Korean bastards threw her from a building like she was a piece of trash. When I heard that, I knew the meaning of hate. All I could think about was killing every one of those motherfuckers north of the DMZ and said so to Yee's face. I was just talking, but the next thing Yee says to me is that maybe there was a way to do exactly that.

"That's how it all started, me helping him. When he told me about getting nukes . . . real fucking nukes, not that fake bullshit we saw on TV . . . and that he planned to fire them at the North, I was all for it. I know it sounds crazy now, hearing me talk about killing millions of people, but that's the way I felt. Like I said, I was filled with hate.

"Anyway, what Yee wanted from me was to talk to the pilots after their flights. Make sure none of them strayed over Chong Do and saw something they weren't supposed to see. Since the island was well south of our normal tracks, I figured it was a no-brainer. That there'd be nothing to tell him.

"Then Olson flew that test flight and everything changed. When I spoke to him after he landed, he told me about these large buildings he'd seen on an island. From the CARSON, he could tell the buildings were completely empty. He thought that was strange as hell and intended to talk to Major Steiner—" the chief's eyes sought her out "—and ask her about it.

"Now, he never told me it was Chong Do, but I knew right away that's what he was talking about. So I gave Yee a heads-up, telling him he might have a problem. Looking back, I should have known what he might do, but to tell you the truth, it never occurred to me he'd want to kill Olson. If I had, I never would have gone along. I swear to God."

His gaze flowed over Steiner, Caralyn, and Coffin, searching for a sign that they believed him. Their expressions remained blank, revealing nothing.

Steiner said, "On the tape, you told Yee when Major Olson was flying."

"Right. He was going to carry the CARSON again. You remember? You requested another test flight, but there was some kind of software glitch—"

"So we rescheduled," Steiner finished.

"Exactly," the chief said. "But the thing was, Major Olson was *supposed* to fly with it and Yee was worried he'd make another pass at Chong Do. And that's what I was doing on the tape, confirming that the flight was a go for the next day."

"So Yee could do what, exactly?" Coffin said.

The chief shrugged. "Yee said he might have me break the CARSON permanently. But it never came to that because I later passed him the word about the change, that the CARSON had been pulled from the jet and wouldn't be on board after all." Noticing Coffin's skepticism, he added, "I spoke to him at his home, sir. That's why that conversation isn't on the tape."

Coffin's skepticism remained. Caralyn's and Steiner's heads were going back and forth; they were similarly unconvinced.

The chief sighed unhappily, watching them. "The sabotage," he concluded quietly. "You still think I was involved in the sabotage."

A statement, not a question. Coffin and the two women said nothing.

"Oh, hell," the chief said, sounding tired. "I know how it looks, but the honest to God's truth is that I had no clue Yee intended to spike Olson's oxygen. In fact, the first hint I got that he was up to something was when I received a phone call from Yee late that night. He wanted me to go to the hangar where Olson's airplane was and help Kwan slip out of it without being spotted. Kwan had crawled over the back fence, snuck into the hangar during shift change. Once the incoming crew showed up, he was stuck. I was plenty pissed, I can tell you. When I confronted Kwan, he gave me this song and dance about how he'd come to disable the CARSON. I knew that was bullshit, since I passed the word to Yee himself that the CARSON wasn't flying. But Kwan insisted Yee never told him.

"So right then I knew I might have a problem. And that Kwan was probably there to mess up the airplane. Still, I couldn't be sure until I checked out the jet completely. And that's what I did, after I got Kwan out of there, in my truck. I came back and inspected the airplane. I concentrated on the engine and the fuel system, because that's what made sense. If you're going to make a plane unflyable, you screw with the engine or contaminate the fuel.

"And that was another fucking mistake. It never occurred to me that he'd tamper with the oxygen system, and the truth is, I never even looked at it. So I guess that's your answer right there. No, I didn't have anything to do with actually killing Olson, but the bottom line was, it was still my fault he died. Just like my baby girl, Song-chee. Both of them are dead because I didn't keep them safe. And that was my job. I knew Yee was up to no good—"

The chief went silent.

He was frowning at Steiner, who was staring at him in horror.

"Charlotte?" Caralyn asked, alarmed. "What is it? What's wrong?"

"Your daughter," Steiner said to the chief, sounding dazed. "The one who was murdered. Her name was Song-chee."

The chief cautiously nodded.

Steiner shook her head, eyeing Coffin. "It can't be coincidence, Ed. That case I told you about, the reason Sun was so afraid. *Song*. That's why it stuck in my head. It was like . . . songs."

It took Coffin a moment. "You're talking about the man who worked for Yee? The one he supposedly had killed?"

"Right. I'm not familiar with Korean names. I *assumed* it was a man."

Coffin felt a chill.

Steiner turned to Caralyn and the chief, intending to break the news to them. But neither needed an explanation; they'd overheard enough to fill in the blanks.

Caralyn began murmuring, "That murdering bastard," over and over, while the chief went perfectly rigid, his face a mask of naked hate.

For a full minute, he neither moved nor even appeared to breathe. Not even when Coffin tapped his arm and said his name.

It was scary to watch.

★38★

Abruptly, the chief returned to life and stuck out his hand to Coffin, demanding his pistol. Coffin advised him that wasn't a good idea, not in the chief's emotional state. The men went back and forth, arguing heatedly. Ultimately, the chief prevailed when he threatened to take off.

Still, before surrendering the weapon, Coffin was able to extract a crucial concession—that the chief take no action until Coffin's plan played out.

Afterward, Steiner and Caralyn seemed skeptical that the chief would keep his word. While it was a valid concern, Coffin was also troubled by an even more worrisome possibility. At his core, the chief was an honorable, decent man, and at some point, he would pay a terrible price for his role in the deaths of his daughter and Olson. It could take a year or five, but eventually the guilt would become a burden too crushing to bear.

Whether he might actually kill himself, Coffin could only surmise. One thing he did know was that from this day forward, the chief's life would be a living hell.

For that reason, Coffin never asked if he'd made the call, warning Yee's men that he and Steiner were en route to speak with Sun. Frankly, Coffin was worried about the effect the question would have on the chief. The man was clearly teetering on the brink of an emotional precipice, and forcing another admission from him could send him over the edge.

Besides, the presence of a bug in Coffin's quarters would provide the answer, so there was nothing to be gained by rubbing the chief's face in it now.

The man was suffering enough.

An hour later, the phone rang again. Coffin suspected it could be Mother, but it stopped after precisely nine rings.

"Twenty-one hundred hours," Coffin said, glancing at his watch. "We need to leave in forty minutes."

"Make it thirty, sir," the chief said, unbuttoning his shirt. "We have to deal with the roadblocks. Major Barlow, where did you put the uniforms?"

"The bedroom closet," Caralyn said, hurrying over to show him.

In twenty minutes, everyone was ready.

As the car approached the police checkpoint at the outskirts of the Ville, the only occupants were the chief and Caralyn. Both wore immaculate Class A blue uniforms, complete with gleaming rank and chests full of colored ribbons.

Caralyn drove, while the chief sat in the back. Tapping the brakes, she slid onto the end of the slow moving queue of vehicles. Ahead, two provincial policemen with flashlights were peering into cars and waving them through. Along the shoulder, a graying officer was barking orders to another cop, who was searching a pickup. Two young American enlisted men stood off to the side, watching nervously.

The line of cars continued to move. From the backseat, the chief said, "Remember, Major. We act pissed off. They have to know we mean business."

"Got it."

"But not too quick. Just follow my lead. And whatever happens, we don't agree to a search."

"If they insist . . ."

"Trust me. They won't."

They crept toward the checkpoint. One car to go . . .

The cop on the left beckoned. As Caralyn rolled forward, she and the chief lowered their windows. The cop casually swung his flashlight around to her and blinked in surprise. He addressed her in Korean; seemed irritated when she didn't respond. The cop had a brief conversation with his partner, standing by the passenger door. The man shrugged.

The first cop motioned Caralyn from the car. As he did, he shined his flashlight in the backseat. At that moment, the chief exploded.

"God *dammit*," he roared. "What's going on here? Why are we being delayed? Didn't you see the placard out front? I am an American two-star general." He furiously gestured to the silver stars on his shoulder. "Now *let us pass*."

The policeman was stunned by the verbal barrage, as was his partner. Though they didn't understand the chief's words, his apparent rage was enough. They nervously stepped back, calling out to the graying policeman.

As Grayhair came over, Caralyn stuck her arm out the window and pointed down to the front bumper, where a two-star placard was attached. She said, "He's an air force general. You understand? A *general*."

The senior man stared at the placard in astonishment. He angrily called out to the two junior men and pointed to it. The men dropped their heads guiltily.

"Now it's going to get good," the chief said softly.

"Good?" Caralyn said.

"You'll see."

Grayhair verbally badgered the first cop. The man responded meekly, and apparently it was the wrong thing to say. Grayhair viciously slapped him across the face. The cop ducked, yelping in pain.

Grayhair dragged him to the chief's window. Both men bowed low and Grayhair rattled off Korean to the chief. He pointed disgustedly to the junior cop and looked at the chief expectantly.

The chief gazed back blankly, pretending he didn't understand.

Grayhair said something else to him and pushed the junior officer forward. The man cowered before the chief, visibly shaking.

"Go," the chief said. "We only want to go."

"*Geu-reo-se-yo?*" Grayhair sounded disappointed.

He glared at the junior man and jerked his head. The man withdrew, bobbing and scraping.

To the chief, Grayhair said, "Yes, go. Sorry. Very sorry."

He backed away from the car, his head bent low.

Caralyn stepped on the gas. As she drove away, she glanced in the rearview mirror, shaking her head. "Jesus, that senior cop is still ragging on the other two."

"Don't feel too sorry for them, Major. They got off lucky." The chief took off his jacket and balled it up. He unzipped a gym bag at his feet and removed another blue jacket, one with stripes on the sleeves.

"Lucky?" Caralyn said.

"You obviously didn't get why the sergeant brought the other cop to me. He was making me an offer. If I was a Korean general, I would have been expected to take him up on it."

"Offer?"

He looked at her in the rearview mirror. "Can't you guess?"

Her eyebrows shot up. "You aren't suggesting . . ."

The chief nodded, donning the jacket. "You got it. The sergeant wanted me to beat on the guy. It's the only way he could save face for the man's embarrassing me. Don't take this wrong, Major, but I think I might have enjoyed it. Kicking the ever-living shit out of someone."

His tone was matter-of-fact. He wasn't making a bad joke; he was telling the truth.

Caralyn was silent.

"We're in the clear," the chief said, looking behind. "Pull over any time, Major."

It was a necessary pit stop; they had to yank the two-star placard from the front bumper. And since enlisted usually chauffeured officers, they opted for a seat swap to avoid raised eyebrows.

They arrived at Osan from the south, avoiding the Ville's main drag, now littered with broken glass in the riot's aftermath. As expected, the guards waved them through the main gate, courtesy of the kitchen pass provided by Mother. A few minutes before nine, they turned down the flight line and drove toward the Jolly Green hangar.

"No one's flying," Caralyn said, remarking on the obvious.

"Tower will still be a problem," the chief said, peering up at it as they drove past. "It's manned around the clock."

"Ed will tell them it's a schedule change. It'll buy a few minutes while they check."

"He'll need more time than that, Major. It will take him at least five or six minutes."

"Actually," she said, "three minutes should about do it."

The chief glanced over, frowning. But once she explained her rationale, he could only nod.

"Hell, I never thought of that," he said, squinting toward the runway. "Now what's he going to do about them?"

She followed his gaze. The chief was looking at an isolated building in the distance. One that sat next to a revetment containing two F-15 fighters.

"Ed never talked about it," Caralyn said.

"He knows they'll be coming, right?"

"He knows," Caralyn said softly. "It's the reason he insisted on going instead of me. Even though I'm the one who's more proficient."

"He's a helluva guy," the chief murmured.

Caralyn only trusted herself to nod. They rode in silence for a few moments.

Finally, the chief said, "You don't have to worry about me, Major."

She looked at him.

"I know you've got your doubts about me. That I might do something crazy. But I owe Colonel Coffin, and I give you my word—"

"Slow down, Chief," Caralyn said, pointing. "There's Colonel Hardy."

After motioning them to stop in front of the hangar, Hardy disappeared through a side door. Seconds later, there was a high-pitched whir and hangar doors started to rumble. Once they were fully open, the chief drove inside, hugging the right wall and constantly checking his clearance.

"You're good," Hardy shouted.

Hardy pushed a button on the wall panel and the giant doors started to close. He came over, as Caralyn and the chief climbed from the car.

They impatiently watched the hangar doors. The instant that they fully shut, Hardy said, "Pop it."

The chief was already pressing the button on the key-chain.

Lifting the trunk lid, Hardy broke into a broad grin. "My, my, don't we look comfy?"

"Go to hell, Colonel," Steiner said, with real enthusiasm.

Hardy and the chief extracted Steiner first, then Coffin. Both stood for a moment, trying to stretch out the kinks and ignore Hardy's wise-ass smile.

"Fine," Coffin said, with a trace of annoyance. "Have a laugh at our expense, Sam."

"Believe me," Hardy said, "I am."

"You wouldn't find it so amusing if it were you, Colonel," Steiner said.

Hardy shrugged. "Never happen. I wouldn't fit."

She smiled sweetly and nodded to the closed trunk. "Let's give it a try, shall we?"

"How about it, Sam?" Coffin said. "We've a got couple of minutes."

"Open it, Chief," Steiner said.

A click. She opened the trunk, contemplating Hardy with what could only be described as a predatory gaze.

Up to now, Hardy had still been smiling, figuring she was joking. But as he looked at her, his smile faded, as if he suddenly wasn't so sure.

Abruptly, Hardy pivoted and hurried toward the maintenance offices at the very back. "C'mon," he said stiffly. "We got work to do."

Steiner flashed a sardonic grin, watching him go. Shutting the trunk, she followed after him, as did the chief and Caralyn.

"Ed?"

Caralyn was looking back at Coffin, frowning. "Aren't you coming?"

The others stopped and regarded him curiously.

"In a minute. It's been a while."

One by one, everyone nodded, indicating they understood. They continued into the offices, leaving him alone.

But Coffin wasn't alone; he was with an old friend. And as he assimilated the familiar image before him, he felt the same sense of belonging that he'd experienced yesterday. When he'd first walked into the U-2 hangar.

It was more than the fact that he was recalling a happier time or somehow reliving his youth. It was also the fact that this was the one thing in his life that he'd truly loved doing. The one thing that completely satisfied him.

And that wasn't all. It was also the realization that he had to encapsulate this moment . . . savor it . . . because this was the last time. Whether he succeeded or failed, he would never be in this position again or have another opportunity.

Moving forward, he was surprised by the emotion he felt. It really seemed as if he was preparing to say good-bye to an old friend.

Smiling, he patted the long black nose of the U-2, then slowly turned and went into the offices.

★ 39 ★

Timing was critical and everyone had to do their part. So for the next twenty minutes, Coffin went through the sequence of events chronologically, beginning at 2230 hours precisely.

When he finished, no one had any questions, but Hardy had a suggestion, one that Coffin halfheartedly argued against, knowing he was wasting his time.

Hardy was determined to go through with it, anyway.

"You'll need help," Coffin said.

"Right. I got help."

"Who?" As far as Coffin knew, everyone was accounted for.

"Let me worry about that, Ed."

"Is it someone from your unit? Are you sure you can trust him?"

"Ed," Hardy said patiently, "it's all arranged. If you need us, we'll be there."

Coffin didn't get it. For some reason, Hardy didn't want to tell him who the person was.

The chief coughed, looking at his watch. "It's time, sir."

Coffin nodded. The chief was indicating they had an hour, which meant Coffin had to get dressed.

The chief trailed him into the office next door. In the middle of the floor sat a sturdy metal-framed chair with neatly folded long underwear and a shiny white helmet on the seat, an orange spacesuit draped over the back.

Coffin parked on the edge of the cluttered desk and took off his boots. After shutting the door, the chief watched him, his expression unusually pensive.

Since deep thinking wasn't the chief's forte, Coffin asked what was on his mind.

"It's Majors Steiner and Barlow, sir. They really *do* look alike."

As if that was a bad thing. "Chief," Coffin replied, "they're supposed to look alike, remember?"

"Yes, sir. But what if someone notices?"

"Pretty unlikely. They're using separate entrances and the odds of anyone seeing them both—"

Coffin's mouth locked in the open position. He now understood what was worrying the chief.

Shaking his head, Coffin angrily kicked off his boots. Once again, he'd forgotten something crucial. When he tried to come up with a solution, his mind drew a blank. There was no solution.

The chief tossed out a suggestion. It didn't solve the problem, but was better than nothing.

"Okay," Coffin said. "But we keep this to ourselves, Chief. I don't want to scare Charlotte and Caralyn unnecessarily. Now, hand me the underwear. You keeping track of the time?"

An hour.

That was the absolute minimum time required for a high-altitude pilot to prebreathe pure oxygen, ensuring the nitrogen gas was flushed from his system, preventing the bends.

And once the chief sealed Coffin in the spacesuit, and plugged the oxygen line from the portable cooler into his helmet, that's all Coffin did for the next forty minutes. He sat alone in the office and breathed, staring at the wall clock and waiting to be placed in the airplane.

The minutes ticked by with excruciating slowness.

It was tedious.

Coffin was tempted to say screw it. To just have them stick him in the jet.

But he couldn't fly bent like a pretzel. So he just sat there breathing and watched the clock.

Until . . .

The door opened and Caralyn entered. She'd changed into a flight suit and looked just like a shorter version of Steiner.

Normally, Coffin would be plugged into a communications console, allowing them to converse. But since that wasn't an option, Caralyn leaned close to his faceplate and shouted: "Preflight is done. Everything is a go." She gestured to the wall clock, spreading her fingers. "The chief and I will take you out in five minutes."

"Do it now," Coffin shouted back.

She hesitated, appearing suddenly uncomfortable. "I promised I'd wait."

"Promised who?"

Coffin heard a garbled response through the faceplate. One that didn't come from Caralyn.

When he looked to the door, he saw the source.

Mother was fixated on him, wearing a curiously melancholy expression. A mixture of sadness and disappointment, with an emphasis on the latter. At that moment, Coffin deduced the problem even before Caralyn left the room and Mother came over to him. Reaching into her jacket and mouthing a single word pleadingly into his faceplate. *Why?*

When Mother's hand emerged from her jacket, Coffin saw what he had expected to see.

The letter—the one he'd placed in the manila folder that he'd given to Caralyn. The one Mother wasn't supposed to have read yet.

She mouthed the word "why?" again and Coffin knew she was asking about last night. Why he hadn't told her then what he'd written in the letter.

There were many things Coffin wanted to say to her. But this wasn't the place for it and there certainly wasn't enough time.

So he made a writing motion, and when she placed a pen and a notepad in his bulky gloved hands, he jotted down a brief explanation that he hoped she would understand.

I didn't want to cause you unnecessary pain. But Charlotte convinced me that you should know the truth and I made the decision to tell you everything, once this was over. To be honest, I thought this might change things between us and I'm tired of being alone.

He handed back the pad. Mother calmly read the words and wrote a sentence of her own. *Do you love me?* When he nodded, she wrote a final reply.

Then you'll never be alone again.

As if to convince him of those words, Mother took one of his gloved hands and held it to her chest. She let go only when Caralyn returned with the chief, signaling it was time to leave.

Sliding into the tiny cockpit, Coffin again experienced the palpable sensation of familiarity. As he scanned the flight panel instruments, he felt a sudden calmness, knowing this was the one place he belonged.

The chief bent over him, attaching the spacesuit hoses to the jet's oxygen system, enabling Coffin to breathe and stay cool. Next came the com line, and once Coffin heard the faint static click, he glanced to the side of the aircraft, where Caralyn stood, wearing a headset, Mother and Hardy nearby.

Keying the transmit button on the throttle, he said, "I'm up."

"Okay," Caralyn replied. "And Charlotte just called; she's in. The Korean guard didn't bat an eye at the ID."

An encouraging first step. But the real test would be when Caralyn joined her.

"We'll crank as soon as the chief gets down," Caralyn added. "You want to fly with the Pogos? Or have us pull the pins?"

Pogos were the small wheels that supported the long wings during taxi operations. Normally, the pins locking them in position were removed on the runway before takeoff, allowing the Pogos to fall free once the jet reached a minimum flying speed. Since Coffin would be without support personnel once he departed the hangar, there would be no one available to pull the pins.

"Leave the pins in," Coffin said. "Can't risk a dropped Pogo on taxi out." Other than burning a tad more gas, flying with them wasn't a big deal.

The chief showed him the red lanyard and pin from the ejection seat; it was now armed. Mother gave him a lingering smile and Coffin hesitantly returned it. Hardy said something to her and they went over to the door controls on the far wall, continuing to talk. Watching them, Coffin had a sudden thought. One that he found both reassuring and unsettling.

"All set, sir," the chief shouted.

Their eyes linked through the faceplate. The chief's heavy face softened and he squeezed Coffin's gloved hand, then moved back and lowered the canopy, locking it shut. As he clambered down the metal stand and rolled it clear of the jet, Coffin consulted the checklist Velcroed to his leg. The engine start procedure was eight lines long and Coffin still knew it by heart.

At a sudden whine, he glanced at the chief, who was powering up the air cart. Coffin checked the engine rpm, saw the needle shiver.

"You got air, Ed," Caralyn said.

"Starting now," Coffin said automatically.

He moved up the throttle and thumbed the start button. As the engine roared to life and stabilized, Coffin flashed Hardy a thumbs-up; saw the hangar doors begin to open.

A minute later, Coffin was ready to taxi and jerked his thumbs outward. The chief darted under the nose and reappeared, carrying the chocks. Throwing them to the side, he jogged over to the door controls and it dawned upon Coffin why.

Hardy and Mother had vanished.

"See you in an hour," Caralyn said.

"Right. An hour." And as Coffin said it, he realized that was all the time they were talking. An hour from now, it would all be over, one way or another.

Caralyn unplugged her headset, threw Coffin a wave, then left by the side door. With his eyes measuring the left wing, the chief signaled Coffin to start taxiing.

Inching up the throttle, Coffin crept forward. Once he cleared the hangar, he looked back and saw the giant doors closing.

Alone again.

★

As Coffin turned onto the inner taxiway, the radio crackled. He'd been spotted by the tower controller. The suspicion in the man's voice was something Coffin had anticipated. What Coffin hadn't anticipated was the controller's comeback to his own somewhat long-winded response—that this was an add-on mission that hadn't made it to the printed schedule.

"Without a mobile officer, Priority?" the man said.

Just like that, the guy had him. Frankly, Coffin couldn't believe it. Controllers tagged for the night shift typically had the mental agility of a rock.

"Priority, hold your position."

"Roger." Coffin could see the man's silhouette staring down at him from the tower. And he was talking animatedly on the phone.

Coffin almost swore. He'd counted on being able to taxi while the controller checked to see if the flight was legit.

So much for buying time.

Watching the controller, Coffin pushed up the power. The U-2 really began to move. In the tower, the controller snatched something from his console.

An instant later: "Priority, you're ordered to stop. You hear me? Stop taxiing *immediately*."

Coffin didn't bother to reply. He was thinking hard, calculating the distance. Call it a mile and change to the runway. And maybe a minute until the Security cops arrived.

No choice. He had to settle for his emergency option.

In his ear, the controller continued to order him to stop. At an approaching intersection, Coffin almost complied, but not out of choice. U-2s turned on a tail wheel the size of a kid's wagon tire. Go faster than a moderate walk, and it was hello shredded tire.

Compounding the problem was the fact that max deflection for the tiny tire was six degrees, resulting in a turn radius equating to half the length of a football field.

The bottom line: the U-2 turned *slowly*.

As the jet pivoted, Coffin impatiently eyed the clock. Twenty seconds, thirty . . .

Finally, the nose straightened and he motored down the intersection, toward the main parallel taxiway, the runway beyond it. It was still a quarter mile and two minutes away, but that wasn't Coffin's primary concern. Not any longer.

Over his shoulder, he saw the flashing lights of the cavalry. And he still had another turn to make.

It was going to be close.

By now, the tower controller was screaming at him. Coffin could have punched him off or switched frequencies but elected to listen. Squinting, he counted the vehicles. Two, no three, Humvees. One cut toward the approach end of the runway; the other two roared straight for him.

Smart, he concluded grimly, watching the first Humvee. That vehicle intended to block the runway and prevent Coffin from taking off.

Reaching the parallel, Coffin cranked into another turn. To his right, he saw the two Humvees race across the tarmac.

Coffin attempted to increase his turn rate. Felt the skid and backed off. The Humvees bounced wildly across the infield onto the parallel and bore down on him. Coffin was still stuck in the turn. He watched the distance close. Under three thousand feet.

Rolling out on the taxiway, he found himself staring into twin sets of approaching headlights. He shoved up the power and the plane shot forward, rapidly picking up speed.

For any other aircraft, this game of chicken was suicidal. With only a thousand feet between him and the Humvees, an impact was a certainty unless the drivers bailed.

But a U-2 was a powered glider, affording Coffin a second option. Within seconds, he had all the speed his long wings needed, and the instant he eased back the yoke, the plane leaped from the ground, thundering over the Humvees. As Coffin climbed steeply into the night sky, he became aware of a sudden panic in the controller's voice, but the man's words weren't directed at him.

Apparently, there was a second unauthorized flight.

On cue, Coffin switched the frequency on the radio.

★40★

Standing outside the entrance to the HTACC, Caralyn felt a twinge of anxiety when the grizzled sergeant at the security window scrutinized her picture ID longer than necessary.

Shrugging, he finally slid it through the opening, saying, "Looks new, Major."

"It is. I lost my other one this morning."

"Gotta try and be more careful, ma'am. Those IDs are gold to the black marketers."

"I'll remember that, Sergeant."

As Caralyn passed through the turnstyle, she glanced back at a deafening roar.

"Funny time for the U-2 to be flying," the sergeant said, checking his watch.

"Yes it is," Caralyn replied.

Hurrying into the building, she took the stairs to the basement and entered the tunnel. As she passed through it, she never once looked at the ceiling-mounted video cameras. Not even when she reached the midway point and a camera swung around to follow her.

In the darkened security center on the third floor of the K-COIC, a ROK captain frowned at a television monitor, watching Caralyn approach the camera. When she passed by, he motored the camera around, briefly followed her, then switched to a second camera, the one over the tunnel exit. As Caralyn came toward it, he zoomed in and froze her image.

Using a remote, he rewound a videotape, eyes fixed on a second monitor. When an image registered, he hit play.

Steiner appeared, walking in the tunnel. At the instant her image filled the monitor, he again froze the tape.

The captain's head swiveled between her and Caralyn. He still appeared puzzled.

Then his eyes went to their nametags.

He snatched up a phone.

Caralyn's clicking heels sounded loud in the silence of the cavernous imagery collection center. Approaching the shiny trailers along the rear wall, she called out and heard a muffled response. Stepping onto the landing outside the nearest trailer, Caralyn paused at the door, identifying herself once more.

"You're alone, right?"

"No. General Yee is with me."

"Caralyn—"

"It's a joke. Of course I'm alone."

Caralyn entered the trailer. Steiner was sitting at the high-tech console, the gun still in her hand. As she laid it on the counter, she said sulkily, "Not funny."

"Sorry." And she was. Sitting in a building full of Yee's people couldn't have been easy for Steiner. "Ed took off a few minutes ago."

Steiner glanced up at a television monitor displaying unrecognizable light green images. "That's the CARSON readout. Ed just turned it on. See those lat/long coordinates in the upper left—"

"Yeah . . ." The numbers were constantly changing.

Steiner clicked on a computer keyboard, then sat back, looking at the screen. "I'm running a continual position check. Ed's eighty-seven miles from the island, over the mountains."

Caralyn frowned at the monitor. "How can you tell what he's looking at?"

Steiner began typing. "What was that? Oh, the CARSON hasn't warmed up yet. When it does— See."

Caralyn did now. The image had abruptly sharpened and come into focus. It was as if she were looking at a green-hued X-ray film. "Definitely mountains," she murmured.

The image began to shift hesitantly. It stopped moving, showing a road and the buildings of a town. Steiner said, "Ed is manually aiming the sensor with the joystick. Trying to get the feel of it. Now he's using the zoom—"

One of the buildings rapidly enlarged. The image became extremely blurred, then gradually began to clear.

"—and adjusting the gain," Steiner said, resuming her play-by-play. "As long as the ceiling is made of a porous material, Ed should be able to burn through it. He's getting there."

Moments later, they could discern what appeared to be long rows of chairs butted against one another, but in actuality were—

"Pews," Caralyn said. "A church."

Both women watched the screen until the image again shifted, returning to the mountain scene. Steiner pointed to a complicated-looking remote at the bank of the video recorders mounted behind her. There was a click and a soft whirr. On the monitor they were watching, the church reappeared.

"Perfect," Steiner said, stopping the tape with the remote, "everything's perfect. All we have to do is wait for Ed to reach the island. When he does, we'll have the proof to bury that bastard Yee."

Her eyes were shiny with anticipation. Caralyn said, "I wouldn't assume we've won yet, Charlotte."

"You kidding?" Steiner glanced at her computer screen. "Yee can't stop Coffin now. Coffin will be at the island in twelve minutes. *Twelve minutes.*"

She was grinning. In her mind, it was the bottom of the ninth. And they were about to score the winning run.

The singular concern that Coffin had refused to discuss was on the tip of Caralyn's tongue. In the end, she didn't have the heart to prematurely burst Steiner's bubble. After all, there was no guarantee the event would transpire.

Maybe.

Caralyn tried to quell her unease. It was going to be a long twelve minutes.

She was about to slide into a chair when Steiner suddenly looked to the door, her grin vanishing.

"You hear something?" Steiner asked, picking up the pistol.

"No."

The women listened, ears straining. They heard only silence.

"Footsteps," Steiner said. "I thought I heard footsteps."

"Cover me," Caralyn replied, already moving to the door.

But as she walked around outside, she saw no one. When she returned, a visibly relieved Steiner set down the pistol, saying, "I'm just a little jumpy. I mean, there's no way Yee could know we're here, right?"

Caralyn felt the unease again.

"Target is ninety-three miles and ten o'clock."

Flying on autopilot in a black void fourteen miles up, Coffin listened to those words from the military controller and felt a sudden fear. Not of dying, but of failing.

Another few minutes would have ensured success. But as the controller guided the fighters to him, Coffin calculated the closure rate and realized they would overtake him, possibly even before he reached the island.

The question was whether they would actually fire. To Coffin, the answer bordered on a slam-dunk certainty. He'd ignored repeated demands to return and he was an accused murderer who had stolen a highly classified aircraft. Add in the pressure being applied by the Koreans and the reality was that the American government's hands were tied.

No, the fighters had a green light to shoot him down. And now Coffin asked himself whether they would succeed.

Again, the answer seemed an inevitable yes. The only protections a U-2 had from attack were electronic countermeasures and extreme high altitude. And while they might help him stave off a missile or two, eventually the odds would catch up to him.

And therein lay Coffin's lone hope. To survive at least the initial fighter passes.

The glowing CARSON display showed him crossing the rugged Korean coastline. On the nav system's time-to-go readout, Coffin saw five minutes remaining. Over the radio, the controller provided the fighters another guidance correction—they would be on him in four.

Focusing on the threat scope, Coffin knew exactly what he had to do. Assuming he had the balls.

The threat scope suddenly screamed shrilly. At the edge of the outermost ring, an F symbol pulsated brightly in red, indicating a single missile had been fired from twenty miles and seemingly imploring the pilot to take violent evasive action.

But Coffin did nothing. Evasive turns would cost him precious time, ensuring that the fighters would intercept him before he could get to the island. And with only one missile to deal with, the odds were in his favor that his electronic jammer could confuse it.

His decision made, Coffin didn't want to be tempted to change it. So he sat back in his seat and closed his eyes.

He never saw the flashing F close on the center of the scope.

He never saw the orange plume come out of the blackness.

He never saw the missile fly by his left wing and detonate in a brilliant flash, a thousand feet above his head.

He never saw or heard anything because his eyes remained closed, the hiss of his breathing loud in the helmet.

It wasn't easy. The survival instinct is powerful, and Coffin couldn't simply retreat inward to resist it. He gritted his teeth and willed himself to just sit there. It took all the self-discipline he possessed. And when Coffin at last heard what he'd been waiting for—the silence of the threat scope—he felt ready to buckle from the tension.

Instead, he calmly opened his eyes and went to work.

He scanned the instruments, checking and interpreting. Threat scope; blank; engine operations and flight parameters, normal; distance to go, nine miles and closing rapidly.

Immediately, Coffin shifted to the CARSON display and, using the joystick, slewed the sensor ahead, stopping on a jagged, luminous green circle.

The island.

He toggled the zoom. The circle became more distinct. Soon, Coffin could make out the compound and felt a surge of hope. In another minute, he would be able to—

The threat alarm sounded again.

★

Two flashing Fs on the threat scope, fired within the five-mile ring. This time Coffin couldn't help it; he had to look. Below his right wing, he saw the two flaming arrows rising up to meet him.

His impulse was to wrench the jet in a turn, in a desperate attempt to make the missiles fly past. But that was as far as it got, an impulse.

There was a blinding flash an instant before a concussion hammered him against the seat. His helmet slammed against the headrest and he felt a wave of pain. Warm liquid slid down his face, blinding him. He heard the howl of rushing wind and the plane staggered, as if mortally wounded. The spacesuit inflated rock hard, automatically compensating for a sudden loss of external air pressure. The nose buffeted and swayed wildly and began to teeter downward.

Frantically, Coffin gripped the yoke and pulled, still unable to see. Slowly the buffeting dampened and the howling noise lessened. Blinking furiously, Coffin saw a blurred image. More blinks and his vision cleared.

He was stunned.

Except for ragged bits stuck to the metal frame, the Plexiglas canopy was gone. And everything in the cockpit, including his checklist and maps, had been sucked out into space.

Eject.

It was a conditioned response. Coffin released the flight controls to grab the ejection ring between his legs. Then his confused mind finally grasped what was right there before him.

His instruments *glowed.* They were working normally, as was the engine. He was *flying.*

Jesus—

The nose dipped. Coffin snared the controls, bringing the jet under control. He was panting in the helmet. The pressure of the wind coupled with the rigidity of the suit made movement an effort. Leveling off, Coffin tried to engage the autopilot. It wouldn't take. *Dammit, he needed his hands free to—* It finally caught. The nav readout showed he'd passed the island, and he banked into a turn, searching for it with the CARSON.

Chong Do flashed by the scope. Rolling out of the turn, Coffin shifted the joystick, reacquired it. As he zoomed on it, he blinked constantly, keeping his vision clear. For now, the threat scope was blank, but it was only a matter of time.

The island's buildings came into focus. He closed in on one and adjusted the CARSON gain. The image fuzzed, then cleared. The interior showed tiny bits of metal, but nothing substantial enough to be a missile or a launcher.

Coffin selected a second building, repeated the process. Again, there were no significant returns.

He was locked on the third structure when he glanced to the threat scope. What he saw turned him cold. *Four* pulsing Fs; because of the wind, he hadn't heard the audible warning. And the symbols were merging on the center of the scope.

Seconds from impact.

For a moment, Coffin sat transfixed, thinking that it was better this way. Easier on him and easier on Mother.

Thinking of her suddenly filled Coffin with a numbing ache in his chest. And with a sudden determination, he reached for the ejection ring.

But the delay proved costly, and as his fingers felt for the ring, the first missile blew off his right wing and the plane flipped over, pinning him against the seat. A second collision sheared off the tail, and the jet hung for an instant, then began a slow tumble into the darkness below.

Watching from a helicopter speeding over the water, Mother screamed.

★41★

In the imagery collection center, Caralyn watched the image on the monitor disappear. At that moment, she knew.

Frantically, Steiner typed commands into the computer, trying to re-establish the connection. Jumping up, she checked the cables leading to the TV. Caralyn rose to help her, sickened. She started to tell Steiner that she was wasting her time, but never got the chance.

Steiner had turned toward the door, her eyes widening in fear.

Spinning, Caralyn saw the silenced automatic first. Then the man.

He stood in the doorway, dressed in a sports coat and slacks, his glasses making him appear more academic than ruthless. Until you noticed his missing ear and fingers.

"My God," Steiner murmured. "Colonel Kwan."

Her eyes darted to her gun on the counter, no more than a foot from her hand. Kwan had spotted it, also. He smiled at Steiner, as if to say, "Go ahead. Try it."

Their eyes locked. Steiner took a breath, then let it out. And again looked at the gun.

Caralyn couldn't understand what had come over her. Since when had Steiner become Joan Wayne? "Don't shoot,"

Caralyn said to Kwan. "I'll give it to you." Reaching around Steiner, she picked the weapon up by the barrel and offered it to Kwan.

With a disappointed sigh, he had her slide it across the floor to him. After pocketing it with the two good fingers of his deformed hand, Kwan smiled malevolently at Steiner. "You are very beautiful, Major," he said.

An obscene compliment, considering the source. Sensing that Kwan sought to rattle her, Steiner kept her face an expressionless mask.

Kwan shrugged, again appearing disappointed. He instructed Steiner to get him the videos from Coffin's flight. When she hesitated, Kwan's gaze hardened through his glasses. "Up to you. I kill you both now or later, it's same to me." Still smiling.

Turning, Steiner ejected a tape from the recorder. When she held it out to him, Kwan's smile froze.

"Don't fuck with me, Major," he growled. "I want the copies also."

Steiner just stood there. Kwan looked suddenly angry. Reaching back, he pulled the door closed and crossed the small space, backing the women against the wall. Kwan had a noticeable limp, but no pain showed on his face. With a man like him, it wouldn't.

He leveled the automatic at Steiner's forehead. "Last time I ask, Major," he said quietly. "You understand?"

For the first time, cracks registered in Steiner's stoic shell. As she gazed into the silenced barrel, she blinked nervously and swallowed often. Yet, despite her fear, she still made no move to retrieve the second tape, not even when Kwan inched the weapon closer, his finger tightening on the trigger.

Caralyn couldn't believe it. It was as if Steiner were daring Kwan to shoot her. It was as if she *wanted* him to shoot her.

"Give him the copy, Charlotte," Caralyn said.

"He's going to kill us anyway."

"So you want to die now?" Caralyn snapped. "This second?" Steiner didn't seem to realize that their only chance was to play along. They had to buy time, hope Kwan let down his guard—

Steiner murmured, "Please, no . . ."

Kwan's hand suddenly reached under his jacket, pulling out a large, gleaming knife.

At the sight of it, Steiner's composure disintegrated completely and she began to shake. Kwan also underwent a dramatic transformation. His face flushed, a psychotic glint appearing in his eyes. Staring at Steiner, he licked his lips and seductively waved the blade in her face. He spoke suggestively in Korean, his breathing becoming labored.

It was terrifying to watch.

Clutching the videotape to her chest, Steiner seemed on the brink of collapse, but Caralyn remained completely calm. To her, this was an opportunity. To use the knife, Kwan would need to move close enough for her to—

Caralyn's eyes slid past Kwan, convinced she was seeing things. The door to the trailer was beginning to open. Once it did, she found herself looking at another man, holding a gun. In a flash, she put it all together and was filled with blinding rage. She wanted to lunge toward him and beat him within an inch of his life. Instead, she glared at him with all the hatred she possessed, screaming that he was a double-crossing son of a bitch.

The instant the words were out of her mouth, Caralyn realized she'd made a tragic mistake. Because Kwan immediately swung his pistol around and there were two coughing sounds. And the chief was knocked flat on his back by the force of two bullets striking him full in the chest.

★

Kwan aimed at the chief's head, intending to finish him off. "No!" Caralyn screamed.

She chopped at his gun hand and Kwan yelped but maintained his grip, squeezing off another round. Blood spurted from the chief's shoulder and he groaned. Grabbing the barrel, Caralyn tried to twist the pistol free, but Kwan was too strong.

"Caralyn," Steiner shouted, "the knife—"

The blade was coming toward Caralyn's head. She ducked and viciously kneed Kwan's left leg—the injured one—and he fell against the console, howling in pain. "Go," Caralyn screamed at Steiner. "Run."

She shoved Steiner past Kwan, who was bringing up his gun. Caralyn swung with both hands and as the gun clattered to the floor, she charged past Kwan. He swore savagely in Korean and thrust out the knife. The blade caught in her coat sleeve and tore free.

Kwan took another swing; by then, she was to the door.

The chief had fallen onto the landing. He was still breathing, but barely. He murmured a word as she ran past. One that made her pause.

"Gun," he said, raising his bleeding arm. "Dropped it . . ."

Except it wasn't on the raised landing. And when Caralyn looked, she saw it had fallen through an opening at the back, wedging behind an aluminum duct.

"No time," the chief said. "He's coming."

Caralyn turned. Kwan was struggling to stand, blood seeping through his left pant leg.

"My girl," the chief murmured. "Had to be him. Should have killed that freak earlier . . ."

The chief trailed off, closing his eyes. His breathing stopped and he became still.

Footsteps behind her.

Caralyn ran.

Steiner was almost to the staircase. Caralyn tore after her, weaving like a broken-field runner. As she raced up the stairs, something whizzed by her head and slammed into the wall. She glanced down. Kwan was perhaps thirty yards behind, dragging his injured leg and taking aim. Caralyn dropped, bracing for the impact of a bullet, knowing he wouldn't miss again.

He didn't.

His pistol coughed and a woman screamed twice. Only it wasn't Caralyn.

The bullet had caught Steiner in the right flank, just as she'd opened the door at the top of the stairs. She'd screamed first in pain and again in surprise, when a second round ricocheted off the wall, showering her with fragments.

"Dive," Caralyn shouted at her "Fall through the door."

Steiner did, another round striking the door where she'd been standing. By now, Caralyn was on all fours, scrambling onto the landing. She threw herself through the opening, felt something tug at her coat.

Rolling clear, Caralyn kicked the door closed and got to her feet. Steiner was trying to stand, clutching her side with bloody fingers.

As Caralyn helped her up, she saw the videotape poking out from the leg pocket of Steiner's flight suit. Taking it, Caralyn zipped it in her coat. Steiner watched her, saying nothing. With her injury, the cold reality was that the tape was safer with Caralyn.

"Can you walk?" Caralyn asked.

"Like it matters?"

They could hear thumping sounds through the door. Kwan was coming up the stairs.

Caralyn said, "Take my arm. I'll help you—"

Steiner was gone, stumbling down the hallway. Caralyn took off after her, shouting for someone to help. At this hour, the only response was the echo of her own voice.

She swore. While Kwan's injured leg meant they could outdistance him, they wouldn't be able to outrun his gun. Then it occurred to her that maybe they wouldn't have to.

"The tunnel," she said to Steiner. "We have to make it to the tunnel."

Behind them, they heard a door open and close. Then Kwan's shuffling footsteps.

"C'mon," Caralyn said, grabbing Steiner's wrist. "Faster."

Somehow Steiner managed it. But with every step, she moaned, blood continuing to seep from her wound.

They came to the stairwell. Going up wasn't an option, because the only way out of the building was through ROK security.

"Almost there," she said to Steiner. "Hang in there."

The tunnel entrance was just ahead. For the first time, Caralyn risked a look back.

Lord . . .

Kwan was running on his injured leg. *Gaining.*

It was going to come down to seconds. Dragging Steiner, Caralyn angled toward the emergency actuators for the tunnel door. She was interested in the second one, the one on the inside of the embedded tracks. They had to reach it before—

With a cry, Steiner pitched forward, pulling Caralyn down as she fell. Both women landed in a twisted heap, no more than a foot from the tunnel entrance. As Caralyn untangled herself, Steiner moaned and clutched her leg.

She'd been shot again.

Caralyn desperately tried to get Steiner on her feet. Steiner almost made it, then her injured leg slipped on the wetness of her own blood. She lay there groaning and Caralyn sagged down beside her, knowing there was no point in running. Not any longer.

Heels were clicking softly. Methodically.

When the women looked, they saw Kwan limping toward them, gun pointed, his face knotted into a snarl. As he came closer, he told Caralyn to move aside, and once she did, he was oblivious to her presence, looking only at Steiner. It was as if for that moment in time, Steiner was the only thing that existed.

Stopping before her, Kwan's expression relaxed into an ominous smile. And again, he reached under his jacket and produced his knife.

Steiner said, "No. God, no . . ." She clawed at the embedded rails in the floor, frantically attempting to crawl. With a guttural growl, Kwan jammed his pistol into his belt and switched the knife to his good hand, straddling her and pulling her by the hair to expose her neck.

Running the knife along her throat, he whispered to her in Korean, getting off on his sadistic fantasy.

Except this wasn't a fantasy, it was real. When Kwan suddenly stopped whispering, Caralyn knew she had only seconds to act and shifted her weight to do so.

That's when she heard a flat cracking sound. As it reverberated through the tunnel, she saw Kwan's body spasm, a red stain mushrooming on his back. An instant later, he went lax, his arms dropping to his side, the knife falling free.

He slowly toppled. "Oh, Christ," Steiner said. "Jesus Christ."

"No," a voice said. "It was me."

★42★

A rag doll.

Lying on his side with his legs and arms splayed out, that was what Kwan looked like—a child's rag doll carelessly tossed aside.

At first Caralyn assumed he was dead, but then she saw him blink. She snatched up his knife and removed the guns from his waistband. Kwan made no attempt to resist. He just lay there, looking at her through askew glasses.

"Make sure," Steiner said, crawling away from him. "For God's sake, make sure."

She was terrified that Kwan was playing possum. But staring at the Korean, Caralyn knew that wasn't a concern.

The chief walked toward them, his injured arm hanging by his side, his good hand holding a pistol on Kwan. Watching him, Caralyn felt relieved and mortified. She said, "Christ, I'm sorry, Chief. When I saw you, I figured you and Kwan were . . ."

She drifted off; the chief wasn't listening to her. He was fixated on Kwan, his face a grim mask. Two bullet holes marked the center of his bulky coat. Peering at them, Caralyn confirmed her suspicion that he was wearing a bulletproof vest and she wondered why.

Now wasn't the time to ask. The chief was still lost in his thoughts. He slowly circled Kwan, staring at the bloody hole in his back. He stepped on one of Kwan's hands and twisted his heel. When there was no reaction, the chief seemed to smile.

"Fucking freak is paralyzed," he murmured.

Caralyn nodded. She was attending to Steiner, relieved her wounds didn't appear life-threatening. Removing her jacket, Caralyn used Kwan's knife to hack off her own flight suit sleeves, then quickly unlaced her boots. As she worked, the chief spoke softly to Kwan, in Korean. Glancing over, Caralyn thought she saw fear in Kwan's eyes.

"This will hurt, Charlotte," she said, securing the bandages with the bootlaces.

Steiner grimaced, but never made a sound.

"Bullets knocked the wind out of me," the chief said, finally coming over. "Knew my only chance was to play dead. It worked. Bastard was bent on stopping you. How is she?"

"The rounds exited cleanly, but she's losing blood." Rising, Caralyn wiped her hands on her flight suit, then zipped her jacket over it. "Good thing you wore a vest," she said, eyeing the chief.

He shrugged off the insinuation, adding, "Agent Hubbard insisted I wear it, when I told her there might be trouble. It was Colonel Coffin's idea not to tell you. He figured if you acted nervous or scared, someone might notice—"

He broke off, looking at the tunnel exit. Abruptly, he said, "You two get going. I'll be right behind you. Once we get to the other side, we'll be okay."

Caralyn did a double-take. "Get going? Charlotte can barely walk. We need an ambulance."

"No time. Hear that?"

Caralyn did now. Faint shouts were coming from the stairwell, in Korean. Steiner made a strangling noise, her big eyes crawling to the ceiling. Locking on the video camera pointed at them.

"You got it, Major," the chief said to her, speaking quickly. "It's why I came here. Yee's security people are handpicked and don't miss a trick. Two women who look identical, they would notice. The reason they're taking their time getting down here is that we're armed. That's what all the chatter is about; they're trying to come up with a plan. It'll take them a few minutes, so you two better get started while I seal off the tunnel. The bastards might have some kind of code to reopen it."

He hurried over to the controls.

Caralyn said, "Chief, wait. We need to move Kwan. He's on the rails and— *Son of a bitch.*"

The chief had startled her by suddenly firing at the video camera. He missed and fired again. The lens shattered.

He looked coolly at Caralyn. "You were saying, Major?"

Their eyes locked. At that moment, Caralyn understood.

The voices from the stairwell grew louder and they heard the squawk of radios. Steiner said, "Caralyn, we need to *go.*"

Her arms outstretched. As Caralyn hauled her upright, Steiner blurted to the chief that Coffin had probably been shot down and might be dead. In the context of the moment, it was a completely unexpected remark, but Caralyn understood why Steiner had made it. It was her way of telling the chief that she believed the ends justified the means, and that whatever he intended to do was fine with her.

The chief accepted her pronouncement with a terse nod. As he prepared to close the door, he looked at Caralyn, anticipating a similar indication of approval.

But Caralyn still needed tangible reassurance that she could live with what he was about to do, knowing she might have prevented it.

Her eyes went to Kwan, lying helplessly on the rails . . . and she immediately received her affirmation. Instead of compassion or pity or even horror, she felt only satisfaction.

Did that make her a bad person? In the eyes of the law or the church, perhaps.

But it also made her very human. And for that reason, she knew she was okay with turning her back on Kwan and walking away.

And that's exactly what she did, with her arm around Steiner. They just hobbled down the tunnel, never looking back. Not even when they heard the hydraulic motors kick in and the massive steel door suddenly thunder closed.

★ 43 ★

The chief joined them before the tunnel's midpoint, and once the small group passed under the video camera, only two of the three faces stared into it, calling for help. By the time it arrived, Caralyn was stepping from an elevator onto the first floor, cinching up her coat and turning away as a pair of security cops blew past and rushed down the stairwell.

Another half turn followed by a short jog took her to the building's entrance. Behind the security window, the master sergeant was simultaneously talking on two phones, while a third rang. He said, "That's right, sir, ma'am. Sergeant Glover is with them now, and he confirmed the two victims were shot. What was that, ma'am? Right, we thought there was a third person with them, but I don't see her on the monitor—"

Had he looked up just then, he would have. But he didn't and Caralyn slipped by him.

Hurrying down the long walkway to the parking lot, she watched a line of headlights speed up the hill. An ambulance was in the lead, and it lurched to a stop out front. Two med techs piled out and ran around to the back, removing a wheeled stretcher.

They jogged it up the walkway. Caralyn sidestepped into the shadows, so they wouldn't notice her bloody clothes. One breathless tech said, "Hey, Major, you know where we're supposed to go?"

"The tunnel."

They went by her. By then, two SP Humvees had pulled up. As the cops hurried past, Caralyn saw a blue staff car turn into the parking lot. One with a distinctive white top.

She swore, measuring the distance to Mother's car.

Too far.

Quickening her pace, she made for the ambulance, ducking behind it just as the white-topped car swung up to the curb. Taking a peek, she watched General Gruver and a full colonel climb out.

Gruver was practically shouting into a radio, saying, ". . . listen closely, Colonel Yu, because I'm going to say this only once. I don't give a damn if General Yee is unavailable, you tell him I want a meeting with him ASAP or I go straight to General Cho. And tell him I want your security videos. That's right. *All* of them."

He angrily clicked off, stuffing the radio in his jacket. The colonel said to him, "First the murders, then Colonel Coffin steals a U-2, and now this shooting. What the hell is going on, General?"

"I wish I knew, Burt. Whatever it is, you can bet that bastard Yee is involved. You know they're saying he could be the next president."

The senior officers hurried up the walkway. Watching them go, Caralyn grimly shook her head, her bloodstained hand caressing the videotape in her pocket.

No, he won't, General.

★

Arriving at her BOQ room, Caralyn immediately checked the messages on her answering machine. General Cho's was there; she knew it would be. Coffin's letter had been hand-delivered to him by the chief's brother-in-law.

Caralyn weighed calling him at once and decided against it. She wasn't ready.

Throwing off her flight suit, she took a quick shower and donned an understated civilian suit and her best pumps—the kind of outfit a person wears when blackmailing a four-star general. Afterward, she hustled downstairs to Steiner's quarters, entering with Steiner's key. Within minutes, she was back up in her room, hooking up Steiner's VCR to her own.

This was an unforeseen step necessitated by Kwan's homicidal interference, which had forced them to leave a second copy of the videotape in the trailer. And everything hinged on their having insurance.

Caralyn opted for two, just to be sure.

Once made, she sealed the tapes in bubble mailers, then reached for the phone. As she did, her hand froze, her eyes focusing on the letter lying beside it.

It was addressed simply, To Caralyn. And below: To be opened in event of my death.

She picked up the letter. The impulse to open it was overwhelming.

In the event of my death.

She shook her head, setting the letter down. It was a condition she wasn't willing to accept . . . yet.

She finally called Cho.

The phone barely rang. She was surprised when Cho himself picked up, voicing her name even before she identified herself.

Obviously, he'd been waiting for her call.

"You have tape, Major?" Cho's broken English was heavily accented, but understandable.

"Yes, sir. Where would you like to meet?"

When he told her, Caralyn had her second surprise. She'd anticipated an hour's drive to either his home or headquarters, in Seoul.

"Sir, I can be there in ten minutes."

"You go outside. To street."

"Street, sir?"

A dial tone; he was gone. Caralyn cradled the phone, frowning. Then her eyes widened when she realized that she'd again been blindsided by the unexpected.

She went to the windows, looking down at the cars. When she'd driven up, she hadn't noticed surveillance and couldn't spot anyone now.

But someone was out there, waiting for her. Maybe more than one.

Turning away, she threw the packets containing the videotapes into a briefcase and on her way out the door, picked up the pistol she'd taken from Kwan. We can trust General Cho, Coffin had told her.

Not this girl.

Caralyn stepped out into the dark, carrying the briefcase. She cautiously moved down the walkway, taking in the scene before her.

In the immediate vicinity, no one was in sight and everything appeared quiet, contrasting with the frenetic activity on the flight line. The ramp lights were cranked up to almost daylight and emergency vehicles raced around helter-skelter, flashers and sirens going full blast. On the runways, a pair of fighters were taxiing into takeoff position even as another two-ship flew overhead and banked into a descending turn, preparing to land.

With a deafening roar, the jets on the runway began their takeoff roll, flames shooting from their tailpipes. As she walked, Caralyn barely gave them a look; she was concentrating on the parked cars, scanning each one. Finally, she saw what she was looking for.

The silhouette of a head.

She eased out a breath, her hand cradling the gun in her waistband. When she was almost to the sidewalk, a man stepped from a black sedan to her left. He was a Korean officer.

She slowed, watching him. He called out her name and beckoned.

She flashed him a big smile, as if intending to join him. Then she suddenly pivoted and darted in the opposite direction, toward Mother's car.

"What you do— Stop, Major." The officer chased her. "You must stop."

Caralyn scrambled behind the wheel, starting the engine. The Korean yanked on the locked door, then rapped on the windows, telling her to get out. Up close, she was surprised to see he was a young captain. His voice became shrill, sounding more panicked than threatening.

She cranked the wheel around. He countered by jumping in front of the car. Caralyn frantically gestured; when he still wouldn't move, she slammed her foot to the accelerator.

The engine screamed. His eyes popped wide and he dove aside.

Calmly, Caralyn put the car in gear and as she drove off, she lowered the window, hollering two words to him.

"Post" and "office."

★

When the black sedan turned into the parking lot outside the base post office, Caralyn was cooling her heels on the bench outside. As the ROK captain jogged up to her, she tossed him another friendly smile. He glared back at her, too smart to fall for it twice.

"General Cho is waiting," he growled. "You must come."

"If I've changed my mind . . ."

"No change," he said. "We go."

He reached for her, then abruptly pulled back.

Staring down at her pistol.

He swallowed twice before managing to speak. "Major, I no understand. I only driver."

"We'll see." Caralyn rose, motioning with the barrel. "Take off your jacket."

He looked at her in shock.

"Easy, Tiger," Caralyn said. "I'm not trying to cop a feel."

He blinked. "Cop a feel?"

"Forget it. The jacket, Captain. Come on."

He reluctantly unbuttoned his service blouse and removed it.

A glance confirmed he was unarmed. Still, Caralyn kept the gun on him until he answered a question: Why was he sent to pick her up?

"Many guards at gate," he said, pointing to the access badge clipped to his pocket. "You must go with me. Many important people with General Cho."

"Important people? What kind of people?"

The captain got a stupid look, sensing he'd said too much. "I no know. I only driver."

"Fine. Then we drive."

But he didn't turn to go. He just looked at the gun in her hand.

She sighed. "I can't take the gun, huh?"

He solemnly shook his head.

She held it out to him in a final test. "Here, you take it."

He got the shocked look again and stepped back. "No. No gun. It make big problem."

The approved answer, and Caralyn knew she should be reassured. But going over to Mother's car to put the gun away, all she could think about was the captain's comment about important people. Ones she was apparently on her way to meet.

What are you up to, General Cho?

★44★

The ROK military headquarters complex was located on the back side of the same hill where the American brass lived, in an enclosed compound surrounded by concrete walls eight feet high. As they rolled up to the gate, Caralyn had to whistle; the captain hadn't been kidding about heightened security.

Normally, a single uniformed guard with a holstered pistol stood out front; tonight, there were four, all armed with M-16s. In addition, two men wearing dark suits and earpieces watched through the gate's grillwork, and as soon as they saw Caralyn, they began to talk into their lapels.

A guard stepped up to the car. Even though he obviously recognized the captain, he still inspected his access badge before saluting smartly and ordering the gate opened.

Passing through it, the captain drove at a snail's pace, and glancing back, Caralyn understood why.

A suit was following.

The compound's architectural theme could best be described as unaesthetic industrial. Approximately a half dozen concrete buildings lined the road, none more than two stories high. The lone exception was a towering bunker-like structure at the very back, fronted by flagpoles and a circular driveway. As they drove toward it, Caralyn noticed limos in a parking area to the left, most with their engines running.

Pointing at them, she said, "Important people."

A silence.

The captain crept around the circular drive, parking behind a line of black Hyundai staff cars.

"I wait," the captain said.

Caralyn nodded; he really was only a driver.

She reached for the door; it was already opening.

The suit stood over her, motioning. As she got out, she noticed the bulge below his left armpit as well as something even more ominous, waving in the breeze behind him.

It was the flag on the staff car parked just ahead. A two-star flag.

Take it easy, Caralyn. It probably isn't General Yee.

But as the suit escorted her toward the building, she felt a twinge in the pit of her stomach. To counter it, she recalled Coffin's advice about dealing with fear: *If you can't go through it, go around it.*

In this case, she split the difference and walked through a glass door.

Two more suits were in the small lobby: one holding a metal detecting wand, the other standing by the elevator.

Caralyn emptied her pockets into a tray. The suit with the wand sprouted a puzzled expression.

"No more metal," Caralyn said, making like she was washing her hands. "That's all."

The wand said something to her escort. Apparently, he was the group linguist and said to her, "Tape?"

Wanting to know if she had it on her. She slowly nodded.

They played the stare game. She waited for him to ask for it.

Abruptly, the man stepped away for a conversation with his lapel.

She said, "I don't speak Korean."

He pointedly blew her off.

Returning, he spoke to the wand, who hurriedly ran his metal detector over Caralyn. Once she was cleared, Caralyn was guided to the elevator.

As she and the suit entered it, the man standing guard reached inside, slid a card into a slot, and quickly stepped back. The doors bumped closed and Caralyn waited for her escort to select a floor, but he never did.

Yet, the elevator went down . . . and down.

The descent stopped; they were several floors underground. The elevator doors opened and they stepped into a long, dimly lit concrete corridor. From the open ceiling, fluorescent lights hissed and air ducts hummed. At the opposite end, Caralyn saw another Korean man in a dark suit, standing outside a steel door.

As they walked toward him, they passed the outline of a second door, which curiously had no visible knob. By now, Caralyn's mind was turning over, cycling through reasons why she was being taken here. Only one explanation made sense, and she felt the fear again.

They stopped before the man. Beside him was a wall phone. He spoke into it, then nodded. Caralyn's escort opened the door and entered, motioning her to follow.

She hesitated, peering past him into the room. Through a smoky haze, she saw soft ceiling lights and little else.

"Okay," her escort said. "No problem."

He actually attempted a smile. It unnerved her even more.

Taking a deep breath, Caralyn willed herself through the door. And as her escort closed it behind her, she found herself confronted with the most startling sight she'd ever seen in her life.

★45★

The room resembled a space-age conference chamber, with enormous television monitors mounted on opposing walls, a glowing floor-to-ceiling map of the Korean Peninsula in between, complete with blinking colored lights. A circular glass table twenty feet in diameter sat in the center of the recessed floor, cushioned chrome chairs angling out from it as if suspended in midair. In front of each chair was a built-in phone and a flip-top computer screen and keyboard. That's where Caralyn was looking now. Specifically, at the people seated in those chairs.

She counted nine. All smoked and wore military uniforms. They also appeared to be staring at her, though it was hard to be certain.

Because they wore shoulder length crimson red hoods, revealing only their eyes and mouths.

All except for one man.

And he was facing the door she'd just come through, curling a finger. Caralyn recognized him by his uniform — more accurately, by the rank on his shoulders.

Four stars: General Cho.

As Caralyn crossed the room toward him, the hooded heads swiveled, puffing and watching. General Cho, too, was smoking, an overflowing ashtray before him. He pointed his cigarette to an open chair beside his and she eased down.

"Tape," he grunted.

From the small of her back, Caralyn freed the tape wedged in her belt and passed it over. As Cho removed the cover, he flicked his cigarette. The ash missed the ashtray, landing on an envelope with Cho's name neatly printed in English and Korean—Coffin's letter.

Cho gave the tape a cursory glance, held it up. Caralyn's escort materialized and bowed low to Cho. He withdrew with the tape and disappeared.

As they waited, no one spoke. The hooded faces smoked quietly, watching Caralyn. Their eyes never seemed to leave her, and Caralyn realized it was a test. When she coolly met their gazes, the hoods dipped approvingly; she'd passed.

A man wearing a naval uniform suddenly grunted. Glancing up, Caralyn saw the monitors flicker.

The videotape began just as Coffin targeted the first building on Chong Do Island. At the instant the CARSON radar revealed an undeniably blank interior, the hoods began to whisper among themselves. As the pattern was repeated on the two subsequent buildings, many sucked air disapprovingly through their teeth.

When the videotaped images abruptly turned to snow, none of the hoods seemed puzzled or surprised. They'd obviously known the U-2 had been shot down.

Cho contemplated Caralyn through curling smoke, his face tight and unhappy. Picking up Coffin's letter, he said cautiously, "Terms are . . . most difficult. I do . . . what I can."

Caralyn sensed another test and didn't hesitate in her response. Squarely eyeing Cho, she said, "Sir, I'm afraid that's not acceptable. You are a powerful figure who can influ-

ence your countrymen as well as your American counter-
parts. Unless everything in that letter—" she pointed to it
"—is satisfied, we go public with the tape. That means all
charges against Colonel Coffin and Major Steiner are
dropped and anyone who helped them—"

She broke off; the suit had reappeared and was speaking
into Cho's ear. Cho turned to Caralyn. "You go, Major. No
time talk now."

Summarily dismissing her? Already?

Four-star or not, Caralyn was suddenly furious. There
was only one reason Cho would feel emboldened enough
to send her packing, and it wasn't because she was a
woman. At least not exclusively.

The suit indicated Caralyn should rise. As she did, she
leaned close to Cho, her voice bitter and sarcastic. "Let me
guess, General—your boy here just got the word that
Colonel Coffin was confirmed dead and you think that
changes the situation. Let me set you straight, sir; it hasn't. I
won't be ignored or intimidated."

Cho seemed more confused than irritated by her remarks. He said impatiently, "You go, Major. Quick."

The suit reached for her; Caralyn froze him with a look.
Around the table, the hoods erupted in conversation and
hissed their disapproval. One said to Caralyn in fluent English, "Major, all is not as it seems. Soon, everything will be
clear."

Caralyn had no idea what he meant and didn't give a
damn. What she did know was that theirs was the ultimate
boys club and she lacked the testosterone to qualify for
membership. With Coffin gone, none of these star chamber
wannabes believed she had the figurative balls to carry out
the threat in the letter.

The truth was, she probably didn't. No way could she

live with herself if she was responsible for a holocaust, lead-ing to the death of millions.

So what was left? Did she tuck her tail between her legs and leave?

Screw that.

"General," Caralyn announced to Cho. "You're forget-ting the FBI is coming here to take over the investigation. And when they show up, you can bet I'll be knocking on their door with one hell of a story and a tape to prove it."

In dramatic fashion, she pivoted away from him and strode toward the door, her face etched in determination. If nothing else, she intended to make them sweat, wondering if she was bluffing.

"Major," a voice said, "you misunderstand our inten-tions."

"Have I?" She disgustedly faced the hooded English speaker. "Well, suppose you enlighten—"

She stopped. The hood was pointing to the back of the room. So were others. And as Caralyn shifted her gaze, she realized she *had* misunderstood.

The suit was holding open a door and beckoning to her.

It was an impressively stocked audiovisual room, with a wide variety of audio and video recorders, and movie and slide projectors. Along the interior wall was a black curtain, and once the suit positioned her in front of it and drew the cord, Caralyn found herself peering through a window into the briefing room.

"You look," the suit said, standing beside her.

"Look for what?"

No reply. Caralyn shrugged and kept looking. The men inside gestured as if conversing, but no sound reached into the audiovisual room.

"Soon," the suit said. He was listening to his earpiece.

This time Caralyn didn't bother with a query. In the briefing room, she saw the circle of hoods turn as one toward the main door. The oneness of movement made her realize that Cho, too, now wore a hood.

For a long moment, nothing happened. The hoods furiously puffed away and clearly felt a tension. Caralyn wished she knew why.

Then the door suddenly opened and three men entered the room. Two wore dark suits and stood discreetly behind the third, a ROK Air Force two-star general wearing a smile that was arrogant and amused.

Yee.

Yee's smile confused Caralyn. He obviously didn't feel threatened by those in the room. In fact, he grinned smugly, walking toward them, indicating he believed this was all some kind of joke.

As Yee approached the table, Cho pointed him to a spot on the floor. Yee continued walking, still grinning. When Cho gestured more emphatically, Yee's grin slowly faded.

He and Cho appeared to have a brief discussion, one that wiped all trace of amusement from Yee's face.

Initially, Yee seemed surprised by what Cho was saying. Then he became visibly incensed.

Turning to the men at the table, Yee made furious, stabbing gestures. He circled them and continued to speak. Most didn't react; they just sat calmly, smoking and watching. On two occasions, Yee stopped and argued with hooded faces who'd apparently disagreed with him.

Finally, he came to General Cho's position and started to walk by. Cho must have spoken, because Yee looked startled. Cho again pointed him to the space on the floor. Yee threw up a dismissive hand and turned away.

Two steps later, he froze.

From across the room, the two suits were coming toward him.

Facing Cho, Yee angrily gestured at the men. A brief argument ensued. Whatever Cho said had the effect of calming Yee, but only slightly.

The suits stopped on either side of Yee. Once again, Cho pointed to the spot on the floor and with a disgusted grimace, Yee finally went over to it.

Up to now, Caralyn had been puzzled by Cho's insistence that Yee stand in that precise position. But once Yee faced the table, with his hands folded, bracketed by the men in suits, she finally processed what she was seeing. The familiarity of the image. And when she saw General Cho rise and read from Coffin's letter, she knew she'd guessed right.

This was a trial. Yee was being put on trial for the crimes listed in the letter.

With her heart pounding in anticipation, Caralyn pressed closer to the window, to watch.

General Cho presented the prosecution's case in its entirety. Once he finished Coffin's letter, he glanced toward the audiovisual window, nodded once, and sat. Immediately, Caralyn's escort sidestepped to a VCR. Moments later, the briefing room monitors replayed Coffin's mission over Chong Do Island. When the tape ended, the escort began another video, one that surprised Caralyn.

She and Steiner were its stars.

The video began with them running toward the tunnel, suddenly falling. Within seconds, Kwan limped into view and straddled Steiner, running the knife along her throat.

At this point, the surveillance camera operator zoomed in on their faces, and viewed on the giant monitors, the effect was chilling.

In vivid, larger-than-life detail, everyone saw Kwan's sexual excitement and Steiner's wide-eyed terror.

The sadistic scene lasted longer than Caralyn remembered. It became too disturbing to watch and she turned away. Finally, she heard a click as her escort stopped the tape. At another click, she watched a screen lower from the ceiling.

A series of slides depicting a stunningly beautiful Asian woman appeared; in several, she was standing beside Yee. A final slide came up; apparently, it was same woman on a morgue slab, her face crushed beyond recognition. Seeing it, Caralyn felt sickened, realizing it was the chief's daughter.

The next photo was also hard for Caralyn to look at. It showed the pretty young security cop, Airman Jeanne Roche, shortly after she'd been butchered, in the park.

Several pictures of Lieutenant Sun followed, as did others of people Caralyn didn't recognize. She counted a total of eleven victims, all apparently killed on Yee's orders.

Major Erik Olson was the last slide shown. Seeing his smiling face standing beside a U-2 was yet another emotional hurdle for Caralyn. She had cared deeply for Olson and he was gone, and in all probability, so was Coffin. Added to the other deaths, it all seemed so damned senseless.

"Why?" she heard herself murmur.

The suit glanced over, his expression sympathetic. He was again standing beside her, indicating the audiovisual display had ended; within moments, so had the prosecution.

After reading from a prepared statement, Cho sat down and everyone at the table looked at Yee, waiting for his rebuttal.

For much of the evidence presentation, Yee had maintained his arrogant demeanor, often interjecting comments. But as his victims' faces kept flashing on the screen, his shoulders dropped and he grew quiet, appearing visibly nervous.

Now, as he scanned the hooded eyes staring at him, he looked small and old and scared. He went over to one man and said something. The man rose to his feet and stared straight ahead. Yee spoke to a second man and got the same reaction.

He turned to a third man. Before Yee could speak, the person got up.

One by one, the remaining men followed the pattern. Watching them, Caralyn understood what was taking place.

They were the jury. By standing, they were casting votes. Seven . . . eight . . .

Cho was the last man sitting. Slowly, he stood.

A unanimous verdict.

Yee seemed to buckle. He looked at the men, his mouth frantically working. Pleading with them. The men around the table showed no reaction. And when Yee stopped talking, they all pivoted in unison and filed past him, out the door.

Cho was the last in line. Before he left, he placed a gun on the table beside Yee. And for a moment, the two men shared a look.

Yee's eyes darted to the men in the suits and he appeared to wilt, sensing there was no escape. Shaking his head sadly, he contemplated the gun before him. Cho must have spoken because Yee slowly nodded.

After Cho and the suits departed the room, Yee lit a cigarette, staring at the gun. Then his eyes went to the map of Korea and he shook his head regretfully. With a last drag, he put down his cigarette and picked up the gun—

The curtain was pulled over the window.

★46★

In the audiovisual room, the sound of the shot was faint, no louder than the rap of knuckles on a wooden door. Afterward, Caralyn's escort reopened the curtain and they watched Cho re-enter the conference chamber, no longer wearing his hood. The two suits trailed, remaining by the door. Caralyn looked for the hooded men, but they never came in.

Yee had come to rest partially on the table, an arm outstretched, his head tilted to the side. Blood oozed from a wound above his temple, pooling out on the glass tabletop. Cho slowly approached Yee, his face tight with emotion. Standing over the body, he reverently gazed at it, then bowed low in an obvious sign of respect. Watching this display, Caralyn was mystified; it was as if Cho genuinely regretted Yee's death.

With a final lingering look at Yee, Cho addressed the suits. One bent his head, talking into his lapel.

Cho began striding purposefully toward the audiovisual room and Caralyn knew why. It was time to finish their talk.

Considering the import, it wasn't much of a talk, lasting no more than ten minutes. All each sought was assurance from the other that they would keep their part of the bargain. For Caralyn, that meant destroying the copies of the tape General Cho knew she must have made, and for Cho, fulfilling the remaining two requirements in Coffin's letter.

The first was a no-brainer; with a phone call, Cho could get the murder charges against Coffin and Steiner dropped. But the second—stopping the air force from coming down on those who had assisted Coffin and Steiner—would be trickier. Caralyn thought the only way would be for Cho to come clean with the American military hierarchy, and she said so.

In response, Cho smiled vaguely and spoke of the history between Americans and South Koreans, explaining that it was a bond forged in war and time and wouldn't be easily broken.

"America and South Korea same boat," he said, finally getting to the punch line. "If one sink, both sink. You understand, Major?"

"I'm beginning to, sir. You're saying both sides have to trust each other."

"Yes, yes. All about trust. General Yee honorable man, but he forget that."

Cho's remark mirrored his earlier display of reverence toward Yee's body. And Caralyn wasn't about to let it pass.

"Honorable man?" she said. "Sir, General Yee was a *killer*."

Cho frowned, as if genuinely perplexed. "Killing necessary in war, Major. General Yee do what he think right. You upset because he kill your friend Olson. But you forget Olson was dangerous man. If he say Chong Do missiles fake, maybe spy find out and North Korea attack. To Yee, decision easy. People not important. Only country."

There it was. With understated eloquence, Cho had rationalized Yee's murderous actions into something noble.

Let it go, Caralyn. But, of course, she couldn't.

"Tell me, General," she said quietly, "would you do what Yee did? Kill all those people for the greater good?"

He seemed amused by the question. "You need ask, Major?"

"Yes, I do, General. Because I don't think you're anything like Yee. He was evil and ruthless and—"

She fell silent; it finally hit her. What she was about to say and how silly it sounded.

She'd just *seen* Cho and a quorum of senior ROK officers prove in dramatic fashion that they could be as ruthless as Yee.

"My country at war and I am soldier," Cho said softly. "You understand now?"

"I understand, General."

Caralyn got to her feet, in sudden need of a shower.

Instead of leaving through the briefing room and walking by Yee's body, Caralyn's escort led her out the back of the audiovisual room and down a narrow hallway lined with cubbyhole offices filled with communications equipment manned by ROK officers. Poking his head inside one, her escort had a brief conversation with someone and received a grunted reply.

At the end of the hall, they hung a right through a door and Caralyn found herself standing in the original corridor, the elevator to her left.

As she followed her escort toward it, she heard an English-speaking voice and turned.

General Gruver was entering the briefing room, saying to Cho, "I got your message, General, but I don't understand why you want us to withdraw the FBI from this— Who the hell is *that*?"

Gruver bolted forward. One of the suits hurriedly closed the door behind him.

"Trust," Caralyn said softly.

Her escort frowned at her, holding open the elevator.

"Trust," she repeated to him, getting in. "I don't suppose you trust me enough to tell me what you told General Cho about Colonel Coffin."

He pushed the button for the lobby, shaking his head. "No speak English."

"Your zipper is down."

He started to look. Reddened.

The elevator doors closed.

"So much for trust," Caralyn said wearily.

★ 47 ★

It was another hour before Caralyn finally returned to her BOQ for that shower, because of two stops she had to make. At the hospital, a nurse told her Steiner was in surgery and the chief was sedated and sleeping.

"They'll both be fine," the nurse said.

That was the good news; the bad came minutes later, when Caralyn drove to the flight line and saw that Hardy's helicopter still hadn't returned. She debated hanging around to wait, but knew Hardy would go through all four hours of his gas, looking for Coffin.

So she went back to her BOQ and took her shower. Afterward, she pushed a chair up to a window so she could watch the flight line, and got comfortable with a bottle of wine, preparing to wait.

For the next thirty minutes, she sat there sipping and staring and thinking. She thought about the nameless faces on the slide show and how the only reason they had died was that a twisted man with even more twisted ethics believed their deaths were justified. She thought of the chief and his beautiful daughter and how fate had delivered them into Yee's control, ruining their lives and ultimately ending hers. Caralyn thought of the irony that, in the end, the same murlerous rationalization that Yee had used to destroy so many had culminated in his own demise. She thought of Cho and the other officers who'd made that call and how they attached a moral, almost noble equivalency to their actions. She thought about Cho's remark that he was a soldier and how much it bothered her because she was a soldier, too.

Staring into the dark as her body slowly decompressed, Caralyn thought about everything that had happened over the past two days and how she would have done anything in her power to change it. She thought about the frailty of life and how nothing is guaranteed. She thought of many things that she'd never considered before, esoteric and real.

But mostly, she thought of the two people, now gone, whom she would miss. Her fondness for Olson had only been a beginning and where it would have led, she would never know. There was an unrequited sadness in that, the kind that comes from a potentially life-changing *what if* that will forever be unanswered.

Then, of course, there was Coffin. With him, she knew what she had—a mentor, friend, and confidant who had always abided by his word to be there for her. And over the years, he had . . . always.

Setting down her wine glass, Caralyn contemplated the letter by the phone, wanting to cry but not being able to. For the next several minutes, she stared at the letter until the pull finally became too powerful to overcome. Maybe it was the booze in her or maybe it was the knowledge that it was winter and the water would be cold and, even in a spacesuit, Coffin wouldn't last more than an hour or two before freezing to death.

Or maybe she just wanted to know.

Whatever the reason, she found herself rising from her chair and picking up Coffin's letter and almost angrily opening it as she asked herself another life-changing question, one with no expectation of an answer.

"Dammit, Coffin, are you alive? Are you . . ."

". . . alive?" Hardy shouted into the boom mic on his headset. "Can you tell if he's alive?"

They were hovering twenty feet over the water, the helicopter's floodlights shining straight down. Mother, now dressed in a full wetsuit, was peering out the cargo door, winching down a rescue penetrator, aiming for a yellow form bobbing in the middle of the swirling waters below.

"I can't tell," Mother radioed back. "His faceplate is closed and he doesn't seem to be moving." Panic in her voice.

"He can't suffocate, Mother; the helmet has a safety valve so he can breathe. He probably passed out from the cold."

The penetrator hit the water. Mother stopped the winch. "Three up and five right."

From the cockpit, Hardy was unable to see Coffin and had to rely on Mother's positioning calls. Slowly, the helicopter shifted up and over, bringing the line within arm's reach of Coffin. But he made no move to take it. He remained slumped forward, arms dangling in the water, his head resting on his life preservers.

"What's happening?" Hardy asked.

"Nothing. He's just lying there." The panic still in her voice.

"There's no chute around him, right?"

"No—"

"Then *he* had to release it, which means he was alive when he hit the water. The suit would give him some protection from the cold. Get on the fins, but give me a final position check before you put on the mask."

They'd discussed this. If Coffin couldn't attach himself to the penetrator, Mother had to do it for him.

In two minutes, she was ready. Peering out the cargo door, she relayed the necessary commands into the headset, allowing Hardy to place the helicopter ten feet above and five to the left of Coffin. Because of the wave action generated by the rotor blast, he wouldn't remain there long.

"Give me three minutes, then start the winch," Mother said.

"Rog." Hardy had winch controls in the cockpit.

Mother swapped the headset for a facemask. Pressing it to her face, she balanced at the edge of the cargo door and jumped.

The cold took her breath away. It was like a wall of knives, cutting to her core. She kicked to the surface and threw out an arm. Nothing. She looked and took another stroke; he was there.

She screamed out his name; no response. Coffin continued to bob, seemingly lifeless. Mother frantically felt for something to cling to. Finally her fingers latched on to the straps running up the back of his spacesuit.

Dragging Coffin, she kicked toward the penetrator and wrestled the safety strap over his head and arms. It seemed to take forever because of the bulkiness of the spacesuit and the life preserver. But she finally made it, and after she squeezed herself under the strap, she clung to Coffin's back, exhausted.

The delay until they were winched up seemed interminable. But finally the line went taut and as they rose together, Mother kept shouting the same thing to Coffin, over and over.

"You can't die now, Ed. I love you."

★ Epilogue ★

THREE DAYS LATER

Viewing the body was something they each felt they needed for closure, to prove to themselves that he was really dead. So once Mother cleared it with the hospital administrator and the morgue supervisor, she led everyone to the third refrigeration unit and opened the door, sliding out the steel slab and pulling back the sheet.

For a long time, no one spoke. They just quietly stared down at the face that had once been familiar, but now had been altered by death.

"It doesn't really look like him," Caralyn said.

"The facial muscles," Mother said. "They relax after a person dies."

"A guy like him who had it all," Hardy said softly. "Makes you wonder what made him . . . drove him to . . ." He left the question unfinished.

There was another long silence. The chief's arm was in a sling and he was struggling to flip to a picture in his wallet, one-handed. He finally managed it, and he held the picture up to the body, becoming visibly emotional.

"Agent Hubbard—"

She turned. The burly morgue attendant was standing in the door, looking mildly puzzled. He said, "Ma'am, a man just called to say he's ready any time. When I asked for his name, he said to tell you, 'It's the general.'"

"Thank you," Mother said.

Caralyn and Hardy started to step away. Mother held them in place with a look. This was the chief's moment. More than the others, it had been important for him to be here.

"Whenever you're ready, Chief," she said quietly.

"I'm ready now." He folded up the wallet, swallowing hard. "Song-chee can rest in peace, knowing the bastard is dead."

"Amen to that," Hardy said.

With a final look at Yee, Mother covered his face with the sheet and they left.

As they took the stairs up from the basement level where the morgue was located, everyone's mood abruptly shifted because of the upcoming celebration. At the lobby, the chief and Caralyn peeled away—he to meet his brother-in-law, who was bringing an important gift, she to confirm everything was in place in the doctor's conference room they were going to use. At the second floor, Hardy split off to get Steiner, who'd insisted on coming and had to be wheeled in her hospital bed.

That left only Mother to continue to the third floor, and when she arrived at the private room reserved for VIPs, instead of entering, she nervously two-stepped outside, waiting for the chief to deliver the gift.

Envisioning the reaction as it was presented, she almost allowed herself a smile. The reason she couldn't quite pull it off was that she was looking at the nameplate affixed to the hospital room door.

Ed Coffin, the placard read.

And to the left: *Brigadier General-select.*

The latter was a source of sadness to Mother, because it reminded her that, while Coffin's name had come out on the promotion list released yesterday, he'd never actually wear the general stars he'd so long sought. Not with what the doctors had told him.

They had said he had an inoperable brain tumor and might last a year.

To Mother, it was all horribly unfair. Coffin had survived being shot down, survived the ejection and the freezing water. And yet, he was going to die anyway.

Yesterday, she and Coffin had shared a lot of tears and hugs, discussing his illness. And after a while, when they were cried out, Coffin began saying things to her that made no sense. He told her that he had no regrets over being sick; in fact, he even considered it a good thing. At first, she believed he was just trying to be strong for her, make her feel better.

But that wasn't it at all; he really meant what he said.

"You see, Mother," he'd told her, "all my life I'd been a striver and an achiever, and along the way, I lost sight of what was important. Becoming sick gave that back to me by refocusing my priorities. A few days ago, Marty Bell told me he'd gotten a tip about the promotion list and that I was on it and . . . I didn't care. At that moment, I knew I had really changed, and my only regret is that I didn't do it sooner. If I had, I would have been open with you from the beginning and told you about my mother, and we would have had those five years.

"It all comes down to the lie I've been living—denying my past, not just to others but to myself. And look how I ended up. Or almost did. A guy who has great professional success but nothing at his core.

"But now I have that core. I know who I am and where
I'm from, and more important, I'm not ashamed of it. And
if it took my getting sick to obtain that kind of insight, then
it's a price I'm willing to pay. I'm not saying I want to die.
God knows, I don't. But when you're faced with it like I am,
you get this . . . clarity. Maybe it will be easier to understand
if you ask yourself the same question I've been asking myself: If you were given a choice between a long empty life
and dying alone, or living a single year with someone you
love and surrounded by friends, what would you choose?"

Mother never hesitated in her response. Because listening to Coffin, she had gotten the clarity he'd referred to.

"A year with you," she said.

As she said it, Mother had another moment of clarity, realizing the preciousness of each day. And that's when she
decided to throw him a promotion party for the general's
star he would never wear and give him the one gift he
wanted above all others.

"Agent Hubbard. Agent Hubbard—"

Mother blinked, turning away from Coffin's door. The
chief was hurrying down the hallway toward her.

He had Coffin's gift.

"Come in, Mother," Coffin said.

But when he looked to the door, an elderly Asian woman
tentatively entered the room, clutching a gold amulet
around her neck. Her face was weathered from years in the
sun and she had stringy shoulder-length gray hair. To Coffin, she was the most beautiful woman he had ever seen.